The light was almost too dim for Susan to see the other side of the room. She was a quarter of the way across when she heard the door leading to the loading dock slam with a dull metallic reverberation. Without slackening her pace, she turned her head and saw what she had expected. Cyberwolf was coming toward her, his amber eyes burning, his blond hair streaming back, and his face still screwed up in fury. He seemed to have lost all human qualities.

Susan felt the chill of fear spread through her body like ice water. She willed herself to move faster. She snatched her breath in ragged gasps, with her chest heaving and her heart hammering wildly. The blank face of the door seemed miles away from her. Suddenly, something hard and solid struck her squarely between the shoulder blades, and a thousand lines of burning pain radiated through her neck and back.

Oh, my God, he's shot me, she whispered to herself.

Ronald Munson

NIGHT VISION

A SIGNET BOOK

SIGNET
Published by the Penguin Group
Penguin Books USA Inc., 375 Hudson Street,
New York, New York 10014, U.S.A.
Penguin Books Ltd, 27 Wrights Lane,
London W8 5TZ, England
Penguin Books Australia Ltd, Ringwood,
Victoria, Australia
Penguin Books Canada Ltd, 10 Alcorn Avenue,
Toronto, Ontario, Canada M4V 3B2
Penguin Books (N.Z.) Ltd, 182–190 Wairau Road,
Auckland 10, New Zealand

Penguin Books Ltd, Registered Offices:
Harmondsworth, Middlesex, England

Published by Signet, an imprint of Dutton Signet,
a division of Penguin Books USA Inc.
Previously published in a Dutton edition.

First Signet Printing, January, 1996
10 9 8 7 6 5 4 3 2 1

PUBLISHER'S NOTE
This is a work of fiction. Names, characters, places, and incidents either are the prod-
uct of the author's imagination or are used fictitiously, and any resemblance to actual
persons, living or dead, events, or locales is entirely coincidental.

To Miriam
Still "Giver of bright rings"

I am deeply indebted to Miriam Grove Munson for help of many kinds. I thank Janet Berlo for her careful reading, and I thank Anne Kenney, Michaela Hamilton, Martin Sage, Jennifer Selesnick, and Marian Young for doing much to help make this a better book. I am particularly grateful to Stephen Selesnick for guiding me through some of the darker passages of cyberspace.

1

The scene was an easy one, and Susan knew that she should be able to go through it without thinking twice.

All she had to do was pick up the red suitcase, open the front door of the house, then stride down the sidewalk. While she was walking, she would have to screw up her face into an expression of angry determination and exaggerate the expression until it became outlandish.

Susan liked the character of Julia McKnightly, and she was pleased to be playing her first comic role. In the last four years, she had done two immensely successful action-adventure stories, and both pictures had been shot mostly on location in Mexico and Costa Rica. During the long hot weeks of filming, she was always sunburned, muscle-sore, insect-bitten, and bruised from spending the day crashing around in the jungle while trying to elude her pursuers.

Working on *The McKnightly Business Report* over the last month had been a welcome contrast. She couldn't ask for anything better than to be here on location with Martin Priestly, the director, and the first-unit crew. They were on a street in Westwood, hardly two miles from her own Bel-Air house, and ready to shoot Julia indignantly marching out of her suburban house after a fight with her husband. Susan would go down the front walk, cross the sidewalk, then get into the dilapidated tan Chevrolet parked at the curb. That would be the end of the scene.

Both cameras would then be moved, and in the next scene she would start the car and drive off. She had no lines, but she knew exactly what to do and how to look. Everything should be smooth and effortless, and she should feel comfortable about it all. But she didn't. Her hands were shaking, and she felt disoriented and scared.

"Hold it a second, Ms. Bradstreet," a makeup assistant said. "I can see a tiny little glow on your forehead and upper lip."

"Marge, what you really mean is that I'm sweating like a pig," Susan said.

She tried to appear casual as she made the joke, but her voice sounded funny in her ears. It was thin and high-pitched, and it seemed to come from someone else, someone standing at the other end of the small living room they had taken over.

She could feel herself sway with dizziness, and she braced her feet so she wouldn't topple over. For a moment everything around her seemed distorted and unreal, and it was as if she had separated from her body and was looking down from some high point. She willed herself to stay absolutely still while the assistant dabbed her face with a tissue and then with a small, downy powder puff.

"That's much, much better," Marge said.

"Thanks for catching it," Susan told her.

Once again it was somebody else, some stranger, who seemed to be speaking. If only this damned scene could be wrapped up, then maybe she could sit down for a minute and recover. She wished she could call everything off for the rest of the day, then go home and go to bed. That's what she really wanted to do.

But what was happening to her? Maybe it was the flu, because her face did feel flushed. Or maybe she was just exhausted. Doing comedy was harder than doing action, and they had been working particularly long hours the last week.

Marge leaned over to give Susan's face a final gentle touch with the powder puff, then stepped away from her. Susan kept her body rigid, and she could hear Larry Blesco, the assistant director, talking into the microphone of his headset. He was standing behind her in the tiny dining room. "We're ready," he reported to the director. "Call it anytime."

The four or five other people behind her were absolutely silent. Susan tried to make her mind focus on Julia and imagine the anger she would feel if her husband had just told her that she was a complete zero.

But she couldn't keep her mind off herself. Her head wouldn't stop spinning, and she was beginning to think she was going to faint. *I'm not going to faint. I'm going to make it through the scene.*

"All quiet," Larry ordered unnecessarily. His voice also seemed thin and remote, and she tried to concentrate on what he was saying. Then he said in a conversational tone, "Action, Susan."

She picked up the red suitcase and opened the door. She stepped onto the semicircular brick porch and slammed the door behind her. A smoky, grayish haze lay over the sky, although at the distant borders of the smog she could glimpse radiant patches of blue. The brilliance of the early afternoon sun gave the haze an almost golden glow. Banks of lights mounted on tall black stands added their own electrical glare to the scene.

She stood still for a moment. She noticed a dozen or so crew members standing outside camera range, but she was careful not to let her gaze rest on them. She took in the long black coils of cable snaking across the small manicured lawn, the power trucks and equipment trailers, and the crowd of spectators gathered in a semicircle around the front of the house.

About twenty feet away, she saw Martin standing by one of the dolly-mounted Panavision cameras. He was whispering earnestly to the cameraman, who was bent over looking through the lens. The second camera was on the sidewalk by the street and was positioned to catch her getting into the car.

She stepped off the brick porch and took two brisk steps down the sidewalk. Then all at once she couldn't breathe. She gasped for breath like a dying fish. She made small wheezing sounds, but her unresponsive chest muscles felt paralyzed. Then she noticed that her heart was beating so hard and so rapidly that she could hear the pounding in her ears.

Sweat broke out on her forehead, but her hands felt

clammy and cold. The dizziness she had fought against earlier came back. The whole world seemed to be spinning around in front of her eyes. She tried to stop the motion by staring straight ahead and keeping her head absolutely level. But it didn't work—the world wouldn't stop whirling.

A feeling of complete terror possessed her. She knew she was going to suffocate. And her heart was pumping so hard that she was afraid it might explode at any moment. Something awful was going to happen to her.

She was going to die.

She gasped and dropped the red suitcase. A vague idea of getting help took possession of her, and she started to run down the walk toward Martin. But her legs were limp and rubbery and would no longer hold her weight. She took only three small steps, then collapsed. She fell onto the lawn by the sidewalk, and she could smell the moist, earthy odor of grass.

"Cut!" She could hear Martin shouting. "For Christ's sake, cut!"

Then she wasn't aware of anything at all.

2

Juan Cortez sat in front of the computer at the admissions desk in the UCLA Medical Center Emergency Room. He punched a few keys, then waited for the "Patient Personal Data" menu to appear on the screen. It popped up exactly the way it was supposed to.

He was installing the software the computer needed to interact with the medical center's new Cumulative Patient Record Database. Now that CPRD was in operation, a staff member or doctor could get access to the records of every patient admitted to the hospital or treated in the emergency room.

Cortez wasn't employed by the medical center or the university, although he spent all his time doing jobs for them. It wasn't the kind of work he should be doing. Somebody with his abilities should be running his own consulting company. That would be the way to coin some real money.

And with the Iceman on his ass, he needed real money. Three weeks ago, in a two-day crap game, he'd lost $6,000, and that was $5,500 more than he had started with. He'd been so sure the odds were going to turn in his favor that he'd given his marker to the Iceman. The Iceman was careful with his money, but he'd been glad to take Cortez's marker, because he knew he could make an easy collection. Cortez had a wife and a job.

He'd skipped the last rent payment and borrowed $500 from Tom Gibson. That way he'd been able to turn over $1,000 to the Iceman, but that was a week ago. Last night the Iceman had called to say he would be "very pleased" if Cortez could come up with another five by the end of the week. Cortez knew he was serious. "I didn't get my name from making snow cones," the Iceman had told him when he took his marker.

Cortez had worked for Software Services for six years, since he was twenty-five. He had been happy to take the job, because it gave him a chance to work with computers. But now he was sick of the work. He'd thought that if he could win enough shooting craps to pay off the debts his wife had run up, he might quit and set himself up in business. If he could get Tom Gibson to come in with him, success would be guaranteed.

Gibson wasn't even working with computers anymore, but he knew ten times more about them than anybody else Cortez had ever seen. When Cortez was just a kid at L.A. Community College, Gibson was teaching there. At first he told Cortez he "sort of" had a degree in computer science from MIT. But whether he had one or not, by the time Cortez met him, he was already a legend among the local hackers. They called him Cyberwolf.

Gibson was faster and better than anybody. Even then

he was a loner, and he stayed away from the other hackers. But they knew about him, and the name they gave him was a good description of what he was like when he was in hack mode.

Watching Cyberwolf tap into the net was like looking into the future and glimpsing the time when the mental powers of people and computers would become intertwined and inseparable. He was unbelievably fast, subtle, and savvy. He prowled cyberspace and lurked in the electronic shadows. "The landscape is silver and gray, and you have to be careful not to get lost in it," he used to warn Cortez. "It's so peaceful, you might not ever want to come out."

Gibson himself gave Cortez the name Backup, because as he said, "If I get lost in the rays, I can count on you to remind me what the fuck I'm supposed to be doing." Cortez liked the name, and he liked it when Gibson called him by it.

But all that was—what? At least twelve years ago. He had been an eighteen-year-old kid crazy about what you could do when you had access to a computer and a telephone line. Gibson was maybe four years older. He was fresh out of MIT and had wanted to go to work for Apple or Data General or maybe get slotted with AT&T, MCI, or one of the Bell operations. But he said they wouldn't touch him.

"I left with bad recs," he told Cortez after they got to know one another. "I worked on my own ideas and refused to take bullshit courses. When they found out I was responsible for crashing the Media Lab machines, they kicked me out."

"Then how did you get a teaching job?" Cortez asked.

Gibson smiled. "The college wanted cheap labor, and they wanted to say they had somebody teaching computer science with an MIT degree. They didn't care about the recs, and I told them I had the degree."

"Didn't they check?"

"I'm sure they did." He smiled. "And I'm sure they found out from the registrar's office that I was awarded a

B.S. in Computer Science." Gibson shook his head in apparent seriousness. "You know, if you can't crack a university computer and give yourself a degree, you don't deserve to have one."

Cortez made it a point to keep up with Cyberwolf. He stopped by his place to have some beers and chew the rag every couple of weeks. He liked Cyberwolf, but he didn't much like what he did to make a living.

When Gibson got out of Chino after serving eight months on the theft-of-services rap, ITT actually hired him. He worked for them for no more than a year, though. "All they wanted to know was what I could tell them about how I could get into the system and make changes without knowing any codes," he told Cortez. "When they thought they knew everything I did, they zapped me."

After that, Gibson had borrowed money from his mother and gone into business—if you wanted to call what he did a business. It was so disgusting that Cortez never even wanted to think about it. The times he saw Cyberwolf, they wouldn't talk about it. They'd just gab about hacking the ITT net or tapping into the Berkeley mainframe. Cyberwolf hadn't lost his touch, and Cortez was always ready to take a lesson.

"Are you almost through?" a male voice asked.

Cortez was startled to realize how long he had been staring at the "Current Patients" list. He looked up at the admitting clerk in the white lab coat standing behind his right shoulder.

"It's done," Cortez said.

"Then what's taking you so long?" the man asked. "We've got patients waiting to be processed."

As Cortez stood up, he heard the high-pitched braying of a siren. He glanced through the tall plate-glass window beside the admitting desk and saw an orange-and-white EMS ambulance with its light flashing pulling into the hospital's circular drive. The noise of the siren was almost deafening. The driver braked quickly, then backed the ambulance up to the dock outside the emergency room.

Then, all at once, roaring down the driveway right behind the ambulance came a convoy of three cars. The first
was a red RX-7, and behind it was a Mercedes convertible with at least five people crammed into it. Behind
them was an LAPD patrol car.

"Uh-oh," the admitting clerk said. "Something big is
happening here."

"What do you mean?" Cortez asked.

"Look at the citizens getting out of those cars." The
clerk nodded toward them. "They are definitely movie
people."

A compact, muscular woman in jeans and a purple
T-shirt climbed out of the RX-7 and began trotting across
the short distance between the car and the ambulance. She
was followed by a wiry, bronzed man, then after him
came the others from the convertible.

The two EMS men became the focus of attention.
While the crowd watched, they opened the back of the
ambulance and slid out the aluminum-framed stretcher.
They held it up and shook it gently so that the wheeled
undercarriage would lock into place. When it did, they
began rolling the stretcher across the receiving platform
toward the treatment area.

The neatly folded white sheet covering the patient's
body was pulled up only as far as her neck. A small,
transparent plastic mask was over her nose, and she
looked fully conscious and alert. Despite the mask, Cortez recognized her immediately.

"That's Susan Bradstreet," he said.

"I told you those were movie people," the clerk said,
sounding triumphant. "Something must have happened
while they were filming. Some of them still have makeup
on."

Cortez looked carefully at Susan's face, and he could
see that her skin looked a heavier shade of peach than
was normal. Apart from the makeup, he couldn't believe
anybody could be so beautiful. Her face seemed so
smooth and delicate that she could have been a statue, or
a painting—anything but a real person.

"I'd say she's had a heart attack," the clerk said. The EMS techs crossed the receiving platform and were now out of sight. Cortez continued to look out the window.

Susan Bradstreet! Seeing her coming into the hospital while he was thinking about Cyberwolf was a strange coincidence. Cyberwolf was always talking about her, as if they were best friends and she told him everything about herself. He knew where she lived, who her ex-boyfriend was, what she and her father talked about—everything.

Wouldn't Cyberwolf be surprised when he told him that Susan Bradstreet was admitted to the medical center. Come to think of it, maybe he'd like to drive over and catch a glimpse of her. The traffic wasn't bad at this time of day, and he could make it in twenty or thirty minutes.

Cortez decided he'd give Cyberwolf a call.

3

David Hightower shifted in his chair and looked across the desk at Ivy Browdel. She was a thin, twenty-four-year-old woman with a long, plain face, but it was her eyes that caught his attention. They had a blank, staring look, as if she were peering into another world that only she could see. For almost an hour he had listened to her describe her fears of this world.

"I'm going to have the nurse show you to your room," Hightower said.

Mrs. Browdel raised her head and looked at him, but she gave no sign of understanding what he said. Hightower nodded to the nurse standing in the doorway, then got up to leave.

"Are you sure there's enough insulation in these walls?" Mrs. Browdel glanced around the small examining room, running her eyes along the ceiling and down the walls. "My husband said the medical center has special insulation so it can't be penetrated by alien radio waves."

"You'll be perfectly safe here," Hightower assured her.

He found it hard not to try to talk delusional patients out of their irrational beliefs. His mentors had taught him that such efforts might even strengthen a patient's delusional structure. Even so, it was contrary to his nature to avoid opposing blatantly false beliefs.

He saw that as one of his many weaknesses as a psychiatrist. When he was a hand surgeon, he had been able to take a direct, straightforward approach to patients. When he saw a problem, his immediate impulse was to try to solve it as quickly and effectively as possible. If someone was suffering from the pain of carpal tunnel syndrome, he would spend a few minutes widening the tunnel and releasing the compressed nerve and, almost magically, the person would feel better.

But that wasn't the way psychiatry worked. It was more tentative and circuitous. The problems were unclear, their causes mostly unknown, and the treatments uncertain. Often, the most you could do was provide patients with support, reassurance, and encouragement. Everything about psychiatry was indirect, and he wasn't sure he would ever be able to acquire the right kind of skills.

Hightower got up from his chair and took Mrs. Browdel's hand. "We're going to give you some medication that will help you feel better soon," he told her.

She looked at him blankly and nodded. Hightower gave her what he hoped was a reassuring smile, then the nurse led her out of the interview room.

Hightower sat back down at the small desk and opened up Mrs. Browdel's chart. He was supposed to have been off work forty-five minutes earlier, but before he could leave he would have to complete his admission note. He switched off his beeper so he could work in peace.

By the time he had finished the note, his right eye was aching from the strain of focusing on the page. He rubbed his eye and massaged the muscles around it with the tips of his fingers.

He had once thought that he would eventually get used to having only one functional eye. But now he knew he never would. He would always feel the loss, and it would always remind him of greater and more painful losses. The bomb blast that had destroyed the sight in his left eye had also killed his wife and put an end to his career as a hand surgeon.

Neither he nor Alma had ever heard of the Algerian Reparation Group. All they had wanted to do was to pay a visit to a Paris department store and buy some presents to take home. The bomb was in a dirty white Citroën sedan parked at the curb. It was just one of those things that happen.

Alma died immediately from massive head injuries and rapid blood loss. "She was never conscious, not even a moment," one of the doctors who spoke English told him. They had been married for three years, and she had been pregnant for two months. The four-day trip to Paris had been a spur-of-the-moment romantic whim—their last escapade as a childless couple.

Hightower himself had been knocked unconscious for four hours. He had suffered a concussion and numerous bruises and lacerations, but his only permanent injury was the damage to his left eye. He must have been turning to look at Alma, because he was hit directly in the face by glass fragments from the windows of the Citroën. Small particles of safety glass had peppered the side of his face and embedded themselves in his eye.

The surgeons removed the fragments and saved his eye, but they could do nothing to repair his damaged retina. For two weeks he could see nothing with the eye, then gradually, in his peripheral field, he was able to discern vague outlines of people and large objects. Since then his vision in that eye hadn't improved.

Hightower closed the manila folder containing Mrs. Browdel's chart and pushed it away from him. He rubbed both eyes with his knuckles, slid his chair back from the desk, and tossed his ballpoint pen on top of the folder.

Every time his eye began to ache, he had to fight hard to keep himself from sinking into depression and self-pity.

When he was well enough to leave Paris and return home to Chicago, he had intended to lose himself in his work. Not only would he increase his operating schedule, but he would take on additional teaching responsibilities at the University of Chicago Medical School. If he filled up each day with activities, he would never have to be alone. He could sleep in the on-call room and take his meals in the hospital cafeteria.

Yet during his first operation, a simple tendon repair, he discovered that, with only one good eye, he lacked the depth perception needed to locate the tissue planes and perform the delicate cutting and tying that surgery required. He let the surgical fellow working with him complete the operation. He realized then that he would have to give up surgery altogether. He resigned his academic appointment the next day.

He spent the next three months doing nothing but sitting at his kitchen table, staring at the TV, and ruminating on the past. He was thirty-two, a widower, an ex-professor, and an ex-surgeon. His whole life seemed behind him.

He knew he was clinically depressed, but it never occurred to him to try to get help from anybody. Surgeons *gave* help, they didn't *ask* for it. Despite the depression he could still think clearly, and he came to the conclusion that he couldn't go on with his life the way it was. He would either have to kill himself or make a concerted effort to put himself back together.

He wasn't sure what putting himself back together involved, but he decided that a reasonable beginning would be to return to Harvard Medical School and get additional training in psychiatry. He had a vague hope that by learning to help others, he would also learn to help himself.

He had to admit that he felt much better after his two years in the residency program at Harvard and a year as a fellow in the UCLA Neuropsychiatric Institute. He was at least well enough trained to be of use to others, so he didn't have to feel that his life was pointless. Yet he still couldn't pretend to be a whole person.

He could handle the pessimism and the depression, but the hardest condition to accept was the lack of restful sleep. He slept fitfully and woke early, no matter when he went to bed. He never made it through the night without being awakened at least once by a recurring dream.

In the dream, he was standing on the shore of a murky ocean and the undertow was dragging at his legs. He was struggling to keep Alma from being swept away, but her arms were too slippery and he couldn't hold on to her. As the waves tugged at her, he fought to yank her back. He grasped her arms tightly, but then they tore loose from her body and came off in his hands. The water swirling around him turned into a dark sea of blood.

Hightower yawned and ran his hand over his face. He needed to start doing things, before he sank into a very low mood. He picked up Mrs. Browdel's chart, went out to the psychiatric admissions desk, and slipped the file into the metal chart rack. He might never know what would happen to Mrs. Browdel, because this was his last day of work. He was taking off for a month to work full time on his research. People who knew him weren't surprised that his project involved evaluating treatments for anxiety and depressive reactions to post-traumatic stress.

Hightower walked to the other end of the admitting desk and stopped in front of the clerk, a short, middle-aged Asian woman. She was sitting behind the waist-high desk, bent over writing in a record book, and the top of her head was barely visible.

"So long, Bernice. I'll see you next month."

Bernice looked up and smiled. "We'll miss you around here, Dr. Hightower. Tell me again where you're going." Her plump face wrinkled for a moment in concentration. "Is it Cleveland?"

"St. Louis."

"I knew it was someplace in the Midwest," she said. "Are you visiting with relatives?"

"My parents," he said. "They're in England now, but

they're supposed to get back Wednesday morning. I'm making them put me up while I sort through some data I've been collecting." He smiled. "I've shipped all my books, and I'm flying out tomorrow."

"Oh, that's wonderful," she said. "I know your family will love having you stay with them for a while."

He smiled, then gave Bernice a wave and walked toward the outside door. Through the glass, he could see the tall, limber palm trees lining the road leading into the campus. Even after almost a year in Los Angeles, the sight of them still startled him. They seemed so strange and exotic, as if they were props erected along the street by a movie company.

"Dr. Hightower!" Bernice called down the corridor. He turned and saw her leaning over the counter holding a telephone receiver. "A call for you," she said. "Dr. Burton in the medical ER said to try to catch you."

"Did you tell him I was off duty?" Hightower asked.

"I did," Bernice said. "He said to get you anyway, because you'd thank him for it later."

Hightower reached across the counter and took the telephone Bernice was holding out to him.

"I know you're trying to get away," Burton said. "But we've got a patient here I think you'll find very interesting."

"What's the problem?"

"So far as I can tell, nothing. So before I order an MRI, I want you to come over and talk to her and see if we agree."

"I'm sure they could spare a senior resident."

"I think she falls in your research area," Burton said. "Besides, our patient is a star, and a resident might feel too intimidated to ask the right questions."

"What do you mean your patient is a star?" Hightower was genuinely puzzled.

"I mean she's a *movie* star," Burton said, with a hint of exasperation. "Have you heard of Susan Bradstreet?"

"Only vaguely." He wasn't sure if even that was true.

"You really were educated on the East Coast," Burton

said. "Anyway, she's in Exam Room Two. So are you coming?"

To his surprise, Hightower found himself feeling excited at the prospect of examining a movie star. It would be a completely new experience.

"I'm on my way," he said.

4

Cortez found a pay phone in the blue-carpeted hallway leading from the emergency room into the main floor of the hospital. A slit window in the cinder-block wall let him keep an eye on the ambulance dock.

"Specialty Books," Gibson said, answering on the second ring. His voice was deep, and he spoke with perfect enunciation. Cortez thought he sounded sophisticated, the way somebody educated at a fancy eastern university ought to sound.

"Hey, Cyber, it's Backup. I just saw something that'll make you shit in your pants with envy when you hear about it. Man, I couldn't believe it myself."

"So tell me about it," Gibson said smoothly. Cortez had never heard him sound flustered. Cyberwolf was always in control.

"I've been checking for software bugs in the ER boxes, and I just saw an ambulance bring in—guess who—*Susan Bradstreet*."

"That *is* interesting," Gibson said, speaking softly and deliberately. "That is *very* interesting."

Cortez glanced outside and saw the two L.A. cops getting into their car. They backed up, then drove off.

"Do you know what's wrong with her?" Gibson asked.

"Maybe a heart attack, the guy on the desk said, but he's not a doctor. She didn't look exactly sick." Cortez stopped to consider. "Worried is the way I'd describe her. Or maybe scared."

Gibson was silent for a long time. Then he said, "I want you to hang around the ER and see what you can pick up. Try to find out what's wrong with her and, if they put her in the hospital, what room she's in." He paused. "Do think you can do all that?"

"If you want me to," Cortez assured him. "But don't you want to come over here? You might get a look at her."

"I'd want more than a look." Gibson sounded very serious. "Come by tonight around eight and tell me what you learned."

"If you say so," Cortez said. "But how come you're so interested?"

"Can I assume you'd like to raise the money to keep the Iceman from flat-lining you?"

"Man, that's for sure," Cortez said. "That mother's ready to put me in the fucking meat locker."

"Then just do what I tell you," Gibson said. "This may turn out to be a better setup than I could have planned myself."

"What are you talking about?"

"I'm talking about making you very rich," Cyberwolf said.

5

Hightower stepped against the wall to get out of the way of a stretcher being pushed rapidly toward the trauma room. A man in a green plaid shirt stained with a dark patch of wet blood lay inert on the white sheet. Hightower turned his head to the side to avoid having to look at the bloody shirt. It evoked too many memories.

Stopping in front of Room 2, he took Susan Bradstreet's chart out of the rack attached to the door. Before he opened the red folder, he glanced around the treatment room. It was obvious that somebody of considerable interest was in the exam room. Everyone who passed by—doctors, nurses, techs, clerks—stared at the door, apparently hoping to get a glimpse inside. The one who appeared most interested was a plump Hispanic man with jet black hair and a thick mustache who was sitting in front of the computer at the billing desk.

Hightower smiled. Susan Bradstreet seemed to have everybody's attention. What would it be like to have thousands of total strangers interested in you? He didn't see how anybody could stand being at the center of so many people's fantasies.

He opened the file and glanced over the top sheet of the patient data form. Susan Bradstreet, he noted, was a thirty-one-year-old white female who was five feet eight inches tall and weighed a hundred and ten pounds. She had gray eyes and dark blond hair. Her place of birth was Cleveland, Ohio, and her occupation was actress. Her next of kin was her father, Kenneth A. Bradstreet of Bay Village, Ohio. She had never been hospitalized, never been treated for a psychiatric problem, and was taking no medication. She was unmarried and had never been pregnant. She had an enviably boring medical history.

Hightower carefully read through Burton's exam notes, then closed the file and tapped on the door. Without waiting for an answer, he stepped into the room.

The room was small, and the six people already inside made it crowded. Most of them were talking, and even though they were speaking in low voices, the sound of their conversation filled the room with a loud, almost mechanical hum.

The noise didn't stop when he walked in, but Hightower could see everyone turn toward the door. They knew he was there, but they didn't seem able to decide what to make of him. He waited a moment, looking around the room at the people.

Near the front, two men were standing close together

and talking to the woman who sat on the edge of the examining table. The men blocked Hightower's view so he could catch only a partial glimpse of her. He felt sure she was Susan Bradstreet, and he started to call her name. But before he could say anything, one of the men turned and stepped toward him.

The man was young, probably in his early thirties, but contrary to the ethos of southern California, he hadn't been taking care of himself. He was apple-shaped, balding, and wore glasses with round lenses and thin gold frames. His blue suit was expertly cut to minimize the bulge of his protruding stomach, but the sidepieces of his glasses were almost buried in the thick layer of fat lining his face and temples.

"Just who are you?" he asked Hightower. He was scowling, and his manner seemed deliberately abrasive. "I'm Howard Simpson, vice-president of Galaxy Films, and I'm in charge of the project this group is involved in." He narrowed his eyes and glared at Hightower. "Are you authorized to be in this room?"

Before Hightower could respond, the man Simpson had been talking to came up and said quickly, "Howard, this must be Dr. Hightower." He turned to Hightower and smiled.

The man was in his middle forties, with neatly clipped silver-gray hair and cheeks as smooth and rosy as a child's. His light gray suit fit perfectly. Hightower was starting to find it strange to be around men who dressed so well. In contrast with them, his summer-weight blazer seemed wrinkled and ill-fitting.

"Dr. Burton asked me to come have a look at Ms. Bradstreet," Hightower acknowledged. Ignoring Simpson, he addressed himself to the man in the gray suit.

"I'm Kenneth Burke," the man said. "I'm Susan's agent and friend." He shook hands with Hightower. "Let me introduce you." He swiveled around and gestured toward the woman sitting on the examining table.

Hightower took a step toward Susan Bradstreet, and she raised her head slightly to look at him. Even knowing that she was a movie star hadn't prepared him for the force of the impact she made on him. For a brief moment, when he looked directly at her, he felt almost stunned. It was all he could do to keep from staring.

Her face was narrow with high cheekbones and so finely shaped that it had an almost unreal perfection. Her gray-green eyes shone like polished jade, and her honey blond hair glowed golden in the light. Her hair was rumpled and tangled, and her face was smoothly coated with peach-colored makeup. Yet none of that mattered. She was beautiful in a striking, almost unearthly, way.

Hightower became aware of something else about her, something that couldn't be explained by her physical appearance alone. She radiated such a powerful psychological presence that the atmosphere in the small, drab examining room seemed charged with energy and possibility. He could sense himself being drawn to her, even though they had yet to exchange a single word.

She returned his smile, but hers was nothing more than a faint, polite twitch of her lips. At first he thought she was expressing arrogance, but as he got closer to her, he noticed that she had an anxious, worried look. The skin around her eyes was pulled into small wrinkles, and the corners of her mouth were drawn down. Her whole face seemed as tight and stiff as a mask. Something was worrying her, and he needed to talk to her in private to find out what it was.

"I'm David Hightower," he said. He took her hand and shook it. He was surprised by the strength of her fingers when she returned his handshake, but he also noticed that her hand felt much colder than it should have. The room was warm from the heat generated by so many people.

While he was holding her hand, he said to her in a quiet voice, "Please ask your friends to leave. We need to talk privately."

He could see her hesitate. She probably didn't want to be left alone, because then she would feel vulnerable to whatever it was that was bothering her. She looked into his face and seemed to study it carefully. He didn't avoid looking at her, but he didn't try to stare her down either. Finally, she nodded.

"I'm sorry, but I have to ask everyone to go now." Her voice sounded weak and shaky, but it also had a sharp edge of authority in it. She turned and glanced around the room. "I need some time with Dr. Hightower. Thanks so much for staying with me, and I plan to get out of here very soon."

No one moved for a moment, then Burke pulled back the door and held it open. A woman and man, both in makeup and wearing ordinary clothes that fit too well to be anything but costumes, came from the back. They each bent and kissed Susan Bradstreet on the cheek before they left.

"I'm perfectly fine now," she told them. Her voice was almost cheerful. "If reporters ask you what happened, tell them I just got exhausted from overwork."

"That's exactly what I want you to say," Simpson broke in. He wagged a finger at the man, then at the woman. "And if you say anything else, you'll be off this picture."

"Yes, sir," the man said. He started for the door.

"Good luck, Susan," the woman said, ignoring Simpson.

"I'd better make a statement to the press, so they'll get the right message out," Simpson said. He gave Hightower a hostile look, then followed the couple out the door. He didn't even glance at the star of his movie.

"So charming," Susan said softly to no one in particular.

A stocky, muscular woman with short black hair, wearing an oversized T-shirt and jeans started for the door. She then hesitated and turned to look at Susan.

"Go ahead, Meg." Susan tried to smile. "Have some coffee and walk around. You can check back later, but I won't leave here without you."

The woman's face didn't change expression. She still didn't move for a moment, but eventually she nodded, then walked out. Hightower was surprised at how lightly and quickly she moved.

"I'll be out in the waiting room, Susy," Kenneth Burke said. "I'll talk to you as soon as Dr. Hightower says it's okay." He gave her a questioning look.

"You don't have to wait around, Ken," she said. "I can phone you later."

"If you think you'll be okay," he told her. He glanced behind him. "I need to make sure Howard doesn't say anything we'll regret later." He smiled and waved to her, then turned loose of the door.

Before the door swung shut, Hightower caught a glimpse of three or four nurses, techs, and the Hispanic man craning their necks to see inside. Now that he had met Susan Bradstreet, he understood a little better why people seemed to go to such great lengths to be around movie stars.

As the door closed, Hightower immediately grew aware of being alone in the room with Susan Bradstreet. He felt an unusual, almost adolescent, shyness. The feeling of being drawn to her was still there. Not only did it surprise him, but it was too strong for him to accept comfortably. He reminded himself that she was somebody with a serious problem and that it was his job to concentrate on figuring out what it was.

"You look uncomfortable perched on the edge of the table," Hightower said.

"My back is starting to hurt."

"Then why don't we sit over there." He nodded toward the two metal chairs on each side of the small desk pushed against the back wall.

Susan nodded and slid off the table. She stretched, shrugged her shoulders, then rubbed her lower back with both hands. Hightower thought her white blouse and pale pink skirt looked too frilly to suit her. She moved with the ease and suppleness of someone who would be a lot more comfortable in jeans. But then she had come directly from a movie set and was wearing a costume, not her ordinary clothes.

Susan walked to the left side of the desk and sat down. When Hightower sat down, they were at right angles to each other.

"Who's the woman you called Meg?" He hoped he wouldn't have trouble getting her to talk, but starting with a neutral topic was always a good strategy.

"Her name is Meg O'Hare, and she's my chauffeur and bodyguard." Her voice still sounded shaky, and she spoke in a hesitant, almost whispery way. She cleared her throat. "She's absolutely loyal and as strong as a tractor."

"She does look strong." He smiled at her comparison.

Susan slid forward on her chair until she was balanced on the edge. She then turned to her left and rested her clasped hands on the desktop. He noticed that she was squeezing her hands so tightly that her fingertips had turned a bluish gray.

"You're a psychiatrist, aren't you?" Her voice sounded firmer, and her tone was almost sharp. The question was more like a challenge.

Hightower said nothing. Raising his eyebrows slightly, he looked at her with an open, expectant expression.

"Dr. Burton didn't tell me you were," she went on. "I'm just guessing."

Hightower nodded. "Does it bother you to talk to a psychiatrist?"

"Not particularly." She shook her head. "But in all honesty, I don't think you can help me."

"Why is that?" Hightower draped an arm over the top of his chair and leaned back. He was feeling tense himself. But if he made himself relax, then maybe Susan Bradstreet would loosen up some.

"Because whatever made me feel so . . . so dizzy and then collapse wasn't something psychological." Then she added in a firm voice, "I'm sure of that."

"What do you think is wrong?" Her resistance to the notion that she might have a psychiatric problem didn't surprise him. It was a common response.

"I don't know what to think, exactly," she said quietly. She unclasped her hands and worked her fingers back and forth. She looked at him without saying anything, and he noticed that her eyes had become moist with tears. She suddenly seemed confused and unguarded. She lowered her eyes, then shook her head and shrugged.

"Do you think you're sick?" he asked gently.

She focused her eyes on the white laminate top of the desk and said in a low voice, "I'm afraid so." Then, almost whispering, she said, "I think it's something very serious."

"What do you mean, 'something very serious'?" he asked. "What sort of problem are you thinking about?"

"Maybe a brain tumor," she said in a strained whisper. Then she started speaking with more energy, as if trying to persuade him she was right. "Nobody can feel the way I did without some physical cause. I think I ought to be seeing a neurologist instead of a psychiatrist."

"Dr. Burton is a neurologist." Hightower tried to sound reassuring. "We can also arrange for you to get a more detailed examination later."

"I didn't know he was a neurologist," Susan said, without sounding wholly relieved. She looked up at him. "Please go ahead and ask me whatever you need to." She sat back in her chair and crossed her arms over her chest. Smiling slightly, she said, "I reserve the right to take the Fifth on some things."

Susan pushed a twisted skein of honey-colored hair off her forehead, and for some reason the gesture reminded Hightower of how beautiful she was. Her eyes flicked about the room, and she was obviously having trouble staying in her chair. She gave the impression that she would like to leap up and run out the door.

"I know you blacked out and collapsed," Hightower said. "Do you mind telling me the details?"

"I was supposed to walk out the door of a house, go down the sidewalk, and get into a car. But while I was waiting behind the door, I started to fall to pieces." She took a shallow breath, then another one. "My head was spinning, and I thought I was going to throw up. And people sounded funny, like I was at the bottom of a well."

"Did you feel as if you were somehow outside yourself and looking down on the scene?"

"Yes, I did, but how did you know?" She looked at him in surprise, as if he had performed a magic trick. "Anyway, things got worse when I started down the sidewalk. I couldn't breathe, and my chest felt paralyzed." She shook her head at the memory. "Then all of a sudden I felt terribly afraid."

"What were you afraid of?"

"I don't know," Susan said. He could see the muscles of her face tighten again. "I felt something horrible was about to happen, but I didn't know what it was. I was sure I was dying, but I didn't know what was killing me." She paused. "Is any of this making any sense to you?" She sounded puzzled and frustrated.

Hightower nodded. "I know what you're talking about. Please go on."

"There's not much more. While I was convinced I was dying, my legs turned to rubber, and I fell down." She shrugged. "The next thing I knew, I was riding in an ambulance with an oxygen mask over my face." She shook her head. "Nothing even remotely like this has happened to me before." She paused, then looked at him with an ironic smile. "So should I sign my living will?"

Hightower ignored the question. "How do you feel now?"

Susan put her elbows on the desk, interlaced her fingers, and rested her chin against them. Her expression was thoughtful, and she seemed to be considering his question carefully. "I feel weak and wobbly," she said at last. "As if I just lived through some public disaster like a plane crash or a hotel fire." She paused to think a moment. "But I'm also very nervous and tense. I think I'm still scared."

He was impressed by the articulate way she gave an account of her feelings. Her description was exactly in keeping with what he had decided was the most probable diagnosis. But he would need a few more answers to test his hypothesis. "Has anything very distressing happened to you in the last year or six months?" he asked. "Anything emotionally upsetting or stressful?"

She nodded her head vigorously, then brushed back her hair as it fell across her forehead. "Several things. Four months ago, I broke up with an actor named Bryan Forbes. We'd been seeing one another for about a year, then I found out that he was using heroin and that he had been stealing from me to get the money to buy it. I couldn't put up with that, and I told him to take a hike." Her face was drawn tight, and her voice was strained.

"Do you use any drugs?"

She shook her had. "I tried snorting coke one time, and until about five years ago I used to drink scotch at parties and wine at dinner." She smiled. "Now I don't even put sugar in my iced tea."

"How do you feel now about breaking up with Bryan?"

"I know I'm better off without him." She drew her lips into a tight line. "But sometimes late at night I miss him so much it's all I can do not to track him down and ask him to come back."

"Any problems with other men in your life?"

She gave him an open, almost defiant look. "I'm not seeing anybody regularly—except for friends, of course."

"Any other upsetting things?"

"My grandmother died sixteen months ago, and that really hurt." She put her hands back in her lap and looked down at them. "I was very close to her, because she sort of helped raise me after my mother died when I was twelve." She looked up. "Then four months after my grandmother was buried, my father had a heart attack and had to have bypass surgery." She sucked in a short breath and bit at the margin of her lower lip. "He seems all right now, but I was certainly scared for a while."

"How about your work?"

"I've been lucky." She smiled. "I've had a couple of hit movies and made a lot of money." She shook her head. "Lots of small hassles, but no real problems."

She slid forward until she was again on the edge of her chair. She brushed back the hair from her face with sharp, quick gestures, then tightly grasped three fingers of her left hand with her right. She seemed about to explode.

"Is something wrong?" Hightower spoke calmly.

"I'm feeling extremely anxious." Her face turned rigid. "I know I said I'd cooperate and talk to you, but it's taking longer than I expected. And it's keeping me from getting a diagnosis of what's wrong with me."

Hightower looked directly at her. Her gray-green eyes caught his, and he found himself staring into them. He could see her fear. "I know what's wrong with you," he said softly.

"You do?" She threw her head back, as if he had said something that shocked her.

"You have an anxiety disorder," he said. "After a few tests I could give you a more exact diagnosis. Maybe it's panic disorder or maybe a generalized anxiety state."

She was staring at him, waiting for him to go on. Her eyes showed intelligence, as well as interest, and he felt sure she would be able to understand whatever he told her. She obviously had a quick mind.

"Without knowing you were doing it, you presented me with a classic description of an anxiety attack. All the symptoms were there." He held up his left hand and began to tick them off on his fingers. "Difficulty breathing, dizziness, rapid heartbeat, depersonalization, derealization, and feeling you were dying."

He spread out his hands. "You also fit two profiles for anxiety disorders. I saw in your chart that you probably have a generally benign heart condition called mitral valve prolapse, and for unknown reasons it's associated with anxiety attacks. Also, you have a recent history of several stressful life events."

Susan sat without saying anything. Her head was bowed, and all he could see was the gleaming gold circlet of hair on top. After a moment, she raised her head and looked up at him. He was surprised to see that her eyes were shining and tears were running down her cheeks.

"Then I don't have a brain tumor?" Her voice was choked.

"Almost certainly not," Hightower told her firmly. "We can arrange for you to have an MRI, but the only function it would serve would be to make you feel better."

"I feel better already," she said, smiling. She used her fingers to wipe the tears off her cheeks and out of the corners of her eyes. She then rubbed her fingers on her pale pink skirt. The tears left dark, wet marks.

"We can put you on a low dose of a tranquilizer," he said. "Then you can get some therapy and behavioral training." He smiled. "You'll be back to normal very quickly."

"You're sure you're right?" She gave him a challenging look. "I definitely don't have some fatal disease?"

"I can't give you a guarantee like that, but I can say that it's highly unlikely."

Susan frowned at him. "What about the tranquilizer? Will it let me go back to work?"

"All anxiolytics are mildly sedating." He shrugged. "I don't know if that would be a problem."

"It would." She sounded definite. "I'd look drugged on film, and I might have a hard time remembering my lines." She shook her head. "But I don't think I can go back to shooting if I'm going to have any more attacks."

"Can you take some time off? Maybe even a week?"

She smiled, and he noticed that the right corner of her lip turned up slightly. The asymmetry seemed to make her more attractive than perfect proportion would have.

"Could I really get over this in a week?"

"Not really," Hightower said. "Anxiety is something you're going to have to learn to live with. But you could take a full dose of medication for a week, then taper off, and you could also learn a number of techniques to help you deal with anxiety."

"That would be great." She sounded relieved. "I've got a clause in my contract that says I don't have to work while I'm sick." She smiled grimly. "Howard Simpson is going to howl about having to stop production, but I'm sure Galaxy's got insurance for just such situations."

"I'll leave it to you to work that out."

"And I'll leave it to Ken," Susan said. "Now, where can I go to get the treatment?"

"You don't have to go anyplace." Hightower smiled. "You can be treated right here."

She looked surprised. "That won't work. I need to go someplace where people don't know who I am. Or if they do, they'll keep quiet about it." She shook her head. "If word got out that I was getting treatments at the Neuropsychiatric Institute, my career would take a nosedive."

"Even if you told the truth?"

"Dr. Hightower, you don't know the film industry." She made it sound as if he were as naive as a child. "I need to sneak away somewhere, get the treatment, then get back before too many people notice I'm not around."

"All right." He couldn't see why the matter was so important, but he was prepared to believe her. "You could go lots of places. Do you want to stay in California?"

"Better not," she said. "Too many people recognize me here. Also, I want a place that's decent. I don't want to spend a week in some snake pit where people yell all night." She wrinkled up her face into a frown. "By the way, there's also security to think about. I've got to go someplace I can take Meg with me."

"Why do you think security would be a problem in a psychiatric institution?"

"Because there will be people there," she said. "When you're famous, people treat you like public property. Even normal people act as if they own you." She waved her hand. "I'm sure the chances that I'll be assaulted in a hospital aren't high, but I also can't afford to pretend it can't happen. With any luck, nobody will know who I am, and that will simplify my life considerably."

Hightower nodded. Susan might be revealing an element of paranoid thinking. He couldn't be sure about it, because he had never been around anyone famous. Maybe people did act the way she was worried about.

He leaned back in his chair and let his mind sift through the names of institutions he could remember.

Then he realized that he knew the perfect spot for Susan Bradstreet.

"Rush Psychiatric Institute in Cambridge, Massachusetts," he said. "Professionally, they're first-rate. Also, they're accustomed to dealing with famous people. I don't know about actors, but they've treated plenty of politicians, writers, and scientists."

"Have you been there?" The question sounded skeptical.

"I spent two years doing a residency there."

"How are the living conditions? This isn't someplace like Gulag Seventeen?"

He smiled. "Rush has a special wing for celebrity patients. It's very posh, and the security is first-rate."

"Will you call them for me?"

Her tone was apprehensive, as though she were suddenly uncertain as to whether they would want her as a patient. Vulnerability was clearly an aspect of her character, and he suspected it was an ingredient that went into making her a successful actress.

"I'll talk to Dr. Burton first," he said. "If he agrees with my diagnosis, I'll make the arrangements."

Hightower stood up and pushed in his chair. "I'm glad to have met you." He stretched out his hand and she took it and held it firmly in hers. "I'll get a nurse to escort you to your room and get you settled."

"Will you come talk to me after you call Rush?" She squeezed his hand gently, and he found himself returning the pressure. Her gray-green eyes focused on his. She didn't seem to be asking for anything, but he found himself wanting to do something to please her.

"I'll stop by later," he promised.

"Thank you," she said softly. She smiled and gave his hand a final squeeze.

He walked to the door, then holding it open, he turned to face her. "How soon could you be free to go?"

"I'd like to leave tonight."

"Tonight? I'm not sure we can set things up so fast."

"Please try," she said in a pleading tone. Then she smiled, and it made her seem calmer and more relaxed.

Hightower thought she looked extraordinarily beautiful.

6

Tom Gibson walked rapidly down the sidewalk toward the black-and-white SPECIALTY BOOKS sign that hung cantilevered over the sidewalk in front of the narrow, two-story stucco building.

He glanced up in disgust at the oily, blue-gray haze that hovered in the air and turned the light of the late afternoon a fiery red. His nose and throat burned from the exhaust fumes coming from the traffic along Davis Street.

The odor of burning gasoline seemed to make the hammering pain in his head even worse. But it was really the glare that bothered him. The reflective matte black lenses of his sunglasses only muted the harshness of the light. He hated the sun, and if he had a choice, he would never go out during the day.

While he walked, he scanned the sidewalk around him. He didn't plan to let himself be blindsided by some cokehead who thought he'd be a pushover. If they tried to fuck with him, they just might end up with a broken neck.

He got a good deal on his rent, but Davis Street was about two cuts below scummy. The two-story red-brick buildings had rotting window-sills and dirty, cracked sidewalks. The floors above the Laundromats, tape-rental stores, and beauty shops were welfare apartments packed tight with old people and single women with children and drop-in boyfriends. Auto-parts stores, a discount supermarket, and a half dozen bars were in the newer one-story cinder-block buildings. Even from the street, the bars smelled like public toilets, and Gibson found the very idea of going into one repulsive.

He spotted the redheaded man lounging against the wall outside a bar before the man spotted him. The man was large, with wide shoulders and big hands, and the pale skin of his face was marked with reddish brown blotches. He was wearing faded black jeans with the cuffs rolled up and a red satin baseball jacket over an olive T-shirt. The jacket was wrinkled and dirty and the fabric collar was frayed at the edges.

Gibson didn't turn his head as he saw the man push himself off the wall and start toward him. He had half expected it, and instead of walking faster, he deliberately slowed down to give the man a chance to meet up with him. He felt his pulse quicken, and his senses seemed to become more alert. The man started walking faster, adjusting the angle of his approach so that he could come at Gibson from the front. Gibson still didn't look.

"Say, let me talk to you a minute," the redhead said in a loud, rough voice. He stood in front of Gibson so that Gibson had to stop or run into him. "I got a little problem." He hitched his thumbs in the waistband of his jeans and spread out his elbows.

"Get out of my fucking way or you're going to have a big problem." Gibson kept his voice level, but his face turned hard as he stared into the man's green eyes.

"Big talk. But don't get your bowels in an uproar." The man stared back at him without smiling. "Listen, I need a few dollars for a bus ticket back to Seattle, and I figure you wouldn't mind helping me out."

"Figure again," Gibson said. He took a step to one side, and so did the redhead, continuing to block his way.

"I been nice," the redhead said. "But I can get rough."

The man reached into his jeans pocket with his left hand and pulled out a knife with a polished black handle. He lowered his hand, and Gibson could hear a faint click as the blade slid out of the handle and locked into place. A gravity knife, he realized.

"Give me the money you've got on you and all your credit cards. If you do, I won't hurt you." The man's blotchy face was screwed up tight, and his green eyes had turned to ice. "Yell, and I'll slit your goddamned throat."

Gibson stared at the redhead for a moment, making an effort to control his expression. He had learned at Chino not to give yourself away by signaling your responses. He could feel the rage building up in him, but he made no effort to resist it. He hadn't been looking for trouble, and then this piece of human garbage had come up to him and started trying to rob him.

"Come on, asshole." The man held the knife low and in front of him. The sun flashed off the blade.

Without saying anything, Gibson pulled his black leather wallet from his back pocket and started handing it over. The man's right hand came out to take the wallet, but just then Gibson dropped it. It landed with a soft thump between them on the dirty sidewalk.

"Pick it up." The man spat out the words, not taking his eyes off Gibson's face.

Gibson knelt down, but instead of picking up the wallet, he grabbed both the man's ankles and pulled hard. The man staggered back on his heels, flailing the air with his arms, then toppled to the pavement with a solid thump. He fell backward, stretched out full length on the sidewalk. As he hit, he made a noise like "Hunh."

The redhead started to sit up, but before he could hoist himself upright, Gibson kicked him. The toe of Gibson's shoe caught him under the chin and made a sharp crack as it snapped his head back. As the man fell backward onto the cement, he threw his arms out to his sides. In his left hand he was still clutching the knife.

Gibson stepped on the man's hand with his right foot. He bore down hard, shifting his weight forward. He could feel the bones of the fingers crunch under his foot, and the man gave a sharp gasp of pain. The gravity knife made a faint metallic tap as it fell to the sidewalk. Twisting his foot back and forth, Gibson ground the fingers against the concrete.

Pain made the man's mouth gape open, but before he could scream, Gibson kicked him on the right side of the head, just above his ear. The redhead stopped writhing and lay sprawled on his back, out cold and with his eyes closed.

Gibson retrieved his wallet, wiped off both sides on the redhead's shirt, then slipped it back into his pocket. Glancing around and seeing that no one was watching, he picked up the gravity knife. He knelt beside the redhead, grabbed his right ear, and pulled it tight. He then sliced off the ear with two quick strokes of the sharp blade. Bright red blood spurted from the stump and ran down the man's cheek. It began forming a small puddle on the dirty sidewalk.

Gibson stood up. Carrying the ear in his left hand and the knife in his right, he walked along the curb until he found a storm sewer. Squatting down, he tossed first the knife, then the ear, into the dark rectangular opening. The knife made a hollow clatter as it hit the concrete, but the ear made no sound at all.

He rubbed his fingers together, trying to rid himself of the feeling of being dirty from having touched the redhead's skin. The asshole wouldn't bleed to death, but it would be a long time before he started thinking of himself as a tough guy again.

Gibson shook his head. Just because he didn't look like the usual street trash, the man must have thought he'd be an easy target. People never seemed to realize that if you looked like an intelligent person, you just might know how to take care of yourself.

Gibson unlocked the door to his shop, stepped inside, then bolted the door behind him. With one smooth gesture, he pulled down the dark green shade and blocked off the rectangle of chicken-wire glass set into the upper part of the door. He took off his sunglasses and slid them into his shirt pocket.

He had just returned from the Federal Express office, where he had been sending out the week's magazine orders. He was trying to conduct his business as usual, but ever since Cortez's call, he had been feeling too excited to concentrate. He couldn't keep from thinking about Susan.

If Cortez knew what he was talking about, fate was presenting them with an unbelievable opportunity. Susan never went anywhere without being guarded or surrounded by dozens of people. But if she was in a hospital, that was a different story. Getting close to her should be easy.

While Cortez had been talking, the idea of kidnapping Susan had come to Gibson all of a sudden. He had realized that would be the only way he could ever expect to enjoy the pleasures with her that he fantasized about. He had also realized that, if he and Cortez did everything right, they could become immensely rich.

Another part of being smart was figuring out how to get what you wanted out of life. He knew his goals, but he was going to have to work out a way to reach them. A good place to start was by reviewing his files on Susan before Cortez came over.

Gibson stood with his back to the door and glanced around to make sure nobody had broken in while he was gone. An attempted robbery and a burglary on the same day would be bad luck, although perfectly possible.

The shop was a single room with walls covered from floor to ceiling by bookcases made of unpainted pine planks. The shelves were filled with an enormous variety of computer manuals. The hardback and paperbound books, spring binders, pamphlets, and loose-leaf notebooks constituted the documentation for hundreds of computers, printers, peripherals, and application programs.

Most of the documentation was for products that were obsolete and had been abandoned long ago by manufacturers. Companies like Texas Instruments, AT&T, and Packard Bell didn't even produce computers anymore, but information about their machines could be found neatly shelved in the mass of material he had accumulated. People and businesses who needed documentation for orphaned equipment and software were happy to pay him high prices for it.

If he wanted to work at the business, he could make a decent living. However, selling documentation would never give him anything like as much satisfaction as what he always ironically thought of as his "cryptic calling." It would never pay as much either. Few things did.

Sometimes he was tempted to get out of the documentation business. He knew, though, that as long as he followed his cryptic calling, he also needed to operate the other business. Selling documentation not only gave him a respectable cover, it provided him with a way of laundering the money that the cryptic calling brought in.

Everything looked just as he had left it, and he walked toward the back of the store. When he reached the back wall, he knelt down in front of the bookcase to the right of the stairway leading up to his apartment. Removing the two-volume, slipcased reference manual for the IBM OS/2 from the bottom shelf, he inserted his hand into the vacant space and ran his fingers along the back of the board. When he encountered the sharp edge of the metal catch, he used his thumb to push it to the left until he heard a click. He replaced the missing volume, stood up, and gave the shelf in front of him a slight tug.

A four-foot-wide section of bookcase swung toward him, its bottom clearing the scarred green vinyl floor by a fraction of an inch. Behind the shelving was a closed and knobless steel door. Painted the same pale gray color as the room, it was set flush with the wall and had no trim or facing. He slid back an inset panel beside the door and revealed the white plastic housing of the electronic control mechanism of the biometric lock.

He tapped out his six-digit access code on the keypad, and waited until the small light on the console glowed amber. Pressing down the yellow "Identification" bar, he simultaneously leaned forward and, using his right eye, stared directly at the red dot in the center of the tiny rectangular glass screen.

In an instant, the infrared beam of the retinal scanner

established his identity, and he heard a sharp click as the
locking mechanism released the door. It swung inward
easily as he pushed against it with his fingertips.

7

For a moment, the darkness in the narrow room was total,
and Gibson felt a wave of relief. He was now inside his
private necropolis. Although it was populated by only images of the dead, he was as sequestered from the harshness of the ordinary world as he would be if he were deep
underground in a sealed vault. In the dark stillness of the
room, the hammering in his head slacked, and he could
feel himself relax.

The necropolis reminded him of his mother's room
when he was growing up. When one of her sick head-
aches started, she would go into her bedroom, pull the
window shades, and turn off the light. She would take off
her dress and stretch out on the bed in her bra and pant-
ies. They were both white, always white, and the contrast
made her smooth skin look very pink.

When he was no more than ten, he started slipping in
through the partly opened door to watch her. Her room
was dark and cool, and she would lie so still that he
would sometimes think she was dead. He would watch
for her slightest movement, a twitch of her hand or the
motion of her chest as she took a breath.

When he was older, maybe thirteen, she would ask him
to massage her neck and shoulders, and as he rubbed his
hands over her smooth skin, she would make little moaning sounds of contentment. He kept up the massages until
one Friday when his father came home from work early
and caught him in her room. His face had turned white
and rigid, then he had grabbed him by the arm. His father

had said nothing but had hissed at him through clenched teeth.

His father dragged him to the bedroom door and threw him into the hall with such force that he had slid along the floor and burned both hands on the carpet. "Don't ever do that again," his father said, speaking in the cold, soft voice he used when he was enraged.

Tom had wanted to tell him that he wasn't doing anything wrong, but he hadn't dared to say a word. He had the feeling that his father was able to look into his mind and see what he was thinking while he was performing the massage.

Gibson shook his head. He shouldn't waste time on ancient memories. He had work to do. He pressed the wall switch, and a faint gray light began to glow from a fixture in the center of the room. The bulb was controlled by a rheostat, and as he turned the knob, the level of illumination rose, but only slightly. He detested harsh, glaring, yellow light, and he had no trouble seeing under conditions that others considered uncomfortably dim.

He looked around with satisfaction. On one wall of the room, he had hung a poster-sized color photograph of the nude body of a slender young woman in her early to middle twenties. The sofa she was lying on had been draped with a black velvet throw.

She was on her back, her arms at her sides. A small red pillow was under her head, and her long black hair fell over her shoulders. The ends of her hair touched the tops of her high, rounded breasts, almost hiding their pink nipples. Her long legs were stretched out straight, and the dark patch of pubic hair between them made her skin look pale, with the pallid, almost waxy color of antique ivory.

Standing next to the woman, at the foot of the couch, was Gibson himself. He was gazing down at her, his lips pulled back in a smile that showed the edges of his very white teeth. Although he hadn't altered the picture, he thought he looked handsome and powerful in it.

He was wearing blue tapered boxer shorts and no shirt. His body was trim and athletic, not muscle-bound but well developed, with clearly defined pectorals and biceps. His amber eyes reflected points of light, making them seem to burn with inner fire. His skin was smooth and pale, with no sign of tanning lines, and his cotton white hair streamed back from his face like the mane of a lion.

He shifted his gaze to the woman. Her eyelids were open, and he looked directly into her deep blue eyes. They were blank and staring in an unmistakable way. A living person's eyes were always shifting, but a dead person's remained fixed. Even in a photograph you could tell.

He thought the corpse in the picture was one of the most beautiful he had ever seen. Of course, he had never actually seen her, in life or in death. All he had had available to work from was a thirty-five-millimeter color photograph he had bought from an embalmer in Ardmore, Oklahoma. Her picture was one of the ten on a roll of film he had paid two hundred dollars to have mailed to him. Twenty dollars a shot—that was the price he had agreed on a year ago when he had gone to Ardmore and had a talk with the oldest embalmer at the Restland Funeral Home.

He glanced from the woman to the image of himself, then smiled. He was impressed by the picture's technical perfection. He hadn't had much experience with the Pix-Wizard at the time he produced it, but he had done an outstanding job of manipulating images to place the body on the couch and to put himself so naturally in the scene. He had liked the result so much that he had made another copy to hang in his bedroom.

He had named the corpse in the picture Sue almost exactly a year earlier. That was after he had gone to Westwood to see *Aztec Gold* on its opening night. The movie was silly, but he had fallen in love with Susan Bradstreet. There was no other way to put it. In some mysterious way, the dark blond color of her hair, the smooth delicacy of her face, and the gray-green color of her eyes combined to make her the most beautiful living woman he had ever seen.

He had been tempted to redo the synthesized image and put Susan's face on the corpse's body, but he decided against it. What most appealed to him about Sue were the empty eyes. He liked gazing into them, knowing they couldn't see him. He didn't think he would be able to change Susan's eyes to get the effect he wanted.

What he would like best was to look into the dead, vacant eyes of Susan herself. He imagined her lying naked on the velvet draped sofa, absolutely still and unresisting, her eyes open in just the way Sue's were. He would want a picture of that. But even more he would want her. She could be his first real woman.

Of course, Susan knew nothing about how he felt. The only thing he had done that came close to revealing his feelings was to send her a picture of the two of them together. They were standing in front of the Chinese Theater with a crowd pressing them from behind. Both were smiling, and he had his arm around her shoulders. She was wearing a black formal dress, and he was in a dinner jacket with a black tie. They looked happy together.

He had bought the picture of Susan from a shop specializing in movie materials, and the man in a dinner jacket he had taken from a book of photographs. He had copied his face from the same photograph he had used in the Sue picture, then synthesized all three. He had replaced his own streaming cotton white mane with short, well-trimmed black hair. He didn't want to make himself too easy to identify.

It gave him a lot of pleasure to imagine how puzzled Susan was when she got the picture. He could imagine her studying his face and wondering who he was. She would try and try to remember meeting him. But she wouldn't be able to, because that was going to happen in the future.

He felt a tug of reluctance as he turned away from the picture on the wall and walked to the middle of the room. He squatted so he could see into the block of pigeonhole shelves he had built against the wall. Each pigeonhole contained copies of issues of the magazines that he produced.

They weren't magazines in the ordinary sense. They were more like special collections of photographs, and he was proud of them. He acquired the photographs, chose the best of them, produced copies, and assembled them in an appealing order.

He also decided what magazines to publish, then made up their titles. *The Crypt of Desire, Still Life, Pleasure Vault,* and *Grave Beauties* were directed to clients interested in pictures of women. The collections he called *Autopsy Room* and *Postmortem* consisted of photographs of bodies of both sexes in various stages of dismemberment and dissection.

One of his least favorite publications, *Mortal Remains,* was made up of pictures of corpses that had been severely burned, dug up from graves, or taken out of the water after weeks of decomposition. He regarded the images as revolting, but if that was what people wanted, he was willing to supply them.

He walked to the boxy Pix-Wizard machine that was jammed into the space between the computer table and the back wall. He had had to sell a lot of magazines before earning enough money to buy the machine, but it was the best investment he ever made.

He picked up a manila folder and flipped it open. He glanced at the picture inside with little more than professional interest. The woman was too fat to appeal to him, but she had red hair and very white skin. She was stretched out flat on a stainless-steel autopsy table, and she had obviously died violently. The flesh on her right cheek was peeled away from her skull and hung down so that her teeth showed through the wound.

He knew people who would be drawn to the woman's hair and skin coloring. Some of his clients would prefer the image the way it was, but for most, he was going to have to take the corpse off the steel table, put it on a bed or a green lawn, then make some cosmetic adjustments to the face.

He would eventually include the picture in a magazine, assuming he stayed in the business, but where he would make real money would be from producing synthetic images, like the picture that showed him with Sue. He could easily sell them for $200 to $400 each. He would circulate the picture to his best candidates and give them a price for setting up a nice scene including them with the red-haired woman.

He raised the flexible gray cover on the digital processor and placed the thirty-five-millimeter negative of the woman's image on the flat glass plate. He looked through the viewfinder and adjusted the film guides until he had the image centered. He closed the cover, sat down at the computer monitor, and got the Pix-Wizard on-line.

He made some minor alterations in the machine's contrast and brightness settings to compensate for the woman's very white skin. He then activated the scanner, and an intense beam of halogen light traveled the length of the glass plate. He could see the light shining from under the gray cover. As the light beam moved over the film, the image from the film was captured as digitized information.

He slid the mouse around and placed the arrow on *Display*. He clicked the control button, and the screen was immediately filled with the image of the red-haired woman. The gaping wound in her cheek looked even larger and rawer than it had in the photograph. He was definitely going to have to fix it up for most clients.

That wouldn't be a problem. The Pix-Wizard encoded an image in a million pixels a square inch. Each pixel was controlled by its own code, so he could turn each one off or on. He could wipe out objects or people from the original image. He could change light, shadow, color— virtually anything.

He moved the arrow onto the "Save" icon and clicked the mouse button. The digitized image was immediately stored on a hard disk. Later, he could make the alterations he wanted, then the machine would transfer the image to film. When he printed the film, he would have a photograph of something that wasn't real, but no one would be able to tell that. It would be a picture of a possible world, one that might have been or might yet be.

He switched off the Pix-Wizard, then typed in the code that put him into one of the computer's hidden directories. He was eager to review his notes on Susan Bradstreet. He wanted to start transforming his favorite possible worlds into an actual one.

8

Susan was lying on the bed gazing up at the acoustical tile ceiling. She was concentrating on counting the holes in the tile directly above her. The pattern of holes was irregular, so the job was harder than she had expected.

Still, the pointless activity distracted her from worrying about herself. The main question was, Would she be able to finish work on *McKnightly*? Even if she did, would a producer even offer her another role? If she got a reputation for having problems that required shutting down production, she wasn't going to be anybody's first choice.

But those were exactly the questions she didn't want to have to face at the moment. The week at Rush should give her plenty of time to think about them. Right now she should take her mind out of gear and concentrate on nothing but relaxing.

She liked being alone in her small hospital room and having people milling around in the social area down the hall. She could feel both connected with them and isolated from them at the same time. It was like being a child and hearing the adults talking downstairs after you've gone to bed. You knew it was safe to go to sleep, because others were awake to keep watch.

She was lucky Dr. Burton had called in David Hightower. He had seen at once that she was very worried, and when she told him that she was afraid she had a brain tumor, he had reassured her without being condescending.

He seemed calm and unshakable, and he was surprisingly good looking. She liked the almost triangular shape of his face and the way the corners of his eyes crinkled when he smiled. He obviously had a quicker, sharper mind than most people she met, and that was refreshing.

He reminded her of the university people who used to come to her parents' parties. Even when she was just seven or eight, some of them would talk to her as if she were a grown-up. They would listen to her opinions about school, her teachers, or the TV programs she watched, then ask her questions. Having such an attentive audience had made her feel very important.

She realized that she felt strongly attracted to Hightower, and that surprised her. Since she had broken up with Bryan in January, she hadn't felt the faintest stirring of emotion for anybody. Bryan Forbes was such a charmer and so incredibly good looking that she had thought she was in love with him. Maybe she had been, but the point was now irrelevant. The anger she felt toward him had burned away whatever love there was and left her feeling scarred and empty.

Bryan had been a big mistake. She had known better than to become involved with an actor. But when she had met him at a party, she didn't think about that. He was just so beautiful that she wanted to take him home with her, and that was exactly what she did. She wasn't disappointed, either.

But if she had been paying attention, she would have realized that from the first month they were together, Bryan was robbing her. He was using the spare bank card from her bedroom desk to take money from her account. She realized what was happening only when her accountant called to tell her that she was going to have to sell some holdings to keep up with her spending.

She was furious, and she felt stupid. She had trusted Bryan, maybe even loved him, and he had betrayed her.

Nothing remotely like it had ever happened to her before, and she felt cheapened and exploited.

"I was short of cash," Bryan admitted when she confronted him. He started crying and actually fell down on his knees in front of her. "I had to have the money to pay for the drugs, and I couldn't ask you for it." Sounding desperate, he said, "The money is just a loan, and I'll pay it back."

"I don't want you to pay it back," she told him. She was crying as hard as he was. "I want you out of my life."

"Don't say anything we'll both regret."

"I already regret many things, but I'll never regret this. Now get up and get out of here."

She knew she was well rid of him, but sometimes she still woke up at three o'clock in the morning and lay in the dark with tears in her eyes. Yet she was also still angry and disgusted, even after six months, and sometimes she was afraid she might not ever find a man appealing again. Now she found herself thinking about David Hightower, and she decided she had definitely been wrong.

She heard a sharp rap at the door, and Meg walked in carrying a white plastic shopping bag with a red UCLA logo on the side. "I thought I'd never find where they put you," she said. "I've got your clothes and makeup, but I had to leave the suitcase at the front desk. Also, no drugs, no scissors, no razor blades, no nail files, nothing made out of glass, and nothing that can be used as a weapon." She paused, then she said incredulously, "It's like a jail here."

"But it makes sense." Susan swung her legs out of bed and sat on the edge of the mattress. She stretched up her arms, then hunched her shoulders as she brought them back down. "After all, this place is filled with crazy people."

"That's why I wish they'd let me stay with you. You never know when some weirdo will get the idea that you're a Martian monster and take a poke at you."

Meg set down the shopping bag at the foot of the bed, then tried to pull out the desk chair. It wouldn't move. "Darn it," she said, shaking her head. "Even the furniture is nailed to the floor."

She shook her head again, leaned her large bulk against the desk, and crossed her arms over her chest. "Why don't they put you in a suite?" she asked. "Or at least an ordinary room. You're not crazy."

"I'm not so sure about that," Susan said. "If I were completely normal, I wouldn't be planning to spend the next week in a loony bin." She made a small wave with the back of her hand. "Besides, if I didn't have deep-seated psychological problems, do you think I'd be in the movie industry?"

"Maybe you've got something there," Meg said. "Only you're not like most of them I've met."

"You're just saying that, because you know who signs your paycheck," Susan said. "Anyway, the real reason I'm here is for security. Dr. Burton said if I had a room on the open part of the psychiatric floor, the hospital might not be able to keep people away from me."

"That's my job." Meg sounded annoyed.

Meg had been with Susan since the filming of *Aztec Gold* two years earlier. Galaxy had decided that she needed a bodyguard while they were shooting scenes in L.A. and Mexico City, and they had assigned Meg to protect her. Susan had found it nice to be able to walk the streets without worrying about strangers assaulting her. So after the production was over, she asked Meg to stay on.

Meg was thirty-six, and before she became a bodyguard, she had been a rodeo performer. Bull riding and calf roping were her two events, and she spent fifteen years on the circuit. "I made about enough money to pay my expenses and give my mama a few dollars to take care of my baby," she told Susan.

When she decided to set up a home for her son, she had come to Hollywood to find work doing stunts. After six months and two small jobs, her money was running out, and she took part-time work as a bodyguard. She discovered that it paid well and that it had enough flexibility to let her spend time with her child.

Meg was still scowling over not being allowed to do her job. "You might not need me here," she said. "But if you go to Boston, I go to Boston."

"I haven't talked to anybody about going yet," Susan said. "We'll see what the setup is like."

She took a tube of moisturizing cream from the shopping bag and walked into the tiny bathroom. Leaving the door open, she turned on the water and let it run for a moment. While the water was getting warm, she squeezed out a blob of cream on a tissue and began to scrub the makeup off her face. A framed stainless-steel mirror was screwed to the wall over the washbasin.

Susan looked up and saw Meg standing in the doorway. The polished steel reflected her image in a blunt, blurred way.

"If you go to Boston, I go to Boston," Meg said again. She hadn't raised her voice or changed her emphasis.

"All right," Susan said, nodding at the image. "God knows I'd like to have you there to talk to, if for no other reason."

She dried her face with the thin hospital towel. "Will you please go out and call Ken and say I'd like for him to be here when Dr. Hightower comes to talk to me?"

"What time?"

"Ask him to come over as soon as he can so he can tell me what he's worked out with Galaxy."

"I'll call from the cafeteria, then grab some supper." Meg started for the door.

"By the way," Susan said, causing Meg to turn around. "There are six-hundred-twenty-eight holes in a piece of acoustical tile."

Meg glanced up at the ceiling. She then looked at Susan, shook her head, and said, "Maybe you're in the right place after all."

Susan showered and changed into a soft, open-necked white shirt and black jeans. She was surprised by how ex-

cited she was at the idea of going to Boston. After the
months of mourning her grandmother, worrying about her
dad, and feeling hurt and angry about Bryan, she felt
trapped in a psychological groove. Maybe a week at Rush
would bump her out of it.

She sat down at the desk and opened the paperback biography of Darwin she had asked Meg to bring from her
bedside table at home. She had read no more than a page
when she heard a light tap at the door.

"Come in," she called out, swiveling around in her
chair.

Ken Burke stepped inside. His light gray suit was still
unwrinkled, but the muscles of his face were slack with
fatigue. She put down the book and stood up to meet him.

"I expected to find you resting in bed," he said. "And
look at you—sitting up reading a book."

"Never underestimate the restorative power of talking
to a psychiatrist." She walked to the bed, then settled herself on it, leaning her back against the wall and tucking
her feet under her. "You look like you just finished the
last round of a bar fight. It must have something to do
with Howard."

"You're right about Howard and the fight, but wrong
about the last round." Ken lifted the tail of his suit coat
and sat down carefully at the end of the bed. "What I can
tell you for sure is that Howard is not happy. He insists
that you not leave the picture, because you're not really
sick."

"Oh, Christ," she said. "It's a good thing I'm on tran-
quilizers. Where did Howard get his medical degree?"
She let her disgust show in her expression. "Do I have to
be vomiting blood to convince him? Didn't he see me fall
on my face?"

"He says if you go away for a week, it's going to cost
a minimum of a hundred fifty thousand a day in down-
time."

"That's bullshit," she said angrily. "They can shoot
around me. And this isn't *Cleopatra*—they aren't paying

a cast of thousands and a herd of elephants to sit around playing cards until I get back."

"He wants Galaxy to recover its losses by withholding its end-of-picture payment to you and taking the rest out of your share of net receipts."

"Why is he after me? They've got insurance, don't they?"

"Howard is trying to scare us," Ken said. "He wants the picture in distribution on schedule, and if he loses a week, that's not going to happen. Because insurance doesn't cover lost revenues, getting you to finish the picture so it'll open on time is what he's really after."

"Can we make Howard turn loose of our money?"

"Somebody else might make him," Ken said. "Howard said he would have to talk to Clarence Goralnic, Galaxy's production vice-president, and explain the situation to him. Howard is supposed to call me back."

"Howard should spend a year where I'm going," Susan said. "And they should give him rabies shots to protect the other people."

Suddenly, there was a single sharp knock at the door and David Hightower walked in. She could feel her mood improve immediately. She sat up straighter and smiled at Hightower. David nodded to Ken, then asked her, "How are you feeling?" His expression was serious. "Did the medication help?"

"Like a miracle. I'm almost back to normal."

"Do you feel up to traveling tonight?"

"Absolutely. The sooner I can start treatment, the sooner I can get back to work."

"That's a good attitude to have," David said. "But don't overdo it and blame yourself if your progress isn't as rapid as you'd like."

He smiled at her, and she noticed for the first time that the skin around his left eye stayed smooth and tight and didn't crinkle up like that around the other eye. The difference gave his face a slightly asymmetric look that she found interesting.

"I called up Dr. Carl Blau at Rush Institute and asked

him if he could admit you this evening," Hightower said. "He said they would be happy to have you as a patient."

"So all she has to do is to show up at this hospital?" Ken asked. "Somebody will be there to take care of her?"

"Rush is staffed around the clock," Hightower said. He turned to Susan. "You can register tonight, but you won't be interviewed until tomorrow."

"At least I can get an early start," Susan said.

A nurse in a short white jacket leaned into the room. "Dr. Hightower," she said. "Mr. Burke has a phone call."

"It must be Howard," Ken said. "Excuse me a minute."

"Another shot in the battle with my producer, who doesn't want me to go." Susan shook her head. "But have a seat and tell me what Rush is like."

She expected David to take Ken's place at the end of the bed, but instead he walked to the desk and sat on the top. He braced one foot against the chair, then shifted slightly so that the right side of his face was turned toward her.

"I've already faxed your chart to them," Hightower said. "But as I told you, you can get excellent treatment right here."

"Don't think I'm waiting to find out what Howard says to Ken. I've made up my mind to go to Rush, and I'm going."

"Dr. Blau says he has space for you in Lowell Division. That's the unit where they isolate dignitaries and other people who have special security and privacy needs. The whole suite has only four or five patient rooms, and it has its own kitchen and social area. By institutional standards, everything is quite elegant." He caught her eye and smiled. "For obvious reasons, the staff call it the Star Division."

He paused for a moment and rubbed the back of his neck. Then he gave her a questioning look.

"It sounds better than Rancho Mirage," she said, giving him an ironic smile. She hesitated a moment, not sure what she was going to say, then she asked, "Will you come with me?"

The question came out in a rush, and she was surprised by it. She had realized that she wanted him to go with her, but she hadn't thought she had the nerve to ask him. She thought she had decided *not* to ask him.

"I'm sorry, but I can't," David said. If he was surprised by the question, he didn't show it. She thought she could detect something like disappointment or regret in his tone.

"I would expect to pay." She did her best to sound brisk and businesslike. "You wouldn't have to stay the week. Maybe just two or three days to help me get settled."

"I suspect you're nervous about going to a new place." His voice became gentle and reassuring.

"I'm sure I'll do well there." She spoke rapidly. "But I've already made a beginning with you."

He shook his head. "I'm leaving in the morning for St. Louis. I'm going on research leave for the next month."

"I understand," she said quickly.

David started to say something else, then he hesitated. He crossed his arms over his chest and looked at her with a pained expression. His eyebrows were drawn down above his nose, and his mouth was pulled into a narrow line.

"I don't think I could accept you as a patient anyway," he said at last.

"Why in the world not?" She was taken by surprise, and she blurted out the question. She had thought they had been getting along very well together.

David shifted around on the desktop and looked uncomfortable. "A psychiatrist shouldn't work with a patient he feels he might develop too personal an interest in."

"Oh," Susan's voice sounded very soft to her. "I think I see what you mean." She smiled slightly and shrugged, feeling almost embarrassed. "I guess I hadn't thought that through myself."

Ken came in, and with relief they both turned to face him. He was smiling, and Susan thought he looked more relaxed.

"It was Clarence Goralnic," Ken said. "He is very understanding. His wife suffers from agoraphobia, and he doesn't have any trouble seeing anxiety attacks as a health problem."

"So he's not going to make an issue of my leaving for a week?"

"He's going to aid and abet you." Ken smiled broadly. "He's ordered a Galaxy Learjet to be ready at seven o'clock to fly you directly to Boston."

"Fantastic," Susan said. "I'm ready to leave now."

Hightower slid off the desktop and walked over to her. He held out his hand, and as she took it, he said, "I'm glad it's all working out for you."

She looked up into his face. He was very handsome, but she thought he also looked sad. He didn't seem to want to leave any more than she wanted him to. Even though they had just met, they seemed to belong together according to some law of nature.

"Give my regards to Carl Blau."

"Thanks for helping me," Susan said. His hand felt very large wrapped around hers. She looked up into his eyes. "When I get back from Boston and you get back from St. Louis, do you mind if I call you?"

"I explained that I can't accept you as a patient." He shook his head, and his face was pulled into a deep frown.

"I didn't say anything about wanting to be your patient."

"Oh." Surprise made his voice go up. He looked puzzled at first, then he smiled. It was a dazzling smile, and she found herself smiling back.

"I'll look forward to hearing from you," he said.

She gave his hand a tight squeeze, then reluctantly turned it loose. Her fingers seemed to tingle from the pressure.

9

Gibson flipped the cap off a bottle of Carta Blanca and handed it to Cortez. He poured himself a glass of Evian, squeezed a slice of lime into it, and sat down at the maple-topped table across from Cortez.

"You're not having a beer?" Cortez looked at him with surprise.

Gibson shook his head. "I've got some ideas to work out. I want to keep my mind sharp."

He noticed that Cortez was still wearing the dark blue pants and light blue shirt that constituted his Software Services uniform. Nowadays he hardly ever saw him wear anything else. Cortez had shown a little talent for computers when he was a student. Now, though, he had become an installer jock, and it was hard to get much lower than that.

Still, Cortez could be counted on to do what he was told and to be efficient about it. But first of all, he was going to have to get Cortez involved.

"Man, you want your mind sharp, I want mine *dull*." Cortez laughed. "I got too many worries." He took a drink from his bottle, then his face became serious as he looked at Gibson across the table. "You know, I'm in real deep shit."

"I know it five hundred dollars' worth."

"You're going to get that money back," Cortez said. "Let me tell you, Cyberwolf, I'm going to pay you back for sure."

"How much does the Iceman want?" He cut Cortez off.

"Oh, shit, I don't know, really," Cortez said. "I think maybe nine thousand, but when I see him, he's going to tell me it's fifteen or some fucking number." He shrugged. "It might as well be a million."

"Do you know his phone number?"

"The Iceman's?" Cortez asked. "I got it in my wallet.

He's got a phone he carries around with him." He then looked puzzled. "What do you care?"

"I want you to call him," Gibson said. "Tell him you're going to come around tomorrow morning and pay him off in full."

"You crazy, man? I can't do that." Cortez gave a snorting laugh. "When I don't show up, he might decide to flat-line me *tomorrow*."

"I'm going to give you the money." Gibson spoke softly, leaning across the table so that his face was close to Cortez's. He then sat back and took a sip of lime water, watching Cortez.

Cortez frowned at first, then his eyes grew wide, his mouth opened, and he shook his head. It was as if he had seen Gibson float up to the ceiling.

"You're not serious?" Cortez cocked his head to the side.

"Absolutely. I told you this afternoon I was going to make us rich. Call the Iceman, then I'll explain what we're going to do."

Cortez took his beer with him into the living room. Gibson could hear the beeps of the phone as Cortez punched in the number. The conversation was short, and Gibson made no effort to listen.

"He says ten-five." Cortez sat back down at the table, tilted up the bottle, and drained out the last of the beer. "Not as bad as what I thought he might come up with."

"Come by tomorrow morning," Gibson said. "I'll give it to you."

"What kind of work you got for us to do? Is this about making us rich?" Cortez sounded interested.

Gibson ignored the question. "Tell me what you learned about Susan Bradstreet."

"Not much." Cortez shrugged and raised his eyebrows. "I hung around outside her room the way you told me. A doctor came to see her, then some people left, movie types in fancy clothes. Then when the doctor was coming out the door, I heard Susan say something about wanting to leave tonight."

"Leave tonight?" Gibson made an effort to keep his voice conversational. "You mean get out of the hospital?"

"I don't know. She sounded like she was talking about going someplace else."

"You didn't hear anybody say where?"

If Susan was leaving the hospital, she might be going somewhere with better security than she had now. He was beginning to get a sour taste in his mouth, and he took another sip of the lime water.

"That's all I heard," Cortez said. "But maybe it's in her hospital record."

"That's an idea." Gibson stood up from the table. "If we go to the medical center, can you check it?"

"I can check it right now, Cyberwolf." Cortez smiled and pushed himself away from the table.

Gibson followed him into the living room, then watched from just inside the door as Cortez knelt down, popped open the lid of his attaché case, and took out a floppy disk.

"Here's the program I've been installing," Cortez said. "It lets you have access to the Cumulative Patient Record Database." He held out the disk to Gibson.

Gibson took it and said, "You're a hell of a guy, Backup." He tapped Cortez on the shoulder with the disk, and Cortez smiled broadly.

"Oh, man, I forgot. We may be in trouble." Cortez's face mirrored his worry. "If you're not in the hospital, you've got to have her Social Security number for an access code."

"That's no problem," Gibson said. "It's 230-45-2788."

Cortez looked at him in surprise. "How did you know that?"

"I reviewed my files this afternoon," Gibson said. "But I knew it anyway. If I've seen something once, I can usually read it off the screen in my mind." He tapped the side of his head.

"I've seen you do it," Cortez said, nodding. "But I mean, where did you get the number?"

"It's in several places," Gibson said. "The Bureau of

Motor Vehicles has it, and so do all the credit-checking companies." He gave Cortez a small, tight smile.

He hadn't even known Susan existed until he had seen her in *Aztec Gold,* but then he had fallen for her completely. In his favorite scene, she had been lying almost naked on a stone at the top of a pyramid, while a modern-day Aztec priest loomed above her with a razor-sharp knife of black obsidian. She had looked so beautiful and yet so helpless that he had felt half sick with desire for her.

A living person had never made him feel like that before, and after the movie, he couldn't stop thinking about her. Her image had become permanently stored in the circuits of his brain, and pictures of her endlessly cycled into his consciousness. That was when he had constructed the picture of the two of them together at the Chinese Theater and mailed it to her. It was an adolescent thing to do, but knowing that she was even aware of his existence made him feel closer to her.

Since then, he had often imagined her walking toward him in Westwood. As they get closer, she stares at him in fascination. Then when she realizes where she's seen him, she smiles, and he smiles back. Without a word, they walk together to his car, and he takes her to his necropolis.

She is standing in the dim room, close to him, looking up at him with her peculiar gray-green eyes. "I'm ready," she says. "I've been waiting for this." At that point the fantasy always blurs, but the scene becomes clear again as he kneels on the floor beside her body.

He begins stripping the clothes off her warm, supple corpse. She is wearing only a yellow T-shirt and red running shorts with an elastic waistband. He doesn't have to struggle with her. He works slowly, taking his time and enjoying the task. He takes off her shirt first, exposing the high, rounded breasts that he had only glimpsed during the movie scene. After a while, he pulls off her shorts. Now she is completely naked, and he sits by her for a long time, studying her carefully, admiring her body. Only when he's ready does he take off his own clothes.

At that point, he usually supplemented his imagination with the image of Sue and himself on the poster. Blending his fantasy of Susan with the picture of Sue, he would throw off his\ clothes, then with barely a touch of his hand, explode into a white moment of oblivion that would quiet for a while the obsessive, hungry thoughts that crowded out all others.

The power Susan exerted over him didn't weaken in the months after the movie. As he began to elaborate and perfect his fantasy, his interest in her grew stronger. Everything about her fascinated him. He set up a database and started compiling information about her. He logged onto InfoSearch and checked through all the on-line publications. The *Los Angeles Times* was his best source, but pieces on her also appeared in *Time, Us, People, Vanity Fair, Cosmopolitan, W Magazine, Mondo 2000, Interview,* and a dozen other magazines and newspapers. He downloaded the text, then worked through it systematically.

The natural next step was to tap into the TRW, Equifax, and Transunion computers and get her credit reports. He learned that Susan had essentially no credit limit, possessed twelve credit cards, paid on time, and had accounts at Bank America and Citicorp. Most of the file was garbage, though, and it didn't even have her unlisted telephone number.

Still, finding that hadn't been a big problem. Late one night he jacked into CALNEX, getting in through a trap-door he had known about for years. After he was inside the system, he ran through the files until he located the equipment-users directory and looked up her number. He used it to crawl deeper into the system and locate her line equipment number. It gave him access to her phone line, and he could listen in on her conversations without any clicks to give him away. That's how he had learned the details of her life, including her experiences with Bryan.

He had known from the start that eventually he was going to do something with Susan. He hadn't known what he wanted or what he was going to do. But when Cortez had called, everything fell into place. Now he knew exactly what he wanted.

He wanted Susan, and he also wanted more money than he had dreamed of. He would go to Paraguay, where he could pay off officials to keep the U.S. from extraditing him. Nazis like Josef Mengele had done it, and so could he. The idea of having both Susan and a vast sum of money was irresistible.

"You install it," Gibson said, handing back the disk.

Gibson's computer was on a white laminate desk pushed against the wall. Cortez sat down in the chair in front of the screen and inserted the disk into the A-drive. Gibson stood looking over his right shoulder.

In less than two minutes, Cortez had installed the CPRD program, then without pausing, he typed in the command that summoned the introductory menu. He moved the arrow to *Current Hospital Patients: Female* and clicked the mouse. An alphabetical list of patients scrolled across the screen.

"Here she is," Cortez said. He clicked the mouse button, and *Enter patient identification number* appeared at the bottom of the screen. He entered the number Gibson had given him, and the screen was immediately filled with the "Patient Data" section of Susan Bradstreet's medical chart.

"Move," Gibson said, taking Cortez's place. "I want to read this."

Gibson skipped the family, employment, and insurance information, then skimmed the section describing Susan's chief complaint. "She fainted," he said to Cortez, without looking away from the screen. He slowed down to read the consultation note carefully, noting the referral to Rush. Then, at the end of the file, he saw that Susan had checked out at 6:12 P.M.

"Goddamn it," Gibson said. He spoke in a quiet voice, but his tone was harsh. He had been expecting her to remain in the hospital for at least two days. His plan was dead before he had even thought through the details needed to make it operational.

And he knew that he could have made it work. That was what was so galling. Now he had to watch everything drift away like smoke in the wind.

"What's the problem?" Cortez asked. He was sitting in the straight chair to the left of the computer, watching Gibson's face and trying to read his reaction.

"She checked out of the hospital a couple of hours ago."

"So what?" Cortez shrugged.

"She was going to be the goose that laid our golden egg. She was going to make us rich."

"Man, what are you talking about?" Cortez asked. "What's she got to do with making us rich?"

"Everything," Gibson said. "We were going to kidnap her out of the hospital, then collect millions in ransom."

"Shit, are you serious?" Cortez's eyes grew wide and he nervously rubbed a finger back and forth under his nose, stroking his mustache. "I don't know if I could do something like that."

"It would have been easy," Gibson said. "You know the layout, and there's no real security at the hospital. We could have walked in, made some threats, and waltzed out with her."

"I know that's right," Cortez said, shaking his head. "But, man, some security guard might have killed us."

"What do you think the Iceman is going to do to you now?" Gibson fixed his eyes on Cortez and pulled his lips into a thin smile.

"You mean now you're not going to give me the money?" Cortez's voice took on a whine, and his face seemed to sag.

"I was going to make you pay me back from your part of the ransom."

"Where did she go?" Cortez asked. "If it's another hospital, maybe it wouldn't be so hard to get in there either."

"She went to Boston," Gibson said. "Cambridge, to be precise."

"Where MIT is?"

"That's it," Gibson said. "Rush Institute is out near Fresh Pond. I've been by it a hundred times."

"Have you ever been inside? Do you know the layout?"

"No," Gibson said, shaking his head slowly.

He didn't know the layout, but he had read something about Rush in the MIT alumni magazine, something to do with computer-aided design. Rush was adding a new research tower to an old building . . . and what? Oh, yes. A CAD program was going to guide the architectural drawings, then the Rush designs were going to be used to train undergraduates.

"Man, we might as well hang it up," Cortez said.

Gibson ignored him and sat motionless, staring into the computer screen. Something was coming to him, one of his ideas that seemed to float in from someplace outside his mind. He was afraid to move or say anything or the idea might evaporate before it had a chance to blossom.

Cortez sat watching him, suddenly aware that he shouldn't say anything to break the spell. He began to turn the pages of a computer-supply catalog.

"It's just possible," Gibson said, hardly aware that Cortez was looking at him. He thought he saw how they might pull off a kidnapping that was more ambitious than his original idea of snatching Susan out of the UCLA hospital. This one would be a much bigger production, but then he could also ask for a lot more money. Wasn't that the way movie people thought? He smiled.

"What's possible?" Cortez shoved away the supply catalog and turned to look at Gibson.

"The Rush designs may still be in the MIT mainframe," Gibson said. He could feel his sense of power slowly returning. "Even if the plans aren't being used as a CAD project, probably nobody took the trouble to dump them."

"Can you hack the MIT system?" Cortez asked. His voice had lost its dull, worried tone and he sounded excited.

"So you're ready to change your tune," Gibson said.

He gave Cortez a smug smile. "You must have been thinking about what you'd say to the Iceman when you dropped by to have a cup of coffee with him tomorrow morning."

"Man, that's nothing but the truth," Cortez conceded. His eyes opened wide, and he shook his head.

"If I can get the Rush architectural drawings out of the MIT system, are you willing to go along with me?"

"How are we going to know where Susan is?" Cortez asked. "I mean, they didn't put her Rush address in her records, did they?"

"We'll get it from Rush."

"Just call them up and ask them?"

"They wouldn't tell us," Gibson said. "We'll social-engineer our way into the Rush computer and find out exactly where Susan is. Then we can use the floor plans and go get her."

"What do we do with her then? Hide her away somewhere and ask for ransom?"

"We ask for ransom, all right," Gibson said. "But maybe we should just barricade ourselves in until they deliver the money."

"Then how do we get out without getting killed?" Cortez shook his head. "Man, I might better take my chances with the Iceman."

Gibson paused, and at the edge of his consciousness, he could sense ideas twisting like plumes of smoke, almost but not quite starting to take shape. "I'm going to have to give that some thought," he said at last.

"If you're thinking about fighting off the cops, we're going to need more help," Cortez said. "At least a couple of guys."

"One more would be enough." Gibson shook his head. "When you have too many people, factions develop. Do you know anybody?"

"Yeah, I do," Cortez said. "He's a gambler named Whipkey, but he's a crazy fucker." He tapped his temple with the tip of a finger. "He's dangerous."

"That's what we need." Gibson smiled. "Talk to him,

and tell him Cyberwolf wants to meet him tonight. But right now, we've got to see if we can get the drawings. If we can, we'll make our move tomorrow." He paused, then said, "This is going to pay off big."

"All right!" Cortez said with sudden enthusiasm. "I'm feeling better already."

"Then let's go shoulder surfing."

10

The TV monitor was bolted to the top of a wheeled metal cart, and the VCR was locked into a frame on the lower shelf. The cart was pulled up to the tapered end of the seminar table.

Hightower sat at the right side of the table in the first chair. His falafel dinner was in front of him on a wrinkled piece of aluminum foil, and a cardboard carton of orange juice with a green plastic straw was sitting at one side.

He was as close to the TV screen as he could get, but even so, he had to turn his head sharply to the left. Otherwise, his left eye produced a fluttering shimmer that interfered with his seeing.

The scene was supposed to be the jungle of southern Mexico in 1955. Alice Davenport, the character played by Susan, was being chased through the bush by the sinister Andrew Morell. Hightower involuntarily held his breath as he watched Susan run down a narrow dirt path, then suddenly encounter a burly man in a loincloth who was brandishing a machete. Barely hesitating, Susan darted off the path and began to weave her way through the dense tangle of vines and tree limbs. Then, directly ahead, only a few feet from her, was a giant rattlesnake, coiled and ready to strike. Susan jumped for a vine and swung over the snake. She hit the ground running.

He glanced away from the TV to locate his falafel-stuffed pita. He bit into it without taking his eyes off the screen. He was alone in one of the medical center's small seminar rooms. He didn't own a VCR, and it was the only place where he could watch the tape of *Aztec Gold*.

After saying good-bye to Susan, he had walked back to his apartment. He couldn't remember when he had been in better spirits. The evening had a warm softness, and the sharp, almost medicinal odor of the eucalyptus trees seemed to invigorate him. He walked unusually fast, bounding down the sidewalk like someone late for a meeting he didn't want to miss.

But as soon as he entered his apartment, he wanted to be somewhere else. The apartment was cleaner than he ever kept it. The nap of the beige carpet was furrowed from his final vacuuming, the white countertop in the tiny kitchen was scrubbed spotless, and none of his personal belongings was in sight. His books had been mailed, and his suitcases were packed.

He took off his tie and jacket, hung them in the closet, then got out a frozen chicken dinner. He had bought it so he would have something to eat on his last night and not have any dishes to wash. He unwrapped the package and started to slide the plastic container into the microwave, then he stopped. Right at that moment he realized that he couldn't stand to be in the apartment even long enough to eat dinner. He was suddenly too much aware of the lonely, empty hours he had spent there during the last year.

He wished he could leave L.A. immediately and fly to St. Louis to see his parents. He would like to tell them about meeting Susan. They would be fascinated to hear that he had been called in to consult about a movie star, and he would like to try to tell them about how strongly drawn to her he had felt. Would they believe she had responded just as strongly? They would probably think he was imagining it, but they would be sympathetic and gently amused. "I guess we can expect to see your name in the gossip columns," his mother would say.

But his parents wouldn't be returning until early

Wednesday morning. So why couldn't he simply settle down and eat his dinner, then listen to some music? He knew the answer. For the first time in two years, he had told a woman that he found her attractive, even if he had done it in an oblique way. Then, to his complete surprise, she had told him, less obliquely, that she also found him attractive.

What had happened was simple, yet tremendously exciting. It was also frightening. He was no longer accustomed to dealing with powerful feelings of sexual and emotional attraction. Patients told him about being in the grip of their emotions, but he had almost forgotten what that was like.

The strong feelings that Susan evoked raised his spirits, but they also generated an undercurrent of guilt that tugged at his conscience. By reacting so strongly to Susan, it was as if he were betraying Alma. Rationally, he knew that was foolish, yet that didn't make the guilt disappear. Perhaps nothing would ever make it go away completely.

In the end, he had put the chicken dinner back into the freezer. He didn't have a car, so he had to walk to Westwood. He didn't mind, though. Walking gave him the chance to dissipate some of the nervous energy he had built up. If he didn't work it off somehow, he wouldn't be able to sleep at all.

His plan was to find a restaurant where he could have dinner. But when he passed by the blinking yellow sign of Spectacular Video, it suddenly struck him that they might have a copy of *Aztec Gold*.

Susan's picture was on the box. She was wearing a gold breechcloth that left her long legs bare up to her hips and a narrow band of red cloth that barely covered her breasts. Her hair was blonder and much longer. Her jaw was set, and her gray-green eyes were calm and steady. The blond hair swirling around her face gave her an untamed, reckless look. He found it hard to believe that the woman he had met that afternoon was the same as the one pictured on the box.

As the end of the movie approached, he watched with frantic tension as Susan was dragged up the steps of an Aztec pyramid by two hefty men. She was half naked, dressed only in scraps of gold cloth, and draped with ropes of jade, emeralds, and rubies. She was about to be turned into a sacrificial victim to please the crowd of Morell's followers milling around by the hundreds on the plaza in front of the pyramid. All hope rested with John Carleton, the man Alice had freed from Morell's secret prison.

The conventions of adventure movies made him certain that Alice would be okay. The real question was whether Susan would find a way out of her difficulties. He suspected that her anxiety attacks could be brought under control quickly. Surely her life would also take a sharp turn for the better. It was hard not to imagine that he was the one who could make that happen.

Now Alice was stretched out on the altar stone. Morell, dressed in a bossed gold breastplate and a headdress of quetzal feathers, stood looking down on her. In his right hand, raised high above her, was a knife of glittering black obsidian. He was going to plunge the jagged knife into her chest and rip out her beating heart.

Just as Morell started his downward stroke with his deadly black dagger, Carleton crawled out of a hollow space under the stone altar. He pointed his revolver toward Morell and yelled at him to stop. Instead, Morell directed the knife's trajectory toward Carleton, who was forced to shoot him.

At the top of the pyramid, Susan's character and Carleton embraced and kissed passionately. The setting sun made the sky glow golden in the background.

Hightower had enjoyed *Aztec Gold* more than he expected. Alice Davenport was a terrific character. She was beautiful, but she was also smart, resourceful, and resilient. He felt sure that Susan had tapped into her own sense of herself in playing Alice.

He pushed the "Rewind" button on the VCR, then stood looking down at it as the tape whirred rhythmically.

Now that the film was over, he was experiencing a sharp feeling of loss. In an almost magical way, he had spent the last hour and a half with Susan. During that time, the illusion was so powerful that she was almost a real presence in the room.

Now, though, she was completely gone, and all he was left with were his memories of their two brief meetings.

11

Gibson liked the atmosphere of Royce Hall. Whenever he needed to make a phone hookup he didn't want traced to his necropolis, he made it on the UCLA campus at Royce. It was a nineteenth-century mission-style building, and the public phone was in its dark, cool basement.

As he and Cortez walked down the marble stairs from the entrance level, the faint sounds of a string quartet reached them from one of the rehearsal rooms on an upper floor. The music was slow and somber and seemed suited to the hollow, echoing sound produced by their footsteps.

He liked the effect. With the music playing in the background, he could imagine that they were descending into the catacomb of an ancient church. He could feel they were leaving the upper world, with all its superficialities, and approaching the darker and more authentic world that lay hidden below it.

The basement floor was paved with red ceramic tile, and the only illumination came from the heavy wrought-iron fixtures hanging from the ceiling. The light was dim enough that Gibson felt no need to put on sunglasses.

At the right of the stairs, two of the three phones were attached to the wall, but it was the third phone that made Royce Hall his favorite jack-in place. The phone was in an old-fashioned wooden booth. It had a folding door with glass panels, a built-in seat, and a narrow metal shelf below the phone. When the door was closed, an overhead light came on and a small fan high up in the corner began to whir.

Gibson pushed the folding door wide open and sat down on the small stool. He put the laptop between his feet on the dark green linoleum floor. They were going to have to do some preliminary work before they could start looking for the Rush drawings.

Cortez stood by the booth and leaned his head through the open door. His black attaché case was between his feet, packed with the various pieces of equipment that they might need.

"Have you got a card number for me?" Gibson asked.

"I've got one, but it's from Radiology." Cortez spoke hesitantly. "I wanted them to think an outsider lifted it."

"Don't act stupid," Gibson said impatiently. "You're not going to be around when the bill comes. You'll be living it up in Cuba or someplace. Now give me the card number."

As Cortez recited the charge-card number, Gibson tapped it out on the buttons. He added the Boston area code and the MIT number. Those he knew by heart. He pulled on the handle of the folding door and snapped it closed. The overhead light blinked on, and the fan began to whir softly.

"Help Desk," a male voice said. "This is Sam."

"Uhh, listen," Gibson said, making his voice higher so he would sound younger. "I'm a summer school student, and I know I'm an idiot." He paused to let the apology sink in. "But I'm trying to do my homework, and I'm supposed to get into the Engineering Design net or something like that—is this making any sense?"

"Just call up the computer and log on," Sam said. "Do you have the dial-up number?"

"Is it 555-5631?" He gave the old number, letting his doubt show.

"I don't know where you got that," Sam said. "The ED

number is 555-6565. Do you have the course ID
number?"

"I guess I could look it up," Gibson said. He gripped
the receiver tightly, feeling beads of sweat forming at his
hairline.

"You really don't know much of anything." Sam
sounded more amused than angry. "The only summer
school course I can think of that you might be taking is
Basic Design Techniques."

"That's it," Gibson said. He tried to make his tone convey the idea that he thought Sam was brilliant for figuring
it out.

"That's 450725," Sam said. "You can use the course
number for the account number."

"Don't I need a password?"

"I can't help you there," Sam said. "But I'd be surprised if the professor didn't tell you to use your date of
birth."

"I appreciate your help." Gibson had no trouble sounding sincere.

He hung up the phone and slumped back in the seat.
The breeze produced by the miniature fan felt clammy on
his face. He pushed on the folding door, and it slid to one
side. The light went off instantly, but the fan blades continued to twirl slowly.

Cortez gave him an inquiring look, then his eyes shifted from side to side. So far no one else had come down
the stairs.

"One more step, and we'll be in the door," Gibson said.

"Cyberwolf, you are an absolute demigod of social engineering," Cortez said. He shook his head. "I'm in awe."

Gibson stood up and stepped out of the phone booth.
"Get out the coupler," he said. "We're going to have to
hack the password. I'm going to start with birthdays."

It shouldn't be a difficult hack. He would need a
number made up of three parts: a month, a day, a year.
The year was the easiest. Assuming the class contained
freshmen, most of them were probably born eighteen
years ago. That would give him the last part of the

number. Only twelve months were possible, so he could combine the number for each of them with the year for the second part of the password. For the third part, he would just have to try all the days for each month. But everything should go fast, because the number of possible combinations was relatively small.

Cortez put the attaché case flat on the floor and clicked it open. He took out a rubber device consisting of two hollow cylindrical pieces joined by a thick cord. Another much longer cord hung from one of the pieces.

"Go ahead and slip them on," Gibson said. "I've got some instructions to punch in, then I'm ready to run."

Gibson opened the lid on the laptop and turned on the power. He booted it, and while he was waiting for the cursor to appear on the computer's small screen, he glanced over at Cortez.

Cortez stretched one of the rubber cups around the receiving end of the telephone handset, then tugged it into place. He picked up the other cup and worked it around the microphone end. The rubber piece didn't slide on the way the first one had, and he was getting nowhere trying to force it.

Gibson finished typing in the instructions for constructing the numbers that he wanted tried as passwords. He looked up and saw Cortez's struggle.

"Didn't you bring any powder?"

Cortez frowned at him, but he didn't say anything. Instead, he leaned out of the booth and picked up his attaché case. Putting the case on his knees, he opened it, and took out a white plastic bottle of baby talcum. He sprinkled powder into the cup that was sticking, rubbed it around with his finger, then slipped the cup onto the end of the phone without difficulty.

"Hand me the tail," Gibson said. "And then let's change places."

Cortez tossed him the end of the long cord attached to the acoustic coupler. Gibson snatched it out of the air and jacked it into the laptop. Cortez stepped out of the phone booth, and Gibson slid past him, holding the computer in front of him as if he were balancing something on a platter. He sat down on the narrow seat of the phone booth and put the laptop on his knees.

"Give me the Radiology number again," Gibson said. Cortez recited the number, and Gibson tapped it out. As soon as he could hear the buzz of a dial tone through the rubber of the coupler, he entered the command to call Boston at the ED dial-up number. A sequence of tones of various pitches immediately followed.

In a moment he could hear a long hiss, then the request to log on appeared on the laptop's screen. He entered the course number Sam had given him and held his breath. The computer seemed to take forever.

Then the number worked, and the request for a password flashed onto the screen. He knew he wasn't going to have much time to supply one, because in about two minutes, the ED computer would disconnect him.

Gibson quickly typed in the command, and the laptop started producing the number-construction sequence built on birthdates. The computer started with January first, then tried one day after another. As each sequence of digits appeared on the screen, he would push the "Enter" key.

Cortez put his head inside the door. "Someone's coming down the stairs," he said in a hurried whisper. Then he added, "It's a campus cop."

"You might have to do some social engineering yourself," Gibson said, without looking away from the computer. He was almost through January, and now the February numbers were starting to flash on the screen.

Gibson could hear the reverberating echo of footsteps coming toward them. He kept working, refusing to let himself be distracted. He heard the buzz and crackle of a belt radio, followed by a few phrases of garbled speech.

"What are you boys up to?" Gibson heard the officer ask. The tone was friendly, but the question was definitely serious. Obviously, he had never seen a computer hooked to the line of a public phone before.

Gibson looked past Cortez and saw that the cop was a

man in his sixties, with hair that was almost completely white. But he was powerfully built, and he carried a pistol in his black leather holster.

Gibson looked back at the screen and realized that he wasn't being prompted for the password anymore. The screen was starting to fill with the Engineering Design welcome-users scroll.

"I'm in," he said to Cortez. The laptop had found it necessary to try only until February 12 before hitting on a sequence that worked. He felt a small thrill of success.

"We're from computer maintenance." Cortez turned to face the cop, and out of the corner of his eye, Gibson could see him tip his university photo-ID badge. "We're checking out the campus phones and making sure they can carry enough information to use with computers."

"Is that what that fellow is doing with that box?" The officer nodded toward Gibson.

Gibson waved a hand at him, then went back to tapping the keys of the laptop. He was long past the welcome scroll and deep into the system, looking through the directory for anything having to do with design or with Rush. He was finding dozens of files, too many to examine one by one. This might turn out to take hours instead of the thirty minutes he had estimated.

"That's right," Cortez said. "The box is hooked to the phone system, and it sends a signal to our facility in the computer center. We've got some equipment there that picks up the signal and shoots it back over here."

Suddenly, Gibson started seeing file names that had RPI as an extension, and he knew he was where he wanted to be. What could RPI stand for except Rush Psychiatric Institute? He called up a file.

"Is that a test for two-way communication?" the cop asked.

"Hey," Cortez said, sounding surprised. "You must be a man who knows about computers."

"I don't know the first thing, and I don't want to," the cop said. "I remember when we didn't even have the damned things. And you know what, the world was a lot better back then."

The document Gibson had called up was headed *Specifications for P4 Level Biological Containment Facilities.* A box in the upper left-hand corner identified the job more completely:

> *Rush Psychiatric Institute Research Building*
> *Architect: Fisher Associates*
> *Contractor: Commonwealth Engineering*

He had found the files.

Gibson felt a shiver of satisfaction. He allowed himself a smile, but he stayed silent. If Cortez kept that fool cop distracted, he could be finished in less than fifteen minutes.

"Yeah," Cortez said. "You got a point, but what can we do now? We don't get paid if the computers don't work."

"I know what I'm going to do," the cop said. "As soon as I can scrape up enough cash, I'm going to move to Oregon and find me a little town in the middle of the woods."

Gibson kept scrolling through the directory. He wasn't sure which RPI files he wanted. The ones that had names like FLOOR PLAN: RESEARCH BLDG., FLOOR PLAN: ORIGINAL BLDG., N.ELEVATION: ORIGINAL BLDG. were obvious, but was he going to need the drawings for the electrical circuits? Still, it was better to get too many than not enough. They could always sort them out later. He started downloading files into the laptop.

"Sounds great," Cortez said. "Get out of L.A. any way you can, that's what I think."

"Give me a floppy," Gibson called to Cortez. The graphical data had already filled the disk he had in the laptop.

"Excuse me," Cortez said to the cop. He reached inside the attaché case, took out a disk, and handed it to Gibson.

"I'd better let you guys work," the cop said. "Been nice talking to you."

"Same here," Cortez said. "I hope you get to Oregon."

"I hope you get out of L.A."

"He will," Gibson called out. "He's on his way now."

The cop glanced back, but he didn't turn around. Gibson could hear the gritty slide of his footsteps going up the marble stairs.

12

Susan laid the Darwin biography on the seat beside her, then slipped off the softly padded headphones.

She was enjoying sitting in the wide leather seat, listening to music, and reading. She rarely had such an opportunity, and it felt like luxury. Even when she wasn't working on a picture, she was always having to meet a producer or an investor, go to a party or a screening, or do something else connected with the business. Staying at Rush for a week was probably going to be more like a vacation than her attempts at actual vacations usually were.

She picked up her book again, eager to get back to the story. She had been afraid that the small dose of Xanax she took at dinner would make her too sleepy to read, but it simply made her feel at ease. She didn't feel euphoric. She just felt . . . normal.

Looking back over the last year, she could remember times when she hadn't felt right. Her heart had seemed to skip a beat or she had found it hard to get her breath. Then she would feel trapped and anxious. It was obvious now that she had been having small anxiety attacks.

She yawned silently and rubbed her eyes. In the back of the plane, directly behind the small galley, were two curtained-off berths. When she got sleepy, all she had to do was climb into one. Meg had even packed her down pillow, and with it she could sleep anywhere.

Susan glanced at Meg on the other side of the aisle.

She was flipping through a magazine called *Rodeo Roundup* that she subscribed to. "I like to keep up with the few old-timers I still know," she had told Susan. "They're the absolute best, and I'm glad I don't have to go out and compete with them." As Meg read she noticed Susan out of the corner of her eye and turned her head.

"I thought you'd be asleep by now." Susan raised her voice so she could be heard over the dull vibrating noise that surrounded them.

"I'm too excited. I've never been farther east than Arkansas. Going to Boston makes me think of the midnight ride of Paul Revere and the Boston Tea Party." Her eyes got as wide as a child's, and she shook her head. "I never thought in all my born days that I'd actually go there."

"After you get me settled at Rush, you can be a tourist for a couple of days," Susan promised. "If they have a special division for celebrities, I'm sure I'll be safe."

"I want to check out the setup first," Meg insisted.

Susan glanced at her watch. They had already crossed the Mountain time zone and now were in the Central zone. She had planned to phone her dad from the hospital, but there hadn't been enough time. If she was going to call him tonight, she'd better do it now. It would be past eleven in Ohio. He would be finished watching the local news and getting ready for bed.

She leaned across the seat and pushed the white call button set into the burled walnut trim surrounding the window. The steward appeared almost instantly.

"I want to make a phone call," she told him, raising her voice above the noise. "And I'd like some water, please."

Her father was regular in his habits, and he would probably be in the kitchen, maybe having a bowl of ice cream before bed. On second thought, it would probably be frozen yogurt. Since his heart attack and surgery, he had been on a low-fat diet, and he assured her he was sticking to it. But whatever he was having, he would be leaning against the kitchen counter staring in the direction of the refrigerator.

What would he be thinking of? Probably something

like how he could make DNA replication more interesting
to his eighth-grade students. After her mother died, she
realized much later, it was her father's teaching that had
kept him going and given him the strength to help her. He
was committed to something outside himself, so when his
personal life got too hard, he could escape into it for a
while.

She was an only child, and both her parents had been
older than her friends' parents. When she was born, her
mother was thirty-eight and her father thirty-six. She immediately became the center of their world, the source of
their delight, and that had made their small family a close
one. When her mother died suddenly of a ruptured aneu-
rysm at the age of fifty, Susan had just turned thirteen the
week before. *It's my unlucky age,* she could remember
thinking.

Her father had been devastated. He was gaunt and un-
steady on his feet, as if he were a sick man, but he had
refused to let anybody take over his classes. Every morning he prepared the day's lessons, then he made himself
go to school, teach, and grade papers.

She now realized that if her father hadn't spent so
much time with her during those terrible early months after her mother died, she couldn't have gotten through
them undamaged. While they talked about her mother,
she remained a real presence for them. With time, her
presence had weakened and dimmed, but Susan knew it
would never disappear.

"The link is already established," the steward said,
handing the phone to Susan. He poured some Perrier into
a glass and set it on the table beside her.

Susan punched in the area code, then followed it with
the familiar number in Bay Village. She could imagine
the long white clapboard house with the three large poplar
trees on the front lawn, the grass beneath them still struggling to grow, and the bushy bayberry hedge separating
their driveway from the Havermeyers.' It was the house
she had grown up in, and she could recall its every detail.

"I'm still awake," her father said, when she apologized

for calling so late. "But you're going to have to talk louder, because the line is crackling. Where are you calling from?"

"I'm about six thousand feet up in the air right now," she said. "I'm in a plane on the way to Boston."

"Those damned radio-phone patches never work very well. There's too much atmospheric disturbance."

"Are you doing okay?" she asked. "Are you getting your exercise and sticking to your diet?"

"I've stopped eating meat entirely, and yesterday it was so hot that I took my walk at the Rocky River Mall. Talk about boring! Are you going to Boston to work on your movie? I thought it was set in L.A."

"I'm spending a week at the Rush Institute getting treated for anxiety attacks." She paused, then quickly said, "I fainted while we were filming, but I'm okay. I went to the UCLA Medical Center, and they said I was just fine."

Her father was quiet a moment, then he asked slowly and hesitantly, "None of the doctors thought this might be anything other than a psychological condition?" She could hear the worry in his voice.

"Absolutely not. I was examined by two outstanding doctors, and one of them was a neurologist."

"Great," he said. The word was almost a sigh of relief. "If you want me to, I'll get Marge Crane to take my classes and come up and stay with you."

"Thanks, but it's really not necessary," she said. "I'm thinking of the week more as a vacation than anything."

"I'm glad you called," he said.

"Me too," she said. "Sleep well, Dad. I love you."

She slipped the phone back into the cradle and pushed the button for the steward. "Did everything work all right?" he asked, taking the phone from her.

"No problems at all." She smiled at him, then picked up her glass of Perrier and took a sip.

"You should have had a strong signal, because we're close to a transmitter site." He nodded toward the window. "We're just coming up on St. Louis."

She leaned across the seat and looked out the window. Through the darkness, in the far distance, she could see a few faint streaks of white light.

He's not even there yet. He had said he was going to be staying in St. Louis for a month. She knew already that she couldn't wait that long before seeing him. She would wait until the end of the week, then call him from Rush.

Maybe she could stop in St. Louis on her way back to L.A.

13

The Cowboy Motel was a single-story 1940s tan stucco structure located on Sunset only a block away from the Hollywood freeway. Gibson was acutely aware of the constant drone of the traffic as he stood by the door in Room 111 and peered through the glass panel, watching for Cortez and Whipkey.

On the tall sign at the edge of the parking lot, a smiling cowboy in a ten-gallon hat twirled a lariat over his head. Faded red neon outlined the figure, but the tubing constantly flickered and quivered so that the cowboy alternately took on a definite form, then lost it. Gibson thought of him as a sort of ghostly apparition shifting between the real world and the spirit realm.

Cortez had waited out front for Whipkey, and as soon as Gibson saw them coming across the parking lot, he pulled open the door. He stepped aside so they could pass, then let the door slam shut from its own weight.

"I'm Whipkey," the stranger said, holding out his hand for Gibson to take. "My first name's Elmer, but just call me Whip."

"You don't need to call me anything yet," Gibson said. He shook hands with Whip and noticed that, despite the warmth of the evening, Whip's hand was not even moist.

"If we come to the right kind of understanding, I'll tell you my name."

Whip looked at Gibson with a steady gaze. "If you're going to be like that, I don't even want to know your fucking name," he said softly. Then, quite unexpectedly, he smiled, and every trace of hostility seemed to be gone. "I'll just call you Charlie, and we'll both be happy."

Gibson nodded, but he didn't smile. Cortez had described Whip as a loner who loved gambling but made his money from selling guns. "I seen him around the games for years. He's what you might call an independent arms dealer," Cortez said. "When military guys get their hands on guns they want to sell, they go see Whip. Then if you need a gun, Whip can take care of you. He's like a retail store."

"Has he been inside?" Gibson asked.

"I heard him tell somebody he's never even been charged with anything." Cortez's brow wrinkled. "I'll tell you something, though. He's not anybody you want to fuck with, and that's a fact. I hear he's killed two people who tried to cheat him. You know, like didn't give him the other half of his money for guns after they picked them up?" Cortez shook his head. "Man, he just hunted them down and—boom! boom!—blew them away."

Gibson studied Whipkey a moment, not trying to disguise what he was doing. Whip had a long sallow face and black stringy hair pulled back from the sides and done up in a little rattail. The tail hung down over the collar of his long-sleeved, red-and-green plaid shirt. Even though the outside temperature hovered around eighty degrees, the shirt was buttoned at the neck.

In his left ear, Whip wore a silver death's-head earring, and on the left side of his upper lip, he had the deep crease of a scar. When he smiled, the scar didn't move, so his lip always curled up in a slight sneer. His eyes were nearly black, with a shiny, glassy look that made them stand out. *Like the eyes of a snake,* Gibson thought.

"Whip, my man, let's not worry about names," Cortez

said, trying to smooth things over. "Just wait till you hear what the Cyber's got to say."

"Want a Dr Pepper?" Gibson nodded toward a six-pack of cans and a white plastic bucket of ice on top of the dressing table.

"I don't care for one, thank you." Whip's tone was formal.

Gibson popped open a can and poured some of the soda into two ice-filled plastic glasses. He waited for the brownish foam to subside, then handed one to Cortez.

"Have a seat," Gibson said, glancing up at Whip.

Whip pulled out the straight chair in front of the blond dressing table. Turning the chair toward the door, he slouched back in it. Cortez eased himself down onto the edge of the queen-size bed.

Gibson turned off the ceiling light, then sat in the upholstered chair beside the door. On the bedside table, a tall Spanish-style lamp of amber glass and black metal gave off a pale yellow glow, but the room was filled with soft-edged gray shadows.

"What's this shit with the light?" Whip asked.

"I can think better when it's dim," Gibson said. "And if you get to hear my proposal, you'll want me to think as clearly as possible."

"Charlie, you can sit in the fucking dark for all I care," Whip said. His voice was slow and easy, but he didn't smile. "So what's your proposal?"

"You'll go crazy for it," Cortez said. "You'll see."

"I said *if* you get to hear it," Gibson said, ignoring Cortez. "I've got a couple of questions first."

"You can ask," Whip said. He smiled and seemed amused. Then he folded his arms across his chest and looked over at Gibson, making a show of waiting for a question.

Gibson heard the sound of voices coming from the room next door. He got up and turned on the TV set bolted to a metal frame attached to the wall.

Nobody said anything as Gibson stood waiting for a picture to emerge. Eventually, a twisted green and yellow band slowly spread out on the screen. It was a scene from *Blade Runner.* Decard was talking to an old woman in the marketplace, trying to identify the scale found in the bathtub of one of the replicants. Gibson turned the control to make the sound louder.

"I hear you know a lot about guns," Gibson said. He sat back down and picked up his glass of Dr Pepper from the floor.

"The army trained me for eight months, then made me a weapons specialist." He tapped his right arm with a finger, as if pointing to a badge. "That's what I was for two years—before they kicked me out." He shrugged, then smiled. "Of course, maybe the army's opinion's not good enough for you."

Gibson ignored the sarcasm. "What did you get kicked out for?" He took a sip of his drink.

Whip uncrossed his arms and leaned back in the chair. "I was at Fort Hood out in Texas, and this girl got killed. Somebody raped her and cut her up real bad. Just because a guy saw me talking to her that night, they thought I might have something to do with it. Of course, they didn't have no proof."

Whip smiled, and his lip curled. "I give them credit, though, they didn't let that stop them one goddamned bit. They said just being a suspect made the army look bad, and anyway I was a borderline personality and never would fit into the peacetime army. So they gave me a psychiatric discharge." He looked toward Cortez. "I'm a fucking lunatic, so you'd better watch yourself." He laughed without making any noise.

"Can you get any guns?" Gibson abruptly asked.

Whip hunched forward and let his hands hang between his legs. "How about an Ingram Mac-10 point three-eight machine pistol," he said. His pronunciation became more precise, and his tone was almost clipped. "It fires six rounds a second, and you can split a man in two with it like a chain saw." He gave Gibson a sly look. "Will that do?"

"I'm not a gun expert," Gibson said, shaking his head. "Can you get a couple of them tonight?"

"Maybe—if I knew why somebody wanted them," Whip said. He pulled himself up in the chair and smiled at Gibson.

Gibson stared at Whip without saying anything for a minute. He was going to have to make up his mind. He had known from the start that any kind of hired weight was going to be low-life garbage. The time he had spent at Chino had taught him that much. At least Whip understood guns, and his psychiatric discharge was actually a sort of recommendation for the job.

"If you're interested, I could tell you about a day's work that would make you twenty million dollars." Gibson raised his eyes and looked directly at Whip.

"I'm interested," Whip said, in a soft, almost drawling voice. He sat up straight. "For that kind of money, I'm very interested."

"It's going to be dangerous," Cortez said.

Whip shifted in his chair and fixed his glassy stare on Cortez. "So's driving on the freeway, and it don't pay nothing."

"I like your attitude," Gibson said. "What I'm talking about is simple. The three of us walk into this particular place and take somebody hostage, somebody famous. We then collect an enormous ransom for this person."

Whip nodded and his face was serious. "I hope you don't have the president of the United States in mind," he said. "Or even a member of his family. I'm a loyal American." He sounded so sanctimonious that Gibson found it hard not to laugh.

"It's not the president," Cortez said. "And I guarantee you it's somebody you wouldn't mind spending a little private time with." He smirked at Whip.

"We're going to take control of the building where our hostage is and barricade ourselves inside," Gibson said. "Then when they give us the money, we hand over the hostage and leave the country."

"Why not just grab the hostage and run?" Whip asked.

He frowned. "Make a phone call later, then pick up the money."

Gibson shook his head. "Having to pick up ransom virtually guarantees that any kidnapping is going to fail. You can look at the record."

"I gotcha," Whip said. "You're saying you can use a hostage to get us the money, then you can get us out."

"That's it," Gibson said. He took a sip of his drink and leaned back in the chair, but he peered at Whip over the glass. "That's the basic plan right there."

"It don't sound like much of a plan," Whip said. "How do we get out of the place? Any fucking idiot with a gun can take a hostage, but to get away, you've got to have it thought through." He leaned toward Gibson. "You know, they give you the money, and while you're running out the back door, they start shooting at you with AK-forty-sevens and grind you into hamburger before you hit the ground."

Gibson smiled at him for the first time. "You're a shrewd guy. That's the heart of the problem." He paused. "But unlike the typical hard-luck yos who kidnap people, I've got the escape problem figured out."

"Tell me about it," Whip said.

Gibson dropped his smile and stiffened his face. "You're going to have to trust me on that." He had decided early on that telling the others too much would jeopardize his plan for himself.

"I don't know what it is either," Cortez told Whip.

"If you can supply the firepower, I can supply the brainpower," Gibson said. He paused and sat back in his chair.

"I know I can supply the firepower," Whip said. "But how the hell can I be sure you've got enough brainpower to get us out?"

"You can't," Gibson said bluntly. "You've either got to take a chance or not go in with us." He jerked his head toward the door. "You don't know enough to cause us any problems, so if you want to take a hike, there's the door."

"How about just telling me the plan," Whip said.

"Then we'd both know, and I could decide whether or not you're full of shit."

"You just gave the reason I'm not telling you," Gibson said. *"Then we'd both know."* He took a sip of soda. "My value is that I know how to get us in and get us out, and I plan on keeping myself valuable."

"I believe I get the point," Whip said.

"You're a gambler," Gibson said. "Do what you're told, and you've got a chance to come out of this with twenty million dollars. It's a big risk, but it's also a big payoff."

"Was that twenty million split three ways?" Whip asked.

"That was twenty million *each*," Gibson said. "Sixty million total."

Gibson stood up and poured himself another glass of Dr Pepper. "There's something else we need to get straight at the start," he said, not looking at Whip. "I make the plans and I give the orders, because I run the show."

He paused, still holding the empty soda can, and looked at the TV set. Decard was talking to an attractive blond woman who was clearly the replicant he had been searching for. The woman suddenly knocked him to the floor and started to run.

Gibson glanced away and stared at Whip. He said in a level voice, "You've heard all you're going to hear, so you've got to make up your mind."

"Charlie, I'm needy and I'm greedy," Whip said, smiling. "And so far as following orders goes, I got lots of practice in the army, and that ain't a problem."

"Does that mean you're in?" Cortez asked.

"I've never been able to walk away from a high-stakes game." Whip shook his head, as if disapproving of a weakness. "I'll go with you."

"All right!" Cortez's voice rose with enthusiasm. He shifted forward on the bed and put his feet flat on the floor. "We'll make a great team, and we'll all have more money than the pope collects on Christmas."

"Just one little thing," Whip said. "We ain't all going to be carrying automatic weapons." He shook his head. "You two don't have no training. You'd kill everybody big enough to die, if I was to give you something like a Mac-10. I wouldn't even want to be in the same *house* with you."

"So what do you recommend?" Gibson asked. "I want a pistol, so I can hide it under a jacket."

"My idea is that I take a Mac-10 and outfit one of you with a shotgun," Whip said. "You want a handgun, I believe a forty-four Magnum would be a good choice. It fires a two-hundred-forty-grain bullet at about thirteen hundred feet a second, and it's got a muzzle velocity of nine hundred and seventy foot-pounds." He nodded his head and looked serious. "You hit somebody with that sucker, he don't keep on coming, and he don't just stop—he gets knocked ass-backwards for ten feet."

"I'll leave the guns up to you," Gibson said. "Can you get them tonight?"

"Does the bear shit in the woods?" Whip said, smiling. "But now hold on a minute and tell me where it is that we're supposed to hole up and fight off the whole fucking police force."

"It's a mental hospital," Gibson said. "And three of us can do just that, too. All the windows have gratings, and the first floor has only one outside entrance. It's got a sliding metal door operated by a computer. The research tower connected to the hospital building has the same kind of door but no windows."

"Does either place have a basement?" Whip asked.

"Sure," Cortez said. "But no outside doors." He smiled at Whip. "We got copies of the plans out of a computer."

Whip looked puzzled at first, then his expression registered understanding. "You can really do that shit? Get inside a computer?" He seemed genuinely impressed.

"To compute is to rule," Cortez said, repeating an expression he had first heard Gibson use in class years before.

Whip nodded. "So where's this nuthouse?"

"Boston," Cortez said.

"Jesus, that's on the other side of the fucking country," Whip said. He shook his head. "Now how about telling me when this is going to happen. If I'm going to be a part of the goddamned group, I imagine I ought to know."

"Tomorrow night," Gibson said.

Whip gave a low whistle and shook his head again. "You're a gentleman who don't believe in waiting for the wedding."

"You never know when our target might change plans," Gibson said. "So I want you to box up the guns and ship them off tonight by air express." He fixed his eyes on Whip. "When Cortez gets to Boston, he'll pick up the rental van and meet you, then you can both go get the packages."

"We're not all going to be on the same plane?" Whip asked.

"Cortez is going an hour later," Gibson said. "After you get the guns, check in at the Cambridge Motel. I've already reserved a room in the name of Bruce Case."

"What about you?" Whip asked.

"I'm not coming in until nine o'clock," Gibson said. "I've got a computer program to write tonight, and if I don't get it finished, we might as well quit now. It's going to be our ticket out of the building, once we get the money."

"Are you going to tell me where we *can* go when we get the money?" Whip asked.

"Cuba," Cortez said. "We can live like kings there and not have to worry about the U.S. government extraditing us."

"I don't know about that," Whip said, shaking his head. "Who wants to live in a raggedy-ass country like Cuba?"

"After we get there, we can go anyplace else we want to," Cortez said. "Man, we can *buy* all the identification papers we need and go over to Europe or we can even slip back into this country."

"You've got a point there," Whip said, nodding his head.

"I'm coming back to L.A. soon as I can," Cortez said.

"I just don't want to live in any foreign country longer than I've got to," Whip said. "Now I've got one more question." He turned to look at Gibson with a critical gaze. "Just who the fuck can we ransom for sixty million dollars?"

Gibson heard the sound of a shot on the TV and glanced past Whip's shoulder. The blond woman Decard had been chasing was dead. She lay on her back in a pile of shattered glass, blood running from under her body.

"Susan Bradstreet," Gibson said.

14

"This is it," Blare, the limousine driver, said.

He slowed the car and turned right into a wide blacktop driveway. Off to the side, a rectangular white sign with a scrolled top hung from a post. The black letters on the sign read: BENJAMIN RUSH INSTITUTE, ESTAB. 1852.

"I don't see anything," Susan said.

Despite the earliness of the hour, she didn't feel tired. Instead, a pleasurable edge of anticipation was making her alert and curious. She glanced out the window on her left, then leaned to the right to look through the windshield.

The sky was cloudless, but everything around the car was hidden in darkness. The dense canopy of arching trees blocked out all but the feeblest yellow glow of moonlight. The flash of the headlights briefly illuminated the smooth black asphalt of the driveway and the rough trunks of the trees growing alongside it.

"Look to the right, up on that rise," Blare directed.

"I can see it now," Meg said.

Susan lowered her head and glimpsed a large circle of light at the top of the steep hill. In a clearing at the center of the circle, she could make out a boxy red-brick tower with a flat roof. At its right was a two-story brick Colonial structure with a high front gable and a portico supported by white columns. Floodlights on the roofs washed the sides of each building with a brilliant white light. Fixtures attached to the tops of tall silver poles illuminated the surrounding open ground and intensified the circle of brightness.

For a moment she thought Rush looked like a magic palace floating above the forest of dark trees encircling it. It would be a haven, a place of safety where, at least for a while, she could escape from the fears and troubles of her ordinary life.

"That's the research tower, with Johnson Hall beside it."

"What are those houses?" Susan asked.

She reached through the partition between the seats and waved her finger toward several structures partway up the hill. Each was inside its own circle of light, and the circles were strewn along a line that followed the curving contour of the hill.

"Those are cottages," Blare said. "That's where most of the patients live."

Susan felt her curiosity suddenly ebb. She leaned back in her seat and rubbed her hands over her face. Her generally good spirits were on the verge of deserting her, and she was starting to feel frightened.

The car stopped in front of the entrance to Johnson Hall, and Susan got out before Blare could open the door for her. She raised her arms over her head and stretched, standing on her toes and thrusting her hands toward the sky. Just moving her muscles felt wonderful.

Over the last three years, she had become accustomed to spending a couple of hours a day in intensive physical training. That was what it took to play a lead role in an adventure movie. The effort had put her in excellent physical condition, but when she missed a training session, she felt sluggish.

Now that she was in front of Johnson Hall, she could tell that the windows on the first floor were all fakes. They were painted frames with clear glass panes, but a few inches behind the glass, she could see smooth white walls. She glanced to her left at the research tower and noticed that it had no windows at all on the first floor. Were people being walled in or out? Probably both.

"Right this way, please," Blare said. "We'll have to ring to get you inside, then I'll come back for your luggage."

Meg walked with Blare, and Susan followed behind them along the herringbone brick path. She was going up the shallow steps and under the portico when she suddenly noticed a woman standing in the corner where the porch joined the building. Susan stopped abruptly, standing completely still, as if frozen. All at once, dizziness rippled through her head, making her sway slightly. She could feel her heart pounding.

The woman noticed Susan looking at her. She moved out of her corner and walked onto the porch so that she was under the light. She seemed to be in her sixties, and she was thin to the point of emaciation. Her white dress was loose and shapeless.

Susan put her hand over her rapidly beating heart and stared in fascination. The time and place were so strange that the woman seemed like an apparition, and for a fleeting instant, Susan wondered if she was real. Then she knew she was as Meg quickly stepped between her and the stranger.

"You shouldn't go in there," the woman said to Susan. Her voice was high and steady, and her dark eyes shifted from place to place, as if she had to keep a watch for things that only she could see.

Susan's heart rate began to slow, and she realized that her body had reacted so violently because the woman had startled her. This wasn't another one of her anxiety attacks.

"Why shouldn't I go in?" Susan asked.

"Excuse me, excuse me," Blare said to the woman before she could answer. "Do you live in one of the cottages?"

"Because the machines won't let you out," the woman said. "The doors don't have keys."

"I'm sure you aren't supposed to be outside at this time of night," Blare said. He sounded more worried than firm.

The woman's eyes stopped darting around, and she stared directly at Susan. "The machines control everything. Everything."

"Thank you for telling me," Susan said. She didn't know what else to say.

The woman gave a weak smile, then slowly walked back down the porch steps and took up her place in the corner.

Susan watched her a moment. "Will you be okay?" she called. The woman didn't look up. Susan turned to Blare. "Should we do something?"

"I'll get somebody to check on her," Blare said.

He held open one of the double doors, and they walked into a vestibule with a black-and-white tile floor. Susan stopped in front of the inner door and looked at it in puzzlement. It was a blank metal slab painted a Colonial cream color and without a doorknob, peephole, or hardware of any kind.

"This door doesn't seem to have a handle," she said.

"It's electronically locked," Blare said. "Somebody inside has to pass you in."

"Is that what she meant about not having any keys?"

"Maybe so." He shrugged, then pushed the red button on the stainless-steel console that was set flush with the wall.

Susan glanced around, and high on the wall in the upper right corner she saw a TV camera trained on them. Apparently the electronic doors weren't the only security precaution. She had noticed something under the roof of the portico, and now she realized that it must be a camera covering the front door.

"This is Blare," the driver said. He was leaning forward and speaking into the perforated circular grill on the console. "I'm here with Miss Bradstreet and Miss O'Hare. Code ninety-two."

"Stand by," came a tinny voice over the speaker.

"What's code ninety-two?" Meg asked. She sounded suspicious.

"Just a number," Blare said. "We change it every day. If I hadn't given the right one, we wouldn't be allowed in, and security would be here in a snap to check us out."

Susan heard a muffled click, then the door suddenly slid into the wall. It made little noises and rolled back so rapidly that it almost gave the impression of simply disappearing.

As they stepped inside, the door immediately slid back into place. When it reached the opposite wall, Susan heard another faint click. Slight as the noise was, it made her feel very locked up.

15

Susan found herself in a broad hallway that ran along the entire front of the building. The highly polished floor was paved with black-streaked green marble, and the opposite wall was a long expanse of white plaster broken only by two wide rectangular doorways.

She glanced left and saw an Asian man sitting at a desk placed at a right angle to the wall. Behind him, farther down the hall, was a set of double doors with inset glass panels. He smiled broadly and waved to them. He then looked down at a TV monitor on a corner of the desk. He studied the screen briefly, turned toward a computer on the opposite side, and typed something on the keyboard.

Directly in front of Susan, through the doorway at the right, was a comfortably furnished sitting room. It was large and didn't seem overcrowded, even though it contained three small clusters of chintz-covered sofas, wing-back chairs, coffee tables, and Persian carpets. An oversized TV screen and various pieces of electronic equipment were grouped together against the back wall. They seemed out of place, and she couldn't help thinking that they marred the graceful character of the room.

In the back right corner were three closed doors, then along the side wall, two more. Very likely they were patients' rooms. A wide archway in the wall opposite the two doors probably led into a dining room.

The computer on the desk beeped sharply. The man then got up and started toward them. He looked young, not even thirty, and he wore a long-sleeved white shirt with a neatly knotted maroon tie. He was short and wiry, and he walked with an obvious limp. When he put weight on his right foot, he lurched forward so sharply he looked as if he were going to fall. Yet he always caught himself in time.

"You're Miss Bradstreet," he said. He bowed his head slightly. "My name is Cho Ling, but people just call me Joe. I'm so glad to meet you."

His name might be Chinese, but so far as Susan could tell, his accent was pure Boston. As she shook hands with him, she noticed that he stood in a peculiar forward-leaning stance. He put all his weight on his left leg and stuck out his right leg behind him for balance.

"This is Meg O'Hare," Susan said, nodding toward Meg. "Thanks for staying up so late to check me in."

"Oh, I'm glad to be here. I'm a big fan of yours." Joe smiled, showing white teeth. "I've even seen *Night Voices*."

"That makes you a real fan," Susan said, smiling back. "I think I had one line."

Suddenly she felt much better about being at Rush. Joe had reminded her that nothing terrible had happened to her. She was the same person she had been before the anxiety attack.

"I'm glad you picked this time to arrive," Joe said.

"I'm the assistant director of Lowell Division, and this is my month to work nights." He looked at Blare. "Is there some luggage?"

"I'll bring it in," Blare said. "But we saw a lady outside, and I think she might need help getting back to her cottage."

"Don't worry about her," Joe said. "That was Doris Krohn, and I saw her on the monitor." He jerked his head toward the desk. "Her doctor gave her permission to stay outside, so long as she doesn't leave the grounds."

"Thought I'd better report it," Blare said.

"I'll key you out," Joe said. He turned to Susan. "I need for you to sign an admission form and a consent form. Please come over to the desk, then I'll show you your room."

Joe turned and started down the hall. His lurching walk was almost painful to watch, but he could move surprisingly fast. Susan hurried to catch up with him, then looked back at Meg.

"I'll help with the suitcases," Meg said.

Susan slowed as they passed the next open door, and Joe adjusted his stride to fit hers. As she had guessed, the room through the arch was a dining room. She glimpsed a polished table of dark wood, a sideboard, and a tall cabinet. The hardwood floor was partly covered with a pale blue and cream rug that looked Chinese. She was struck by how elegant, and no doubt expensive, the furnishings were.

"Is this where we eat?" she asked.

"That's right," Joe said. He twisted around and motioned toward the back. "The kitchen is straight through that door. For safety reasons, we keep it locked when the staff isn't working there."

As they reached the desk, Joe walked around to the back and put his palms flat on the surface. Supporting himself with his hands, he eased himself down into the chair. He then swung around to face the computer and typed out something.

Susan glanced over her shoulder in time to see Meg

and Blare going out the front door. She hadn't even heard the door open.

While Joe was looking through a stack of forms, she walked down the hall beyond his desk. She was curious about the double doors she had glimpsed earlier. When she reached them, she leaned forward and peered through one of the glass rectangles.

She could see nothing but a brightly lighted hallway with white walls and a floor covered in a pattern of pale gray and dark green vinyl tiles. Along the hall on the right were several windowless metal doors painted charcoal gray. At the end of the hall, she could make out the wide doors of an elevator.

As she walked toward the desk, Joe turned to glance at her. "Is the research tower through there?" She jerked her head toward the doors.

"That's it," he said. "Patients aren't allowed inside, but if you want to visit, I'm sure Dr. Blau can arrange a tour."

"Is it worth it?" Susan sat down beside the desk.

"Absolutely," Joe said. "Get Dr. Simon to show you his pool of moray eels. He's studying their nervous system, and they're the scariest-looking creatures in the tower. A couple of researchers are working on seizure disorders in monkeys, and sometimes you can hear them screaming even in this building."

"Sounds like a jungle in there," Susan said, smiling.

"Some world-class research goes on here," Joe said. "The tower has fully equipped labs, surgical suites, and a freezing chamber to preserve whole specimens." He sounded proud to be associated with Rush.

"I always like to hear scientists explain their research."

"As I say, talk to Dr. Blau," Joe said. "Now if you'll answer a few questions, we can get finished here."

Susan put her hand over her mouth to stifle a yawn. The day was catching up with her. Then she remembered something that Joe said earlier that had puzzled her.

"How do you know Doris Krohn won't leave the hospital grounds?" she asked.

"We track her on the monitoring system," Joe said.

"When you came in, I was sending a message to Hope Cottage to tell them I had visual contact with her outside. But Doris also has on one of these." He opened the center drawer and took out a clear plastic hospital bracelet with a slight bulge in the middle. He held it up by the metal clasp at the end so she could see it. "This has a chip in it that emits a continuous signal at a fixed frequency," Joe said. He waved the bracelet back and forth in front of him, then held it far out to one side. "We can check the computer, and it will display a map and pinpoint exactly where Doris is. If she gets out of range, an alarm sounds."

"Sounds like she's wearing a beeper in reverse," Susan said.

"I hadn't thought of it that way," Joe said. "But I guess she is the one who's sending the signal." He smiled.

Joe passed over the single-page hospital-admission form and pointed to the line at the bottom where she was supposed to sign. She signed, then did the same on the consent form. She didn't bother to read either.

"That's all there is," Joe said, as she handed him the papers. "I've made arrangements for Miss O'Hare to stay at the Sheraton. It's only a mile down the road, and Blare can drive her there."

"I don't think you understand," Susan said. She told herself to speak calmly and not get angry—at least not yet. "Meg is my bodyguard. She stays with me."

Joe looked surprised. "Oh, I thought she was just a friend," he said. He dropped his gaze. "But I'm afraid there's some confusion about this. You see, the only people allowed to stay in rooms at Rush are either patients or staff." He looked up at her and smiled, showing his very white teeth. "You're not going to need a bodyguard while you're here. Our security is excellent."

"I want her with me anyway." Susan allowed no doubt to creep into her voice. "I guess Dr. Hightower didn't make that clear when he talked to Dr. Blau."

"Dr. Blau told me Miss O'Hare would be escorting you, but he didn't say anything about her staying here." Joe's forehead wrinkled in uncertainty.

"Then let's wait until tomorrow to work it out," Susan said. She spoke as though the issue was settled. "Meg can stay in my room tonight or sleep on one of the sofas in the lounge."

She could see Joe hesitate, and his smile was fixed and formal. She suddenly realized that now that she had signed the admission form, she had put herself under hospital rules. Joe was probably considering whether he should assert his authority and order Meg to leave or accept a compromise.

"That's a good suggestion," he said smoothly. "Counting you, only three patients are in Lowell right now, so why don't I put her in the room next to yours. You can both get some sleep, then you can discuss the matter with Dr. Blau in the morning."

Joe nodded, as though giving approval to his own action. "Sometimes we do let a family member stay the night, when patients have special problems. I think I can stretch the point."

"Thank you," Susan said, smiling. Then before Joe had a chance to think any more about the matter, she asked, "Who are the other two patients?"

"Clara Rostov is one," Joe said. "You'll enjoy her. She's like a grandmother in the movies."

"They're the best kind," Susan said.

Even as she said it, she realized that her own grandmother hadn't been like that. She had been sixty pounds overweight, highly opinionated on topics she knew little about, and a chain-smoker. But she had also indulged her only grandchild and kept up a barrage of praise and compliments that didn't end until the day she died. It was only during the following year that Susan realized how much she had depended on her grandmother's steady stream of unqualified approval to sustain her self-confidence.

"The other patient is Tim Kimberly," Joe said. "He's only fifteen, but he's a bright kid. You'll like him too."

"Shouldn't he be in with other kids?"

"Ordinarily he would be in one of the juvenile cottages," Joe said. "I can't tell you any details without violating confidentiality, but his dad and mom are having a custody dispute, so we're keeping him here."

"It must be boring for him."

"It's not bad," Joe said. "He gets to mix with other kids during the day, when he's in group or goes to OT— occupational therapy—but he has to come back here to spend the night."

"Speaking of spending the night, if you don't have anything else for me to sign, I'm ready to try to make the best of the rest of it."

The computer emitted a sharp beep. "This is Blare," came out of the speaker. "Code ninety-two."

Joe leaned across the desk and typed in something. It was obviously a command for opening the door. "Here comes your luggage," he said. "I'll take you to your room."

"I don't mind going by myself." Susan stood up.

Joe hesitated, then said, "The rules say I have to go with you." He lowered his head slightly, looking embarrassed. "I also have to go through your luggage and make sure you're not bringing in any nonprescribed drugs or anything that could be used as a weapon."

Susan felt a momentary shock at the idea of a stranger searching her luggage. Then she caught herself. She had forgotten for a moment what sort of place Rush was.

"Of course you do," she said. "I should tell you right now that Meg carries a gun, but she has a license."

"I can't let her keep it." Joe shook his head. "I'll have to lock it up in the desk."

"She's not going to like being unarmed."

"This isn't one of those B-movie madhouses with maniacs threatening to knife people," Joe said. "Nothing is going to happen to either of you here."

"I'm not worried." Susan smiled. "I'm just anxious."

16

Gibson pulled on the thick leather strap attached to the back of the bookcase. As soon as the bookcase swung forward and clicked into position, he stepped to one side and gave the steel inner door a push backward. He then waited, listening, until he heard a sharp snap that meant the biometric lock was engaged and that once again he was sealed into his necropolis.

He could sense the darkness seeping into him, and at another time, he would enjoy sitting quietly and letting it wash away his stress. Now, though, he was beginning to feel a raw excitement spreading in him like a warm glow, and he was eager to get on with his project. He still had to install the Chernobyl program.

That wasn't all, either. He had to transfer the money from his local bank to the numbered account in Bahrain and get his passport out of the safety deposit box. He also had to make sure Cortez paid off the Iceman so he wouldn't put out the word that Cortez had disappeared. Gibson's plans depended absolutely on keeping his identity a secret, and he couldn't risk the cops linking Cortez to him.

He groped for the round knob of the rheostat left of the door, then slowly turned the switch until the light became an opalescent gray gleam. He squinted until his eyes adjusted to the brightness.

He dropped his clipboard on the vacant surface of the worktable, then sat down at his computer beside it. The computer was booted and running, and he switched on the screen. As soon as the screen began to glow in a soft dark blue, he adjusted the clipboard so that he could read the program that he had been working on nonstop since leaving the Cowboy Motel. It covered twelve single-spaced pages. Fortunately, he hadn't had to start from scratch, because over the years he had written a number of routines to let him get onto Internet and then into NYNEX—the New York–New England Exchange.

The hole in NYNEX that he used to get past the "ice"—the intrusion countermeasure electronics—and inside the system had been there for five years to his knowledge, and very likely it had been there since the system was established. Probably a long-gone designer had left it so he could get in and out without causing ripples in the net.

Sticking the subroutines together had been easy enough, but after that he had to start writing the UNIX code to let him do what he wanted in the NYNEX system. He began running the net, following out branching paths into local and regional areas and searching in strange domains. He had spent hours scanning directories and looking for files that would be useful in a final routine.

Eventually, he solved his problem elegantly by locating a superuser—a system-manager—program and getting it to recognize him as a friend. He had then descended to root mode and inserted routines that became just more sets of files inside the vast multiplicity of code lines making up the instructions necessary to keep NYNEX operating.

He had devised a Trojan horse program that he could neatly inject into the gigantic ice program that was supposed to keep people like him out of the system. To cap the irony, somebody running the directories would find the Trojan horse identified as an antivirus agent.

He pulled the keyboard toward him, and in a final, almost superstitious, test to see if the NYNEX back door was still open, he keyed in the command that should get him inside. After a few seconds the dull buzz of an empty phone line sounded. The blankness was interrupted by the pulsating pattern of *eeep, eeep, eeep,* then came the sharp static of a connection.

The blue screen of the monitor was suddenly filled with a boxed message in heavy bold lettering:

WARNING
Access to this computer and to the computer data
and the computer materials accessible by use of this
computer is restricted to those whose access has
been authorized by NYNEX or its subsidiary companies. Use by unauthorized persons is a violation of
federal and/or state laws.

He typed in another command, and the screen was immediately filled with an array of alphanumeric patterns.
He smiled with satisfaction, then immediately got out of
the system. No need to put himself at risk for a trace. The
hole was open, and there was no reason it should disappear in the next day or two.

He started keying in his program, and by the time he
had typed out the first line and hit "Enter," he was feeling
almost light-headed. He felt so sure that everything was
going to work that he would stake his life on it. Actually,
that was what he was doing.

But everything was going to work in an even grander
sense. His life was going to become what he wanted it to
be. He would have enough money to retire from the world
and live a life remote from the narrow constraints of a
moralistic, hypocritical, and sex-obsessed society.

Maybe when he got established in Paraguay he would
hire people to build him a house underground. It would be
a large, elaborate structure with smooth blank walls and
no windows. There would be no way for the sun to get in.
All the light would be artificial and completely under his
control. The inside of the house would be cool and dark
and elegantly furnished. Maybe he would even build an
underground swimming pool.

He would have tunnels with tiled walls going deeper
into the earth. They would lead to computer rooms, store-
rooms, a movie theater, and a dungeon. Then farther away
than any of the other rooms, he would install a private
morgue. He could do that in Paraguay. He would have an
enormous amount of money, and government officials

were always ready to take bribes. He would buy bodies the way people bought chickens at the market.

He would finally become free to be himself.

When he finished entering the first page of the Chernobyl program, he went back to check over each line. He couldn't afford to make a mistake, but it was hard to keep his mind on checking. He kept thinking about the house in Paraguay.

He would be able to take Susan there and show her around. They could stroll through the tunnels together, and in the darkness and silence, he could talk to her. He could tell her about his idea of alternate worlds, worlds that could be brought into existence by imagination and determination. Having her with him would fulfill the thousands of fantasies he had invented since his experience with a silent friend when he was sixteen.

He had been a junior at Hillcrest High School in Dallas. One Friday night during the spring, maybe April, a boy named Dennis asked if he wanted to go with him and one of his friends to the Starlight Drive-In theater across the river in Oak Cliff.

He knew Dennis only because their mothers had worked on a Red Cross blood drive, and the families had gotten together a few times. He thought Dennis was a stupid loudmouth, and he didn't like hanging out with him. Still, he couldn't think of a reason to say no, and he didn't have anything else to do. It wasn't as if he had any real friends likely to ask him to do something.

Dennis's friend Bert was so fat around the middle that his belly hung over his wide tooled-leather belt, but at the same time, he was tall and broad enough not to be taken for a fat boy. He was eighteen, and he held down a full-time maintenance job at Parkland Hospital. "I went to Crozier Tech, but I never graduated," he told Gibson when Dennis introduced them. "I just quituated."

Bert came stocked up with a gallon jug of red wine and Dennis with a half ounce of marijuana. The three of them sat in Dennis's red Mercury Cougar on the gravel parking area of the drive-in and sipped and smoked. Gibson did

some of both, but not too much of either, because he
didn't like to lose control of himself. He didn't like the
feeling that time was slowing and the world was slipping
from his grasp.

The marquee of the Starlight advertised its hours as
"From Dusk to Dawn," and during that time, five or six
movies were shown. That night it was all science fiction,
and B-movies from the fifties filled the screen one after
the other. They watched *It Came from Outer Space, In-
vaders from Mars,* and *The Body Snatcher.* But by the end
of the third film they were hardly paying attention to
what was happening on the screen. Everything had turned
into background for their crude comments and wise-
cracks, and they giggled at whatever anybody said,
whether it was funny or not.

Nobody wanted to stay until dawn, but it was nearly
two by the time they left. He could still remember the
way the tires crunched on the crushed white rock of the
exit road.

As they pulled onto the road leading across the river
and into Dallas, Bert suddenly asked him, "You want to
be scared?"

"That's an idea," Dennis said. "I hadn't thought about
it."

"You mean scared like when you jump off a bridge into
the river?" he had asked. "Something like that?"

"No, no," Bert said. He sounded half serious and half
teasing. "I mean scared by spooks."

"Right," Dennis said enthusiastically. "Let's see if you
can take it without running for your mom."

"I don't believe in ghosts."

"I didn't say anything about ghosts," Bert said. "I
mean real, solid things that can scare the piss out of you."

"If you can take it, I can," he told them.

Dennis drove to an older residential area in the city that
was made up of two-story duplexes mixed in with single-
family houses. The houses were substantial red-brick
structures, with narrow 1930s driveways and neat lawns.
Along one street, though, some of the houses were no

longer being used as residences. Signs for an insurance
agent, an exterminator, and a dentist were staked on the
lawns or displayed across the eaves.

Dennis turned the corner and swung into a brick alley
running behind the row of houses. He immediately cut
off the headlights and slowed the car to a crawl. Hedges
from the backyards had grown long branches that
scratched at the fenders and slapped through the windows
as they drove past.

"Lots of people back out of this," Bert said. He
hunched his shoulders as if he were shuddering. "Whoo,
mama, I don't know if I can do this my own self." He
jerked his head around to look at Gibson in the back.
"You sure you want to go through with it?"

Gibson could hear the taunt in his voice and didn't answer him. He had already figured out that if Bert and
Dennis had done whatever it was, it wasn't anything to be
genuinely scared of.

"Here it is," Dennis said.

He pulled the car off the alley and onto an asphalt slab
beside a two-story brick building. The moon wasn't out,
and it was impossible to tell anything about the building.
Either no one lived in it or the people had gone to bed
and turned off all the lights, because no light shone from
anyplace.

When they got out of the car, Bert took the lead, and
Dennis came last. "Now don't knock me down trying to
run past me," Dennis told him in a whisper. He knew they
were teasing him. He didn't like it, but he knew better
than to try to make them quit, because that would just
make things worse.

Bert stopped in front of a window at the back of the
building. The small rectangular panes had been painted,
but Gibson could tell that the building hadn't been abandoned. He could hear the noise of a ventilation fan running directly overhead. After a moment he also heard a
compressor start up. Probably a refrigerator, he thought.

"Keep quiet now," Bert said in a breathy whisper. "We
don't want to scare anybody inside."

"What is this place?" he asked Bert. He was beginning to feel uneasy about what they were doing. He wasn't so much worried about what they might find inside as he was afraid that a police car would drive by and see them.

His father would be furious if he got arrested and would never stop criticizing him for his stupidity in getting into a position to let it happen. "I've wasted my time and money raising an idiot," his father would yell at him. "You had a brilliant future ahead of you, and now you've thrown it away."

His mother would look sad, shake her head, then say in her maddeningly soft voice, "I'm sorry to have to agree, but no sir, your father spoke the truth, and that's all there is to it."

His father would go on to say more, making his words sharp and hurtful. He would speak to his son the way he didn't dare speak to any of the lawyers at the firm. He had worked there as a clerk, then as an office manager, since poverty and a pregnant wife had forced him to drop out of law school during his first year. Gibson had realized early that his success was supposed to be his father's revenge for the years he spent being subservient to attorneys, for his years as "Gibby," the underling who had to do whatever shit work the lawyers didn't want to do.

Bert pushed on the wooden window frame and the window slid up smoothly. The opening was unscreened and hardly more than waist-high. Bert lifted his right leg, twisted his body around, and stepped through the window.

"You go," Dennis whispered, nudging his arm.

He did exactly as Bert had done and found himself standing in darkness so dense he could almost feel it. He could smell an acrid, slightly sweet odor that he couldn't identify. It seemed almost pleasant at first, but it immediately became so overwhelming he would have welcomed a breath of fresh air.

Although he could see nothing in the darkness, he heard the slight wheeze of Bert's breathing and moved toward it slowly. He took mincing little steps, sliding one foot forward, then pulling the other up level with it. The floor felt hard, and he could feel the grit on his shoes scraping against it. He stopped when he could sense Bert's bulk close to him.

Just then, Dennis stepped inside, blocking the pale blue rectangle of light that marked the opening.

"Shut the window," Bert said.

He could hear the creak and rattle of wood as Dennis pulled down the sash. The pale blue rectangle disappeared, leaving in its place only more darkness. The painted panes screened out even a glimmer of light.

"Here goes," Bert said. He spoke in a normal voice, which sounded very loud. "Get ready to do whatever you've got to do."

The absolute darkness began to be replaced by a faint yellowish glow from overhead. The glow became bright enough for him to see that they were in a room lined with white rectangles of ceramic tile. Not only was there tile on the floor, but three of the walls were covered with tile up to the ceiling. Tall metal cabinets with glass fronts took up most of the fourth wall.

In the exact center of the room stood a table with a stainless-steel top that had gutters running along its sides. At the bottom of the table, the gutters curved around and came together at a drain. A black rubber tube attached to the drain led from it into a chrome pipe sticking up from the tile floor. At the top of the table was a hose that looked exactly like the vegetable sprayer in a kitchen sink.

"This is where they take out their blood," Bert said. He put his hand on top of the table.

"Is this an operating table?" he asked.

"You might say that." Bert's tone was teasing, and he opened his mouth in a grin that revealed large yellowed teeth.

"Show him where they keep them," Dennis said. His voice sounded high and nervous.

He was beginning to catch on, and he was almost amused that they expected him to be scared. Dennis had a fixed smile, and he still stood near the window.

Bert walked to the wall with the glass-fronted cabinets, and Gibson noticed four stainless-steel doors arranged in a grid. They each had a handle on the front, like drawers in a filing cabinet. Bert grabbed the handle on the lower right drawer.

"Come over here," Bert ordered Gibson.

Bert waited until Gibson was standing beside him, then he began tugging on the handle. The drawer started sliding open in a smooth, easy way. Gibson stepped back to allow it to glide past him unimpeded. He could then feel a draft of cold air coming from the opened door, and a dank, slightly sour odor floated over him.

The woman that lay on the slightly concave metal shelf was young and attractive. Her hair was a dark honey blond and it lay spread out from her neck like a frame for her face. Her eyes were closed, and her head was turned somewhat to one side, as though she were a sleeper who had just dozed off. Her skin had an almost translucent ashen hue, as if it had been bleached to that color from some darker shade. But her lips were still red, and they were parted slightly.

"I just delivered her this afternoon," Bert told him. "That's when I unlatched the window."

He was dimly aware that Bert and Dennis must have planned to take him to the building before they started talking about it. Dennis's suggestion had seemed spontaneous, but it wasn't.

"The reason she looks so good is, she died of an overdose of some goddamned drug," Bert said. "Nobody claimed the body, so she goes here for students to practice on."

He paid no attention to Bert. He was fascinated by her. She was lovely, a genuine Sleeping Beauty. Her breasts were small, with pale pink nipples, and she was slender, with slightly flaring hips, a narrow waist, and long legs. He noticed with interest that the triangle of tightly curled pubic hair between her legs was the same dark blond as the hair framing her face.

As he studied her body, he could feel himself becoming

aroused. He had never seen anyone living who could exert such a powerful attraction over him. She was like a doll, a life-sized doll that he could play with and that would stay with him as long as he wanted. He wouldn't have to talk to her, and she wouldn't be able to say anything that would make him feel shy or inadequate. Her body would be his to do with as he liked.

"What sort of place is this?" he asked Bert without looking up. Even to himself his voice sounded remote and distracted.

"It's an embalming school," Bert said. "The Dallas College of Mortuary Sciences."

"Touch her," Dennis said. His tone was challenging, and he walked over to stand beside Gibson. "We want to see you do it."

"I don't think he's scared," Bert said. "Look at the way he's staring. Shit, man, your fucking eyeballs are going to lock up like that." He sounded amused.

"I dare you to touch her," Dennis said.

"Show him you're not scared," Bert said. His voice had a knowing tone that was both a goad and an invitation.

Without looking up at either of them, Gibson leaned over and kissed the partly opened lips of the corpse. They felt cold, yet soft and yielding, and he could taste a faint saltiness. Was it from sweat or tears? While he kissed her lips, he ran his hand across the smooth and supple skin of her abdomen, then gently squeezed one of her breasts with the tips of his fingers.

"Oh, my God," Dennis said in a raspy whisper. "That's disgusting. You're a fucking pervert."

"Time to go, Jack," Bert said.

Bert took his arm and pulled him away. He didn't want to go. The kissing and fondling had excited him even further, and all he wanted was to be left alone with the corpse.

"Leave me here," he said to Bert. It was almost a plea.

"No way, no way," Bert said. "This place has got a patrol that comes by on the hour, and we're crowding the limit."

Bert shoved past him and pushed the drawer closed. Gibson stood staring for a moment at the blank grid of stainless steel. He felt a terrible sense of loss.

Dennis gave him a ride home, but he never called him again. A month or so later, Gibson had tried to locate Bert at Parkland Hospital, but he was told that Bert no longer worked there.

During the next several weeks, he was tempted many times to go back to the Dallas College of Mortuary Sciences, and once he did. He parked where Dennis had parked and tried the painted window that Bert had raised. The window was locked, and so was the back door. He thought about breaking in, just one time, but in the end he didn't do it. He was still afraid of his father.

But even now, sixteen years later, he could remember exactly what the corpse looked like and how it felt. It was the only dead body he had actually touched. When he looked at the images of others and fantasized about what he would like to do with them, he was forced to rely on his tactile memories to make the imagined experience more real.

He was sure Susan's skin would have the same smooth delicate feel to it. He was also sure that kissing her lips while they were still warm and supple from body heat would be even more exciting. Of course, that would be only the beginning, because now he was eager to go beyond the bounds of his previous experience.

Body heat, he thought, liking the sound of the phrase. *Susan's body heat should last long enough.*

Gibson keyed in the final line of the Chernobyl program and felt a sudden rush of exhilaration. He lifted his hands above his head with his palms together, as if he were a boxer who had just won a fight. He would have to do some test runs without actually getting on Internet, and maybe a little debugging, but the real work was finished.

He still had to copy the program and install it on the machine in his living room. He was going to run the program on that machine. The computer in the necropolis was going to serve as a backup in case of some technical glitch, but the necropolis computer was also the key to his plan.

The two computers weren't networked with each other, and more important, they had different telephone lines. The line in the living room was a regular one, assigned a number in the usual way. However, the line hooking up the necropolis computer ran through the wall and into the adjacent building. The line was then attached to the service coming into that building. The line existed only because he had wired it himself, then assigned himself a phone number so deep inside the Caltel system that no regular equipment check would ever locate it.

Once the cops learned that he had the power to melt down the entire NYNEX system, they would go crazy trying to find his computer before it injected the Chernobyl program. He smiled as he thought of the frustration he was going to cause them.

17

Hightower sat at the desk in his father's study and looked at the stack of floppy disks piled beside the computer in front of him. He let out his breath in a long sigh, shook his head, and pushed his chair back. He wished his parents were already home so he would have somebody to talk to.

The disks contained the patient charts he was using for his research project, and each chart represented a person diagnosed with some form of anxiety disorder. To turn the cases into data, he had to read through each chart and classify the patient's symptoms and history according to his criteria. He then had to assess the relative effectiveness of drug treatments versus behavior therapy.

He knew what he needed to do, but he didn't feel like doing it. He didn't have the energy or, if he was honest with himself, the inclination. He was exhausted to the point of being dizzy and slightly ill. Part of his fatigue, he was sure, was due to the usual underlying depression, but he had another reason to feel tired. He had slept poorly again.

The irony was that he had been in such a good mood after being with Susan that he had expected to sleep well. He was extremely tired and had fallen asleep immediately, but he had slept fitfully, because the dream about Alma had come again. Only this time it was a disturbingly altered version of the usual dream.

He was standing alone on the shore of an ocean, and the clouds overhead were shaping up for a storm. The sky was darkening and the surf was rushing in with a loud *whoosh,* getting closer and closer to where he was standing. His heart pounded and he felt such panic that he could hardly breathe. He wasn't worried about himself, though. Instead, he was looking out over the water, searching for someone he had seen swimming nearby.

He at once caught sight of a woman's head bobbing in the froth of the surf, a head with honey-colored blond hair. He then rushed heedlessly into the ocean, and as the water swirled around his feet, it turned red, as if suddenly stained by an immense spill of blood.

He ran through the water, feeling it tug at his legs, but he pushed on. Finally, he was near enough to lunge forward and grab the woman with the blond hair. Relief flowed through him as he felt his hand wrap around her arm. But as he dragged her toward him, he saw that he was pulling in Susan. She opened her strange gray-green eyes and smiled at him. She seemed happy and unworried.

He wanted to smile back at her, but he suddenly realized that he had forgotten someone else, someone being dragged away by the powerful tide of bloodred water. He could see her sleek dark hair just a few feet from him. He knew that it was Alma, even though he couldn't see her face.

If he turned loose of Susan, he might be able to capture

Alma. But he couldn't get himself to loosen his grip on Susan's arm. Instead, still holding her tightly, he stretched out as far as he could and grabbed for Alma. But his reach was too short and the undertow too powerful. He watched helplessly as the red water sucked her away, and he knew he would never see her again. The last thing he saw before he awoke, shaking and sweaty, was her pale, anguished face.

The remainder of the night he lay in bed, neither asleep nor awake, turning from side to side, looking for a comfortable position. He was relieved when around five-thirty the dark sky began to lighten to a leaden gray and the first faint streaks of pink appeared. But now he was exhausted and depressed.

He got out of the desk chair and walked to the window. The study was at the rear of the house, and from its window he could see the swimming pool. The blue-green water was perfectly still, and the harsh brassy light of the early afternoon sun glanced off it as if it were a sheet of polished steel.

He leaned against the window frame and shook his head again. Would he ever be able to stop dreaming about Alma? He needed to accept her loss and go on with life. It wasn't as if he had a genuine choice.

Hightower turned away from the window. The harsh glare from the swimming pool hurt his eyes. He rubbed the corner of his right eye. He was neither hungry nor thirsty, but he needed to eat lunch. It might even make him feel better.

He sat at the kitchen table with a slice of Gruyère and an apple. To distract himself, he switched on the small TV perched at the end of the table. Using the remote control, he surfed through the channels, seeing nothing he wanted to watch.

He paused at a "Continuing Medical Education" film on cataract surgery. The surgeon used a diamond-tipped scalpel to cut along the edge of the cornea, injected sodium hyaluronate gel, then extracted the lens and the hard nucleus. He slipped the lens implant into the capsule and sutured shut the corneal incision.

The whole procedure had taken about fifteen minutes, and now somebody who was virtually blind would be able to see again. Without surprise, Hightower realized that he was jealous of both the patient and the surgeon. He wished surgery could restore his vision, and he also wished he were a surgeon again.

Feeling himself slipping into self-pity, he got up from the table, snapped off the TV, and carried his dishes to the sink. As he did so, he caught sight of the red cordless phone recharging on the kitchen counter. His immediate impulse was to snatch up the phone and call Susan at Rush.

He knew it wouldn't be a good idea. She had barely gotten there, so he shouldn't distract her from her primary task of learning to deal with her problem. Still, he felt sure that she'd be glad to hear from him, and realizing that made him feel better about himself.

Still, there would be nothing wrong with calling Carl Blau and asking if Susan had arrived all right. He searched in his wallet and took out the yellow slip with the Rush phone number written in large red letters. He had put the number in his wallet after talking to Blau, and at the time, he wouldn't have said that he had any intention of calling again. Sometimes it seemed that Freud was right about a few things.

"She's settled in nicely," Blau told him. "She wanted her bodyguard to stay with her, and I bent the rules and said she could stay one more night."

"Do you think she'll get along with the other patients?"

"Oh, she'll be a tonic for everyone," Blau said. "She's completely charming, and I see her as a welcome addition to our therapeutic milieu. I thank you for sending her to us."

"I could think of no better place for her."

"Are you calling because you're a terribly conscientious psychiatrist, or do you have a personal interest in Susan?" Blau's question sounded slightly teasing.

"I'd have to say it's more the latter." Hightower knew he sounded awkward. "She's no longer my patient, really. But I wanted to know how she was doing."

"I had a reason for asking," Blau said. "Susan asked me if it would be all right for her to call you and let you know how she was doing. I told her to wait a few days, but you two seem to be thinking along the same track."

By the time Hightower slipped the telephone into its recharging cradle, he was eager to get back to work. If he could sketch out a draft of his paper by the beginning of next week, he could return to Los Angeles to finish the final draft. He would still have three weeks of research time left before going back to the hospital. He was looking forward to seeing his parents, but a week with them would probably be enough to satisfy them all.

He was whistling as he headed back to the pile of floppy disks waiting for him in the study. A lot could happen in three weeks.

18

Mrs. Rostov sat at the head of the table, with Susan at her right. "I'm getting a bit deaf, and I want to hear everything you say," she said.

Mrs. Rostov was a small, thin woman in her early seventies with a narrow powdered face, pale blue eyes, and a carefully arranged wreath of iron gray hair. She was lively and seemed so normal that Susan wondered why she was at Rush.

"Where do you make your home, Miss Bradstreet?" she asked.

"Los Angeles, but please just call me Susan."

Susan glanced at Tim Kimberly. He sat across the table between Mrs. Rostov and Joe Ling, but his head was bowed over his plate, and he didn't look at anyone. He had a wide face, large brown eyes, and curly sandy-colored hair.

"I was in Los Angeles thirty years ago," Mrs. Rostov said. "It was a marvelous city." She turned toward the red-faced woman in a white kitchen uniform who was holding out a bowl of green peas. Mrs. Rostov put a spoonful on her plate. "I loved the climate. I wanted to move there, but my husband had to stay in New York for professional reasons."

Susan took some peas from the bowl. "Did you grow up in New York?" she asked Mrs. Rostov.

"If you're making soup and put in too much salt, boil a potato in it," Mrs. Rostov said, leaning toward Susan as though imparting a family secret.

Susan stared in surprise, but then she remembered that Mrs. Rostov was a little deaf. "Did you live in New York when you were a girl?" she asked again.

She heard a snorting laugh and glanced across the table at Tim. He was watching Mrs. Rostov, but as soon as he noticed Susan looking at him, he bowed his head again.

"They wouldn't let us go out in the rain," Mrs. Rostov said. She took a slice of roast beef from the tray offered to her.

Susan turned her head slightly and looked at Meg. Meg gave a barely perceptible shrug.

"Mrs. Rostov responds like that to questions," Joe said. "It's connected with her illness."

"It's Ganser's syndrome," Tim said, looking directly at Susan for the first time. "Ask her a question, and she says anything that pops into her head. She's weird, but she's not really crazy." He smiled slightly. "Me either. I just have a shaky sense of self-identity." He looked at Mrs. Rostov. "We're not nuts, are we, Mrs. R.?"

"Have some roast beef, Tim," Mrs. Rostov said.

"I don't eat corpses."

"My goodness!" Mrs. Rostov gave him a disapproving look.

"Tim," Joe said, cutting in quickly. "Dr. Mallory asked you not to talk like that."

"All right, then I don't eat dead bodies," Tim said. He sounded petulant and he scowled, like a small child reacting to a scolding. "I'm a vegetarian."

"I should be," Susan said, trying to smooth out the situation. "I often feel guilty about eating meat."

"God put animals on this earth for us to use for our needs," Mrs. Rostov said. "And eating is a basic need."

"So is sex," Tim said. "But I bet you don't think we should ..."

"Tim," Joe said sharply. "I'm sure you don't want to lose your privilege of going into town to buy science fiction."

Tim's eyes narrowed, and he clenched his jaw tightly. He glowered, but he said nothing.

"I used to read science fiction," Susan said.

A moment passed, then Tim glanced up and realized that she was talking to him. "Yeah?" he said. She saw his face relax a little. "Who did you read?"

"You probably never have heard of them," Susan said. "How about Philip K. Dick?"

"*Do Androids Dream of Electric Sheep?*" Tim said immediately. "Did you know *Blade Runner* is based on it?"

"I saw it in college," Susan said, nodding. "What do you read?"

"Lots of stuff." Tim shrugged. "I used to like Heinlein and Spider Robinson, but now I like cyberpunk best."

"Cyberpunk?" Joe said. "Is that what you said?"

"*Blade Runner* was real good cyberpunk," Tim said.

"You should say *really* good, dear," Mrs. Rostov said. She smiled at Tim, who ignored her.

"What makes something cyberpunk?" Susan asked.

"It's got to be a story about the future, when technology is so advanced it seems like magic to us, but the main characters are kind of crazy and dangerous." Tim shrugged, then looked down at the table, as though embarrassed. "Cyberpunk people sort of blend together with computers."

"I'm surprised your parents let you read such trash." Mrs. Rostov looked at Tim with concern.

"They don't pay any attention," Tim said. "I'm just a toy for them to fight over." His voice turned angry. "The funny thing is, they fight over me, but neither one of them really wants me around. Dad hires a nanny when I stay with him, and Mom puts me in boarding school." Tim laughed harshly, then suddenly focused on his plate and began eating quickly.

"Can you recommend a book?" Susan asked.

He gave no sign that he had heard the question. Then without looking up, he said, "Read *The Neuromancer*. That's the start of it all."

She felt pleased to get a response from him, and she thought she had a glimmer of why people become psychiatrists. She would ask David if it was the feeling of getting through to someone that had led him into psychiatry.

By the time they had finished dessert, she was feeling tired. The food and conversation had kept her distracted, but it felt like a long time since she had started the day. She hadn't gone to sleep until five-thirty, then a nurse knocked on her door at nine-thirty. "If you want breakfast, you'll have to move fast," the nurse said. "Service ends at ten, and you're scheduled to see Dr. Blau at ten-thirty."

Her queasy stomach hadn't let her eat anything more than a bowl of cold cereal and a cup of tea, and by ten-thirty she was sitting in a red leather chair in front of a mahogany desk stacked high with books and papers. Dr. Blau sat in a creaking swivel chair, looking at her across the desk. She had been prepared to like him, because David obviously did, and she hadn't been disappointed. He was in his sixties, completely bald except for a fringe of gray hair, and quite stout. He had a plump round face, and his manner was informal and friendly.

"I'm sorry you didn't get a longer rest," he said. "But we're not going to have much time with you." He smiled at her. "It's like touring Europe in a week—you've got to visit three countries and see six cities, even if you're tired and sleepy all the time."

"I'm used to showing up for work at six and not finishing until ten at night."

He looked at her in exaggerated surprise. "I'm not sure I like hearing that. You're going to ruin my fantasies about the easy life of a movie star."

He had spent almost two hours with her, and she had left his office feeling optimistic. She realized that her career wasn't over and that she wasn't going to be disabled by panic attacks for the rest of her life. With her worries eased, she had found herself thinking about David Hightower, and she felt sure that he was also thinking about her.

"We usually go into the lounge for coffee or hot chocolate," Joe said. "Join us if you want to."

"I'd like coffee," Susan said. "But I hope nobody will mind if I take it to my room tonight. I'm running out of steam."

"Oh, my dear, you *should* retire early," Mrs. Rostov said. She gave Susan a look of worried concern. "We can talk some more tomorrow."

"I'll bring you some coffee," Meg said. "I'm going to turn in too."

"I've enjoyed talking to you all," Susan said, getting up from the table.

She walked through the arch leading into the living room. The light from the chandeliers was a soft yellow, and the vacant room looked quiet and peaceful. At the moment, the only thing that really interested her was sleep.

But of course she would read a little before getting ready for bed. She always did.

19

The living room of the suite in the Cambridge Plaza Motel had dark green carpet, blond furniture, and a swirled plaster ceiling. Gibson leaned over and switched off the tall table lamp at the end of the couch so that the only light in the room was the pale glow coming from the shell-shaped plastic wall sconces.

He took the pistol that Whip held out to him and weighed it in his hand. He had never before held one that was so heavy, but he liked the feel of it. It was matte black with a boxy rectangular grip and a peculiar, almost triangular-shaped barrel. No one would ever think that the .44 Magnum was designed just for target practice.

"This right here is the safety," Whip said. He reached out and pushed on the protruding round button just above the trigger guard. "Now watch this," he said to Gibson. He spread his feet, bent his knees, and held an imaginary gun in front of him with his arms extended. "Stand just the way you see them in the movies, and be sure to use both hands, because this bastard's got a kick like a young mule."

He tapped the back of the barrel. "Look through this notch and line up your target with the knife blade at the front. Squeeze off a round, and—bam!—you got another trooper knocking at the pearly gates."

The boxes Whip and Cortez had picked up from Rapid Express were open and the contents spread out on the round motel table. Cortez sat on a stool at the high counter separating the room from the small bar area.

"This sucker will blow a hole big as your fist in an engine block," Whip said, tapping the pistol with his index finger. He focused his flat, glassy eyes on Gibson. "Just keep that in mind, Charlie."

Gibson nodded, then strapped the canvas pocket holster on his left side. He slid it toward his back and slipped in the pistol. He was wearing a summer-weight blue jacket, and its skirt fell into place without leaving a bump.

He had worn the jacket as part of his costume, along with a blue oxford shirt and a maroon-and-gold striped tie. He was going to act the part of a supervisor, and Cortez and Whip were going to be the technicians.

Cortez had on his usual work clothes of dark blue pants and light blue shirt, and Whip was wearing the same outfit. Gibson had made him take off the death's-head earring but had let him keep the little rat's tail of hair. Whip's clothes belonged to Cortez. The shirt hung loose on his shoulders, and the pants were slack around the waist. But nobody had to be fooled very long.

"Now what you got for me, man?" Cortez asked Whip. His voice was high with excitement. He slid off the stool and walked over to the table.

Whip picked up a bulky package and began stripping off the heavy brown paper. In a few seconds he held up a gun for Cortez to see. The blue-steel barrel was a foot or so long, and attached to it was a round metal canister like an oversize tuna-fish can. In front of the canister, a pistol grip jutted down. A second pistol grip curved slightly backward behind the trigger.

Holding on to the barrel with one hand, Whip pulled back on the folded metal-frame stock. It snapped into place with a sharp click, and the short awkward gun was suddenly transformed into a formidable-looking weapon.

"This is a Street Sweeper," Whip said. "It's not just an ordinary shotgun." He smiled, and the scar at the left corner of his lip turned the smile into a sneer revealing his upper teeth.

"So what's so special about it?" Cortez asked.

"This weapon is available only to the police and military," Whip said. He sounded didactic, as if he were still an arms instructor. "It's modeled on the South African Armsel Striker." He patted the round canister. "This here is a revolving drum magazine that contains twelve rounds. If you hold down on the trigger, you can empty the magazine in thirty-two seconds."

Whip held out the gun to Cortez. Cortez hesitated a moment, then wrapped his hand around the stock. "What does it shoot?"

"These right here," Whip said. He bent down and extracted a shotgun shell with a green casing and a shiny brass rim from the box on the floor. He held up the shell for Cortez to see.

"I'm going to load you up with double-ought buckshot," Whip said. "In each shell you've got twelve thirty-three-caliber slugs." Whip held up a finger and wagged it at Cortez as though teaching him a lesson. "Now you don't have a whole lot of range with this weapon, but when a man gets his street swept with this fucker, they don't put him back together. They just hose him off the ground."

Gibson was starting to feel anxious. They still had a lot to do. He turned to Cortez. "Boot the laptop and jack into the Rush system. Check the registration file and find how many patients are in Johnson Hall."

"You got it, Cyber," Cortez said, laying his shotgun on the table.

"That reminds me," Gibson said. "No real names once we get operational." He then pointed at the guns on the table. "Whip, I want you to pack up the toolboxes."

Whip nodded. "I'll start with Backup's little baby here." He picked up the Street Sweeper and folded back the stock.

Cortez sat on the sofa by the end table and snapped off the laptop's hard plastic lid. He unwound the line cord, then got down on his knees and plugged it into the wall outlet. He put the computer on his knees and began stroking the keys.

"I'm in the system now," he said after less than two minutes. "The same password as before."

Gibson sat on the opposite end of the sofa and watched Whip carefully arranging the guns and ammunition in the two long metal toolboxes. Along with a ladder, they were among that afternoon's purchases, and their bright red paint was shiny and unscratched.

Cortez was hunched over the keyboard of the small computer. The keys made soft clicking noises as he pushed them.

Gibson could feel the stirring of anticipation in his stomach. He would be seeing Susan within the next hour, and after so much waiting and longing, he could hardly believe it was finally going to happen. Would she recognize him? Surely she must have studied his face in the photograph many times, puzzling about when she might have met him.

Cortez suddenly turned around and said, "I've got the registration list. Susan's name is here. And two more— Clara Rostov and Tim Kimberly. You want me to check their medical charts?"

"Not necessary," Gibson said. "If there had been a dozen patients, I'd be worried. Even if there are a couple of staff people around, we'll be able to handle the situation with no problem. Now get out of that file and let me take over."

Cortez nodded to show that he understood as he tapped several keys. "All right, I'm signing it over to you, Cyberwolf." He lifted the laptop, slipped from under it, and stood up. "What are you going to do?"

"Remember the automatic doors on the drawings?" Gibson asked. "I'm going to find the codes for the device drivers. Then I'm going to change all the protocols so I can initiate the interrupts. That'll give us control over the doors, phones, air conditioning, and everything else." He sat down on the couch and balanced the laptop on his thighs.

"Man, that's going to take some heavy wizardry." Cortez frowned and shook his head. "If anybody can do it . . ."

"What kind of machine are we dealing with?"

"IBM VM nine-point-two."

Gibson nodded and looked down at the screen. As soon as his fingers touched the keys, his mind began floating free of the world of motel rooms, people, and guns. The light in the room seemed dimmer, and the small noises

Whip was making began to fade away. He was speeding off into a darker, quieter world. Within seconds, his surroundings seemed obscured by the diffuse gray light of a dense fog.

Gibson's fingers made familiar automatic gestures, tapping into the system. He started by reviewing the directories, and as he searched, he could feel the pull of the system. He sensed himself merging with it. As he merged, he felt liberated, freed from the materiality of the world, from the disgusting solidity of the physical. He was pure mind, pure spirit, a part of the infinite and eternal.

Directory after directory scrolled past, but he wasn't finding what he needed. He would have to take the plunge and go deeper. He selected an accounting program and called up its codes. He started reviewing the lines one by one, then he saw his chance—a crack in the ice. He explored it cautiously at first, wary of a trap, but nothing happened. He ran along the fissure in the code, and it led him even deeper into the system. All at once, he was far past the ice and surrounded by dot files.

As the start-up instructions for application programs flashed past, he saw exactly what he needed: a large fragment of a rejected shell program. It had been deleted, but not overwritten. He hit the scroll lock and froze a block of command lines on the screen. He felt himself smiling. With no trouble at all, he could now go anywhere in the programs. He had access to every file, and maybe, just maybe, he could follow the shell down to the root.

He began to stroke the laptop's keys, barely touching them with the pads of his fingers. Almost immediately, he spotted the maintenance file, and as if by magic, a bright outline map of the Rush complex appeared on the screen. He took in the entire diagram at a glance and clicked in on the Johnson Hall schematics. He identified the doors, then went down the file register to locate the interrupt lists.

He located the protocols governing the interrupt loops. Without pausing, he began making changes in a systematic way, replacing the system code with his own. As he typed, he could feel himself getting taken up by the system. It was wrapping itself around him, drawing him inside. Then it was pulling him down—or was he diving? Whatever was happening, he was going straight for the center, straight to the core of the system. He was entering cyberspace. He felt a thrill of elation.

In ten minutes, he had done what he had set out to do. It was time to get out of the system, but he found it hard to leave. He could feel the pull of the machine, and he wanted to stay where he was. He didn't want to return to the sick world of substance. He wanted to remain inside the system and stay abstract, pure, and clean.

He forced himself to log off.

"Did you do it?" he heard Cortez ask.

He looked up to find Whip and Cortez standing over him. Both were staring down at him. Cortez looked excited, but Whip's face revealed puzzlement and confusion.

"Hey, Charlie, you in a trance or something?" Whip asked.

"Start loading up the van," Gibson said. "We're going to walk right through the front door."

20

Hightower held the knife by the blade, drew back and took aim at the heart, then rapidly snapped his arm downward in a short, sharp arc. The knife spun out of his fingers and twirled through the air, tumbling end over end. Then with a dull thud, the point struck the carotid artery on the left side of the neck.

He shook his head in disgust at the result. Once he had been able to put the knife into any one of the four chambers, and now he couldn't even hit the heart itself. Once he could have severed the carotid artery deliberately, instead of hitting it by accident.

The damage to his left eye had put an end to those skills, along with his surgical ones. His depth perception was almost completely destroyed, and he had essentially no binocular vision. Now he had to rely on guesses rather than trusting to his body.

The target tacked to the wall with surgical staples was a full-size Frank Netter anatomical chart showing the internal organs of a male body. Now that he was no longer a surgeon, the chart struck him as almost grotesque. The skin and muscles of the figure were peeled away from the neck, upper body, and torso, and the organs were drawn in a realistic way. The body had no face, because the covering tissue and bone had been stripped off to reveal the brain, sinus cavities, and mouth.

He walked the twenty feet from the line of yellow tape on the basement floor to the back wall. The chart and the wall around it were marked with dozens of nicks and perforations where the knife point had struck.

He grabbed the knife and pulled it out of the cork-covered pine. It had an eight-inch blade of highly polished surgical steel that tapered to a daggerlike tip. The handle was forged from the same piece of steel, so the knife had no tang and no need of fasteners. It was part of his father's autopsy kit.

So far as Hightower knew, though, his father had never used the knife for any purpose other than throwing at anatomical charts. Like all surgeons, Lawrence Hightower was comfortable using knives, but he also had a good eye and a sharp aim. During years of play, his father had almost invariably scored more points than he could, but then when Hightower was about seventeen, he had found himself able to beat his father the majority of the time. But those days belonged to the past.

His father had devised what he called "the anatomy game" when Hightower was in the eighth grade and taking general biology. He wasn't a very involved student, but in the second semester, when they were studying the human body, his father had seen a chance to get him more interested in the subject.

His father had taken him to the basement and pointed out the anatomical chart he had stapled to the wall. "If you can throw this knife so that it both hits an organ and sticks into the wall, that's an automatic point," he said. "If you can tell me the name of the organ, that's another point."

"Is that all?" Hightower asked him.

"That's for the first round." His father smiled. "And that guarantees you two dollars—one for the organ and one for its name. If you hit that organ again on any other round, you don't make any money. You always have to hit a new organ."

"How do I know if I've got its name right?"

"Because I'll be here to tell you," his father said. "We're going to do this every Thursday night after dinner."

Hightower made enough from playing the game to keep himself in spending money. He also learned a lot of anatomy, because after a while his father started replacing the gross anatomy charts with ones of fine structures. Hightower learned the parts of the eye and the names of the cranial nerves in that way.

Eventually, by the end of the school year, he and his father began playing the game just for fun. There were weeks and even months when they didn't play it often, but they kept playing it over the years, even after Hightower had graduated from medical school and became a practicing surgeon.

He slipped the knife back into the cracked leather instrument case, then put the case itself into the drawer of the workbench where his father still kept it. This was the first time Hightower had played the anatomy game since the damage to his eye. Even though he was disgusted by how poorly he had done, he had to admit that it was better than he expected. Maybe if he challenged his father to a game, he could improve with practice. Whether he did or not, his father would like playing with him.

He was feeling almost happy, and he had no doubt about the cause of it. He had put in a good day's work and managed to get another twenty cases coded. That wasn't what had put him in such a good mood, though. That was the result of his feeling sure that Carl Blau would decide to let Susan call him tomorrow. Or if not tomorrow, then the day after.

He didn't know when she would call, but he felt certain that she would.

21

"I see the sign coming up," Cortez said.

He applied the brakes, then twisted the wheel and guided the gray van into the driveway. The tires crunched on the white limestone gravel. Then they were running on the smooth asphalt, and the van glided silently through the darkness.

Gibson leaned out the window and looked behind them. The road they had turned off was now nothing more than a small ragged patch of brightness, but he saw no sign of another car coming after them. Turning around, he peered through the windshield, letting his eyes follow the moving brightness of the headlights. The moon was hidden by heavy clouds, and the branches of the trees formed a dense arch. The van seemed to be traveling through a long, dark tunnel.

The driveway began to slope upward at a steep angle. Then suddenly at the top of the hill in front of them, Gibson caught sight of two large lighted buildings. From the MIT computer drawings, he immediately recognized the taller one as the research tower. The graceful two-story Colonial building joined to it was obviously Johnson Hall.

"Stop right here," Gibson said.

Cortez drew the van to a complete halt. He turned off the headlights but left the engine running.

Whip leaned forward, and as he drew closer, Gibson caught a whiff of the pomade he used to keep his little rat's tail twisted together. It was a heavy, sweet odor, like the smell of decaying flowers, and Gibson shifted away from him.

"Is that the target?" Whip asked.

"The one that looks like a big house is Johnson Hall," Cortez told him. "That's where little Miss Susy's spending the night."

"She probably ain't expecting company, neither," Whip said. "But after her and me snuggle down in that bed for an hour or two, she's going to be glad we come." Then changing to a high, mocking voice he said, "Oh, Whip, won't you please do that again? It feels so good." He gave a short, explosive laugh like a bark.

"That's enough," Gibson said. He spoke at normal volume, but he made his tone sharp and commanding. "Susan is our winning ticket, and nobody—and I mean nobody—touches her." He turned in his seat to look at Whip. "We may have to show her to the cops, and she's got to be in perfect physical condition."

"I gotcha," Whip said. He sat back and leaned his shoulder against the sliding door.

Gibson picked up the laptop and put it flat on his knees. He popped off the cover, then turned on the van's overhead light. The illumination from the bulb was dim, but it was enough to let him see the keyboard.

"Strap the coupler to the phone," he ordered Cortez.

Cortez retrieved the acoustic coupler from under the seat and unfastened the small coil of wire attached to one of the rubber cups. He handed the end of the wire to Gibson, who popped the jack into the laptop's modem.

Cortez picked up the phone from the holder between the seats and with difficulty tugged one of the cups over one end of the handset. "I could do without these goddamned square-end phones," he said.

Gibson looked down at the pale blue screen, then he

began to stroke the keyboard gently. Within a second he heard a series of high-pitched beeps. Then a sudden harsh hum was followed by a sharp click. Lines of print suddenly appeared at the top and bottom of the screen. Gibson let his breath out slowly. He was in the Rush system.

He entered the shell program, asked for the maintenance file, and called up the schematic drawing of Johnson Hall. He looked over the thin yellow lines with their machine symbols indicating the status of the devices governed by the interrupt protocols. The door he was interested in had a solid circle over it, showing that it was closed and locked.

He typed out an interrupt message, hit "Enter," then immediately got back into the maintenance file. He quickly found the schematic showing the status of the door.

The solid circle had changed to an empty one.

"That's it," Gibson said. He kept his voice flat, but he could feel a building sense of excitement.

"Way to go, Cyber." Cortez sounded proud and thrilled.

"That's what?" Whip asked.

"The front door of Johnson Hall is unlocked," Gibson said. "Unlocked and wide open."

Cortez braked slowly and brought the van to a gentle stop a few feet beyond the herringbone brick path leading to Johnson Hall. He turned off the headlights and then the engine. The hot metal gave off tiny crackling noises as it began to cool in the night air.

The floodlights on top of the buildings cast a wide circle of light over the surrounding area. The light streaming into the van was bright enough to make Gibson's eyes water. He took out his handkerchief and pressed it against his closed eyelids.

Gibson carefully folded his handkerchief and put it in his back pocket. He then turned in his seat and tapped Whip on the arm. "It's time to make our move. Have you got the Trojans?"

Whip nodded, then pulled on the door handle and slid

the door open. He climbed out of the van, then leaned back inside and pulled out the aluminum stepladder that was on the floor between the seat and the right side of the van.

Whip carried the ladder straight up, with his arm through the steps to support it. When he reached the end of the brick walk, he climbed the shallow stone steps to the portico.

"Let's start after him," Gibson said, nodding at Cortez.

They got down from their seats, and Gibson stood blinking in the brightness. The glare from the light spilling down the sides of the buildings was painful and distracting. He took his matte black sunglasses from the inside pocket of his jacket and put them on. He felt an immediate sense of relief.

Cortez grabbed the two red toolboxes out of the van, then stepped to the side. Gibson pulled out the laptop and slipped its strap over his shoulder. Once inside the building, he would have access to computers and terminals, but he wanted a backup.

While they were walking up the brick path toward the building, Gibson kept an eye on Whip. He was in front of the double doors. He spread the ladder's legs, then, glancing up, he pushed the ladder a foot or so until it was in position.

Gibson stopped and held his hand to the side to signal Cortez. He lowered his head to peer under the roof of the portico, then straightened up when he saw what he had expected to see: the black, boxy shape of a mounted television camera.

Whip climbed halfway up the ladder then took the small Trojan packet out of his pocket. He tore open the foil and removed the condom. He stretched the top open wide, then slid the thin rubber over the barrel of the camera to cover the lens.

Gibson smiled at their first success. He had been sure that a surveillance camera would be trained on the outside door. Soon, dozens of cops would be working feverishly to identify the people who took over Johnson Hall, and some bright guy would remember to check the tape from the cameras.

As Whip came down the ladder, he glanced toward Gibson. Gibson jabbed his finger rapidly in the air, pointing toward the vestibule. Whip nodded. He folded up the stepladder, then pulled open one of the doors. He walked inside, turning the ladder on its side to get it through the opening.

"Let's go," Gibson said, starting toward the portico. He pulled off his sunglasses and slipped them into his inside jacket pocket.

It wouldn't do to look suspicious.

22

Gibson was the first through the door.

He walked briskly inside, then stopped to survey the situation. To his relief, the lights were dim, and the long hallway was in semidarkness. He teetered on his toes and turned his head from side to side, glancing around. He tried to convey the restrained impatience of a busy repair supervisor.

He looked across the hall and through the rectangular doorway opposite him. According to the computer schematic, that should be the living room. He could see two people sitting in the dim gray light watching a large-screen TV. They looked like the old lady and the boy—Clara Rostov and Tim Kimberly.

He felt a fleeting moment of panic. Where was Susan? Had they transferred her to some other hospital? Then he caught himself. She might already be asleep in her room. He would find out where she was as soon as he established control. That was what he needed to concentrate on.

He stepped to the side to let Cortez slip past him. Whip

was supposed to go back and pull the condoms off the surveillance cameras before joining them. Gibson could hear the metallic scraping of the legs of the aluminum ladder as Whip slid it around on the bricks.

Cortez put down the toolboxes and stood very still. His breathing was rapid, and as he inhaled through his mouth, he produced a frail whistling noise. He was obviously scared.

Gibson heard a dull flapping sound and glanced to the left. He saw a thin Oriental man in a long-sleeved white shirt and dark trousers making his way toward them. The man was some kind of cripple, and every time his right foot slapped against the marble floor, he seemed on the verge of tumbling down.

Behind the man, more than halfway down the long hall, Gibson noticed a desk with a computer monitor on it. He nodded to himself. That was where he needed to be to initiate the interrupt and shut the outside door. And the sooner the better. He would then have Susan in a small sealed world where he controlled all the variables. She might resist him at first, but eventually she would want to please him. That was the way power worked.

He turned toward Cortez and said in a low voice, "Wait here for Whip, then leave him to cover the door. Meet me by the computer, and be ready with the tools."

"Got you, Cyber," Cortez said. His voice was strained, and he was nervously tugging the hairs of his mustache. Gibson picked up the laptop, then started down the hall to meet the man coming toward him.

"I understand you're having computer trouble," Gibson said loudly. His voice reverberated in the dim emptiness of the hall.

"The front door just flew open," the man said. They were now hardly ten feet apart. "I couldn't get the computer to shut it, and now the surveillance cameras are on the blink."

"Sounds like some computer code got erased by the gremlins." Gibson nodded and caught his lower lip between his teeth as if thinking about the problem.

"I called the Computer Center, then phoned Security," the man said. "Security's dealing with an out-of-control patient, but they're supposed to send some officers over as soon as they can."

"We can probably get the door shut before they get here," Gibson said, taking pleasure in the irony. "My name's Bob Dodd, and I've got my crew with me." He nodded toward Cortez. "We're going to fix your door and put your computer back in control."

"Are you from the Computer Center? I've never seen you around before." The man shifted his weight to his left foot and put his right foot out behind him.

"We do contract work for them," Gibson said. "We were there installing new hardware."

"When I talked to Phil Krass, he said he wouldn't be able to send anybody until tomorrow morning."

"We sort of volunteered." Gibson smiled and shrugged. "We had just finished our job there when you called Phil, and we thought since you were in a bit of a bind, we'd come by and take a look." He stopped, then quickly added, "I can't guarantee we can fix whatever's wrong tonight."

"I understand," the man said. He held out his hand to shake. "My name is Joe Ling, Bob. I'll show you the computer."

Ling started down the hall, lurching from side to side. Gibson kept up with him for a few steps and then slowed and allowed Ling to get ahead of him. He glanced around and saw Whip standing beside Cortez. Gibson jerked his head sharply to signal Cortez to follow him, and Cortez bent over and picked up a toolbox. In two quick steps, Gibson caught up with Ling.

Ling walked behind the desk, then eased himself into the swivel chair. He took a key from his pocket, unlocked the center drawer, and pulled out a solid circle of yellow plastic about six inches in diameter. Two keys were attached to the steel ring dangling from the circle.

"We don't want somebody dropping the keys in his pocket and going home with them." Ling held up a small barrel key with a flat rectangular top. "We keep the computer locked so unauthorized people can't tamper with it."

"Good idea," Gibson said, lowering the laptop to the floor beside the desk. "Erase a system command and you could tie this whole hospital up in knots."

He was chattering to keep Ling distracted. But he felt like screaming. If only Ling would hurry so he could close the goddamned door before Security arrived.

Gibson glanced at Cortez. He was squatting down on the floor beside the open toolbox a few feet in front of the desk. His face was as stiff as a painted wooden mask.

Ling saw Cortez and nodded, then swiveled his chair around to face the computer. On the monitor, abstract patterns of red and yellow took shape on a blue background, swooped from side to side, then dissolved. Ling inserted the barrel key into the base of the machine.

"Unlocked," he announced. He put the key with its oversized yellow tag back in the center drawer, then looked up at Gibson. "But hang on, I forgot to ask you today's code number."

"What do you mean, code number?"

"You know," Ling said. "The security code for today."

"But I'm not a regular employee," Gibson said, realizing immediately what he was supposed to know. "Phil just told me you had a problem with the door. He didn't give me the code number."

"That can happen." Ling nodded. "People get in a hurry." His voice had become smooth and uninflected, and he kept his eyes turned away.

Ling clearly didn't believe anything he had said. Ling was probably going to try to stall him until Security arrived. So it was time to stop screwing around. Whatever it took, he had to get the door closed. He started to reach under his jacket for the Magnum.

Suddenly, a short stuttering burst of gunfire came from the end of the hall. The noise was almost deafening in the closed space. While the sound was still reverberating, four or five single shots, distinct but muffled, came from outside the hall.

Gibson took his hand off the Magnum and swiveled around to look toward the front door. He saw Whip standing half crouched and holding the Mac-10 close to his body and aiming the stubby muzzle toward the outside door. He fired another burst, then stepped out of the doorway and put his back against the wall.

"Cops!" Whip yelled down the hall. He didn't take his eyes off the opening, and his voice seemed unnaturally high. "Two of them. Both with weapons drawn."

Gibson turned toward Ling, then was so surprised that he took two steps backward. Ling was standing up and pointing a snub-nosed, blue-steel revolver at him.

Gibson felt a surge of anger at his own stupidity. He had let himself be distracted by the gunfire, and probably because Ling was a cripple, he had underestimated him.

"I don't know who you are," Ling said. "But I'll shoot you if you move." His face was drawn so tight that his eyes seemed to bulge, and the hand holding the gun was quivering. Keeping his eyes fixed on Gibson, he reached out for the telephone.

Then the world seemed to explode. Three shattering blasts occurred in rapid succession. Gibson automatically jumped away from Ling.

Ling was thrown into the air. His head, arms, and legs jerked violently like those of a malfunctioning mechanical toy, and he appeared to hover above the green marble floor. Then, after what seemed like minutes, his body tumbled backward over the desk chair and fell to the floor.

Ling's chest was a welter of blood. His white shirt had turned a deep red, and the cloth was shredded as if steel claws had ripped through it and torn at the flesh beneath. His face was splattered with his own blood, and his eyes still bulged. Now, though, they were vacant and unmoving.

Cortez was standing with the butt of the Street Sweeper braced against his shoulder and his left hand wrapped around the pistol grip. An empty stare was frozen on his face, and he seemed to be waiting for Ling to get off the floor.

"Backup!" Gibson yelled in a sharp voice. "Go help Whip cover the door." He paused until Cortez lowered the shotgun, then he shouted, "Run, goddamn it!"

Gibson pushed past the dark chair to get to the computer, and from the corner of his eye, he glimpsed Cortez moving at a fast trot. Bending over the keyboard, he tapped the "Space" bar to get rid of the screen-saver display. He became aware of the slick, sticky feel of blood on the soles of his shoes.

As soon as the screen cleared, he got into the shell program, called up the maintenance directory, and typed out the interrupt command for the front door. He hit the "Enter" key, then waited with his hands tightened into fists while the computer made faint clicking noises.

He heard a soft *thunk* as the door slid into place. Feeling a surge of relief, Gibson straightened up from his crouching position. He looked at the video monitor on the opposite end of the desk. It was displaying an image from the security cameras.

The grainy black-and-white picture was blurred, but he could make out the stepladder. It was standing on the front porch, with no one and nothing else near it. Beyond the ladder, he could see only the top one of the shallow stone steps leading up to the porch from the brick path.

The scene abruptly shifted to the entrance area. He could see the stainless-steel speaker grid and the closed door. At the edge of the field, on the floor nearest the outside door, he could make out the crumpled form of a body. The dark clothes were obviously a uniform, but he could see only part of the torso.

All at once he saw motion. The body was moving out of the semicircular area covered by the security camera. Either the person was alive and crawling out the front door or someone was dragging out the body, alive or dead.

Gibson bent closer to the monitor, trying to figure out what was happening. Then suddenly he heard the sounds of scuffling and Whip yelling, "Goddamn it, get her off me."

He looked down the hall, but he couldn't get a clear view of what was happening. Whip and somebody wearing black sweatpants were struggling together on the floor. Cortez crouched over them, dodging around and trying to pull them apart.

Gibson pushed back the rolling chair, but he felt it wedge against Ling's legs. He shoved harder and the chair turned over on top of the body, clattering as it hit the floor.

Gibson hurried toward the fight. He started to run, but then slowed down. The bottoms of his shoes were too slick with blood to run safely on the polished marble. He didn't need a broken leg or a cracked skull right now.

Who the hell was Whip fighting with? It wasn't Susan or the boy, and the Rostov woman was too old to be rolling around on the floor like that. Maybe it was a maintenance worker who was working late.

When he got within ten feet of the struggle, he could see that Whip was struggling with a woman. As she pulled loose enough to strike Whip under the chin with the heel of her hand, he got a good look at her: it was Meg O'Hare. He had never seen her before, but he had seen her picture dozens, if not hundreds, of times. She was in almost every wide-angle picture taken of Susan in public for the last two years.

Meg was breathing hard, but she had her legs clamped around Whip's waist. "You little asshole, I'm going cut you in two," she said between clenched teeth.

Cortez was pulling on Meg's arm, trying to yank her off Whip. She was squeezing his stomach with her knees, and Whip was twisting like a snake, trying to break free. The Mac-10 was rattling on the floor, attached to him by a shoulder strap. The gun was half under him, and there was no way he could pick it up.

"Get out of the way," Gibson told Cortez.

Cortez looked at him in surprise, then dropped Meg's arm and stood back. Gibson pulled out the Magnum.

"Man, I've already threatened to shoot her," Cortez said. "She just keeps right on."

Gibson wrapped his hand around the butt of the heavy automatic and took a step closer to the fight. He raised his hand above his shoulder, then, clenching his teeth, he brought down the gun barrel in a short arc. The metal made a loud crack as it struck Meg on the side of the head above her left ear.

Meg's body stiffened, rose a foot off the floor, then collapsed on top of Whip. Whip pushed at her, but he was unable to shove her off him. Then half shoving and half crawling, he inched sideways until he got out from under her.

"Son of a goddamned fucking bitch," Whip said. He got up from the floor and adjusted the strap of the Mac-10 so the gun swung under his right arm. "That crazy fucking woman jumped me from behind and knocked me down before I knew what the fuck was happening."

Whip rubbed his lower back with both hands, then turned to look at Cortez. "How come you didn't shoot the stupid bitch? She like to've killed me."

"Well hell, man, I didn't want to shoot you." Cortez shook his head. "She was swarming over you like stink on shit, and I could've just as easy blown a hole through you as her."

Gibson slid the Magnum into its holster. He then looked down at the bulky figure of Meg O'Hare sprawled on her stomach. She was barefoot, and with her black sweatpants, she was wearing a black T-shirt with *Aztec Gold* printed on the back. The shirt was faded to charcoal gray, and the gold letters were flaking.

He thought about shooting her in the head right then. She would always be a potential threat, a coiled rattlesnake waiting to strike. Even so, keeping her around might be a risk worth taking. If he killed her now, he would get nothing in exchange. If he waited, he might be able to use her life to buy something he needed—maybe credibility, maybe time. He would have to do something to show her that she was under his strict control.

Whip came over to him. "No wonder the bitch knocked me to the floor. She's big as a pregnant sow." Whip drew back his right foot and gave Meg a sharp kick below her ribs. She didn't move, but the toe of his shoe sank into her soft flesh.

Whip knelt down and grabbed her by the hair. He lifted her head and twisted it around so he could see her face. "God, she's so ugly she didn't have to fight me," he said. "She could've looked at me and scared me to death." He let her head drop, and it hit the marble floor with a sharp crack.

"Stop it!" a woman screamed in a high, harsh voice. "Leave her alone!"

Gibson looked up and saw Susan. She was standing framed by the living room doorway, as if she were on a stage with a proscenium arch. He stared at her, almost unable to believe how beautiful she was. He had studied hundreds of images of her, poring over them again and again, yet she looked more attractive than any of the pictures had ever suggested. None of them had captured the soft but angular delicacy of her face.

She was thinner than he had imagined, yet she looked as lithe and supple as she did on the screen. He liked the way her dark blond hair was cut short at the back, and he even liked the way it was rumpled, as if she had just gotten out of bed. Yet she was still dressed in jeans and a black knit shirt.

"Just stay where you are, Miss Bradstreet." Gibson spoke in a firm voice, but he tried not to make it unkind. "Meg is going to be okay."

As though the words were a cue, Susan began to collapse. She seemed to fall in stages. At first she wavered on her feet and grasped the door-facing to steady herself, then her body sagged and her grasp was broken. She slipped to the floor and lay unmoving.

"What the fuck is going on?" Whip asked.

23

Hightower bounced hard twice in the darkness and launched himself upward from the diving board. As he plunged into the depths of the lighted pool and glided through the water, he could feel power and energy running through him like an electric current.

He had always loved swimming, and at UCLA he tried to go to the pool four or five times a week. In the last few years, though, swimming had become more an ordeal than a pleasure. When he dived, he was anxiously aware of the hissing noise of the water rushing past his ears. Water blocked his nose, and he could feel its massive weight pressing against his chest. He was sure then that he was drowning.

This time, though, he wasn't feeling anything like that. He had enjoyed spending the day working on his research. Part of what had attracted him to surgery was the prospect of dramatically relieving the despair of patients coming to him for help. If this project was successful, he might experience that satisfaction once again.

Would he be able to sustain his good mood through the long days of work ahead? He could if he was able to talk to Susan every couple of days. But would she want to talk to him? They barely knew each other. Wasn't he rushing things?

He felt sure he wasn't. He and Susan seemed to have had the same strong and immediate attraction to one another. He knew his own feelings, and the way she had openly expressed her wish to see him when he returned to L.A. showed that she felt the same. And hadn't she told Carl Blau that she wanted to call him?

He gave a powerful flutter kick and shot to the top. His crawl stroke was strong and regular, and in a few seconds he was holding on to the slick chrome of the ladder and hauling himself out of the water.

He stood in the bright spray of light coming from the

fixtures attached to the garage roof and slowly dried himself with a beach towel. The night was hot and humid with no hint of a breeze. The moist air felt too thick to breathe, and the brick patio surrounding the pool radiated the heat it had absorbed during the day.

He sat down at the wrought-iron table a few feet from the edge of the pool and poured out a glass of lime seltzer. When he and Alma had visited his parents, they would lounge by the pool in the evenings and drink gin-and-tonics. His father bought expensive gins with distinctive flavors, something like Tanqueray or Bombay, and the drinks had seemed better than those at other places.

Now he drank no alcohol at all. He refused to take antidepressants because he didn't want to experience the world as blunted by drugs, so it didn't make sense to use a depressant that would produce the same result. Yet he still missed the icy sharp bite of the tonic water mixed with the peculiar flowery flavor of the gin. After just one drink, he'd feel the gradual relaxing of his tense muscles and the softening of the tight focus of his concentration. Maybe that was what he really missed.

From another backyard pool down the street, he could hear the sounds of splashing and laughter. The rattling, teasing voices were young—probably teenagers—and they suddenly made him aware of his isolation.

He reached across the table and clicked on the radio. He slowly twisted the dial until he found a clear station playing a Mozart horn concerto. The music had brightness and clarity, but what was most appealing was its quality of absolute precision. In the complex changing structures, he was aware that immensely detailed abstract patterns were somehow being perfectly realized.

"That was Mozart's Horn Concerto in E flat, Köchel listing four-forty-seven," a sonorous male voice said. "And this is KWMU, community-supported radio of the University of Missouri—St. Louis, your National Public Radio station."

Hightower took a sip of seltzer and put the glass back on the table. He began to wonder if he shouldn't go inside and try to code a few more charts. He could put in at least two more hours before bedtime.

"This just in from the Associated Press," the announcer said in a formal voice. "The actress Susan Bradstreet has apparently been taken captive along with several other people at the Benjamin Rush Institute in Cambridge, Massachusetts."

"Oh, no, no, no," Hightower said in a rising voice. His face tightened, and he leaned toward the radio. He felt dizzy, and he could feel the blood pounding in his ears.

"One security officer was killed and another injured during the seizure of the building," the announcer said. "So far nothing is known about the captor or captors or about their motives."

The announcer paused, then added in a softer and more conversational voice, "Susan Bradstreet is a favorite of a lot of people, particularly since playing Alice Davenport in *Aztec Gold*. We'll give you the details as soon as they come in."

Hightower picked up the radio and hurried across the patio and through the back door into the kitchen. He felt sure the radio report was correct, but he had to know more. How could such an incredible thing happen? And what was the real situation? He had to talk to somebody on the scene.

He located the card with Carl Blau's number on the countertop by the telephone, but his eyes were blurred from the pool water, and he couldn't read even his large scrawled writing. He held the card close to his eye, hardly an inch away, then began moving his hand outward, extending the distance. He still couldn't read it.

"Goddamn it," he said in a harsh, loud voice. He slapped the card down on the countertop in angry frustration, then ran into the study to get a magnifying glass.

Rushing back to the kitchen, he snatched up the cordless phone and rapidly tapped out Blau's number. On the fourth ring, an answering machine took the call. He didn't wait to hear the message. He pressed down the switch hook and called directory assistance for the Boston area.

"For what city, please?" a male voice asked.

"Cambridge," Hightower said. "The home number for Dr. Carl Blau—B-l-a-u."

The pause was longer than usual, then the operator said, "I can give you the office number, but the home number is unlisted."

"This is a medical emergency."

"I can let you talk to a supervisor."

Suddenly, trying to get to Blau didn't seem worth the hassle. He knew what he had to do. He had to find out for himself what was happening and see what he could do to free Susan. He had to go to Cambridge.

He called TWA first. "We don't have any more departures to Boston this evening," a Mrs. Smith told him.

"Can you see if any other airline has a St. Louis–Boston flight tonight?"

"Sorry," she said after several minutes. "The last departure was nine-thirty-five. I also checked for connections from Chicago, New York, and Newark. and there's nothing available until six-thirty tomorrow morning. That's on TWA. Will you be needing a round-trip ticket?"

"Not yet," he said. "I've got to think."

He dropped the phone back into its cradle and sat down at the kitchen table. Could he charter a plane at night? Did he know anyone with a private plane he might persuade to fly to Boston?

Something at the back of his mind was nagging him.

Then all at once he realized he did know somebody who might help. His name was Milton Weiser, and he was the transplant coordinator at Barnes Hospital. Because Weiser's job was to arrange for organs to be flown to transplant centers, he might know if he could charter a flight.

Hightower called Weiser at home. "He's still at the hospital," his wife said. "He's got two status-one cases tonight, and I don't expect him home until past midnight. If you need to talk to him, you'd better beep him."

Hightower dialed the paging number, then while he waited for the callback, he got dressed. Just in case

Weiser might know somebody to call for an immediate charter, he packed a change of clothes and his shaving kit into a small bag he found in his father's closet.

Taking the bag with him, he went to the basement and removed the long chrome-steel autopsy knife from the leather instrument case. He smiled ruefully. Did he really need to take a weapon? Was he going to storm a building single-handed with a knife between his teeth? Maybe he would. Anyway, knowing he would have the knife with him made him feel better.

He carefully wrapped it in a rag torn from one of his father's blue oxford shirts, then dropped the bundle into the bag on top of his own blue shirt. In case he needed to strap on the knife where no one could see it, he added a roll of self-adhesive bandage. He then went upstairs to the kitchen and turned on the coffee maker.

While the coffee was dripping, he called Pamela Fine's number. She had been a friend of his parents for over thirty years, and she wouldn't mind meeting their plane. Even though he felt a mixture of guilt and regret at not being there himself, he had no doubt that he was doing the right thing.

He got Pamela's answering machine. "This is David," he said. "Will you please pick up Mom and Dad at the airport tomorrow? It's TWA flight 222 arriving at 8:42 A.M. Their London flight is TWA 101, and it's supposed to get into Kennedy at 3:30 A.M. Then they leave on 222 at 5:18. I'll call and explain later. Thanks, Pamela."

He poured a cup of coffee and sat down at the kitchen table. He was halfway through the cup when Weiser called.

"I need to get to Boston immediately," Hightower told him. "I've got a patient who's being held captive by somebody who has taken over a building at Rush."

"Are you talking about Susan Bradstreet?" Weiser interrupted him. "Somebody just mentioned the Rush situation to me. She's your patient?"

"I sent her there."

"I'll be goddamned," Weiser said. "Now that you're in L.A., you do move in high circles."

He was surprised Weiser already knew about the take-over, but he wasn't inclined to explain that Susan really wasn't his patient and that his interest in her was personal. He was willing to use whatever worked, if it would get him to her.

"Can I charter a plane tonight? Is it possible?"

"This may be your lucky day," Weiser said. "I'm waiting for a heart that's being harvested even as we speak. I suspect it's going to be out in about fifteen minutes, then it's going to take ten minutes more to get it to me and for me to ice it down."

"So?" Hightower asked impatiently.

"So then I'm sending it by ambulance to the airport, where I've got a Cessna Citation jet waiting to take it to Mass General." Weiser paused. "If you can get down here before the ambulance leaves, you can go with it."

"I'm out the door now," Hightower said.

"Wait," Weiser said. "One more thing."

"Yeah, what is it?"

"Drive carefully," Weiser said. "I'm trying to get home early tonight."

24

"Listen to me very carefully," the man in the blue blazer said. His voice had a sharp edge, but he sounded educated. "I don't have time to repeat everything."

Susan was sitting at one end of the long sofa, and Mrs. Rostov was at the opposite end. Tim Kimberly sat next to her in a low club chair. Susan's hands were in her lap, and they were trembling. Mrs. Rostov and Tim looked as frightened as she felt. The older woman appeared to be trying to sink into the deep corner of the sofa, and her

cheeks were wet with crying. Tim sat up straight, but his
eyes were wide and his face was white and pinched.

Susan kept thinking about Meg. She had left her lying
motionless on the floor like a heap of dirty clothes. At
least she hadn't been shot, but she needed to be taken
care of.

The man in the blazer sat opposite them in a high-
backed wing chair. He had a calm, intelligent face and
white-blond hair that swept back from his forehead. He
wasn't particularly tall, but he was well built, with powerful shoulders. His hazel eyes had a yellowish cast, like
the eyes of a cat, but they were hard and steady as he
looked at them.

At his right, behind the chair, stood the man with the
scarred lip and the greasy tied-back hair—the one who
had been kicking Meg. Hanging under his right arm from
a canvas sling was what looked like a short, stubby machine gun.

"Are you awake now, Susan?" The man in the blazer
was looking directly at her, and he sounded concerned, as
if he were a close friend worried about how she was
doing.

"I'm awake," she said. Her voice was hoarse and indistinct. She cleared her throat and nodded at him.

She had never really slipped into complete unconsciousness, the way she had on the *McKnightly* set. She
had been unbelievably angry at what the three men were
doing to Meg, but just as she was stepping out to rush at
them, her legs lost all their strength. As she lay on the
cold granite, she had teetered on the edge of complete
darkness for a moment. Then it passed, and someone
pulled her to her feet and guided her to the sofa. She
thought it must have been the man in the blazer.

"I'm Cyberwolf," he was saying. "Whip is behind me,
and Backup is out in the hall. Those aren't our real
names, of course." His smile was nothing more than an
automatic twitch. "But we know your real names: Susan
Bradstreet, Clara Rostov, and Tim Kimberly." He nodded
to each of them in turn. He then jerked his head to the

right. "And Meg O'Hare out there with Backup keeping an eye on her."

"I always thought Hoover was the best president," Mrs. Rostov said. "He was such a gentleman."

Susan saw Whip and Cyberwolf turn and stare at Mrs. Rostov in complete surprise. She was blotting the tears off her powdered cheeks with a small white handkerchief and didn't seem to be addressing anyone in particular.

"She's got Ganser's syndrome," Tim said hurriedly. "She always acts this way." He reached over and gently patted Mrs. Rostov's thin shoulder. "You're okay, Mrs. R. These guys aren't going to hurt us."

"You're so young," she said, shaking her head. "You don't know anything."

Cyberwolf nodded to Whip. Whip took a step backward, and in a swift, easy-flowing movement, he rotated his weapon through a half-turn, twisted his body to the left, then fired a burst of shots at the living room wall.

Susan automatically put her hands over her ears. The bright flashes from the muzzle were as frightening as the staccato raps of the exploding shells, and Mrs. Rostov threw herself sideways, facedown on the sofa. The bullets raked the wall, sending up puffs of plaster dust.

The deafening noise ended abruptly, but Susan's ears were still ringing. Mrs. Rostov had sat up again and was pushing herself farther into the corner of the couch, as if seeking its protection. Tim was sitting very straight, his face paler than ever.

"I said we don't have time to waste," Cyberwolf said. His tone had become harsh. "Now keep quiet and listen." He paused and glanced around. "We are the action arm of the Association for Psychiatrically Disadvantaged People—the APDP. We're seeking justice for people society calls mentally ill." He gave each of them an earnest look. "We don't believe mental illness exists. We think society identifies behavior it doesn't like, then labels people who act that way crazy, so it can justify locking them up in hospitals and controlling their minds with drugs."

Susan gazed at him with full attention. She was listening to what he was saying, but she also had something else on her mind. Cyberwolf looked familiar. Maybe she had met him at a party or maybe just seen him briefly while she was out promoting one of her movies.

"We've taken over Johnson Hall to call attention to our cause," Cyberwolf said. "We want publicity for APDP, but we also want to raise money to defend the rights of people who dare to be different from the social norm."

"You're holding us for ransom," Tim said. His eyes were wide, and his voice sounded excited.

"Not everybody, kid," Whip said. He showed his teeth in a smirk. Susan noticed that a silver death's-head earring was now dangling from his left ear.

Cyberwolf made a half-turn in his chair and faced Whip. "Let me do the talking." His voice was sharp.

"I'm the one they want," Mrs. Rostov said in a tone of complete certainty. She nodded her head. "My daughter, Maria, is an assistant attorney general. She knows a number of wealthy and important people in Washington. She could raise a lot of money."

Cyberwolf turned to face them, and Susan noticed that he was looking at her with an almost apologetic expression. She suddenly realized that the point of the invasion was to take *her* hostage. And of course Tim was right about the ransom. That's why they wanted her.

It made sense. Tim's parents might be rich in the way that a million dollars made people rich, and Mrs. Rostov's daughter might have political influence. But when it came to producing money, they couldn't compare with the amount that Galaxy could come up with.

"I'm the one you really want." Susan spoke directly to Cyberwolf. "Let everybody else leave, and I'll cooperate."

He stared at her for a moment, then shook his head. "We need all of you," he said. "And everybody has got to cooperate, not just you."

Cyberwolf's face suddenly hardened. He leaned forward, and his voice became a snarl. "If you don't cooperate, we'll blow your fucking heads off." He tilted his head to look behind his chair. "Won't we, Whip?"

"Time for lesson two," Whip said. He left his position and stood in front of Tim. Looking down at him, he said, "Open your mouth."

"What are you going to do?" Tim's face was ashen, and his voice shrill.

"Leave him alone," Susan said. "He's just a child."

Her face was suddenly hot and flushed, and she could feel her heart thumping again. Despite her anger, she couldn't trust herself to stand up, much less do anything. A part of her didn't even want to try to do anything. She was deeply afraid of these people.

"We ain't going to hurt him—least not right this minute," Whip said. "Now drop your jaw, buster."

Tim leaned back in the club chair and opened his mouth slightly. He stared up at Whip with frightened eyes.

"Make a bigger hole," Whip ordered. "Like you was swallowing an apple."

Tim opened his mouth wide, and the strained muscles pulled his face into a distorted caricature. Whip inserted the muzzle of the machine pistol between Tim's teeth. His finger was on the trigger.

"If I put two pounds of pressure on this trigger, I can blow off the back of your skull and scatter your brains against the wall." Whip gave a sudden laugh, then glanced around. "And the barrel doesn't even have to be in your mouth."

"That's enough," Cyberwolf said. "Do the rest of you need a personal demonstration?" He glanced at them and waited. "No? Okay, let's say we understand each other."

Tim rubbed his mouth with his hand. His face was red, and Susan saw that he was crying. He was obviously trying not to make any noise, but his body shook with suppressed sobs. Mrs. Rostov put out a thin, bony hand and rested it on his arm.

"Stay in this room," Cyberwolf said. "If you go into

the hall, you'll be shot." He got up from his chair. "Whip will be in charge here."

"What about Meg?" Susan asked.

Cyberwolf looked at her. "Backup will take care of her. She's going to have a bad headache for a while."

"I want to make sure she's all right," Susan insisted. She felt light-headed, but she didn't stop. "I want to see her."

Cyberwolf turned to leave, then hesitated. "All right," he said. "You can come with me."

As she stood up, she held on to the top of the couch. But she seemed steady on her feet, and she felt she could walk without collapsing.

She followed Cyberwolf through the archway and into the dimly lighted hall. The odor of vomit hit her immediately, and she noticed a small irregular puddle splattered on the floor where Meg had been lying. Meg was sitting with her back against the wall by the outside door. Her legs were stretched out in front of her, and her head was tilted to one side, as if she were sleeping.

Standing a few feet away from Meg was the plump Hispanic with the thick mustache—Backup, Cyberwolf had called him. He was leaning against the wall and cradling what looked like a comic-book submachine gun in the crook of his right arm. When he saw Cyberwolf walking toward him, he stood up straight and took a step forward. He balanced the gun on his shoulder.

"Any trouble?" Cyberwolf asked.

"Nothing," Backup said. He tapped the left side of his head with an index finger. "She's still woozy from the hit."

Susan knelt down on the floor beside Meg and smoothed back the hair from her face. Meg slowly raised her head. Her eyelids were droopy, and her eyes looked dull and unfocused.

Susan's fingers touched the short matted hair above Meg's left ear. Although the light was dim, she could see blood on the tips of her fingers. She looked up at Cyberwolf, wanting to scream at him for the horrible thing he had done. He was talking to Backup, paying no attention to her, but she didn't scream. She was afraid of making him angry.

"Are you okay?" Meg suddenly asked. Her speech was slow and thick.

Susan glanced down. "I'm fine." She spoke as earnestly as if she were talking to a child. "But I'm worried about you."

She tried to recall what she knew about head injuries. There was something about people's eyes you were supposed to check. Then she remembered: see if the pupils were dilated or were different sizes.

"Let me look at your eyes," she said to Meg.

She took a tissue from her pocket and wiped the blood from her fingers. She then used her thumb to raise the lid of Meg's right eye and stared into it. The pupil was a small black circle against the blue-green of the iris. The left eye looked exactly the same.

"You're going to feel better soon." She patted Meg's arm. "A lot better."

"How is she?" Cyberwolf asked.

Susan looked up. In his blue blazer, khaki pants, and striped tie, he looked like some official who had come to help them. It was only with difficulty that she could make herself remember that he was the one who had deliberately hurt Meg.

"She's suffering from shock and needs to be put to bed." Susan looked directly into Cyberwolf's face. "Please help me carry her into her room."

"Not yet." He shook his head, then turned to Backup. "Bring me a pillow off one of those sofas, and get me a towel."

Backup nodded. As he walked toward the living room, his shoes grated on the polished floor.

"I don't want you to watch this," Cyberwolf said to Susan. He sounded vaguely apologetic.

"What are you going to do?" Susan had assumed he was going to put the pillow under Meg's head so she could lie down.

"I've got to help her remember not to fight us," he said. "The lives of all of us depend on how we act tonight."

His face had a thoughtful expression. He seemed to want her to understand and accept what he was telling her. He almost seemed to want her approval, and she felt puzzled.

"I want us all to stay alive," she said.

He nodded as if he agreed with her, then reached under his blazer and pulled out the pistol he had used to hit Meg. He studied it a moment and pushed in a small pin in front of the trigger guard. He squatted down beside Meg.

He was on the opposite side from Susan, yet close enough for her to feel the heat coming from his body. She hated that sense of intimacy and moved away from him.

Backup returned with a blue bath towel and a large white throw pillow. Cyberwolf stood up, and Backup handed him the pillow. Backup flipped the towel off his shoulder, and Cyberwolf caught the end of it.

Cyberwolf knelt down by Meg's ankle and put the pistol on the floor beside him. He picked up her right foot and placed it on the pillow. He then slid the towel between her big toe and the second one. He pulled the towel tight so that her big toe was isolated from the others.

He glanced up at Susan. "Stand up," he told her.

"What are you going to do?" she asked again. She could hear the desperation and fear in her voice.

"I told you I don't want to have to repeat myself," he said. His face was a frozen mask as he looked at her. He waited until she stood up, then said, "Backup, get behind her and keep her eyes pointing away from me."

Backup covered the distance between them in two steps. He put his hand at the base of Susan's skull and wrapped his fingers around her neck. She felt as if her head were locked in a vise.

Before she could guess what was going on, the hallway was suddenly filled with the hollow booming noise of

Cyberwolf's pistol. Meg screamed, and her bare feet thudded against the floor.

Susan struggled to turn around, but Backup tightened his grip. She could feel his fingers digging into the flesh of her neck, and her skin burned as she tried to twist free.

"Let her loose," Cyberwolf said.

She whirled around to see him standing and staring down at Meg. The white pillow was drenched with blood. More blood was running out of Meg's foot where her big toe used to be.

25

"Need some fresh coffee, Dr. Hightower?" Sam Brand asked. He held up a glass carafe and looked back at Hightower from the galley at the front of the plane.

Sam was a courier for the Organ Sharing Network. He was a husky black man in his early thirties with an open, friendly manner. During the ambulance ride to the airport, he had chatted with Hightower about the satisfactions of working as a courier. He had also very politely not asked him why he needed to get to Boston in such a hurry.

Hightower was glad, because he wasn't sure he could explain it. The police would surely be doing everything possible to free Susan, so despite his impulse to help her, he couldn't imagine what use he could be. He seemed to be responding to the same sort of atavistic drive that made relatives of trapped miners hurry to the scene of a disaster.

"No, thanks." Hightower raised his voice so he could be heard over the plane's vibrations. "My stomach can't take it."

"You get used to it." Sam smiled and leaned against a bulkhead to steady himself as the plane suddenly swung to the right and dipped.

The Cessna was fast and the weather relatively clear. He couldn't have gotten luckier than being able to hitch a ride. Still, compared to the commercial aircraft he was accustomed to, the Citation was alarmingly small, and he was unpleasantly aware of eddying currents and downdrafts. The plane might suddenly pitch from side to side or plunge straight down, then halt abruptly, as if somebody had pushed the emergency stop on an elevator. He had been able to nap for an hour or so, but reading was out of the question.

Hightower glanced at the red-and-white plastic picnic cooler on the floor between Sam and the bulkhead. He had been present when Sam had pulled back the lid to check the contents before they got into the ambulance. The cooler held a heavy glass lab jar in which the heart floated motionless in a sterile saline and potassium solution. The jar was sealed with a leak-proof rubber gasket and surrounded by mounds of crushed ice. Kept at the freezing point, the organ would stay alive for about five hours. If it hadn't been implanted by then, it would soon be as dead as the rest of the donor.

Usually, though, hearts reached recipients on time, and the result was a medical miracle. Yet such miracles were routine in only a few special cases. Hearts, kidneys, livers, and even lungs could be transplanted, but eyes couldn't. The eye was an extension of the brain, and a successful transplant would require much more than getting the plumbing right.

Sam took a sip of coffee and put his cup down on the stainless-steel counter. He slid open the door of the pilot's compartment and leaned inside. Hightower could hear him talking to the pilot, but he couldn't understand the words.

"Okay," he could hear Sam say, as he pulled his head out of the compartment. "I'm going to call Mass General, then." Sam closed the door, then flipped open the cover of a small niche next to the galley and took out a beige telephone with a short black antenna. He rapidly tapped out a number.

"This is Sam Brand in transit from Barnes, St. Louis," he said. "We're twenty minutes ahead of schedule. The pilot has informed air-traffic control, and I'm notifying you so the ambulance will be waiting."

After Sam hung up, he started to close the cover of the niche, but then hesitated and looked back at Hightower. "Was there anybody you wanted to call, Dr. Hightower?"

"I don't think so," Hightower said. Then he stopped himself. "Maybe I do need to call somebody. Let me find the number."

He unzipped the outside pocket of the shoulder bag he had tossed his clothes in and took out his address book. He had stuck it in as an afterthought, in case he needed to call people in Los Angeles. He hadn't thought about Don Lindsley at the time, but Don was exactly the person he needed to talk to. Don was in Cambridge and in a position to know something.

He clicked on the light above his seat, and a circle of intense brightness spread over his lap. He opened up the address book and located the "L" section without any trouble. But he had kept the book for years, and the names and numbers were written in characters too small for him to read without a magnifying glass. He turned to the second page of the section and recognized *Lindsley* by the general pattern of letters.

He had been a second-year fellow in surgery at Mass General when Don was brought into the emergency room. Hightower wasn't actually in the emergency room, but the supervisor called him after a glance at Don's hand. Ten minutes later, Don was in a third-floor operating suite. Hightower introduced himself while the anesthesiologist was giving her monitoring equipment a final check. Don was sleepy from the preop injection.

"Please do your best to save it," Don said. "Even if the hand's just a hook, I want to keep it."

Don had been on an arrest call with two other officers, and they hadn't expected trouble. The suspect was a man in his thirties, the owner of an office-supplies shop, who was being picked up for failing to pay child support. He would have been back on the street after posting bond, but something snapped in him. Don was hardly a foot away from the suspect when he pulled a gun and pointed it directly at Don's stomach. Don later said he could see the trigger begin to travel. That was when he pushed the flat of his hand against the gun's muzzle and shoved upward.

And that was when the suspect pulled the trigger.

The .38-caliber slug was fired at point-blank range, which meant that it simply bored through Don's hand. Had Don been even a few feet away, the slug would have had time to start tumbling through the air, moving end over end. Then when it hit, it would have blown his hand apart.

Even so, the bullet did a great deal of damage. On entry, it tore through the soft tissue, severing nerves, muscles, tendons, and vessels, then broke the third and fourth metacarpals and shattered one of the carpometacarpal joints. It damaged more soft tissue as it exited. By the time Hightower saw the hand, it was a bloody, pulpy mass, turning purple and beginning to swell.

The first round of surgery took nine hours, but by the end Hightower was feeling almost cheerful. The CM joint couldn't be made as good as new, and Don's fourth finger would always be a little stiff. Still, Hightower was confident that, in time, Don would have almost complete use of his hand.

"It looked so bad, I thought you'd just want to chop it off," Don told him later. "I wanted to keep it for looks, but I never thought I'd be able to use it again." He shook his head and flexed his fingers. "If it hadn't been for you, I would have had to go on disability and give up on making detective."

That was at least ten years ago. Hightower hadn't done much to stay in touch, but Don and his wife, Sarah, had sent Christmas cards with notes telling about their two children and Don's progress in the department. When they read about Alma in the *Globe*, Don had written him a moving letter.

Still, when Hightower had gone back to Harvard for his residency in psychiatry, he hadn't even let them know he was in town. Seeing Don would have reminded him too much of his old life as a surgeon, and he didn't think he could stand it. He had wanted to cut himself completely free from the past. Now, though, it looked as if he might need the past to help with the future.

Hightower snapped loose the buckle on his seat belt and took the address book up to Sam. "Lieutenant Donald Lindsley," Hightower said, speaking above the plane's steady hum.

Sam glanced at the address book, then tapped out a sequence of numbers on the phone. Hightower leaned his back against the opposite bulkhead, bracing himself so the plane's dips and swoops wouldn't knock him over.

"It's ringing," Sam said.

He started to hand over the phone, but Hightower waved it back. "You go ahead," he said. "I don't want to get involved in talking to his wife." That was only partly true. In fact, he was embarrassed not to have written the Lindsleys.

Sam nodded. "Lieutenant Lindsley, please. Dr. Hightower wants to talk with him." Sam listened quietly, his face wrinkled in concentration. "Just a sec, let me get that down." He bent over the galley counter and wrote a telephone number on a white scratch pad. "Thank you," he said into the receiver. "Yes, I certainly will."

He moved a switch on the phone, then turned toward Hightower and leaned close. "She says virtually the whole department is at Rush Institute and that Lieutenant Lindsley is with them." He tapped the pad of paper. "He called and left the phone number for where he was at the time. She says you can try it if you want to, but she doesn't know if he's still there." He paused. "She also wanted me to tell you hello for her."

Hightower smiled automatically. "Let's try the number."

Sam dialed the new number, and when he held out the

phone, Hightower took it. Sam picked up his coffee cup and sat down, giving Hightower some privacy.

"Command post. This is Brody," a male voice said.

"Lieutenant Lindsley, please. Tell him it's David Hightower."

"Hold on," Brody said.

Hightower could hear a mumble of voices and the strangely amplified sounds of chairs creaking and people moving around. Then somebody picked up the phone.

"Dr. Hightower," Don Lindsley said. "This is a total surprise." His voice conveyed his astonishment, but Hightower thought he also caught a hint of annoyance.

"I know you're in the middle of a tense situation," Hightower said. "I wouldn't bother you, except somebody I know is one of the hostages—Susan Bradstreet."

"Is she your patient?" Lindsley asked. Hightower was impressed by the way he hadn't missed a beat. The annoyance was instantly replaced by professional curiosity.

"In a way," Hightower said. He couldn't think of how to explain his relationship with Susan. He decided he would have to tell Lindsley more, although maybe not everything.

"I don't know if you've heard that I left surgery and went into psychiatry," he said. "I'm now at the UCLA Medical Center, and yesterday I was called in to consult on Susan Bradstreet. I'm the one who recommended that she spend a week at Rush."

"And it sure didn't turn out the way you expected," Lindsley said. "You must be feeling mighty guilty."

"You put your finger on it," Hightower said. "I'd like to do whatever I can to help get her out of there safely."

"I can't talk about that over the phone," Lindsley said. "Where are you now?"

"In a plane about half an hour from Logan."

"It sounds like we may be able to get some useful information out of you. If you're willing to come out here, I'll introduce you to the officer in charge."

"That's why I called you."

"How about I just say you're Susan Bradstreet's psychiatrist?" Lindsley suggested. "Is that too far from the truth?"

"No, that's okay," Hightower said.

"I'll have a police car meet you at the airport and bring you straight here."

"That's not necessary," Hightower said. "I'll rent a car, but if you could tell people at the police line that you're expecting me, I'd appreciate it."

"I can certainly do that, Doctor," Lindsley said. "Just ask for me." He paused, then said, "It'll be good to see you."

26

Gibson saw Susan's face freeze with shock as she realized that he had shot Meg. He watched her for a sign that she might faint again, but she seemed steady on her feet.

"You're an animal," she said in a low, fierce voice.

Her words hit him like a slap. He had done something for *her*, and she didn't appreciate it. She apparently didn't even realize it.

"I could have killed her." He tried to sound calm and reasonable. "I had to keep her from interfering, but I kept her alive as a favor to you."

He tried to catch Susan's eye, but she wouldn't look at him. As he gazed at the smooth profile of her face against the white wall, his anger was replaced by frustration. He didn't want her to think he was brutal or insensitive, but he didn't know how to show her what he was really like. Being close to her made him so uncomfortable that he couldn't think clearly.

Susan seemed not to hear him. Instead, she started trying to reach Meg. She took a step forward, but Cortez's hand snaked out and grabbed her arm. She struggled to jerk loose, but he tightened his grip.

"Let me go. At least let me try to stop the bleeding."

Meg had passed out and slumped to the side. The blood spurting from the ragged flesh where her toe used to be had become a slow ooze. Gibson tried not to look at the floor in front of her. Bits of skin and muscle mixed with fragments of bone were strewn in a semicircular pattern, and the whole area was splattered with blood. But he couldn't block out the sickly sweet smell of blood combined with the acrid odor of gun smoke.

"I can't spend any more time here," he told Susan. "And you're coming with me."

The clock was ticking, and he needed to tap into the net and get out the ransom demand. The people at Galaxy had access to enormous amounts of money, but they wouldn't have millions sitting in their checking accounts. He would have to give them a few hours to arrange loans with the banks.

"Leave me here," Susan begged. She twisted around in Cortez's grip and gave Gibson a pleading look.

He had been about to tell Cortez to take her back to the living room. But Whip would be standing guard, and he didn't trust Whip to keep his hands off Susan. What was more, he wasn't sure she would want him to. She might find a low-life piece of shit like Whip appealing. After all, she'd fallen for that dope addict. For a brief moment he saw the two of them lying in bed together, Whip with his long sallow face and little rat's tail of greasy hair and Susan with her sleek body and bare skin. He shook his head in sudden angry disgust.

"You're coming with me," he said in a curt tone. "Backup will take care of Meg."

Susan looked fully at him. Her eyes were red-rimmed and bright with tears, and her face was lined with worry. Yet she was still so beautiful that he found looking directly at her upsetting. He could hardly keep from turning away.

"I want to take care of her myself," she insisted.

"Don't argue with me," Gibson said. He realized that

his voice had turned cold and flat. More gently, trying to be reassuring, he added, "You'll be safer with me."

He didn't give her a chance to respond. Instead, he turned to Cortez and said, "Wrap up Meg's foot and get her into bed."

"No problem, Cyber," Cortez said.

Gibson started down the hall without looking at Susan. Then out of the corner of his eye, he saw that she was coming with him, and he felt a sense of relief. He didn't want to have to force her. He wanted her to *want* to be with him; he wanted her to find him interesting and take pleasure in his company.

The phrase reminded him of words from "Greensleeves"—"for I have loved you oh so long, delighting in your company"—and he started whistling the tune. He whistled softly, and the mournful melody seemed to float down the long, dim hall like a plume of smoke in an airless room.

His whistling trailed off as he approached the desk, then stood looking down at the sprawled body of Joe Ling. The man's eyes were open in a fixed gaze, as though he couldn't believe what had happened to him. The thick puddle of blood under his body was starting to turn dark brown. The blood on the front of his white shirt looked almost black.

"I'm not coming any closer," Susan said. She stopped a few feet from the desk, then backed against the inside wall, as if seeking shelter. "I don't want to have to see another of your victims." Her tone was a mixture of defiance and resignation.

"I didn't do this. Backup did." He knew he sounded defensive. "Ling had a gun and was going to shoot me." He lowered his gaze. "I've got to find it so nobody else gets hurt with it."

He straightened up the fallen desk chair, then walked around Ling's body, scanning the floor for the small blue-steel revolver. He then walked down the hall, looking along the wall behind the desk.

At the end of the hall, he saw it. The gun must have

been flung from Ling's hand, because it had slid at least twenty feet along the marble floor. He dropped the revolver into the side pocket of his blazer.

Finding himself in front of the double doors leading into the research tower, he tried turning the doorknobs. Both doors were locked, but that didn't surprise him. The staff wouldn't want Lowell Division patients wandering into the labs.

Eventually, he was going to have to get into the research building. Once the ransom money was in his possession, Cortez and Whip would be trying to escape by following the plan he would give them. They would be making a very public exit out the front door, and the cops would be focusing attention on them. He would then make his own escape, but he had to find a private way out. The best place to look would be in the research tower, because cops were going to be swarming around Johnson Hall like hornets.

He noticed a slot for inserting a magnetic key card below the right doorknob. Using a card would be faster than searching for the right computer interrupt, and a card was sure to be in Joe Ling's desk or wallet. As soon as he sent his message, he'd look for it.

Susan had watched Cyberwolf pick up the gun and try the door, and she could feel a shiver of dread run down the back of her neck as she saw him coming toward her. Her anger over Meg had temporarily insulated her from her fear, but now she felt vulnerable again.

Cyberwolf had never directly threatened her. In fact, he spoke to her in a soft, almost hesitant manner that reminded her of shop clerks, hotel managers, and naive fans. He was obviously giving her the star treatment, but even so, she could sense powerful, hidden emotions influencing his behavior toward her. Exactly what they were she didn't know, but she could feel him making an effort to restrain himself. She felt sure that she was looking at the thin crust over a pool of molten lava.

"I found Meg's toy," he told her as he came up to the

desk. He gave her a triumphant smile, then took the pistol from his jacket pocket and held it up for her to see. "Now I'm going to fix it so nobody can get hurt with it."

He flipped open the cylinder of the revolver, turned the pistol upside down, and dumped the shells out in his hand. He dropped them into his pocket, then slid the gun in after them. Just then the telephone began to ring.

She looked at the phone, then glanced at Cyberwolf. He stood frozen, obviously as surprised as she was. The sound was completely ordinary, yet in the circumstances it seemed peculiar. Her first idea was that David Hightower had found a way to get through to her. Yet even while the thought was crossing her mind, she realized how foolish it was. He probably hadn't even heard about the takeover.

Cyberwolf moved nearer the desk, but he still wasn't close enough to pick up the phone. It was on the opposite side, and the swivel chair was blocking his way. He pushed on the chair arm nearest him, but the rollers on the chair's spidery legs jammed against Joe Ling's outstretched body.

The phone kept on ringing, its long, shrill peals painfully loud in the silence of the dim hallway. Cyberwolf swiveled the seat of the chair around, placed his foot on the front edge of the cushion, then shoved it backward with a violent kick.

The chair hit Ling's corpse, bounced over it, then toppled toward the wall. As the chair fell, its back caught on the two thin black cables leading from a metal-edged panel in the floor into the back of the computer perched on the edge of the desk. For a moment the cables supported the chair, then one of them pulled loose from the computer, and the chair fell the rest of the way to the floor.

Cyberwolf stared at the fallen chair for an instant, then picked up the phone and said, "Johnson Hall."

No one would have been able to guess from his level, expressionless tone that he had been frustrated in trying to get to the phone. His control seemed so complete that it was frightening, and she realized again that under Cyberwolf's smooth, polite surface was a seething cauldron of rage.

With the phone to his ear, he twisted around so that his back was partly turned toward her. She found herself moving closer to the desk, as if by doing so she could get closer to the person on the other end of the line. The world outside was already growing unreal, and whoever was on the phone, even a complete stranger, was a reminder that she shouldn't forget it was there. If she let Cyberwolf define her world for her, she would become like one of those abused women who lose their own identity and even refuse to leave their tormentor when they have the chance. She clenched her hands into fists. She was never going to be like that.

Cyberwolf held the phone and listened for what seemed a long time. At last he said, "I can tell you that so far no patient has been harmed, but that's all I can say. I'm not authorized to answer any questions, make any statements, or conduct any negotiations. You'll be receiving instructions from our representative shortly." He turned so he could see her.

"I can't make any comment about that," he said curtly. "But you can facilitate matters by giving me the E-mail address for a computer at your location." He paused. "All right, but I'll wait no more than two minutes." He looked at his wristwatch.

He sounded so formal and unbending that he might have been parodying a press secretary determined to give away as little information as possible. Yet there was nothing humorous about his imitation. His eyes were narrowed in concentration, and the expression on his face was completely serious.

"I'm ready," he said. He picked up a yellow ballpoint pen from the desk, and Susan watched as he wrote down HOPECOT.2 @ RUSHIN.BITNET on a small yellow pad. "Say it again for confirmation." He put the point of his pen on each letter and number in the series, one after the other.

Susan began to repeat the address silently to herself.

She was a quick study when it came to scripts, and if she just kept saying the address, she would remember it. She was comfortable enough with computers to know how to use a communications program, and if she could recall the address, she might be able to contact the police. At the least, memorizing the address made her feel that she was doing something to fight back.

Realizing that gave her a boost of inspiration. She suddenly saw that she could fight against Cyberwolf. She didn't have to remain passive, simply waiting for other people to make the effort to rescue her. She should start looking for chances to help herself. She might even escape.

For a moment she wondered whether, if she did escape, she wouldn't be abandoning Meg, Mrs. Rostov, and Tim. Wasn't it her duty to stay with them? No, thinking that way was foolish. She was the one who was crucial to Cyberwolf's plans, and if she could get away, he might be forced to turn the others loose to buy freedom for himself. Staying a hostage wouldn't do anybody any good, but getting away might help them all.

"Stand by to receive a message," Cyberwolf said, then abruptly hung up the phone. Turning around, he bent over and, with no apparent effort, picked up the desk chair, lifted it level with his chest, then threw it down the hall toward the double doors. The chair hit the marble floor with a sharp metallic crash and slid into the front wall with a solid bump.

Susan felt a surge of fear. She stepped back from the desk, but Cyberwolf ignored her. He calmly rotated the computer so he could see the back, then picked up one of the black cables the chair had caught on. She had no idea what had triggered his outburst, but apparently it was over.

She watched him examine the loose end of the cable, rolling the chrome coupling between his fingers. She expected him to look angry, but except for a slight tightness around his mouth, his face showed no expression at all.

He dropped the loose end, then traced the cable down

to the floor. She closely watched what he was doing but tried not to look at Joe Ling's body, with its vacant, staring eyes. The cable disappeared through a hole in the metal-edged panel that was set flush with the floor. Cyberwolf knelt down and lifted up the panel, as if taking the lid off a box. The cable ran along a rectangular metal channel that was a foot or so deep and maybe eighteen or twenty inches wide.

"Some droid forgot to screw in the connector, and the cable just popped loose," he said scornfully. "At least the cable's not broken." He put the panel back in place, then straightened up and shook his head. "I hate hardware."

She stood quietly, saying nothing, and he stared at her for a moment with a blank expression. His narrow amber eyes seemed focused somewhere in the space between them. She realized that he wasn't so much talking to her as thinking out loud.

He bent over the computer and pushed the chrome coupling into one of the five or six variously shaped holes. She couldn't see much of what he was doing, but he seemed satisfied when he stood up. He meticulously straightened out the wires, then turned the computer around. The blank screen of the display stared at her like a blind eye.

Gibson was relieved that the cable wasn't wrecked. He wanted to be able to send and receive E-mail, and the easiest way to do that was with the computer on the desk.

The cops had rattled him a little by calling on the phone. He hadn't expected them to respond so quickly—at least not before he had sent the demand letter. Still, he thought he had handled the situation well. If he talked to them for long, he might inadvertently say something they could use to identify him. They might then be able to locate the computer with the Chernobyl program and shut it down. If that happened, he might as well shoot himself in the head and save the cops the trouble.

He shoved the computer over so that he could sit on the edge of the desk. "Will you please come over and stand in front of the desk?" he asked Susan. "I'm going to send a message, and I need to be able to see you."

"Do you think I might escape?" Susan gave him a scornful look. "I can't imagine where you think I could go."

"You couldn't go anywhere." He gave her an almost apologetic smile. "Everything is sealed as tight as a tin can."

She didn't argue with him, but he kept his eyes on her as she walked around the desk and sat on the floor. She crossed her legs, leaned against the wall, and closed her eyes. With her head turned up slightly in a way that showed her fine smooth features, she could have been modeling for a sculpture of an angel. He had seen faces like hers carved from white limestone. The faces always represented the graceful beauty and simple charm of death, and in Susan's face, he could see both qualities. She wouldn't be the angel of death, though—she would be the dead angel.

He started to imagine what the rest of her body would look like if she took on the stillness of a statue, with her blood drained away and her skin as pale as moonlight. Her shoulders would glow like polished marble, and her nipples would retain a pink hue against the ashen color of her breasts. Then he caught himself. He couldn't let himself be distracted now.

He booted the computer, then tapped into UUCP-NET, the network made up of all connected UNIX machines and emulators. He typed out a bang path that would route the mail in three hops. First it would go from Rush to MIT, then from there to the Oxford Mathematical Laboratory, and finally to the address at Rush the cops had given to him.

He already had the dial-up number and password to gain access to the MIT computer, and the Oxford machine was virtually a public facility. So by banging the E-mail through MIT and instructing Oxford to readdress and forward it, he could create the impression that it was originating there. He was also covering his tracks, because somebody checking the Rush outgoing traffic would see the MIT address and assume that was the final destination of the transmission.

He would sign the ransom letter "John Armstrong," and in addition to making his demand for money and setting a deadline for delivery, he would put in the crap about the Association for Psychiatrically Disadvantaged People. The scheme offered enough smoke and mirrors to keep the cops from learning his identity right away, and that was the most effective way of protecting the Chernobyl program.

He smiled with satisfaction as he faced the computer screen and looked at the bang path he had specified. He shifted the keyboard on the desktop so he could reach it better, then began typing the ransom letter. When he finished, he would activate the interrupts and shut down the phones. If the cops could call in, they would be pressuring him all the time. He wanted to be the one in control of communication.

While he was waiting for an answer to his letter, he would be able to spend time with Susan. He would leave Cortez and Whip with the others and take her with him to the research building. They could find a comfortable and private place, and maybe he would tell her about the scenes he had imagined between the two of them.

Susan watched Cyberwolf hunched over the keyboard. He was typing steadily, and he didn't seem to be aware of her or of anything except the computer in front of him.

She again had the feeling that she had seen him somewhere, but she still couldn't place him. She had to admit that he was physically striking, even attractive. His pale face and strange amber eyes gave him an exotic, alien look, as though he were literally from some other world. His swept-back blond hair emphasized his pallor, but it was his eyes that she noticed most. They appeared to observe everything and assess it with a shrewd, deeply buried intelligence.

"Now it's done," Cyberwolf said abruptly. He reached

behind the computer and turned it off. Picking up the disk
of yellow plastic from the desk, he bent over the computer for a moment. He slid the yellow disc into his jacket
pocket, then stood up.

"What's done?" The marble floor was getting hard, and
Susan also stood up.

"Whatever happens now, your fate and mine are bound
together." His voice was serious, but then he suddenly
smiled. "There's no way out but forward."

"I'm not sure that sounds good for me," she said. She
had guessed that he was writing a ransom demand, and
what he said seemed to confirm it. She approached the
desk.

"My shoes are a mess," he said.

He lifted his right foot to examine it, and she could see
that the bottom of his shoe was smeared with Joe Ling's
blood. She glanced away quickly.

When she looked back, Cyberwolf had turned his attention to searching the desk. He opened the top drawer on
the right and rummaged around in it. He discovered the
short, chunky box of shells that Meg had turned over to
Joe Ling. After glancing into the box, Cyberwolf put it
back into the drawer. Fishing the other shells out of his
pocket, he dropped them inside with the box.

"No gun, no good," he said. He glanced up at her and
smiled.

He grabbed the large center drawer and pulled on it until it came free from its runners. Then in one smooth
movement, he turned the drawer upside down, spilling its
contents on the desk. Paper clips, ballpoint pens, pencils,
floppy disks, a box of staples, index cards, rubber bands,
and a variety of other small items scattered across the
desk. Several slid off the flat surface and onto the floor.

Susan caught a glimpse of the clear plastic bracelet before it hit. When it landed, she took a step forward and
covered it with her left foot. She then bent down and
quickly tugged on her shoelace to untie her shoe. Much
more slowly, she began to tie it. She glanced up at
Cyberwolf, but he was absorbed in looking through the

heap of materials from the drawer. She lifted the ball of her left foot slightly, pulled out the bracelet, and slid it into the top of her sock.

She raised her eyes to see Cyberwolf staring at her. Her heart stopped, then beat several times in rapid succession. She felt slightly dizzy, but she looked back down and went on tying her shoe. When she stood up, he was still hunting through the scatter of materials.

"Ah-ha, here it is," Cyberwolf said, sounding pleased. He held up a red plastic card. "The key to the magic kingdom."

27

Hightower shaded his eyes against the glare as he followed the young uniformed policeman into the narrow band of light that encircled the red-brick cottage.

The halogen bulbs shining down from the roof gave off a stark white illumination that bleached out the color of everything it touched. The grass growing along the sidewalk had faded to a muddy gray, and when he glanced at his hands, he saw that the skin on his fingers had turned a sickly shade of white.

The entrance to the cottage was at one end, and the sign above the door said HOPE in blocky red letters. He ignored the doorbell and rapped on the metal door with his knuckles. When a plump man in shirtsleeves opened it, he said, "I'm Dr. Hightower. Lieutenant Lindsley expects me."

"Wait here a minute," the man said, then shut the door.

In even less time the door opened again, and Don Lindsley stood in the entrance. He had lost much of his tightly curled black hair, and what little was left was fluffed up on top to cover the bare brown skin of his scalp. His heavy round face now had a few wrinkles

across the forehead. Yet his shoulders were as broad as
Hightower remembered and his body as powerfully muscled.

"Dr. Hightower." Lindsley's rich, resonant voice sounded very formal. His smile was equally formal, and his face
looked strained with worry. "It's a pleasure to see you."

"You're looking well, Lieutenant," Hightower said. As
they shook hands, he could detect the slight rigidity of
Lindsley's middle finger. But he could tell from the pressure Lindsley was exerting that the hand had plenty of
strength.

"Come on back, and I'll introduce you to the head of
the Hostage Negotiating Team," Lindsley said.

"I hope he's willing to tell me what's going on,"
Hightower said. He paused, then said what he had
planned to say since their phone conversation. "I want
you to know that my interest in Susan Bradstreet is more
personal than professional."

"I figured that out from the start," Lindsley said. "By
the way, the HNT head is a *she*—Lieutenant Katherine
Murphy. I told her who you are, and she wants to tell you
about the situation herself." He hesitated, and a troubled
look crossed his face. Then in a softer voice he said, "But
do come and see me later."

Hightower followed Lindsley down a long hall with
doors on both sides. Loose bundles of gray telephone
wires ran along the floor and into some of the rooms.
Several people passed them, some dressed in jackets and
ties, others in jeans, and a few in police uniforms. They
all seemed in a hurry, and they brushed past one another
in the narrow corridor without speaking.

"We moved the patients into other facilities," Lindsley
said, glancing over his shoulder. "Have you been here before?"

"I worked here for almost two years. This is where I
did part of my training in psychiatry."

"A psychiatrist," Lindsley said. Disbelief was in his
voice, and he looked back again with a frown. "I sure
don't know how to figure that."

"After the accident, I couldn't do surgery anymore."

"That's a shame," Lindsley said. He stopped and turned around. "I didn't know."

"I should have told you." Hightower felt embarrassed. "But I'm doing okay now, and I'll fill you in on the details when all this is over."

"Sure," Lindsley said, nodding. He turned and started walking again.

The supervisor's office was in the middle of the building. The door was pushed back against the wall, and two thick books were on the floor to keep it from slamming shut. Hightower could smell the odor of stale cigarette smoke coming from the room. He followed Lindsley inside.

Seated in front of a wooden desk was a thin woman in her early forties, with a sharp face, freckles scattered across both cheeks, and frizzy strawberry blond hair. She was dressed in jeans and a short-sleeved khaki work shirt that had a gold badge pinned above the left pocket. She was tipped back in the swivel chair and turned sideways so she could look at the man she was talking to.

The man sat hunched forward on a cracked brown leather sofa pushed against the side wall. His elbows rested on his knees, and his hands were clasped together as if he were praying. He had lank black hair that touched his collar, an olive complexion, and calm dark eyes. He was wearing black jeans and a black T-shirt with CAMBRIDGE POLICE on the front in large gold letters. Both he and the woman were smoking cigarettes and using the white china saucer on the corner of the desk as an ashtray.

"This is Dr. Hightower," Lindsley said. "Meet Lieutenant Murphy. This is all her show." Hightower thought he detected a trace of resentment or maybe even anger in Lindsley's voice.

"Have a seat, Dr. Hightower." Lieutenant Murphy's voice was low and husky, but it had a light, easy lilt. She gestured toward a straight-backed chair against the wall diagonally opposite the sofa. She eased her own chair down, then rolled it backward a foot or so to open up the space.

"I'll be down the hall, Doctor," Lindsley said. "Third door on the right." He rested a heavy hand on Hightower's shoulder, making it clear that he expected Hightower to come see him.

"Close the door, Don," Murphy called after him.

Lindsley halted, then used the toe of his shoe to push aside the heavy books. The door jerked inward rapidly until the pneumatic closer went into action and slowed it down.

Murphy waited for the latch to click, then said, "That's George Augustine over there." She inclined her head toward the couch. She sounded almost cheerful, as if making an introduction at a party. "He's our negotiator, if we ever get that far."

Hightower nodded to Augustine, then shifted in his chair. He could feel time pressing on him like a heavy weight.

"Can you tell me what's happening with the hostages?" He looked at Murphy. "All I know is what I heard on the radio."

Murphy bit at the cuticle on her left thumb. Then, without raising her eyes, she said, "As a favor to Don, I'm giving you a one-day ticket for all the rides." She looked at him with a sly smile. "But you wouldn't talk to reporters and try to become a TV star, would you?"

"I won't talk to anybody," Hightower promised.

She smiled again and nodded. She then brushed her hair away from her ear. "Maybe we can trade information. Don says you're Susan Bradstreet's psychiatrist."

"I recommended that she come to Rush for treatment." That much was true.

"I see," Murphy said, drawing out the last word. She looked into his face a moment. Then apparently dismissing the topic, she said, "We've got five hostages: Susan, her bodyguard, a staff member, and two other patients." She swiveled her chair around and pointed through the window. "The takers have gone barricade in that building on the right."

Hightower lowered his head and looked where she was pointing. On the top of a steep rise, through a thin screen of trees, he could see the graceful Colonial lines of Johnson Hall. Joined to the end of it was the awkward stub of the research tower. Like the cottages, the buildings were surrounded by a nimbus of light, and for a moment Johnson Hall seemed to float above the dark landscape like Sleeping Beauty's castle.

"I say five hostages," Murphy said. She held up her left hand with her fingers fanned out. "But we haven't had direct contact with any of them."

"You mean they may be dead by now." Hightower kept his voice calm, but he could feel the muscles in the back of his neck tighten.

Murphy leaned over and tapped the ash off her cigarette. "It's possible," she said, not looking at him. "But I don't think so—at least not everybody." She turned and looked at Hightower. "And certainly not Susan, if that's worrying you."

"Why not?" Hightower asked. "Wouldn't it be easier for a hostage taker if he didn't have to keep a group of people under control?" He pushed the worst-case interpretation because he wanted Murphy to prove him wrong.

"But this is a ransom deal in a barricade situation," Augustine put in. His voice was surprisingly gentle, almost soothing. "The takers have to be able to prove they've got goods to ransom." He shrugged. "If they can't, they know we'll starve them out or go in with a tank and blast them to hell and gone."

"And Susan is what it's all about," Murphy said. She shrugged one shoulder. "Face it, nobody's going to pay out megabucks for an old woman, or a kid, or a couple of flunkies. But a movie star—well, that's something else."

"Have you asked for proof that she's alive?"

"We're not ready for that," Murphy said. "We're at the waiting stage." She rested the heel of her right foot on the edge of the chair seat. "We're waiting for the takers to get tired, get into fights, and decide they've bitten off more than they can chew. After first contact, we don't *talk* to them this early."

Murphy put her foot on the floor and took a long drag on her cigarette. She blew out the smoke in a thin, ragged stream. "That's hard to accept when some maniac's got a gun to your girlfriend's head or your kid's. A lot of hot dogs—including cops—want us to rush in with guns blazing, shoot down the takers, and drag out the hostages."

She looked at Hightower, brushed the hair away from her face again, and nodded her head. "That's exactly the way to get the hostages killed. Either the takers panic and kill them or the cops kill them by accident."

Hightower started to speak, but he held himself back. What Murphy said made sense, but he wasn't convinced. Sometimes it had to be right to take the risk of going in for the hostages. Besides, you didn't have to go in with guns blazing. You could go in with stealth and cunning.

"Is there anything you can do except wait?"

"We've got the area secured and the takers contained in the building," Murphy said. She held up a finger. "We've got everybody cleared out of the kill zone in front, and we've spotted snipers around so we can make sure the takers stay where they are." She held up two more fingers.

Augustine leaned back on the couch, stretching out his legs. "Usually, about now we start to aggravate them. We turn off the electricity and put them in the dark, or maybe turn on the heat and sweat them. Or we shut off the water, so they don't have anything to drink and the toilets start to stink."

"Enough harassment and even the hard guys crack open like a rotten watermelon." Murphy snapped her fingers. "They get so miserable, they'd do most anything to get out of there."

Augustine sat up straight again. "But we can't play any games with these takers." He shook his head slowly and made a sad face. "They've got complete control of the computers."

Hightower gave him a puzzled look. "What do you mean?"

"A computer program runs everything in those buildings," Murphy said. "And I mean the whole shebang. The doors, lighting, air conditioning, telephones—even the pumps that circulate the water from the storage tanks." She leaned forward and put out her cigarette with short, hard stabs.

"Surely that's not a big problem." Hightower tried to put hesitancy in his voice so he wouldn't sound like a smug doctor educating dumb cops. "You should be able to operate the program from a terminal here at the hospital." He glanced at Augustine. "Has anybody tried that?"

"Just since we got here this evening." Augustine's gentle, soothing voice had acquired a raspy edge of irritation. "I don't know how the takers did it, but they changed the program. Even the people who run the computer operation here can't make the damned thing work."

"We're trying to locate the guys who wrote the software," Murphy broke in. "But they haven't worked here in four or five years, and now nobody knows how to find them. We've got to check the records even to get their names."

Hightower got out of his chair and walked closer to the desk. He bent down and glanced through the window at Johnson Hall. The building looked as peaceful as an illustration on a Christmas card. He tried not to think too much about what might be going on inside. He was getting impatient with all the talk, and he had a strong urge to act—to do something. Still, he was hearing things he wanted to know, even might need to know.

He looked down at Murphy. "You've said 'takers' several times. How many are involved?"

"We think two," Murphy said. "They came in a rented van that we traced to Logan Airport. It was reserved from L.A. and picked up by a Hispanic male who showed a California license and an American Express card in the name of Oscar Gonzales. We figure they flew in from L.A. for the purpose of taking the hostages."

She paused, struck a match, and touched it to the end of another cigarette. She took a drag, then fanned the smoke away from her face with short chopping motions. "Both cards are phony baloney. The Hispanic also used the AE card to pay at the Cambridge Plaza Motel, but the suite was reserved on the phone by somebody calling himself Bruce Case. The Hispanic could have been using that name, but one of the security officers who tried to stop the takeover gave us a Caucasian-male description." She looked over at Hightower. "He was lucky and only got a bullet in the arm. The other officer got killed."

"I heard it on the radio." He nodded his head and paused a moment. "That's terrible." Then the obvious question struck him. "Did you get fingerprints? Either in the motel or the van?"

"Hunh," Augustine said, giving a kind of snort. "We got zip on the rooms, because they took a towel and wiped everything down. On the van, we got a couple of fulls and a few partials. We're running them, and I suspect we're going to learn they match up with the prep crew at Avis." His mouth grew tight and his face wrinkled up in distress. "This is an unusual case."

"We're in what we call a mastermind situation," Murphy said. "We're dealing with a very smart guy who's got everything planned down to a tee." She wagged the two fingers holding her cigarette at him. "And we're not even sure the mastermind is in that building over there. He might be at Oxford University."

"Oxford?" Hightower shook his head. "Are you serious?"

Murphy looked at him with a fixed stare for a moment. The smoke from her cigarette curled upward in a wavy, irregular line. Eventually she nodded, as though she had made up her mind. "Less than an hour ago, we got the ransom demand."

Hightower suddenly felt his breath catch in his chest. "What do they want?" He searched Murphy's face, trying to discover if she was going to continue to make free with her information.

"No reason you shouldn't know," Murphy said. "Half of Los Angeles knows already." She rubbed her forehead, as if she had felt a sudden pain. "They want three million in cash—in hundred-dollar bills packed in three suitcases and delivered to them."

"Three suitcases?" Hightower felt himself starting to get agitated as he tried to piece together everything he had heard. "That sounds like three hostage takers."

"Maybe," Augustine agreed. "But that doesn't mean all three are in Johnson Hall." He rested his calm eyes on Hightower. "The third one could be calling the shots from some other place."

"But, listen," Murphy said. She pointed a finger toward him, as though to keep him in his chair. "The three million is for bus fare. The kicker is that they want *twenty* million dollars transferred by wire to a numbered bank account."

She flipped open the black plastic cover on a yellow legal pad that lay on the desk. "Just a second, and I'll tell you where." She glanced at the notes on the pad. "To the International Bank of Bahrain in Al-Manamah, Bahrain." She pronounced the names syllable by syllable, like a child learning to read.

"The transfer has to be made and the cash delivered to the front door by six in the morning," Augustine said.

Hightower glanced at the large, white-faced clock above the desk. "That's in about six hours. Is that enough time?"

He could feel the muscles around his eyes starting to ache. The cigarette smoke was irritating, and his left eye was watering. He closed the eye and wiped out the tears with his handkerchief. He massaged his temples with his fingertips.

"Probably not," Murphy said.

"So will they kill the hostages?" Hightower could feel blood rushing to his face, and he was suddenly too warm. "Then they couldn't get away, could they?"

"They've got a gimmick," Augustine said.

"We can't tell you any more than that," Murphy cut in

quickly. She caught the ash from her cigarette and dropped it into the saucer. "I think the gimmick is total horseshit anyway."

"Who's supposed to pay the money? Susan can't be that rich."

"Galaxy Films," Murphy said. "They wanted us to get in touch with Kenneth Burke and tell him to talk to the people at Galaxy."

"He's Susan's agent." Hightower suddenly recalled the polite, elegantly dressed Burke and remembered how concerned he had been about Susan. He must be worried sick now.

"The mastermind even gave us the phone number," Murphy said. She lifted her right foot and rested her ankle on her left knee. "And he told us to get Burke to tell Howard Simpson that *Aztec Gold* netted Galaxy seventy-five million and the twenty-three-million ransom isn't a third of that." She looked down and started tying her shoelace. "I guess that's in case Galaxy balks at coming up with the money."

"Mastermind has got it all figured," Augustine said.

"That's right." Murphy pulled the bow tight and put her foot back on the floor. "Burke is also supposed to tell Simpson that Galaxy's going to benefit from the publicity. So then they'll make a lot more on Susan Bradstreet's new movie."

"So what's going to happen?" Hightower asked. The smoke was burning his eyes, and he could feel a headache starting to build at the back of his head. "Are they going to pay the money?"

"They'll pay," Murphy said. "They'll get it back, because we're going to deliver the suitcases ourselves." She smiled. "There's no way we're going to let these guys get away."

She put out the second cigarette with the same violence as the first. "That's the problem in all ransom situations, you know. The taker has got to get away." Her face grew rigid, and she gently tapped her fist against the arm of the chair. "And when he walks out the door, that gives us what we call the possibility of armed interdiction."

"If there's a mastermind, he must have worked that out," Hightower said.

"That's where his gimmick comes in," Augustine said.

"That's where I know he's bluffing." Murphy raised an eyebrow. "And we're going to blow his ass out of the water. Do you remember *Dog Day Afternoon*? The movie with Al Pacino? Right when the guy is driving off in the limo—bang!—they get him with a head shot." She nodded solemnly.

Hightower nodded at Murphy, but he said nothing. Her confidence sounded like pure infantile thinking. She seemed most concerned with killing the hostage takers, but all he wanted was for Susan to get out safely. And the others too, but he didn't know them, so he didn't think about them in an emotional way. He couldn't think about Susan in any other way.

Murphy leaned back in her chair and swiveled around to face him. "Did Susan ever mention the name John Armstrong to you? Or have you ever heard it yourself?"

"I've never heard the name from anybody."

"How about the Association for Psychiatrically Disadvantaged People?" Murphy rocked the chair back and forth in short arcs.

"I've never heard of it either," Hightower said. "It sounds like a civil rights organization."

"It does, doesn't it?" Murphy said. "John Armstrong is the name on the ransom letter, and he claims he's demanding the money on behalf of the association. We've already got people checking, but George has got his doubts." She looked at Augustine. "Tell him, and let's see what a psychiatrist has got to say."

"I think it's a con." Augustine's voice sounded calm and soothing once more. "I think we're supposed to waste time trying to track down Armstrong and this association, and that makes me think there's nobody in Oxford either." He paused. "Maybe somebody sent the E-mail from there, but that doesn't mean it was the mastermind."

"Let me get this right," Hightower said. "You think the takers in Johnson Hall want you to think you're dealing with this Armstrong so you won't try to find out who they are?"

"Right, right," Augustine said, nodding his head vigorously. "Most takers don't give a shit if you know who they are." He shrugged. "But then most takers are either stressed-out ordinary joes or psychos, so they don't even think about it."

"Maybe the takers want to get the money, then go back home," Hightower suggested. "They don't want to be fugitives."

"I can buy that." Augustine nodded, then sat back on the couch. "Yeah, that would figure."

Murphy fixed her eyes on Hightower. "Now let me ask you about Susan Bradstreet. Is she nuts or what?" She stopped and waved her hand as though dismissing what she had just said. "Do you think she'll crack up under the stress?"

"If you mean, will she become psychotic, the answer is no." Hightower hesitated a moment, wondering how much he could say without violating confidentiality. He also didn't want to say anything that would hurt Susan's career if the media picked it up.

"She suffers from an anxiety disorder," he went on. "She could have one or more anxiety attacks and maybe even faint." He shook his head. "Then again, after the initial shock of being taken hostage, she might not have any attacks at all. When some people get flooded by anxiety-producing stimuli, they stop reacting to them."

Murphy picked up the yellow pad on her desk and flipped to a fresh page. "You mean the experience might actually cure her?" She took a ballpoint pen out of the pocket of her shirt and began making notes.

"More accurately, she would unlearn some reactions that produce anxiety." Hightower considered whether he should say anything else about Susan's anxiety attacks and decided that was enough. "She's an intelligent, capable person with a strong personality structure, and I don't think she's likely to go to pieces."

Hightower stood up, so they would know he was on his way out. Murphy seemed to be staring at some place on the floor. He asked, "What's the waiting time?"

"What do you mean?" Murphy lifted her eyes to meet his.

"How long before you do anything? You said you did things in stages."

"I'm not real sure," Murphy said. "We're going to wait a while, then send a message saying we need more time." She bit her thumbnail again. "We'll just play it by ear."

"When would you decide you have to go in?"

"Never," Augustine said immediately.

Murphy started to say something, then hesitated. Finally, she said, "We consider that the action of last resort. That's when all negotiation and communication have come to an end." She smiled. "Then maybe we'll be forced to go in with an assault team and take them out."

"You don't think it's possible that you could sneak somebody into the building who might be able to surprise the takers?" Hightower asked. "Maybe that way the situation could be defused in an hour or so."

"First, you couldn't get anybody into that building," Murphy said. "With those automatic doors, it's shut up tighter than a package of weenies. It's like, vacuum sealed."

"What if somebody could get in?" Hightower pressed. He could hear his voice getting louder. "What if somebody could get past the doors?"

"Then I'd say, second, we still wouldn't do it." Murphy gave him an exasperated look. "Listen, I told you, we use the Chinese-water-torture method. We wait until there's nothing else to do but go in, then we do it."

"But by that time the hostages might be dead." Hightower could feel blood rushing to his face, and he stopped trying to sound polite. "If the ransom isn't delivered or if the takers decide they don't need the hostages to get away, they might kill everybody."

"I can't tell you you're wrong." Murphy seemed almost regretful. "I can just tell you what usually works, and what usually works is what we do." She held out her hands, palms up, in a gesture of helplessness.

"But you said yourself this is not the usual kind of case," Hightower objected. He clenched his teeth to keep himself from shouting.

"I did," Murphy agreed. "But it's not totally different." She wasn't smiling, and her voice had taken on a sharp, defensive tone. "We're not dealing with abductions by creatures from outer space, so we're still going to do it by the book."

Hightower suddenly saw that nothing was going to come of further discussion. If he continued to push the topic, it would continue to go around in the same tight circle. He crossed his arms over his chest and squeezed the muscle of his left arm with his right hand.

The image of Susan came into his mind with the vividness of a snapshot. He felt a gentle wave of tenderness and sadness pass through him. *Susan couldn't die. He wouldn't let her.*

He was going to have to do something he had only fantasized about before. He was going to have to find a way into Johnson Hall and get Susan out.

"Thanks for talking to me," Hightower said. "I'd better go visit with Don a little."

"These things usually work out," Murphy said. "If you don't push too hard."

28

Susan found it depressing to sit in the semidarkness of the living room, but she knew it would be foolish to object. Cyberwolf himself had turned off all the table lamps. The only illumination left was the yellow-green light filtering down from the fluorescent fixtures high overhead.

"I want everybody in front of the TV," Cyberwolf had said. "No news shows, but anything else is okay—religion, sitcoms, movies, whatever you want."

Susan thought she understood his plan. He wanted to distract them and reduce the possibility of conflict. He was using TV as a kind of social tranquilizer.

"You heard the man," Whip said, sounding like a drill sergeant. "Move in some extra chairs, and we'll have us a little TV party."

With Whip and Cyberwolf standing back and watching, they had moved a few additional chairs into position. Susan helped Mrs. Rostov drag up a Boston rocker with a cushioned back, and Tim turned around a love seat. Whip sat at one end of the semicircle next to Tim. Susan sat at the opposite end, but Cyberwolf didn't sit at all. Instead, he strolled back and forth behind them, like a prison guard keeping an eye on the convicts.

"You get cable here?" Whip slid the strap of the automatic pistol off his shoulder, but he held the gun cradled in his lap.

"Sure," Tim said. He had stationed himself in front of the group, ready to turn on the TV. "We even get the science fiction channel. Is it okay to take a look?"

"I guess so," Whip said.

"Well, it's not all right with me," Mrs. Rostov said. "Let's see something with good characters." She turned to Susan. "What about you, Miss Bradstreet?"

"I don't really care."

"Turn on the TV and put it on the fucking channel." Whip sounded impatient. "Just ignore the old bitch."

"That's rude," Mrs. Rostov said. "You don't have to talk to me like that."

"Yeah, but I like it a whole lot." Whip leaned forward and looked past Tim's chair to where Mrs. Rostov was sitting, staring straight ahead. Susan caught a glimpse of his dangling death's-head earring and his dead eyes.

"Now shut the fuck up, old woman, or you're going to get your brains splattered on the floor."

Tim stood immobile, his face a sickly white. He glanced at Mrs. Rostov, then at Whip. He then quickly turned on the TV and changed the channel to thirty-eight.

Susan recognized Walter Pidgeon immediately. He was standing in the living room of a 1950s version of a futuristic house, and with him was a tall, dark-haired man dressed in a baggy gray uniform. "I tried to warn you away from this planet," Walter Pidgeon was saying.

"It's *Forbidden Planet*," Tim said. "This is Dr. Morbius, and that's Commander John Adams." He tapped Walter Pidgeon and the dark-haired man in turn.

"If I want any shit out of you, I'll knock it out," Whip said. "Now sit down and shut your goddamned mouth."

"Whip," Cyberwolf said curtly. "Remember your manners."

Whip looked over his shoulder and stared at Cyberwolf for a moment, his face unreadable. Then he turned around without saying anything.

Susan was suddenly glad Cyberwolf had made them watch television. It would minimize the friction and reduce the chances of any of them getting killed. Whip was obviously a psychopath, ready to explode. She was particularly glad Meg was still in her room so Whip wouldn't have a chance to provoke her and maybe end up shooting her.

When she and Cyberwolf had come back, she had insisted on going into Meg's room to check on her. She thought he might refuse to let her, but he didn't. He seemed surprisingly ready to do what he could to please her. That was useful, but it was also frightening. He seemed to be trying to draw her closer to him.

Meg was conscious when Susan saw her, but she was weak and her forehead was hot to the touch. Susan took a look at Meg's foot. Somebody, presumably Backup, had wrapped torn strips of a white pillowcase around it. The splotches of blood on the dressing were dark brown, which suggested that the stump of Meg's toe was no longer bleeding.

"I'm sorry, Susan," Meg had told her. Her voice was thick and choked. "Some bodyguard." Her eyes brimmed over with tears, and she wiped her cheeks with a corner of the sheet.

"You were very brave," Susan assured her. "You tackled Whip with your bare hands."

"With my pistol, I could've put a bullet between his eyes."

"Don't think about it," Susan said. "We're going to get out of here, but right now you've got to rest."

Meg was shivering, despite her fever, and Susan covered her with a heavy blanket from the chest of drawers. She wanted to give her some aspirin, but all drugs were kept out of the hands of patients. The best she could do was wet a towel in cold water, wring it out, and put it on Meg's forehead.

"That feels nice," Meg said. Her voice was indistinct, and she seemed to be drifting off to sleep.

Susan had wanted to sit with her, but Cyberwolf had given her only ten minutes. He hadn't allowed them to be alone, either. Backup was guarding Meg, and he didn't leave. He sat by the window with his strange gun on the floor beside him. He stroked his black mustache with his index finger, saying nothing but watching everything she did.

"Time's up," he told her. "Cyber said ten minutes, and that's it. You got to go back in the other room now."

Meg was asleep, and Susan made no objection. She was committed to doing whatever she could to escape, and leaving when she was told was a crucial element in the only plan she had been able to come up with.

If she did everything she was told, Cyberwolf would probably allow her to visit Meg again. She would do that two or three times, and he would get used to seeing her moving from one room to the other. Then on the next trip, she would walk toward Meg's room, but quickly duck into the hall.

If she was lucky, she would have ten or fifteen minutes before anybody missed her. Cyberwolf would think she was in Meg's room, and Backup would think she was in the living room. That might be enough time to figure out how to use the computer to open the front door. She had watched Joe Ling do it.

If she got caught, she would just have to try something else. She felt sure they wouldn't kill her until they got the ransom money. She had been able to switch the clear plastic bracelet from her sock into her front pocket, and maybe she could do something with it.

In another ten minutes, she could ask Cyberwolf to let her see Meg again, and she was starting to get nervous. She could feel her heart pulsing in her ears, and her hands were trembling. She forced herself to pay attention to the TV screen.

It was night, and Commander Adams and his crew were standing outside their saucer-shaped ship in the desert. Suddenly, their radar showed that something large had broken through their defensive perimeter—something invisible.

All at once, the stillness of the night was shattered as they began to shoot at the radar target. Their energy-beam weapons produced sharp crackling noises, and when the red and blue streaks hit the intruder, they revealed the shifting outline of a giant fanged beast with slanting yellow eyes. A hollow howling sound came from the creature's mouth.

"Forces from the id," Tim said. He was leaning forward in his chair, and he seemed to be talking to himself.

"What do you mean?" Whip asked. He seemed as wrapped up in the movie as Tim.

"Dr. Morbius is using the machine left behind by the people who used to inhabit that planet," Tim said. "It taps into the mind and transforms forbidden thoughts into destructive energy. He wants them all dead."

Susan glanced behind her and noticed that Cyberwolf had slipped away while they were watching the attack.

Then she saw him coming through the arch from the hall. He must have been doing something with the computer.

"Any response?" Whip called out.

"Nope." Cyberwolf sounded unworried, almost casual. He walked to where Whip was sitting and stood behind his chair.

"How do we know they got the message?" Whip swiveled around and hooked an elbow over the back of the chair.

"There's no way they couldn't have gotten it."

"You sure of that?" Whip asked suspiciously. "I don't trust all this computer shit."

Susan saw Cyberwolf nod slightly. His face was impassive, but his strange amber eyes were hard and fixed, as though daring Whip to doubt him.

"Then they've got to be fucking us over," Whip said. "We're going to have to do something to show we're serious."

"If we have to," Cyberwolf said. "But right now, try to keep from acting the way they expect us to."

"What do you mean?" Whip asked.

"They want to rattle our cage." Cyberwolf's smile was condescending. "They think we're going to get worried and panicky. Maybe even start fighting about what we should do."

"What should we do?"

"Wait," Cyberwolf said. He raised his hand with the palm outward, as if stopping traffic. "We've made our demands and given them a deadline."

Mrs. Rostov spoke up. "You're all going to go to jail." She turned to look at Cyberwolf. "My daughter has a high position in the United States government, and she won't rest until you're behind bars where you belong."

Susan saw Whip lean out of his chair and stretch his arm past Tim. Suddenly, she heard a flat cracking noise. Mrs. Rostov gave a cry of pain, grabbed at her cheek, and fell to the side. Only then did Susan realize that Whip had slapped Mrs. Rostov in the face.

"You won't listen, will you?" Whip's voice was cold. "When I say shut the fuck up, I mean shut the fuck up."

Susan expected Cyberwolf to tell Whip to leave Mrs. Rostov alone, but he said nothing. He seemed to be watching the TV screen, oblivious to everything that was taking place around him.

Susan knelt on the floor by Mrs. Rostov's rocking chair. She took a tissue out of her pocket, unfolded it, and put it in Mrs. Rostov's hand. The old woman had a hand over her eyes and was sobbing quietly. The left side of her face was a livid red. Her thin shoulders were shaking uncontrollably. Susan rubbed her back and patted her gently.

Tim reached across and put his hand around one of Mrs. Rostov's wrists. He moved cautiously, as though afraid that by comforting her he would bring trouble on himself. Susan could see the fear in his eyes, and she wanted to tell him that she admired him for behaving so bravely. But she didn't want to do anything to provoke Whip. His next display of brutality might be worse.

Mrs. Rostov's shoulders stopped shaking, and she dabbed at her eyes with the tissue. She began rocking gently in her chair.

"Are you okay now?" Susan asked.

Mrs. Rostov said nothing, but she nodded her head slightly. Her eyes were rimmed with red, and her cheeks quivered.

Susan sat back down and looked at the TV screen. Commander Adams and Alterra, Dr. Morbius's daughter, were on a shuttle car speeding through a long tunnel. They were going to the underground city containing the machinery that had been operating the entire planet, untended, for two thousand centuries. Adams had realized that the planet's inhabitants had destroyed themselves by hooking up their minds to the machines. The machines transformed unconscious desires into actual monsters, and he was going to have to destroy them to save Alterra and his crew.

Susan felt a tap on her shoulder. Startled, she jerked her

head around. It was Cyberwolf, bending over her with his hands on his knees to be nearer to her level.

"Could you come over and talk to me a moment?" He was so polite he seemed almost obsequious.

Her initial impulse was to refuse, but then she realized it might help to spend some time with him. If he started to trust her a little, she might get a better opportunity to make her escape.

29

Hightower walked into the patient-room that had been turned into a temporary office. Lindsley was sitting at the student desk sorting through a stack of papers. He glanced at Hightower, then got up and shut the door.

"You look busy," Hightower said.

"Faxes from LAPD and New Scotland Yard." Lindsley waved toward the desk. "No Armstrong, no Association for Psychiatrically Disadvantaged People, and no suspects that fit our descriptions." He leaned his back against the door. "Did Kathy treat you right?"

"She gave me a good sense of what's going on."

"Maybe so," Lindsley said in a skeptical tone. "Take a seat for a minute." He sat at the desk and pointed to an upholstered chair next to it.

"I'm in a big hurry," Hightower said, not moving. "But I want you to show me a floor plan of Johnson Hall. I need to know the layout so I can—"

"Don't tell me." Lindsley cut him off. He picked up a yellow pencil and rolled it awkwardly between his stiff index finger and his thumb, then raised his eyes and gave Hightower a long, steady look. "I know why I'd need to see a floor plan if I were in your situation." He dropped the pencil and held up his hand with the palm turned toward Hightower. "But I'm the police, so don't let me know about anything that I might have to stop you from doing." He nodded at Hightower. "Now just sit down and let me do some talking. Okay?"

Hightower caught a sharp edge of urgency in Lindsley's voice. "All right." He sat down, then turned his head slightly so that he could focus on Lindsley with his right eye.

"Kathy told you about the ransom demand and the deadline?"

"Right," Hightower said, nodding.

"Did she mention anything about the Chernobyl program or the possibility of a meltdown?"

"No." Hightower shook his head.

"I didn't think she would." Lindsley puckered his mouth as if tasting something bad. "She told you what she wanted you to leak to the media."

"She specifically asked me not to talk to the media."

"I'm sure she did." Lindsley shrugged his shoulders and smiled slightly. "But why do you suppose she was so happy to talk to you?"

"She said it was a favor to you."

"Yeah, well, I did ask her, but I expected her to say no," Lindsley said. "Police command operations aren't usually real anxious to give detailed briefings to civilians." He tightened his lips into a small smile.

"Couldn't she just hold a press conference?"

"I'm sure she'd like to, then she could tell them how smart she's being. But if she tried it, the chief would come down on her like a load of lumber." Lindsley raised his eyebrows, making his dark brown eyes look enormous. "So I'm willing to bet she couldn't wait to talk to you, so you could get her story out."

"What do you mean, get her story out? What story?"

Lindsley picked up the pencil again and gently drummed it against his cheek. "This is a big case. It's the biggest Kathy will ever get. So if she screws it up, she screws up the rest of her career." He shook his head. "Nobody will make her chief here or in Miami or anyplace where they watch TV, and she's not going to be happy frozen in rank for another ten or twelve years."

"Are you saying she's not handling this right?" Hightower glanced nervously at the door to make sure it was closed.

Lindsley hesitated, clearly trying to choose the right words. "Let's just say she's handling it by the book. She's going to stick to the standard routine for dealing with hostages. If something goes wrong and the situation blows up in her face, nobody can fault her." He nodded and tapped the pencil eraser on his teeth. "That's the inside story she wanted you to put out—that it's all by the book."

"But you don't think the routine fits the situation?" His own doubts made him ready to agree with Lindsley.

"About like diapers on a dog," Lindsley said in a disgusted tone. He threw the pencil back on the desk. "She's completely underestimating the seriousness of the situation, because she doesn't take the meltdown threat seriously."

"Wait a minute." Hightower was starting to feel frustrated. "That's the second time you've mentioned meltdown, and I still don't know what the hell you're talking about."

"It's in the ransom letter. The guy who calls himself Armstrong isn't just threatening to kill the hostages if we don't deliver on the money. He's got some more extensive plans."

"What else?"

"He wants to make sure the takers can get away," Lindsley said. "So he's demanding a helicopter to shuttle them from here to Logan Airport, then a plane and a pilot to fly them to Cuba."

"Murphy told me that getting away was always the weak point for any hostage taker."

"She's right," Lindsley said. "But this guy has got it all worked out perfectly—this Chernobyl program gives them a free ticket out." His eyes hardened, and his expression turned angry.

"So what's the Chernobyl program?"

Lindsley shook his head. "I can't even imagine the technical details, but it's a computer program that totally overloads a communications network so that it can't function anymore. It melts down the system—that's why it's called a Chernobyl program."

"I'm missing your point," Hightower said.

"Let me put it bluntly," Lindsley said. "Armstrong—or whoever the mastermind is—says he's written a program that will destroy the New York–New England Telephone Network—NYNEX."

Hightower nodded. "So if he doesn't get the helicopter and airplane, he'll activate his program."

"Right, except he says the program is already running. So to stop it, he's got to send a canceling command."

"If he doesn't send the command, then NYNEX will shut down?"

"You've got it," Lindsley said. "And that completely ties our hands." He tightened his hands into fists. "If we kill one of the takers or maybe even capture him, the mastermind might not cancel the program." He gently hammered a fist on the desk. "And if we happen to kill the mastermind, we're really screwed, because then there's nobody to initiate the cancel command."

"So what would that mean?" Hightower felt almost dazed. "What would happen if NYNEX shut down?"

"It would be a total disaster," Lindsley said. "It would be so big, I can't even guess at some of the things that would happen." He pushed his chair away from the tiny desk. "Look, NYNEX has twelve million customers, so first off we lose all phone service. You can't dial nine-one-one and say you're having a heart attack or that the Hancock Tower is burning down. You can't call a cop and say somebody's shooting at you or smashing out the window at Shreve's."

"So a lot of people will die who might have been saved, and a lot of crimes will take place."

"Cops might as well stay home and hide under the bed, for all they can do." Lindsley's face went slack for a mo-

ment, and he spread out his hands in a gesture of helplessness. "But that's just the beginning. Because, you
know, that twelve million isn't just me and my cousin
Jimmy. It includes all the hookups between computers in
the entire region."

He nodded. "That's where the big disasters come in."
He held up his left hand and touched the tip of his ring
finger. "Consider this: the air-traffic controllers in thirty-
seven airports from here to Bangor and down to Manhat-
tan and New Jersey are suddenly going to lose their
computers. Are planes going to crash?" He gave Hightower an exaggeratedly quizzical look. "You bet your ass
they are, and some of them could kill hundreds of people."

He touched another finger. "The power grids supplying
electricity throughout the Northeast depend on a computer network to direct the distribution and tell them
when they need to shed load." He threw up his hands.
"They're all going to blow, and then there'll be a complete blackout over the whole East Coast."

The seriousness of what Lindsley was telling him was
beginning to sink in.

"And all the hospitals that don't have backup genera-
tors are going to lose patients in surgery, the emergency
rooms, and the ICUs," Lindsley added.

"People will die," Lindsley said flatly. "Lots of people
will die."

"Wait a minute." Hightower's voice was strained, and
his chest was so tight that it was hard to talk. "When is
this supposed to take place?"

"At six tomorrow morning." Lindsley gave him a
searching look. "What's the matter?"

"My parents are on a plane that's landing in New York
at three-thirty."

"You're lucky, then." Lindsley gave him a bleak smile.
"They should be on the ground before anything is likely
to happen."

"Right," Hightower said. His muscles relaxed, and he

took a deep breath. "You've already talked to computer experts?"

"I had a discussion with three computer scientists from Harvard right before you arrived," Lindsley said. "Before that, I met with two people from NYNEX. They all agree it's possible *in principle* to write a Chernobyl program and shut down the system, but nobody thinks it's likely."

"Because it would be hard to do?"

"They all think it verges on the impossible," Lindsley said. "But they also say that NYNEX regularly sweeps the system, just for the purpose of picking up programs that don't belong there."

"But what if the program isn't in the system? What if it's in some other computer, just waiting for the right time to be injected into NYNEX?"

"They don't see that as a serious possibility," Lindsley said. "They think their security is so tight that nobody could get deep enough into the system to do any significant damage."

"You obviously take the threat of meltdown seriously," Hightower said. "How come Murphy doesn't?"

"A couple of reasons." Lindsley leaned back in the small chair. "First, the computer scientists, including those from NYNEX, don't take it seriously."

"So she's got the experts on her side," Hightower said.

"Right," Lindsley acknowledged. "The second reason is that she doesn't believe the E-mail was actually sent from Oxford. She doesn't think Armstrong is a real person, and she doesn't think the Association for Psychiatrically Disadvantaged People is a real organization." He frowned and tapped the stack of paper on the desk. "Since we can't confirm anything, she thinks the whole business is a con from beginning to end."

"And that makes her think the Chernobyl program is a con?"

"Exactly," Lindsley said. "And here I am, dumb as a stump when it comes to computers, and I believe it's real."

"Including the part about Oxford and Armstrong?"

"No, not that," Lindsley said. "That feels like a con, and the experts say it would be easy to route E-mail from someplace else to Oxford." He pursed his lips and shrugged. "I don't have any good reason to believe the rest of it's not a con too—but I don't."

Hightower nodded. He could see Kathy Murphy's point. She was relying on expert advice and acting prudently. Lindsley didn't seem to be relying on anything but intuition, on nothing more than a hunch. Yet it was hard to believe that Lindsley wasn't right. Or was that just his fear for Susan speaking?

No, not really. Something about the ransom demand was unusual, something was hard to grasp. But what?

Suddenly, Hightower glimpsed what it was. So far as the likelihood of truth was concerned, there was an almost inverse relation between the Oxford part of the E-mail demand and the part threatening a meltdown of NYNEX.

"I can give you a reason," Hightower said. The idea wasn't quite clear in his mind, and he hesitated a moment, trying to work through the logic. Then he really did see it. "I think the very fact that the Oxford address is a con indicates that the Chernobyl program isn't."

"You'll have to explain that," Lindsley said. He wrinkled up his face and shook his head.

"The con was supposed to make you think that somebody—Armstrong—was in Oxford running the show," Hightower said. "But if it's a con, chances are that whoever masterminded the crime is in Johnson Hall with the hostages. The Oxford part was just a case of misdirection, a kind of computer sleight of hand."

"Yeah, yeah." Lindsley nodded his head. "So what?" He looked puzzled.

"So Armstrong—or whatever his name is—is going to be very interested in escaping," Hightower said. "And if he knew enough about computers to take control of the Rush computers and to pull the Oxford trick, that's persuasive evidence that he knows enough to write a Chernobyl program."

"So the Chernobyl program is his only guarantee that he makes it out safely." Lindsley vigorously nodded his head. "I believe you've got it, Doctor." Lindsley smiled, then all at once his face clouded. "But that's not proof. Even if it's reasonable, I can't convince anybody of it."

"Probably not," Hightower admitted. "But you've already got the NYNEX people searching the system for a Chernobyl program."

"Right," Lindsley acknowledged. "But I think your idea that the program is sitting someplace in a computer just waiting to inject itself into NYNEX is more likely." He held up a finger. "This mastermind is too cautious to risk NYNEX locating the Chernobyl program while he's still depending on it."

"Maybe, but I don't think you can do anything about that."

"Yeah, but here's what I can do." Lindsley hesitated a moment, frowning, then his face noticeably brightened. "I can get the L.A. detectives to step up the effort to identify the takers. If we can find out who the mastermind is, we might be able to locate his computer and shut the damned thing off."

"Are you going to tell them what's at stake?"

"I'm going to tell them what *I* think is at stake," Lindsley said. "But I'm going to keep Murphy's name out of it." He tightened his lips. "That program is ticking like a time bomb."

Hightower nodded, but his mind was elsewhere. Somewhere at the edge of his awareness was another implication of the Chernobyl program that Lindsley hadn't mentioned. What could it be? He glanced idly around the room. The patient-occupant had been forced out in a hurry, and his possessions were still in place. A bookcase half filled with paperbacks stood by the head of the narrow bed, and a red baseball cap hung from a metal clothes hook screwed to the wall.

A large poster pinned above the desk showed the sun as a dark orange ball sinking below a smoky horizon. The horizon was at the edge of a bleak urban landscape of collapsed buildings and smoldering fires. BEFORE IT'S TOO LATE was printed in heavy black letters across the top.

Hightower was sure that the idea hovering at the edge of his awareness didn't have anything to do with the mass destruction meltdown would produce. He was thinking about some result on a smaller scale, something that had to do with Susan. He was starting to feel frustrated and angry, because the pieces weren't falling into place.

Then he saw the implication with complete clarity. Something caught in his chest, and his eyes went out of focus. He forced himself to take a deep breath and let it out slowly. Then he was able to talk.

"Once the takers have the ransom money, they don't need to keep the hostages alive." Hightower's voice was breaking, and he cleared his throat. "The mastermind has a two-step plan. He'll use the hostages to get the money, then use the Chernobyl program to get away."

Lindsley stared at him hard for a moment. His dark eyes seemed blank, as though he had suddenly gone blind. "That's right," he said softly. "I should have thought of that. The hostages will become a liability, because they're the only ones able to identify all the takers."

"They'll kill them," Hightower said in a flat voice. He had divided himself from the present and was hardly aware that Lindsley was sitting beside him. If he was going to do anything to help Susan, it had to be now. Time was running out, and there might not be any "later."

He felt a physical urge to get up and run out of Lindsley's office. But run where? Johnson Hall was sealed tight by the computer-controlled steel doors. He stood up.

"I need to see the plans for Johnson Hall."

"Kathy Murphy's got the only set." Lindsley shook his head. "She's not showing them to anybody who doesn't have a need to know. So far that's just her and Augustine."

"How about members of the assault team?"

Lindsley gave him a grim smile. "We don't use assault teams."

"Not even when negotiations have broken down and the hostages are almost sure to be killed?" Hightower bent forward and looked into Lindsley's face. "That's when Murphy said you used them."

"If Murphy said it, I wouldn't call her a liar in public," Lindsley said. "But statistics show that assault teams produce a net loss of innocent life—civilians plus cops. So I can promise you it's going to be a cold day in hell before we send one in." He shrugged. "That's what I mean about doing things by the book."

"Goddamn it." Hightower spoke softly, but he put his bitter feelings into the words. Murphy hadn't actually said she would use an assault team. When he had asked when they would go into the building, she had danced around his question, leaving him to draw the conclusion he wanted to.

Suddenly he felt tired and depressed. He rubbed his left eye and wished he could see better. He had wanted to believe that eventually the police would storm Johnson Hall and try to rescue Susan. Murphy herself had held out little hope of that, and now here was Lindsley saying there was no hope.

"That's why I'm talking to you this way," Lindsley said. His face was screwed up tight. "We're facing destruction on a massive scale, and I can't get Kathy Murphy to take it seriously." He shook his head in disgust. "If things were different, I'd say leave everything to the police."

Hightower took a deep breath, then sighed. "Can you at least tell me what the layout of the building is?"

"I don't know myself. But this will help: one of the people in the computer center told me that the whole set of plans is stored in an MIT computer."

"That doesn't do me any good." He sighed again. "Maybe if I had a week, I could get somebody to find the plan for me."

"You can get somebody right now. I've already called up Pete Salter and asked him to meet you at what he calls his image lab."

"You called before you'd even talked to me?" He looked at Lindsley in surprise.

"Hey, I'm a detective," Lindsley said. His expression was mock-serious. "I know what kind of surgeon you are, and I know you think the way to solve problems is to jump into the middle of them and start swinging." He held up his right hand. "If you weren't like that, I'd be showing you my steel claw right now."

"Can Salter get the plans?"

"He can do better than that. He can damned near get the whole building." Lindsley passed a slip of white paper to Hightower. "Here's his address."

Hightower glanced at the paper, saw that he could read it, then stuffed it in his shirt pocket. He got up to leave.

"One more thing," Lindsley said. He reached behind him and picked up a leather briefcase. He clicked open the brass clasp and took out what looked like a thin black plastic box. It was hardly larger than a deck of cards and had a raised metal stud at one end. He handed the box to Hightower. "Take this with you."

"What is it?" Hightower weighed it in his hand and found that it felt solid but wasn't particularly heavy.

"It's a cell phone. Flip it open."

Hightower pulled on the end with the stud, and the phone unfolded like a clamshell. A keypad with numbers too small for him to read was on the lower part. When he tugged on the metal stud, a stubby antenna slid out.

"I want you to stay in touch with me," Lindsley said. "I doubt if I can help you, but you might be able to feed me some information."

"I can't read these numbers without a magnifying glass."

"You don't have to," Lindsley said. "The phone's got a voice chip, and all you've got to do is say my first name twice right into the receiver." He pointed at the phone. "Try it."

Hightower held the phone up to his ear and said "Don, Don" in a clear voice. Immediately, a sharp buzzing sound came from the leather briefcase. Lindsley reached inside and took out another phone. He flipped it open, pushed on something, then closed it again.

Lindsley slipped the phone into the side pocket of his seersucker jacket. "From now on, I'm going to be carrying this with me," he said.

30

Susan followed Cyberwolf to a part of the room where two armchairs were pulled up to a coffee table. She sat down without being told, and he took the chair at her right.

He looked at her for a long time, as though studying her face. "I've seen your movies," he said at last. He quickly turned his eyes away from her. "If you don't mind my saying so, you're not just beautiful, you're talented." He looked back at her, as though checking her reaction. "I admire that."

"You've got a funny way of showing it."

"It's nothing personal," he said. He smiled shyly, inviting her to say that she understood. When she didn't respond, his faced turned serious again. In a sympathetic voice he said, "I felt very sorry about the way Bryan treated you."

"Bryan!" Susan was so astonished she almost shouted the name. "Bryan Forbes? How do you know Bryan?" She was completely puzzled, and for a moment she even wondered if Bryan himself had something to do with what was happening.

"I know everything about you." Cyberwolf's smile broadened and turned sly. "I know about Bryan stealing money from you and about the tuition you pay for Meg's son at that school in . . . is it Arizona?" He looked smug. "I know you worry that your father might not be completely recovered from his heart attack."

"Have I met you?" Susan stared at him, dumbfounded that he should be familiar with details of her life that she had talked about with only a few close friends. She studied his face, peering through the dim light, trying to place him.

Then she suddenly realized that she had seen him before. Not him, really, but a *picture* of him.

"Your hair looks different, but you're the man in the photograph," she said with certainty. "The one at the Chinese Theater." She leaned toward him. "You're standing next to me, wearing a tuxedo, and you've got your arm around me. But I don't remember meeting you." She shook her head. "I've stared and stared at that picture."

"I hoped you would." Cyberwolf's voice was quiet and sincere. "That was the only way I could get you to think about me." He suddenly stopped talking, as though he had said more than he had intended.

He got up and knelt beside her. He glanced up at her face, then leaned forward and rested his forehead on the cushion beside her leg. She moved to the side, trying to avoid touching him.

"Why did you want me to think about you?" She felt strange talking to him when she couldn't see his face. She glanced down and noticed that the left pocket of his blazer was bulging open.

"Because I think about you so much." His voice was muffled. "I can't go five minutes without having some fantasy about you."

"I see." She tried to sound neutral and not reveal the shock she felt. She began to realize that it was no accident that Cyberwolf had selected her as a victim. He undoubtedly wanted the ransom money, but he obviously also wanted her. He had come for *her,* and even if the money was paid, he wouldn't let her go. A shiver ran through her. Getting away—escaping—seemed even more important than before.

"The picture of us was clever, don't you think?" Cyberwolf sounded surprisingly direct, like a child asking for praise. He raised his head and glanced up at her. He smiled, then put his head down again.

She gently shifted her weight to her left hip, then pulled the plastic wristband from her right pocket. Doing her best not to move her left leg and disturb Cyberwolf, she bent forward and slipped the band into the pocket of his blazer. She then deliberately moved her leg, as if changing to a more comfortable position.

"How did you do it?" she asked. "Sit up and talk to me."

Cyberwolf raised his head and looked at her with his amber eyes opened wide. "I'm enjoying being close to you." He sounded hurt. "I'm not pawing you or anything."

"But I want to see you when I talk to you."

"If that's what you want," he said, smiling gently. He got up and sat back down in the other chair.

"So how did you get the picture you sent me?"

"By transforming reality." Cyberwolf laughed softly. "I used a machine called the Pix-Wizard to digitize the photograph of you at the opening, one of a man in a tux, and another of my face. I manipulated the images and edited them a little, then printed out the result."

"And it looks just like an original photograph?" Susan was surprised. "Not like it's been doctored?"

"It's perfect," Cyberwolf said. "I think of it as a picture of a possible world."

Then Whip suddenly shouted, "Hey, Charlie. I need to get into the kitchen."

Cyberwolf looked annoyed at being interrupted. He stood up and faced Whip across the width of the room. "What for?"

"To get something to eat. I'm hungry. I'm going to shoot off the lock."

"Don't do that. I've got some keys, and I'm sure one of them is a master."

Cyberwolf and Whip walked toward each other. She had watched Cyberwolf put the yellow plastic disc with the keys into the pocket of his blazer. But which pocket was it? Was he going to reach in and find the bracelet? She held her breath, trying to remember how he had stood by the desk. She was almost sure he had put the disc in his right pocket.

Cyberwolf patted both pockets, then reached into the right one and took out the keys. As he handed them to Whip, she finally let out her breath.

"Take the other two with you," Cyberwolf said. "I'm busy."

"I can see what you're busy doing." Whip glanced at Susan and gave a knowing smile. The corner of his lip curled up in a sneer. "Maybe the old woman knows how to cook."

Cyberwolf turned abruptly away without saying anything.

"What was I telling you?" he asked Susan. He sat back down and gave her a quizzical look.

"Something about possible worlds."

"Oh, right. I was saying that the Pix-Wizard makes pictures of possible worlds." He spoke earnestly, and his eyes looked into hers. In the dimness they seemed almost to glow. "What we experience as actual is not the way things necessarily are. There's a possible world in which you and I are . . . very close." He looked up at the ceiling, not meeting her eyes.

"I guess so," Susan agreed. "But I don't get the point."

"I want us to inhabit that possible world." He hesitated a moment, searching for words. "I want to make it an actual world, one where you and I . . ." He hesitated again, running out of words. "Where you and I could become . . ."

He shook his head violently. "I'm not expressing myself well. I get nervous when I talk to you, and I can't come out and tell you what I really mean."

"I think I understand what you're getting at." She made a point of sounding remote and cold.

Suddenly, a chattering burst of gunfire came from the direction of the kitchen. Then almost simultaneously, a high-pitched wailing scream followed.

"Oh, my God!" Susan exclaimed.

Cyberwolf said nothing, but he was immediately out of his chair and running toward the dining room. Susan hesitated, then hurried behind him. Running down a narrow aisle, she hit her hip painfully against the back of a sofa, but she didn't stop.

The door to the kitchen was wide open, but she resisted the inclination to rush inside. She stood with her back against the dining room wall and cautiously peered around the corner.

Whip was holding a white kitchen towel up to his face and pointing his automatic pistol toward the ceiling. A gallon can of peanut butter with a red-and-yellow label stood on the white countertop. Cyberwolf was beside Whip. Both had their backs to her and their heads bowed to stare at something on the floor. The air was filled with the odor of burned gunpowder and a sickly sweet stench.

"The fucking old bitch stabbed me," Whip said. His voice seemed curiously high and light, as though he was either scared or excited. "She cut me right along my cheek." He held out the bloody towel and turned his head slightly so Cyberwolf could see the wound. "She got the knife out of a drawer, but I sure as shit didn't see her."

Susan looked down and saw Mrs. Rostov sprawled on the floor. She was on her back with her hands thrown to the sides and a long-bladed chef's knife beside her. She lay absolutely still, and her face was a mask of blood. A pool of blood in the shape of a pork chop had already formed under her head.

Susan leaned back and pushed her shoulders hard against the wall. She allowed the air in her lungs to escape slowly. Then she made herself breathe in and out in a deliberate way until the dizziness she felt disappeared.

Mrs. Rostov was dead, but where was Tim? She looked around the corner again and frantically searched the room for him. To her relief, she spotted him standing at the right, slumped against the institutional-sized refrigerator. He was staring at Mrs. Rostov's body with a look of horror.

She poised herself to rush into the kitchen and wrap her arms around him. Then she suddenly realized that while everybody was distracted, she had a chance to get away. She was sure Cyberwolf hadn't seen her following him. So far as he knew, she was still sitting in the living room. Tim was upset, but she could do him more good by escaping than by comforting him.

"I wish you hadn't killed her," Cyberwolf said.

"She was fucking going to kill me." Whip's voice was angry.

"You've just thrown away one of our bargaining chips. We can't buy anything with a dead body."

Staying close to the wall, Susan crossed the dining room and stepped through the arch into the hall. She began walking quickly toward the computer. She could feel her heart beating rapidly, and at every moment she expected to hear someone shouting for her to stop.

The computer seemed an immense distance away, and she wanted to run. But running would make too much noise, so she compromised by breaking into a jog.

When she reached the desk, she went behind it, but she kept her eyes turned away from Joe Ling's body. *Just focus on what you've got to do.* The computer's power switch was on the front, and she pushed it toward the small vertical line that indicated the "On" position.

Only the switch wouldn't move. She pushed even harder, but when it still wouldn't move, she realized something was wrong. She examined the lock on the right side of the computer. The small slit in the rotating cylinder was lined up with an icon depicting a closed padlock.

She squeezed her hand into a fist and pounded it softly on the top of the desk. *Goddamn it, goddamn it, goddamn it,* she said under her breath. She remembered the keys on the yellow disc, the one Cyberwolf had put in his pocket. He must have locked the computer.

She glanced nervously up the hall. So far it was still empty. *Not that it makes any difference,* she thought bitterly. What could she do now except sneak back to the living room? She could wait for a while, but what was the point? Either Whip or Cyberwolf would just march her back at gunpoint.

In desperation she looked behind the computer, wondering if she could find some way to bypass the lock. She tugged on one of the black cables, but she couldn't move it. She moved the computer back a few inches to free up some slack.

As she glanced down, she saw, set flush with the floor, the metal-edged panel the cables led out of. She had seen Cyberwolf lift it up, and she suddenly remembered that under the panel was an entrance to the distribution channel the cables ran through.

She stuck a finger into the round hole at the end of the panel. She tugged, and the panel moved a little, but it didn't come up. The metal frame was covered with a veneer of the same green marble that was on the floor, and the piece was heavier than she had expected. She jammed three fingers into the hole and yanked hard. The panel popped loose, exposing an opening about three feet long. As the panel came away, she noticed that blood from Joe Ling's body had stained one of the metal edges. She leaned the panel against the wall, trying not to get blood on her hands.

She bent over and looked inside the galvanized sheet-metal channel. It had to lead someplace where there was another panel she could use for an exit. The research tower seemed most likely. If she could worm her way down the channel, she could head in that direction. Once she got into the tower, she would surely be able to find a way out.

She started to step into the opening, then hesitated. Could she squeeze inside? Even if she could, was the channel large enough for her to crawl through? It was hardly more than twenty inches wide and maybe twelve or fourteen inches deep. And what if she got stuck somewhere under the floor? No one would know where she was, and she would lie there until she died of thirst.

As she gave a nervous glance up the hall once more, she realized that she didn't have a choice. She either had to risk getting stuck in the channel or let herself be killed by Cyberwolf. Maybe he wouldn't simply kill her either. The way he knew so much about her and wanted to get close to her in a "possible world," he might do anything.

She would have to go into the channel feetfirst, because that was the only way she could have her arms free to pull the panel back into position. But then she would have to crawl through the channel without being able to see where she was going. Still, it would be so dark inside that wouldn't make any practical difference.

She sat down and inserted her feet and legs into the channel. The thin metal gave off a dull *thumm* as it buckled under her weight. She worked the rest of her body inside until she was able to lie flat. Just as she was stretching out her legs, she heard voices in the hall. She couldn't understand what was being said, but they sounded angry and excited.

Her pulse was pounding in her head, and she quickly reached for the panel. She pulled it toward her, pushing the computer wires through the hole so they wouldn't hang it up. She maneuvered one of the metal edges into the supporting lip and cantilevered the panel over the opening.

"Look behind the desk!" she heard Cyberwolf shouting. "She can't get out of here."

Her hands were shaking so much that she could hardly control them. She succeeded in gently lowering the panel toward the other lip, but then the panel caught on something and wouldn't settle into the groove. She put her finger into the hole and jerked, but the panel refused to go into place.

The hard slap of footsteps began to sound on the marble floor. Somebody was definitely coming. He wasn't running, but he was moving fast.

Tears of frustration sprang to her eyes, and for a brief moment she felt like lying back and giving up. Her hand brushed against the computer wires, and only then did she realize that the panel wouldn't go down because it was

held back by one of them. She was lying on the wire, and
it didn't have enough slack to slip through the hole.

She arched her back to raise her body, then pulled more
wire up the channel. When three or four inches were
bunched up beside her head, she tried again to close the
panel.

This time it fell into position with a satisfying click.

31

Hightower's head swam, and he squeezed his toes hard
against the floor to make sure his feet were securely
planted. Yet after only a minute or two of disorientation,
his mind made the necessary adjustments, and he began
to notice his surroundings.

The hall stretching in front of him seemed immensely
long. The walls were pale pink and unnaturally smooth,
as though constructed of molded plastic. Yet they also
seemed strangely unstable. The lines where they inter-
sected with the floor trembled, and sometimes the whole
surface appeared to undulate. *It's not real,* he reminded
himself. *It's only virtually real.*

He lifted his right foot and slowly took a step. Then,
very cautiously, he took another. He could hear the
echoing sound of his movements in his ears, but nothing
else. It was just as well the Berserker hadn't come upon
him right at first or he would have been killed. Now he
might have a chance. Feeling more confident, he sped up
his walk, and after a few steps he was looking through a
rectangular arch.

The room beyond was large and windowless. Its walls
had the same strange plastic sheen as those in the hall.
Clusters of sofas, chairs, and small tables took up much
of the space, leaving only narrow paths between the
groupings. But the shapes of the furniture looked slightly

wrong, and none of the brightly hued colors of the wood or the upholstery seemed quite right.

He looked around the room. Along the right of the wall in front and continuing around the corner, he saw a series of five doors. Pete Salter had told him that the Berserker was someplace in the building. The creature was nothing more than a computer-controlled combination of digitized images projected onto his retina, Dopplered stereo sounds, and physical sensations produced by his force-reflective data suit. Even so, in the excitement of the hunt, he found that hard to remember. As he curled his right hand, he could feel the gun, its knurled butt rough against his palm. He was going to try to shoot first. That was his only strategy.

He threaded his way along the narrow aisles until he reached the first door. Using his left hand, he reached out and grasped the doorknob. He twisted the knob and simultaneously pushed forward. He felt pressure in his wrist as the door resisted him, then opened a crack.

He saw a single bed and a chest of drawers. On the back wall was a window with a decorative grate over it. A strange yellow light, not quite like sunlight, came through the intricate punched pattern of the screen.

Slowly, cautiously, he pushed the door open farther. Suddenly, a large dark shape came rushing at him from the left. He felt his breath catch in his throat and his heart stop as he whirled to face it. Cold sweat broke out on his forehead.

The creature was tall and wearing black clothes and a black cape. Its head was skull-like, with long pointed ears and shriveled skin that was dead white and seemed to glow with a greenish look of decay. From deep sockets, the creature's reptilian eyes, with their round black pupils, stared directly at him. Its thin lips curled up in a snarl of hatred, and as it came toward him, it seemed to slither with a dry, rustling sound.

Salter hadn't told him that the Berserker would look so gruesome. He fought back the impulse to run. If he was going to accomplish his aim, he would have to play the game.

Glistening strands of saliva hung from the Berserker's pointed teeth. Its yellow eyes blazed with hatred, and in its white skeletal hand it held what looked like a long pistol with thin steel hoops around the barrel. The Berserker gave a loud hiss and pointed the weapon at him.

Hightower heard a high-pitched sizzling sound and saw a flash of intense blue light. He felt a wave of heat on his right cheek. The shot had barely missed him.

Reacting almost automatically, he raised his right hand and pulled the trigger of the gun. A long blaze of white flame shot out. The creature grabbed its right arm and let out an ear-shattering roar. Then Hightower felt a sudden sharp pressure against his left upper arm and shoulder as the Berserker shoved him aside and raced across the living room with unbelievable speed, somehow dodging all the furniture.

Hightower took a deep breath for the first time in what seemed an hour. His knees were weak and his hands were trembling. He could still feel the force of the Berserker's shove, but he needed to get through the whole building as quickly as possible. He had to find the Berserker and kill it without getting killed himself. He didn't have time to be killed.

"We know that you're more likely to remember something if it has emotional significance," Salter had told him. "You could study a floor plan for an hour and remember most of it, but even so, you would have to work at retrieving the information. It wouldn't be deeply processed, so you couldn't count on its being retrievable when you needed it."

"So you do something to evoke an emotional response," Hightower concluded. "Is that the idea?"

"That's right," Salter said. "We put you in a kill-or-be-killed situation for ten minutes, and that focuses all your senses and hooks up your emotions with what you're learning. That the situation isn't real doesn't make much difference, because the emotional part of the brain is easy to fool."

Pete Salter was small and wiry, with a pinched face and closely cropped brown hair. "He's a professor at MIT," Lindsley had told Hightower. "He also started his own company. It's called HIT—Human Interface Technologies—and it's located between Kendall Square and the MIT campus, down close to the river."

When Hightower arrived, Salter was sitting in front of the computer and searching through the MIT files. In a few minutes he found what Hightower needed.

"We've got two file sets for Johnson Hall," Salter told him. "One is for the basic CAD course, and the other is for advanced design. The basic files don't include the basement, because no changes were made in it when Johnson was remodeled and attached to the research tower. Which set do you want?"

"The one that's most complete," he had said.

Hightower jerked his attention back to the present. Leaving the door to the small room open, he turned and crossed the living room. The Berserker had gone through the arch in the middle of the wall, and Hightower went after him.

A long shimmering table in an almost iridescent brown stood in the middle of the room. The dining room was empty. He stood in one place and turned around slowly, surveying every part of the room. At one end was an arch leading back into the hall, and at the other end was a swinging door.

Holding his gun at the ready, he pushed against the front edge of the door. His fingertips registered the pressure he was exerting, and the door silently swung open. He rushed through the opening, then turned rapidly from side to side, pointing his gun in all directions.

But the Berserker was nowhere to be seen. Without letting up on his vigilance, Hightower relaxed a little and let his gun hang down by his side.

He was in the kitchen. A white countertop ran the length of the back wall. At one end of it, a black restaurant-style stove stood next to a double-door refrigerator. At the other end, a small rectangular door with a handle like one on an oven was set into the wall.

He pulled on the door's handle, but nothing happened. Then he realized he couldn't expect everything to work. He wouldn't be able to open the refrigerator, take out an egg, and fry it on the stove, either. He was in a virtual world, not the real one.

Salter had warned him about that. "After a few minutes, you'll start trying to interact with the virtual world as you do with the real one. But don't expect to be able to drink a glass of water, even if you hear it poured and see it in the glass."

Hightower realized that he had made the transition into the virtual world. From the first, the computer-controlled sounds, images, and sensory impressions had been easy to accept as realistic. Now, though, he accepted them as *virtually* real. If he stopped to think, he knew he wasn't actually in the world he was experiencing. Yet with the Berserker trying to kill him, he didn't have time to stop and think.

He would have to start the game over if the Berserker was successful. "We've got to build in something of real value to the human," Salter had said. "If you were doing virtual surgery, I'd fix it so that if you made a surgical error, everything would go dark for you. You'd be suited up, then—bang—everything's black for two minutes."

"I have a crucial reason for needing this information," Hightower said. "I don't have time to start over."

Salter wasn't moved. "Then don't let yourself get killed."

Hightower suspected that the rectangular door in the kitchen wall was nothing more than the trash chute. If so, it didn't matter that he couldn't open it, because it wouldn't do for his purposes anyway. He needed to find a way into Johnson Hall.

At the front of the room, in the area between the wall and what might be a pantry jutting into the room, was a set of narrow stairs leading to the upper floor. They were set back, with several feet of space between them and the door of the pantry.

The pantry door was closed. He stood to one side, held his gun at the ready, and pulled the door open. He slowly put his head around the corner and peered inside. He could see shelves on both walls, but nobody had bothered to give the computer the data needed to stock them. Beyond the shelves was a set of stairs leading to the basement.

Hightower let his left hand slide against the rough texture of the wall. Then his fingers found the light switch, and he turned it on. A glaring light flooded the stairs, and standing at the bottom and staring up at him with its dead white face and yellow eyes was the Berserker.

Hightower fired first, but he was too late. The Berserker had dodged to the left and disappeared. Hightower hurried down the stairs, raising his feet clumsily at first. He stopped at the bottom, crouched, and peered cautiously around the corner.

A flash of blue light burst directly above his head— about where his waist would have been—and he could feel an almost painful warmth on the left side of his face. He crouched even lower, then raised his gun and fired back at the Berserker. A streak of white flashed from his gun barrel. The burst of light blinded him, but not before he saw that he had missed his target.

He closed his eyes so he could adjust to the dim light of the basement. He could hear the sound of footsteps running away from him. The Berserker was making no effort to move quietly. That might be because it wanted him to follow. Maybe it was planning a trap.

It was strange to think about the Berserker as planning or making an effort. After all, it was nothing more than an illusion created by a complicated interactive computer program. Still, it was only by thinking of the Berserker as a creature with will, desires, and intentions that he could plan his own strategy.

He stood up in a crouch, then stepped away from the stairs and looked into the dim gray light of the basement.

With difficulty he could just make out the figure of the Berserker running toward the rear of the building.

Hightower started toward the creature. He didn't run, but he walked rapidly. Even though the basement looked large, the Berserker would soon have to reach the back wall. He would eventually catch up with him, and then he would have to test his accuracy with the gun against the Berserker's. His recent performance in knife throwing didn't increase his confidence.

As he drew nearer to the back wall, he continued to hear the footsteps. But instead of sounding closer, they seemed to be getting fainter. It made no sense—unless the Berserker was running parallel to the wall.

Hightower reached the wall, stopped, and looked along it. He then turned and looked the other way. He could see nothing in either direction but the long shimmering gray of the wall. Yet he could still hear the footsteps.

The noise seemed to be coming from the left, and he began working his way in that direction. He kept close to the wall. Now and then his shoulder brushed against it, and as he slid his right hand along it, he could feel its solidity with the tips of his fingers.

He stopped for a moment and listened. He could hear his own breathing and a sort of buzzing electronic background noise, but he couldn't hear the Berserker's footsteps anymore. The Berserker was hidden someplace and waiting for him. He was sure of it.

He started to move again. Suddenly, the hand he had been sliding along the wall slipped into empty space. He was so startled that he jerked back his hand and stopped dead in his tracks.

He listened again and still heard nothing. He quietly eased himself down flat on the floor, then began to crawl slowly along the wall until he was in the opening.

The opening seemed to lead into a completely dark room, and he could see nothing. Trying to make no noise, he switched the gun from his left hand to his right. He then fired one shot through the opening and into whatever was beyond it.

The brief flash of light showed him what he needed to see—the Berserker was standing at the left against the wall.

Hightower saw no details, but he didn't need to see them. He pointed his gun at the Berserker as if he were pointing a finger. When the darkness came again, it was total and profound, but he made no effort to focus. Instead, he started firing white flashes at the spot where he had pointed the gun.

The first flash proved he had the direction correct, and he caught a glimpse of the cadaverous white face of the Berserker. The Berserker had also seen him, and streaks of blue light burst over his head. Hightower put his second and third shots in the same target area, then for the next two he moved the gun muzzle slightly to the right.

After he fired the last shot, he suddenly heard a long, high-pitched wail. "You've killed me this time," an eerie quavering voice said. "But beware! There will be another game." A maniacal laugh followed.

The laugh made Hightower feel cold all over, even though he understood that, like the voice, it was synthesized.

Without warning, an intense white glow, like iron heated to the melting point, began to come from the crumpled body of the Berserker. In the glow, Hightower could see that the opening in the wall was an entrance into what seemed to be a long tunnel with a vaulted ceiling. He touched his fingers against one side and took a few steps forward. He could see nothing, but he was ready to go on and explore the tunnel in the dark.

Then the wall that he was touching seemed to dissolve, and he was left with his hand raised uselessly in the air. The darkness surrounding him turned to a blank whiteness, and the animated world was suddenly empty of all forms and figures. Strapped into his helmet, he could see nothing.

"Congratulations, Hightower." Salter's voice sounded in his ears. "You've got good reflexes. You could have handled Skill Level Two without any problem."

"What's that tunnel I was in?" Hightower asked. He could feel the thrill of the discovery starting to build inside him.

He waited impatiently for Salter's answer. Then he realized that Salter was fussing around with the data suit and wasn't listening to him. He could feel Salter pulling on the flat connector wire at the back of the helmet.

"The tunnel—tell me about the tunnel." Hightower was vaguely aware that he was on the verge of shouting.

"Oh, yeah," Salter said. "That's one of the Berserker's favorite hiding places."

"Where does the goddamned thing go?" It took a deliberate effort not to grab Salter by his shirt front and shake him.

Salter looked startled. "I can tell you what I've heard," he said. "Johnson Hall is the original building at Rush, and it was built as a private lunatic asylum in the nineteenth century."

"For the very rich," Hightower said. "I knew that."

"Insanity was a stigma then, and families didn't want anybody to know that one of their members was crazy. So when they committed the patient, they used the tunnel to smuggle him in. Later on, since they didn't want to be seen visiting him, they'd go through the tunnel, too."

"Where's the entrance?" Hightower asked, cutting short Salter's explanation.

"I'm not exactly sure. I think it's in a little park on the north side of the Rush grounds." Salter gave Hightower a quizzical look. "Maybe I could find it on a map."

"Get the map while I take off this suit," Hightower said. "I've got to hurry."

32

Susan forced herself to lie completely still in the darkness of the channel. The slightest shift in her weight would cause the thin galvanized steel to flex, then pop into position again. If the metal snapped back while someone was near the desk, it would be an invitation to pull up the access panel and check inside.

The hole for the computer wires let in a small spot of light that kept the darkness from being absolute. With her eyes opened wide, she watched dust particles swirling in the grayness. Straining her ears, she listened to the footsteps coming closer.

Each step hit the marble floor with a distinct slap, which was immediately followed by a rasping sound as the walker twisted on the ball of his foot to take another step. She focused on each sequence—*slap, rasp, slap, rasp*—hearing minor variations of tone in every one.

She fought down the impulse to climb out of the grave she had buried herself in and run. But she had nowhere to go. Her best hope—her only hope—was to stay calm and keep quiet. Who was coming to look for her? It wasn't Cyberwolf, because he was the one yelling instructions. Backup was with Meg. So that left Whip—Cyberwolf was sending out his Doberman.

Hunting her down was the kind of assignment somebody like Whip would relish. If he caught her, he could slap her around, maybe even rape her. She would be at his mercy, and that alone gave him a powerful motive to find her. However, it gave her an even more powerful motive to make sure he didn't.

Her right hand was beginning to ache. It was jammed between her thigh and the metal wall so that her weight was against it. At first she had noticed only a slight pressure, but now her hand was throbbing. With every beat of her heart, a pulse of pain shot through it. She tried to ignore it.

The footsteps stopped abruptly. They were close, no more than five or six feet from the desk. Whip must be looking around, surveying the scene. She tried to keep herself frozen into immobility. That's what rabbits did; they would freeze and wait until danger went away.

The footsteps suddenly started again. They sounded louder, as if they were almost directly over her head. Whip must be coming behind the desk.

Sure enough, the steps were replaced by gritty shuffling noises. She could almost see Whip standing in one place and looking around—looking for her. She tightened her shoulders, pulling her arms in against her body. She did her best to ignore her throbbing hand.

Probably by now Whip was bending over and peering into the kneehole of the desk, half expecting to find her curled up like a scared puppy. She hardly dared to breathe, and she clenched her teeth so tightly her jaw hurt.

Scared as she was, she felt a sense of something like power. She might get caught, but at least she had gotten away. She wouldn't have liked herself if she hadn't tried. Even poor, frail Mrs. Rostov had fought back. And by attacking Whip the old woman had made it possible for her to escape.

"She's not here!" Whip shouted. His voice was so loud that he must be only inches away from her.

Her hand was hurting so much that each pulse of blood was like a stab wound. She longed to pull it from under her leg and flex her stiff fingers. Her back was also starting to hurt. The sheet steel was hard and unyielding, and the bony ridge of her spine was aching from the pressure of lying still.

Suddenly, she could stand the pain in her hand no longer; she had to do something or scream. She shifted her right leg to take the pressure off her hand, then pulled it free. But as she changed positions, the sheet metal buckled, making a small dull thumping noise, like a heating duct when the furnace comes on.

She froze into immobility again, holding her breath and

squeezing her eyes shut. She kept the muscles of her legs tensed, sure that if she relaxed them, the thin metal would snap back into position with a loud crack.

"Check the research tower doors!" Cyberwolf shouted.

She curled and uncurled the fingers of her hand, trying to get the blood to start flowing again. When it did, her hand began to tingle, as if a thousand needles were pricking her skin. But that was infinitely better than the throbbing.

Yet now her leg was beginning to hurt, and she didn't know if she could keep it pushed flat against the bottom of the channel. *Leave! Go do what you were told,* she screamed at Whip in her mind. But he seemed in no hurry. She heard small scratching sounds, then a few soft thuds. He must be searching through the desk, opening and closing the drawers.

After what seemed an eternity, he slammed the last drawer, and she heard him walking toward the end of the hall. She relaxed her leg, and the metal under it popped loud enough for Whip to hear. She froze again, and this time even her heart seemed to stop beating. She waited for him to halt, walk back to the desk, and start searching for the source of the noise.

But his footsteps kept on going down the hall, growing fainter at each step. She gave a shudder of relief that made her whole body quiver.

Then the footsteps abruptly stopped, and she could imagine Whip trying the doors. She held her breath and listened, but she couldn't detect the faintest noise. Whatever he was doing didn't take long, because he immediately started up the hall.

The footsteps grew louder, and again every muscle in her body seemed to tighten. She wondered if she would be able to stay completely quiet again if he decided to stop at the desk. She was even more tired now; her back was hurting, and her legs were cramped.

Whip's steps were suddenly much louder, then the sound became progressively fainter. He wasn't stopping.

Relief flowed through her like a soothing drug. For the

first time in what seemed hours, she let herself take a deep breath. She almost laughed.

Soon, she could no longer hear the sharp, repetitive slap of Whip's shoes, but she still waited a long minute before allowing herself to move. Tightening her shoulders, she raised her back to relieve the aching pressure on her spine. The metal popped, but the noise no longer seemed loud. She let her body go limp and forced herself to relax.

She dreaded the idea of crawling feetfirst into complete darkness, but she couldn't stay where she was. At any moment, Cyberwolf himself might come running down the hall and jerk up the access panel. Eventually that was going to happen, and when it did, she didn't want to be there. She had to move fast.

She arched her back, raised herself on her elbows, and pulled with her heels. She succeeded in moving forward a few inches, and she lifted herself again to repeat the same torturous process. This time she shoved hard with her hands, but at the apex of the movement, her face rammed into the top of the channel. Sharp pain shot through her nose. Tears came to her eyes, and she fell back flat onto the metal surface. Her nose hurt as if someone had smashed it with a hammer, and she could feel blood seeping out of one nostril.

Oh, God, I've broken it, she thought in despair. Her nose might be so damaged that even a plastic surgeon wouldn't be able to put it back into shape. Then nobody would give her a job.

She lifted her right hand, but the space was too confining for her to reach her face. She slid her hand along her body and touched her nose. Her skin was slick with blood, and her nose felt tender. She gently squeezed the bridge and searched for the bone and cartilage with the tips of her fingers.

Nothing seemed broken. The bleeding was already stopping, and even the pain was letting up. She gingerly wiped off the blood as best she could, then rubbed her hand on her pants.

She was afraid to start moving, afraid she would smash her face again. She lifted herself up slowly on her elbows, then stopped when she sensed that the top of the channel was almost touching the tip of her nose. That was high enough to let her move forward, but it would be difficult to get leverage.

She pushed with her elbows and hands and pulled hard with her heels. The galvanized metal warped and snapped as she crept forward. It worked. She was advancing.

She repeated the same contorted sequence of moves, then did them again. She could breathe through only one nostril, and her back and shoulders were already beginning to hurt with the strain of supporting her body. But she was moving, inching herself along. That's what counted.

She tried to establish a rhythm in her movements. She arched her back, propelled herself forward, then lay flat. This allowed her muscles to rest a moment. Time and again, she repeated the pattern. But she was so slow, so pathetically slow. She could feel frustration and despair building up. If she didn't hurry, Cyberwolf might not only realize where she was, he might figure out where she was likely to come out of the channel. Then he would be there waiting for her. She had to go faster.

The faint light coming through the cable opening had disappeared. She was now surrounded by darkness so complete it felt like a physical thing, something lying on top of her, pressing her down and making it hard to breathe. She ignored the feeling, bowed her back, and pulled herself forward another few inches.

Suddenly, something brushed against the left side of her face. She recognized at once that it was a cobweb. She rolled her head from side to side, trying to pull free, but the sticky silk of the web was tangled in her hair and wouldn't come loose.

Reflexively, she raised her right hand to wipe it off. But she had forgotten how confined the space was, and her hand hit the top of the channel with a solid thump. *Don't panic. You're perfectly all right. A cobweb isn't dangerous.* She slid her hand up to her face and pulled on the sticky strands until she managed to pull most of the web loose. She rubbed it between her fingers, forming a small ball that she flicked to the side.

She wanted to lie still and recover for a moment, but she had to go on. She had lost too much time already. She put both hands on the metal floor and raised herself on her elbows, ready to make the next move forward.

It was then that she felt something crawling on her neck, creeping up toward her left cheek. It moved slowly, touching her skin so lightly that at first she hadn't noticed anything.

Obviously it was a spider, the one that had spun the web she had demolished. But what kind was it? Maybe just a common brown house spider. However, on the East Coast, inside a building in a wooded area, it could be a black widow.

She suddenly recalled a textbook picture of the black widow spider's long spindly legs and furry two-lobed body with a red hourglass marked on its back. She saw its small round head with its glassy compound eyes and its tiny white hollow fangs for injecting poison. An uncontrollable tremor shook her, and she eased herself down flat. Beads of sweat sprang out on her forehead, and she simultaneously felt hot and cold.

If she threatened the spider, it would bite her to protect itself. But what if she didn't threaten it? Then the spider should keep on scurrying away to make its escape. Since she couldn't run away herself and couldn't see what was happening, the safest course was to leave the spider alone.

She lay completely still, suppressing every instinct to try to smash it. The drying blood made her left cheek feel tight, as if the skin were stretched. Then she felt the spider move from her neck to her face. The delicate touch of the soft hairy pads of its feet seemed to burn her skin like acid as it walked on her cheek. She tightened the muscles of her face to keep from crying out, but she couldn't avoid making a hoarse, strangled noise deep in her throat.

The spider moved rapidly across her cheek and onto her forehead. As it began climbing into her hair, her whole scalp prickled. She could almost see the black furry body, with its two thick lobes, getting tangled up in her hair. It would bite her again and again, trying to struggle free from what it would instinctively sense as a trap.

She clamped her jaw tighter, but she could no longer stand to do nothing. Careful not to make any sudden moves that would signal danger to the spider, she gently slid her right hand along her body and over her face. She reached her hairline, and then it was time to act. With her fingers spread, she rapidly rubbed her hand through her hair.

At first she felt nothing, then she sensed a movement on her scalp near the crown of her head. She raised her hand as far as the cramped space would allow and slapped her head.

She didn't hit the spider directly, but she did hit it. The soft body squirmed under her fingers. The spider was trapped by her hair, and she could feel the creature struggling, its legs tugging at loose strands.

Her body shook, and she was choked with fear. At any moment she would feel a sharp bite in her scalp or on a finger. She pushed harder, rubbing her fingers back and forth against her scalp, as though scrubbing her head. Then all at once she felt the pulpy body of the spider tear apart, and something wet and sticky covered her fingers.

The mess felt disgusting. She lowered her hand and wiped it on her pants. She couldn't bear to think about what was still tangled in her hair. Even so, she was dizzy with relief. She hadn't been bitten.

She felt the need to lie back and relax a few minutes, but she couldn't let herself. Slowly, painfully, she hoisted herself off the sheet metal and started her slow crab-walking crawl.

She seemed to be moving incredibly slowly. Was she making any real headway? She focused on her next move, paying close attention to the distance between the place her hands were at the start and where they were when she slid them up by her hips for the next move. She did the same for the next two moves.

The best she could estimate, each of her awkward maneuvers gained her about four inches. It seemed like a pitiful distance. For the price of straining her arms and arching her aching back, she got less than half a foot.

But she didn't have to go far, just to the other side of the doors to the research tower. She formed a picture of the scene, seeing the blank section of polished green marble stretching between the desk and the doors. How many times would her father fit into the space? Somewhat more than three times. He was six feet tall, so she had to cover roughly twenty feet.

That didn't sound bad. She had moved more than half the distance already. Or had she? Four inches a move meant she could cover a foot in three moves, so twenty feet would take sixty moves. Yes, she was surely more than halfway.

She felt a surge of satisfaction. *You can do it if you stick to it.* It was the saying her mother had used to encourage her when she felt hopeless about something like long division. Later, though, her mother would tell her the same thing when the problems were on a bigger scale. "You can do anything you set your mind to," she would say. "If you want to be a biologist, that's what you should do. Just stick to it."

One of her permanent sorrows was that her mother hadn't lived to see her become an actress. She would have been proud if her daughter had become a biologist, but she would have been delighted that she had become a successful actress. Sometimes Susan wondered if she hadn't gone into films just to please her dead mother.

She began searching for any sign of light that would indicate an access panel. She felt sure she had gone far enough to be inside the research tower, but she could still see nothing but darkness. Perhaps she had been too optimistic in judging the distance. She couldn't expect an access panel right by the door, and maybe she would have to go twice as far before finding one. Well, she would just have to keep going.

As she pulled herself forward with her heels, the toe of her left foot kicked something hard. She stopped, then used her feet to explore what she had run into. She seemed to be at some kind of barrier. Keeping her left leg against the wall, she extended her foot. It moved freely. She pressed her right leg against the wall and extended her right foot. It also moved freely.

She felt her stomach sink. She was at a fork in the channel, and the possibilities were frightening. One branch might lead out of the research tower and down into some underground switching facility. Maybe it wouldn't even have any access panels, and she would find herself reaching a dead end. Or either of the branches might split off into other branches. If that happened, she could get lost in a maze of distribution channels. Her initial fear would turn out to be justified, and she would die of thirst, like a cat trapped inside the wall of a house.

A feeling of absolute hopelessness came over her. Her shoulders began to shake with sobs, and hot tears ran down the sides of her cheeks. "Oh God, Oh God, Oh God," she repeated over and over. Her voice was blurry with crying, and the words were virtually unintelligible in her own ears.

She writhed in the narrow space, kicking out her feet and rolling from side to side. She could no longer tell if she was standing up or lying down, whether she was on her face or on her back. Her head swam with dizziness, and the metal coffin she was in seemed to be growing smaller, the sides pushing in toward her.

Her heart pounded like a machine out of control. She grasped for her chest with both hands, but they hit the sheet-metal roof with a solid *thumm* that reverberated through the channel.

Suddenly, she couldn't breathe. She gasped for air, her chest heaving and her mouth opened wide. The darkness surrounding her seemed thick and gelatinous. It filled her nose, making it impossible for her to breathe in enough

air. The harsh whistling noises coming from her mouth
frightened her. Her head was spinning around, and she
could feel herself dissolving into the blackness around
her.

She came awake slowly, wondering where she was and
why she could see nothing. Then she began to remember.
She slid her right hand to her face and rubbed her eyes
with her fingers. She felt a sharp jolt of pain as she
bumped her nose.

She had no idea how long she had been unconscious. It
could have been two minutes or an hour. She felt
strangely embarrassed about fainting, as if someone had
seen her do something shameful. Even so, she was still
alive and free. That meant she had a chance—at least she
did if she could mobilize herself.

"You can do it if you stick to it," she repeated to herself. It seemed a childish thing to say, but it also seemed
to help. She was thinking more clearly and ready to try
again. She had to get moving, though. If the fork in the
channel that she chose led to a dead end, she would need
even more time.

She lifted herself to her forearms and gasped with the
pain. Her elbows felt raw, and the muscles in her back
and legs were so stiff she wondered if she could bend
them. She moved her left foot toward the right, then
arched her back, dug in her heels, and pushed and pulled
herself into the right-hand fork. Her only reason for
choosing the right was that it seemed to lead in the general direction of the rear of the research tower.

She counted each time she moved, and at the ninth
move she stopped to rest. She lay flat on her back and
shrugged her shoulders to loosen up her muscles.

As she stared up at the sheet metal above her, she noticed something—*she could see it*. She couldn't see it
clearly, but she could tell that there was something there,
something that was slightly lighter in color than the surrounding darkness. The galvanized sheet metal was re-

flecting light, and that meant she must be close to someplace where the light was coming in.

She suddenly didn't feel as tired and stiff as she had. She raised herself on her elbows, arched her back, and pushed and pulled herself forward.

Then she saw it, not five feet from her: a small circle of light forming a bright spot on the metal floor of the channel.

33

Gibson paced back and forth under the arch at the entrance to the living room. The cool dry air blowing from the air-conditioning duct made his eyes burn and itch, and even the weak light seemed harsh. He squeezed his eyes shut, enjoying a moment of velvety blackness.

Susan was gone. No doubt about it. He had checked the fire exit at his end of the hall and discovered that the steel door was still sealed shut. That didn't surprise him, because she couldn't have activated the computer interrupts.

He glanced down the hall, and less than fifty feet away, he could see Whip coming back. He didn't need to wait for a report to learn that Whip had been unsuccessful. He could read it in his disgruntled expression and his hunched-over, slouching walk.

Gibson shook his head. Susan had completely surprised him by running off. Since kicking Bryan out of her life, she had been behaving like a zombie, unable to make even tiny decisions without talking them over for two days with her agent. Yet when she got the chance to escape, she had been absolutely decisive and leaped into action. Something had happened to change her.

But what really hurt was that she had abandoned him. When the two of them were alone and talking in the living room, she had seemed to understand the way he felt.

Even though he hadn't been able to come out and tell her how much he cared for her, she sensed it. And then to do what she had done . . .

What he hadn't been able to tell her was that because he loved her so much, he was going to have to kill her. Could she have sensed it? Was that why she ran away? Well, he was going to get her back. It was just a matter of a little time and inconvenience. She was mistaken if she thought she was a match for Cyberwolf.

"Hey, Cyber," Cortez called. Gibson turned around. "She's not in any of the rooms." Cortez came toward him, talking as he walked. The Street Sweeper was tucked under his right arm.

"You're sure you looked under the bed in Meg's room?" Gibson saw that Whip was only a few feet away from them.

"I looked under all the beds." Cortez stroked his mustache and shook his head. "Man, there's no place to hide around here. She couldn't have turned invisible or evaporated, so where the hell is she?"

"That's what I want to know," Whip said, coming level with them. He sounded angry, as if Susan, not Mrs. Rostov, had slashed his face. The long cut had left a blotchy, irregular line of dried blood on his cheek. "She's not under the fucking desk, and the doors to the research building are both locked."

"I'm not surprised," Gibson said.

"All right, Mr. Fucking Genius," Whip said. "Suppose you just tell us where the fuck she is."

"She's in the research building." Gibson's voice was even, almost bland. "That's the only place she can be."

"But how?" Cortez asked. His dark eyebrows were pulled inward by a puzzled frown.

"Did you give her a key?" Whip made the question into an accusation. "I noticed the doors open with a card."

"Was that what you were looking for in the desk?"

"I was just checking," Whip said. "But you'd been there before me, pawing through that top drawer."

"I've got the card to open the door," Gibson said. "I'm planning on checking out the research building to make sure the cops aren't trying to sneak through it." He shrugged. "I knew we'd have to do that when I looked at the floor plans and saw that the buildings are connected."

Whip cocked his head and gave Gibson a suspicious look. "Are you trying to put something over on us?"

"Like what?" Gibson kept any suggestion of challenge out of his voice. Arguing with Whip would be a waste of time at best; at worst, it might be dangerous.

"Like you tell Susan you're going to help her escape and she should go hide in the tower and wait for you." Whip's face got darker. "Then while we're sitting around here with our fingers up our ass, you slip away and meet her there."

"Interesting," Gibson said, nodding. "But I've got the card here." He reached into his back pocket and took out the red plastic card. "So how did she get past the locked door?"

"You opened the door when the two of you went down the hall," Whip said. "Then when all the commotion started in the kitchen, you told her to take off."

"Can she escape from the research tower?" Cortez asked.

"Impossible," Gibson said. "We locked the doors there when we locked them here. The tower doesn't have windows on the first floor, and you can't get to the other floors without a key to the stairway doors or to the elevator."

"So we've got her trapped," Cortez said.

"You mean you've got her where you want her." Whip kept his eyes on Gibson. "Let me hear you deny it."

"What am I supposed to be up to now that I've got her in the building?" Gibson met Whip's gaze as he slipped the red card back into his pocket. "Now that she's waiting for me?"

"You double-cross her and you double-cross us," Whip said. "You get on your computer and tell the cops to drop the sixty million in front of the research tower." Whip's scarred lip curled into a sneer. "Since Cortez and me can't get past them doors and can't get out the front door here, you leave us where we are to catch the shit." He reached up and stroked his death's-head earring. "You pick up the ransom and get on the plane. Then while the cops are trashing our asses, you're sitting in the sun someplace counting the money."

"That's a good story," Gibson told him.

"Maybe you're not the genius you fucking well think you are." Whip rested his hand on the Mac-10 stuck into the top of his blue pants. "You computer bozos think you know everything, but you don't know shit about how real life works."

"But you do," Gibson said.

"I know a little something about it." Whip pulled out the automatic pistol and slipped the canvas sling over his shoulder.

"I don't believe Cyberwolf would double-cross us." Cortez glanced nervously at Gibson, then back at Whip.

"So what's he got to say about it?" Whip was smiling, but his eyes had a blank look. "I ain't heard him deny it." In a smooth, almost careless motion he pulled back slightly on the jutting magazine of the machine pistol so that the muzzle pointed toward Gibson.

"I've already said part of the story's true."

"What do you mean?" Cortez asked in surprise. "You gave her a key so she could meet you?"

"I said she's got to be in the research building," Gibson said. "But I didn't give her a key."

"Then how the fuck did she get in?" Whip asked. "You said the doors were locked when you was there, and I know goddamned well they're locked right now."

"I was turning that over in my mind while I was waiting for you to get back," Gibson said. "I believe she crawled through the floor channel where the computer cables are laid." He swept his hand through his hair, pushing it off his forehead. "She saw me lift off the service plate."

"It would be a squeeze," Cortez said. "But she's thin."

"That sounds like bullshit," Whip said. "You can fake out your buddy Backup, but you can't shit an old shitter like me."

"We don't have to argue about this," Gibson said. "If we're going to ransom her, we need her back." He gave Whip a sharp glance. "So Backup and I will wait here while you go find her."

Whip said nothing for a moment. He stared hard into Gibson's face, then glanced at Cortez. He was obviously weighing the odds that they were plotting against him.

"Why don't you and me both go in," Whip said cautiously.

"Because I've got to send a message to let the cops know that we're running out of patience and need a response."

"So Cortez could go with me."

"Backup," Cortez said sharply. "Don't use my name, man."

"Shit, nobody can hear us," Whip said.

"Backup needs to keep an eye on Meg and the boy."

"Where is the boy?" Whip looked past Gibson and into the depths of the living room.

"I put him in the room with Meg," Cortez said.

"I don't trust her," Gibson said. "She's strong, and she's tough."

"What the fuck, just shoot her," Whip said.

"I keep telling you we may need some live people to bargain with," Gibson said. "But that's beside the point. The question is, are you going to go in and find Susan and bring her back?" He looked Whip directly in the face, then added, "If you don't want to go for any reason—any reason at all—you can stay here on guard duty and Backup can go."

"No problem," Cortez said. "I wouldn't mind getting out of this place and doing a little quail hunting." He laughed and patted the barrel of the Street Sweeper.

Whip looked at Gibson, then at Cortez. Finally, with his eyes narrowed, he fixed his gaze on Gibson. "Charlie, I'm going to gamble on you," he said. "But if I find out

you're trying to screw me, I'm going to cut off your balls
and make you swallow them whole." He nodded and
raised the Mac-10 so that it pointed toward Gibson's
heart. "Then I'm going to kill you dead."

"Are you going to go or not?" Gibson ignored the gun
and looked into Whip's face.

"Man, I'm happy to go," Cortez said. "I want to get ac-
tive. I'm going nuts shut up in here."

"I'm the best one to go," Whip said. He reached up to
his left ear and tugged gently on the dangling silver
death's-head. "Charlie's right about that."

"How come?" Cortez asked.

"Because the army trained me to stalk the enemy,"
Whip said. "You'd probably shoot your own ass off. Besides, I've had lots of experience persuading reluctant
women to cooperate with me." He smiled, and dark red
blood began to ooze out of the cut along his cheek.

34

Susan lay on her back on the carpeted floor beside the
open access port. Just being out of the dark sheet-metal
trench made her feel almost light-headed. If she had to
die, she wanted to do it in the light, not trapped somewhere under the floor like some night-crawling grub.

The muscles in her back, legs, and arms ached, her
nose was tender, and the scrapes on her hands burned.
Still, she had stuck to it—and she was free. She wasn't
absolutely free, but that would come, if she just didn't
give up.

She couldn't stay where she was. Cyberwolf had probably figured out where she was and was hunting her already. She needed to find a way out of the building or at
least get to a phone.

She pushed herself up on her elbows. She was next to

a white plaster wall in a very large room, but it was dim
and shadowy. High above her, behind egg-carton gratings,
a row of long fluorescent tubes gave off a feeble yellow-
green light.

The room was hot and humid, and the sweat beading
up on her face ran down her cheeks in warm trickles. The
thick, swampy atmosphere was permeated with the rank
smell of rotting fish.

She stood up slowly, feeling weak and dizzy. She
braced herself against the wall with her right hand. She
looked around, expecting to find a computer near the access panel, but none was there. The cables were simply
sticking up out of the floor. A few feet away, though, was
the end of a long laboratory bench consisting of tan
wood-grain laminate cabinets topped by a thick slab of
black plastic resin. It was just like the benches she remembered from her days as a biology major.

She was obviously in a lab and apparently in its back
corner. In the middle of the room was some kind of circular framework, and coming out of the floor below it
was a bright, almost incandescent glow. At her left was
a solid door, and directly across the room, she could see
a glint of light reflected from the glass-paneled door of a
lab office. To the left of the office, on the adjacent wall,
was another solid door.

She remembered looking down the hall of the research
tower while Joe Ling was busy at his computer. She had
seen doors opening to the right, and she must be behind
one of them now. Only it probably wasn't so simple.
Most likely, each door led into a warren of rooms—a lab-
yrinth of interconnected laboratories, storage rooms, and
animal facilities.

Animal facilities! Of course, that's what the smell had
to be. Either it came from the animals themselves or from
their food. She must be in or near some animal lab.

She started making her way along the wall. She saw no
windows anywhere. Maybe the research tower didn't *have*
windows or maybe they were in one of the other rooms.
But before rushing into another room, she should try the

telephone. The office on the other side of the room was sure to have one.

Halfway across the room, she paused. She was no more than twenty feet from the circular structure in the middle, and she could see now that it was a low metal railing surrounding a pool of water. The bright glow came from the water, shining upward like a fountain of light. She crossed the open space.

When she reached the pool, the odor of spoiled fish was so strong that she had to swallow hard to keep from gagging. The pool was ten or twelve feet in diameter, and the water was the murky gray-green color of the ocean.

She looked over the railing into the depths. At first she wasn't sure what she was seeing. Swimming in endless looping patterns were what looked like giant snakes, seven or eight feet long, with loose flaps of skin along their backs and bellies. As the snakes moved in sinuous curves, water resistance made their skin flaps ripple.

Then she realized that they weren't snakes. They were moray eels. Joe Ling had mentioned that somebody on the staff was studying them as part of a neurological research project. She stared down at the eels with a mixture of fascination and dread. They gave the impression of being totally alien, like creatures from another planet. Constantly moving, they wove in and out of each other's way so that the pool seemed filled with them. However, she guessed there were no more than a dozen.

As she watched she found she could make out three different varieties. One was jet black, another an iridescent emerald green, and the third clay colored and mottled with irregular dark spots. No matter what their color, they all had the same kind of mouth, a narrow lipless slit that curved slightly upward at the end of their blunt noses. They swam with their mouths open, showing dozens of needlelike teeth crowded together in their jaws. Their lidless eyes were round, with pale yellow irises and tar black pupils.

Despite the heat in the room, a shiver ran up her back. Something about the eels terrified her. They were so utterly alien—there was no other word for them—dangerous, pitiless, and monstrous. She crossed her arms over her chest and gave herself a hard squeeze.

As she turned to go, she saw a small perch lying on the floor just inside the railing. On an impulse, she kicked the perch into the pool. As the fish hit the surface, a speckled moray lunged for it, sinking its teeth into the thickest part of the fish's body. Then a large black eel changed direction and, twisting around like a corkscrew, locked its jaws behind the head of the speckled eel.

The speckled moray dropped the fish and rotated its body, trying to pull loose. Blood streamed into the water, and all at once, six or eight eels began to tear at the body of the speckled moray. The entire pool turned into a writhing, twisting mass.

Susan stepped back in disgust and horror. When she had kicked in the fish, it had never occurred to her that it would trigger a cannibalistic feeding frenzy. She quickly turned away and hurried toward the glass-paneled door of the office.

The office was unlocked. She pulled open the door, then stood at the threshold peering inside. The interior was so dark that she could see only the vague forms of a desk, a table, and a tall bookcase against the back wall. She hesitated, not wanting to turn on the lights. But it was so dark that she would have to waste a lot of time searching for the telephone. She ran her fingers along the metal frame by the door and found the switch.

The light dazzled her. She blinked several times, and when at last she could see, she spotted the telephone on the metal desk. Instead of trying to find the police number, she would just call 911. She walked to the desk and snatched up the phone.

The line was dead. She tapped on the switch hook, but she got no dial tone. She pulled on the phone cord and followed it until she located the wall plug. She slid out the jack, then pushed it back in. Still no dial tone.

She shook her head in anger and frustration. Somehow or other Cyberwolf must have shut off the telephones.

Now what was she going to do? She stood by the desk, staring down at the litter of papers and glossy lab-equipment catalogs scattered across the top.

Then she remembered—she had seen the E-mail address the police had given Cyberwolf. She glanced around the office, and on a table in the opposite corner, she saw the blank screen of a computer monitor.

She pulled out the typing chair, sat in front of the computer, and flipped its switch to "On." While the computer was booting up, she tried to recall the E-mail address. She had made a special effort to memorize it, in case she got a chance like this. So what was it? The address had "Hope" in it, she was sure. But that was part of a longer name, one that included a number and Rush. Remembering that triggered the rest: the address was HOPECOT.2 @ RUSHIN.BITNET.

She glanced at the menu displayed in yellow and red letters on the blue background of the screen. Most of the names meant nothing to her, but she guessed that *COMMTALK* had to be a communications program. She moved the mouse until the arrow pointed to the name, then clicked the button to load the program.

The menu disappeared, and in crisp yellow letters she was offered three options: *Send? Receive? Read?* She pointed at *Send* and clicked. At the next prompt, she typed in the HOPECOT address and entered it. She expected to be able to start typing her message, but instead she was offered more options: *Text? Talk?*

She selected *Talk,* and the screen displayed *Please Begin Speaking Message Now. Press <Enter> to Send.*

She hesitated, looking for a place to speak into. Then on the left side of the beige plastic housing, she saw what had to be the grille of a condenser microphone. She leaned forward.

"This is Susan Bradstreet," she said into the grille. "I'm in a laboratory on the first floor of the research tower." She kept her voice low, but tried to speak clearly. "Meg O'Hare and Tim Kimberly are still prisoners in Johnson Hall. Clara Rostov and Joe Ling are dead. I am okay and am about to start searching for a way out of here."

She hesitated. What could she say that would be of any help to the police? Obviously something about the kidnappers, but she knew so little. Still, she would have to do her best.

"Three kidnappers, all men, and they only use nicknames. The leader is called Cyberwolf—repeat, Cyberwolf. He is a white male in his early to middle thirties. I never met him before, but there is a picture of him with me in one of my photograph albums. We are at a movie opening outside the Chinese Theater, and he's got his arm around me."

Then she thought of what Cyberwolf had said about how he had put the two of them together. "Cyberwolf faked the picture by using a machine he called the Pix-Wizard. I think it's like some kind of computer."

Suddenly, she was sure she had heard something. Or maybe she'd felt it. It wasn't so much a distinct noise as a slight vibration, like a heavy door closing. It seemed to come from the front wall of the lab. She glanced out the office window, looking toward the door near the corner. But the lights inside the office were so bright they kept her from seeing anything.

She pushed the "Enter" key and heard the clicking and popping of computer sounds as her message was processed. She reached for the red "Off" switch, then decided she didn't want to risk the slight noise that shutting down the computer would make. Moving quickly, she got up from the chair and turned off the lights.

Even before her eyes were adjusted to the shadowy gloom, she opened the door and stepped outside. She kept the doorknob turned to prevent the latch from clicking. When the door was solidly against the jamb, she slowly allowed the doorknob to unwind in her hand, letting the spring bolt silently slide into the plate.

Moving quickly and quietly, she crossed the room to the back wall. If she could reach the end of the lab bench, it would give her some temporary cover. Somebody coming in the front door would be distracted by the fountain of golden light shining in the center of the room, and she might have a chance to escape through the door in the back wall.

When she got to the end of the bench, she paused and listened. Her heart was hammering so fast and loud in her ears that it was hard to listen for anything else. She still couldn't hear anyone coming, so she started across the remaining few feet to the back door.

She hadn't crossed half the distance when she heard the door at the front click open. The sound was faint, and if she hadn't been listening with intense concentration she wouldn't have noticed it. Her heart was pounding as if it were going to break out of her chest, and her hands were shaking. Whoever was looking for her was making a deliberate effort to move silently. She was being stalked.

Looking toward the front, she saw the door slowly opening. The very slowness gave her the chance to get to the rear door. She turned the doorknob and pulled. The door moved a little, but it didn't open. She bit her lip to keep from crying in complete frustration. She pulled harder, and the door came slowly toward her. She then realized that the metal door was much heavier than she had allowed for.

She slipped through the narrow opening, then turned and glanced toward the front. She was expecting to see Cyberwolf, with his pale face and swept-back white hair, but the figure standing just inside the room didn't completely surprise her. Although the dim light made it impossible to see details, judging by his height and general build, she was sure it was Whip.

Suddenly she heard a high-pitched squeal coming from behind her. As she instinctively swung around, the heavy metal door slipped out of her hand. She lunged for the doorknob, but she was too late. The door slammed shut with a solid thump that made the whole wall shake.

Now he knows exactly where I am.

35

Hightower pulled the rented Ford into the small asphalt lot by the entrance to the park and turned off the engine. Two mercury-vapor lights attached to the tops of tall metal poles bathed the area in a luminous yellow-green glow.

The hair on the back of his neck prickled. The peculiar greenish shade reminded him of the sallow waxy look of embalmed bodies and newly dead corpses. He could feel the closeness of death, sense its coldness and emptiness. Death felt as real and palpable to him now as it had on the day he lost Alma. He thought of it as a ghastly invisible creature hovering over Susan, ready to snatch her life and leave her body limp and motionless, her skin bloodless and ashen. He shook his head. He had to keep his mind focused on the problems at hand.

He unzipped his carry-on bag and took out the autopsy knife and the roll of self-adhering bandage. Working quickly, he wrapped the bandage around the bare skin of his left leg. Holding the knife flat against the outside of his calf, he strapped it down with another layer of bandage. He then stamped his foot on the carpeted floor of the car. The knife didn't move. Hightower got out of the car and closed the door without slamming it. A block down the street he could see a row of two-story frame houses. If someone called the police to report a strange noise in Brooks Park, he might not be able to persuade the cops to wait until Don Lindsley arrived. They might take him to the police station, and he would lose an untold amount of time.

He was feeling the pressure of time. Don had said on the phone that he would come immediately, and it had taken Hightower close to twenty minutes to get to the park from Salter's lab. He had expected Don to be waiting for him.

Don was at least close by. The stands of trees and the

scrub bushes and vines at the back of the park screened off the Rush buildings, but they were no more than one long block away, straight through the park. From the road, just before turning into the park, he had seen the boxy brick top of the research tower rising above the trees. Now he was down too low to see it, but he thought he could detect a faint smear of light against the dark clouds about where the tower should be.

The area illuminated by the lights was a small playground. Crammed into it were a swing set, a merry-go-round, and a short slide. The ground was covered by a thick layer of shredded bark and wood chips. Against the darkness of the bark, the chips shone almost as white as bone fragments in the light.

Hightower hurried across the playground, climbed a shallow bank, and began to walk parallel to the ragged line of bushes running along the opposite side. He pushed back the branches of one of the overgrown bushes and shone the weak yellow beam of his pocket flashlight into the hidden area behind it. He saw nothing but patches of coarse ankle-high grass and the thin trunks and pale gray bark of trees that he couldn't identify.

He wished he knew exactly what he was looking for, but at least he had a good idea of where to look. If the entrance to the tunnel still existed, it would have to be in the area of the playground. The CAD plans on Salter's computer showed that the tunnel ran straight to the park from Johnson Hall.

He couldn't see Johnson Hall, but using the research building as a marker, the tunnel entrance should be to the left of the tower. That's where he was starting his search. He hoped some park department official, acting in the name of public safety, hadn't decided to seal the mouth of the tunnel with poured concrete or bury it under fifty tons of topsoil.

Using the beam of his flashlight to guide him over the rough ground, he began to walk a zigzag path. Starting at the edge of the clearing and extending into the woods, it covered a swath of land fifteen or twenty feet wide. Tan-

gles of vines wrapped themselves around his ankles and
briars tore at his clothes. As he wove his way through the
underbrush, he systematically pushed aside the limbs of
the larger bushes, then checked to see if they were hiding
the entrance. The bank grew steeper as he walked away
from the center of the playground.

Suddenly, Hightower felt the toe of his left shoe kick
against something hard. He stumbled forward a step, then
caught himself. He looked around to see what had tripped
him. At first the beam of his light showed him nothing
but a litter of leaves and small dead twigs. But then he
noticed the corner of a block of smooth limestone sticking out from the gnarled roots of a large tree. The block
looked like a paving stone. When he shone his light beside the tree, he saw what he had been searching for.

"Thank God," he said in a low, fervent voice. He
wouldn't have to comb through the woods for hours,
searching behind every bush for the tunnel entrance.

The stone was part of the small paved platform in front
of the door leading into the tunnel. Most of the pavement
was intact, but leaves and debris littered the platform, and
tufts of thick grass grew in the dirt that half covered it.
Mixed with the natural litter were fragments of brown
glass from smashed whiskey bottles and two shiny aluminum beer cans. The pavement was obviously a place for
local teenagers to sit and drink in seclusion.

The tunnel was virtually invisible. A semicircle of red
brick vaulting showed at the entrance, then the tunnel immediately disappeared into the steeply sloped hillside. A
profusion of vines, bushes, and small saplings grew
around and above the entrance. The thick vegetation
blended in with the scrub growth covering the entire area.

Hightower stepped onto the pavement and turned the
beam of his flashlight on the entrance. The door consisted
of a metal frame covered by a solid sheet of iron. The
iron was unpainted and scaly with thick orange rust. The
door's hinges were cemented into one of the limestone
posts that faced the red brick.

The door had no handle. Where one might have been,

a ragged hole had been cut into the plate with an acety-
lene torch. A heavy chain ran through the hole, then
looped through a thick iron staple set into the limestone.

The hardware had an old-fashioned hand-wrought look,
but there was nothing old-fashioned about the padlock securing the chain. Hightower examined it in the flashlight
beam. It had a gray metallic sheen, probably a steel-
molybdenum alloy. If so, it would be impossible to cut
the hasp with an ordinary hacksaw. He'd have to ask Don
if he could get him a diamond blade.

He heard the crunch of gravel as a car turned off the
road. He crouched down to look through the bushes, but
the foliage grew too thick. He would have to work his
way forward, toward the playground. As he twisted
through the brush, he glanced over his shoulder several
times, noting the shadowy shapes of particular trees and
bushes. Now that he had located the tunnel entrance, he
didn't want to waste time searching for it again.

Don had parked his unmarked car beside Hightower's
rented one. He was standing by the right fender, his bulky
shape making him look vaguely threatening in the faint
greenish light. He spotted Hightower as he broke free of
the bushes and started across the playground. They met at
the merry-go-round.

"I found the entrance." Hightower could hear the pitch
of excitement in his own voice.

"Can you get in?" Don asked.

"It's going to be a struggle. The door is chained and
fastened with a molybdenum padlock. I'm going to have
to have a diamond hacksaw."

"Not to worry," Don said. "I've got an easy way to get
you past the lock." He lifted a large foot and rested it on
the steel platform of the merry-go-round. "And I've got
something interesting to tell you."

"What is it?" Don spoke in his usual deliberate way,
but Hightower was sure he could catch an undertone of
agitation.

"We got a message from Susan. She's okay, and she's
broken loose from the takers."

"Thank God for that." Hightower felt the muscles around his eyes relax. "Where is she? Is she out of the building?"

"No, but she's someplace in the research tower."

"So she's still vulnerable." Hightower felt his face grow tight again. "She must be scared. Did you talk to her?"

"Nobody did. She sent us a computer message. She says there are three takers, and the leader is a guy called Cyberwolf." He gave Hightower a quizzical look. "Have you heard the name?"

"Never." Hightower shook his head. "But did Susan say she was okay?"

"She didn't say she wasn't." Don shrugged his large shoulders. "She said the resident supervisor and Mrs. Rostov are dead and that Meg's been injured. She didn't say how."

"So are the police going to change their plans?"

"I'm changing mine," Don said. "Susan gave us a couple of pieces of information that will help identify Cyberwolf."

"In the next couple of days?"

"In the next hour, if we're lucky. It turns out she's got a picture that he faked to show him and her together. She told us where to look for it, so the L.A. police are going after it."

"But even if you get a picture, you still have to hit it lucky to find somebody to identify him."

"I haven't told you the rest," Don said. "Susan said he faked the photo with a machine he called the Pix-Wizard." He paused. "Machines like that can't be all that common."

"I see," Hightower said, nodding. Don's optimism suddenly made sense. "You can find out from the manufacturer who bought the machines."

"There can't be many of them," Don said. "We can limit our search to L.A., because the car and hotel reservations came from there." He gave Hightower a steady look. "If we can ID this guy, we should be able to locate his computer and shut off the Chernobyl program."

"You think so?" Hightower didn't hide his skepticism.

"We've got to find it," Don said emphatically. "No two ways about it." His face took on a grim look.

"How about Murphy? Is she ready to storm the tower and get Susan out of there?"

"Not while the takers have got other hostages," Don said. "She wants us to find out who this Cyberwolf is, because then she'll be able to use some of the standard moves to psych him out and talk him into giving it up."

"I don't believe that will ever happen."

"I agree with you," Don said. "Otherwise I wouldn't be out here doing something of doubtful legality and putting my career on the line."

"The threat really hasn't changed," Hightower said. "Even if Susan is loose in the research building, they'll hunt her down." He turned his face toward the ground, biting the edge of his lower lip. "She may be in more danger now than she was before. They might kill her trying to capture her again."

"It's possible," Don admitted.

"I've got to get going." Hightower felt his stomach tighten with anxiety. "What did you bring me for the lock?"

"Walk over to the car with me."

Hightower followed Don across the playground and stood beside him while he unlocked the trunk. Don took out a gun with a barrel that was hardly longer than the stock. Keeping the muzzle pointed straight up, he passed the gun to Hightower.

"This is a ten-gauge shotgun with a chopped barrel," he said. "Have you ever used one?"

"I've fired a shotgun, but that was twenty years ago."

"This one's a slide-action, and its got a big kick. Be careful you don't let it knock you on your ass."

"A gun's fine, but I need something to cut off the lock."

Don reached over and patted the barrel of the shotgun.

"That's what this puppy is going to do for you." He turned and picked up something from the floor of the trunk. "These are as scarce as hen's teeth, and I could only get a couple."

Hightower held out his hand and accepted what seemed to be two shotgun shells. He hefted them, and they felt quite heavy, heavier than he remembered shotgun shells weighing.

"These are Shok-Lock rounds," Don said. "Load them in your weapon and fire them like ordinary shells."

"What are they?"

"They're ceramic projectiles. Instead of fragmenting and showering you with lots of dangerous metal, they vaporize on impact. And they get the job done, too." Don turned back to the trunk. "Now wait a second, and let me get you some real rounds."

Hightower slipped the Shok-Lock shells into his front pocket, then Don handed him a green canvas ammunition belt. Its loops were filled with shells, and the polished brass on the ends of the casings gleamed in the faint light.

The belt fit perfectly, without any adjustment. The shells were heavy, but just wearing the ammunition belt gave him a sense of power. Had the people who planted the bomb in the Citroën had the same experience?

"Won't the Shok-Lock shell make a lot of noise?"

"I'll call dispatch and tell them to ignore any complaints." Don turned to the car again. "I've got one last present for you. I wouldn't have it, except I found I'd left it in my car."

"What is it?" Hightower took the oval-shaped object Don was holding out to him. "It feels like a hand grenade."

"It's a flash-bang grenade," Don said. "It's a distraction device that produces a lot of light and noise." He paused, then gave Hightower a long, serious look. "Do your best to avoid trouble. Just remember, Rambo was crazy."

Hightower nodded to show Don that he understood the unspoken message. "I don't know how to thank you."

"I believe I told you the same thing after you put my hand back together." Don's face was still serious. "Now don't say anything else, because I don't want to know it."

"I know you're risking a lot," Hightower said. "Good luck tracking down the computer."

"When you get inside, give me a call. I won't call you. You don't want the phone in your pocket buzzing at the wrong time." Don fell silent and looked at Hightower a moment. He then gave his hand a firm shake and said in a formal tone, "Good luck to you, too, Doctor."

36

Now he knows exactly where I am.

An image of Whip's long sallow face with its twisted smile and dead eyes came into Susan's mind. Then the world suddenly shifted out of focus, and she felt herself swaying. She put a hand against the door to brace herself.

Oh, God, it's another anxiety attack. Was she going to faint again? That would be perfect for Whip. After everything she had been through, her body was now going to betray her.

From someplace deep inside, she felt a surge of anger. Whip wasn't going to take her so goddamned easily. She had seen what he did to Mrs. Rostov. He was at least going to have to work for his prize.

Her lips tightened as she realized that an important change had taken place in her. Her experiences as a captive and an escapee had peeled off the veneer of civilization and made her tougher and more resilient. She was in a situation in which the survival of the fittest had its most primitive meaning. If she had a weapon, she wouldn't feel any compunction about killing Whip. It was kill or be killed, and she was going to survive.

She began to feel steadier on her feet, and her eyes

were coming back into focus. She was going to have to start moving quickly. She would try to find a way out, but if she couldn't, she'd need a place to hide.

Suddenly, she heard another squeal. She whirled around, but she couldn't see where the noise was coming from. It must be some sort of animal, but she couldn't imagine what.

Her eyes darted from place to place, looking for a weapon or a hiding place. The room was small. Metal supply cabinets with glass fronts lined two walls, and a narrow operating table covered with a green drape stood at the opposite end.

She crossed over to the cabinets and glanced through the glass at the shelves. Green sheets and boxes of gauze pads and bandages were stacked on the bottom one; a variety of plastic bottles stood in rows on the top. If she had time to read the labels, she might find some kind of acid to throw in Whip's face. But she didn't see anything else that might be a weapon.

She turned to look at the operating table and saw that it was too narrow for her to hide under. Even if she hung a sheet over it, part of her would stick out. Directly to her right was an open door, and without wasting any more time, she ran toward it. For the third time she heard a squeal, but she was in such a hurry that it barely registered.

As she stepped into the room and closed the door, she was assaulted by smells. The air was filled with a rank animal odor mixed with the acrid scent of urine. Suddenly, she heard high-pitched squeals, then loud chattering and *ee-ee-ee* sounds.

Susan turned left and saw rows of metal cages stacked three high at the end of the room. Behind the stainless-steel mesh covering the doors, she could see the bright staring eyes, black noses, and grizzled brown-furred faces of at least two dozen large monkeys.

The monkeys increased their chattering. Their faces were twisted with either anger or fear, and they drew back their lips to show long yellow canine teeth. Some stuck delicate black fingers through the mesh and furiously rattled the cage doors.

Susan caught her breath and backed away from the cages. These weren't pet monkeys, but large wild animals for use in research. They were making threat displays, and if they got loose, she was sure they would attack. She remembered from her primate zoology class that monkeys were aggressive and had no particular fear of fighting with humans. They were extremely strong, and their bites could kill.

Yet the monkeys didn't so much frighten her as make her nervous. She ran her hand along the door's front edge, trying to locate a dead bolt. There wasn't one; it had only a slot for an electronic key card. She was wasting time.

She hurried across the room to the opposite door and jerked it open. She was starting to feel desperate. She had to do something to protect herself, even if it was only to run. If she ran far enough, fast enough, she might find a way out.

She let the metal door slam behind her. She was in another large lab, but she saw nothing of interest there except another door directly across from her. If she could get to the hall at the front of the building, she would surely be able to find a fire exit or some other route to the outside.

She grabbed the polished brass doorknob and turned it, but the door refused to budge. She pulled harder on the doorknob, feeling the sweat break out on her forehead. Nothing happened. She slapped the door with the flat of her hand, and tears blurred her eyes.

Despair spread through her body like a chill. She couldn't go forward, and she couldn't go back. Whip had her cornered. All at once, she seemed too tired to move. Maybe she should just give up. After all, she couldn't win a fight with Whip.

She turned and walked toward the center of the room. To her left, rising up from the floor near the wall, was a cylindrical stainless-steel tank four or five feet in diameter. The cylinder was covered by a domed lid polished to a mirror finish, and the enameled metal plate on top of the lid caught her eye. The message was in black and red letters against a white background:

CryoTech Tissue Preservation Equipment
WARNING: EXTREME LOW-TEMPERATURE HAZARD
THIS UNIT CONTAINS LIQUID NITROGEN AT -200° C.

As soon as she saw the temperature of the nitrogen, she began to piece together a plan. She wouldn't give up. Maybe Whip would kill her, but she wasn't going to make it easy for him. It was going to be her wits against his machine pistol.

The latch on the domed lid was like the fastener on an ice chest. She flipped up the hasp, then grabbed hold of the lid and pulled. It was heavier than she expected, and her first tug didn't move it at all. She bent her knees, braced her feet, and shoved upward with both hands. The lid moved an inch or so, and she shoved harder, using the power in her legs. She strained until she felt her muscles giving out. But just then the lid suddenly seemed to become weightless as a counterweight mechanism took hold. Relief swept over her, but she kept pushing, not stopping until the lid was balanced upright.

She was stretched over the open tank and could feel the heat draining from her body. She jumped away, and glancing down, she saw that the tank was filled to within six inches of the gray gasket around its rim. The liquid nitrogen looked less white than blue, a dark aqua that made her think of ancient glacial ice.

The nitrogen appeared to be on fire. Billowing white clouds boiled off its surface, and an endless smoky stream spewed out of the cylinder. The process was going faster than she had expected. Wisps were floating through the room, and soon the fog would become dense, maybe even impenetrable.

She hurried to the back of the room and scanned the

lab bench running the length of the wall. She saw only a few odds and ends of glassware, a hot plate, a scale, and several small pieces of electronic equipment. Nothing looked usable as a weapon.

Just then she heard the high-pitched sounds of the monkeys squealing and chattering. *It's got to be Whip.* They were yelling at him the way they had yelled at her.

She crouched on the floor beside a heavy wooden table that was set at right angles to the back wall. It was almost directly in front of the nitrogen tank, so the white haze around it was already thick. Hardly daring to breathe, she looked nervously toward the door. *Where in the hell is he?* Waiting for something to happen was almost worse than having it happen.

She started crawling behind the table so she would have more cover. All at once her left hand plunged into a nest of loose wires and thin black hoses. She jerked her hand back, glad that she hadn't pulled some piece of equipment down on her head.

Glancing up, she saw a rectangular gray metal box about a foot tall and two feet long. Protruding four or five inches from its front was a short cylinder. The instrument looked familiar, then she realized that it was a twin of the laser she had used in a geology seminar her senior year at Barnard.

Suddenly, she glimpsed a slight movement at the side of the room and jerked her head around. The fog was growing heavier, and objects were becoming difficult to make out. But she could see well enough to tell that the door was opening slowly. Just as a small crack showed between it and the jamb, the movement stopped. Whip's eye was sure to be peering through the narrow slit. He would be surveying the room, searching for her.

Moving as quietly as she could, she continued to crawl around the table. When she reached the side opposite the door, she raised up to a crouching position and looked at the door. It was open much wider, wide enough for someone to walk in, but she still couldn't see Whip. She glanced at the printed metal label on the box on the table and she saw that she had been right: it was an argon laser.

She strained her ears, but she heard nothing. Even the monkeys had stopped their chattering. The room was deathly quiet. The only sound was the noise of her pulse beating a regular rhythm against her eardrums. The drifting clouds of white fog and the complete silence made her think of the Arctic. She could be isolated in some remote plot of icy wasteland and feel no more helpless than she felt now.

Then she realized that she wasn't helpless. She had a weapon at hand. *She could use the laser as a weapon.*

If she aimed it at Whip, she might not be able to hit him. If she did, the beam probably wouldn't even burn his skin. But if she could blind him with the flash, she might have a chance of getting out of the trap she had run into.

She reached up and rocked back the switch that turned on the laser system. A steady throbbing sound started up. It wasn't loud, but in the silence it was like a scream. The sound brought back memories of her lab days. The throbbing was the pump circulating the coolant. To fire the beam, she would have to press the red button on the opposite side.

She glanced toward the door, but she could no longer see if it was open or closed. The door itself had become indistinct. The frozen nitrogen was still boiling out of the steel tank, and the fog filling the room was as woolly as cotton candy.

She felt a prickling on the back of her neck, and her jaw quivered. She had thought the fog would protect her by making it difficult for Whip to locate her. But now she realized that the fog worked both ways. He was out there someplace, hidden in the white blur and silently searching for her.

She held her breath, then strained her ears for the smallest sound. She could hear only the steady thumping of the coolant pump. She raised up high enough to peer over the top of the table. The area around the door looked like a field of clouds seen from the window of an airplane.

Some patches of fog were denser than others, and at first they gave the impression of being physical objects. But as she stared at them, they shifted and changed, adopting new forms as drafts of air strayed into them.

The thumping sound was going to give Whip something to home in on. He would be curious about the noise and want to investigate it. She had to be ready to lift the laser, point it at him, and press the red button. She would have to catch him at a distance, because if he got too close, he would simply knock her makeshift protection out of her hands.

She needed another weapon so she would be ready for close-in fighting. She turned toward the lab bench. Maybe she should get one of the glass flasks. If she broke off the bottom, she could use the jagged neck the way people did in movie fight scenes.

Still crouching, she turned around slowly and moved toward the bench with both hands held out. She counted her steps—six of them—then her fingers touched the front of the cabinets. She ran her hands along the smooth top of the bench, stretching as far as she could reach in both directions. She found nothing, not even a petri dish or a sponge.

Desperation swelled up in her chest like an inflating balloon. She had to find something quickly. She took three small sideways steps. Suddenly, a hand gripped her ankle. *She hadn't seen him because he crawled through the door, then along the floor.* Her heart stopped beating, and she found it hard to get a breath. The white fog appeared to ripple, and for a moment she thought again that she might faint.

"Hello, you sweet little bitch." Whip seemed to be speaking through clenched teeth. "You shouldn't want to hide from me."

She heard herself making tiny incoherent cries, almost like the whimpering of a puppy. Her mind disengaged from her surroundings, and for a fleeting moment, she felt uninterested in what was happening. Then her body took over, and it was as if a program designed to ensure survival was directing her actions.

She lunged forward, trying to jerk her leg free, but Whip's fingers were welded to her ankle. She twisted her leg from side to side, but his grip was like a steel trap. He was holding her so tightly she couldn't even feel her skin slip under his fingers. They seemed clamped to the bone.

Whip suddenly gave her ankle a sharp pull. She teetered in the air for a moment. Then with a sickening sensation in her stomach, she felt herself falling facedown.

She threw out her hands to protect her head, but her chest hit the concrete floor with an impact that knocked the breath out of her. Gasping for air, she pulled herself forward on her elbows, scrabbling along the floor like a crab. She could sense Whip's hand groping for her, yet she didn't feel scared. She was too preoccupied with surviving.

Whip caught the toe of her shoe, but she twisted her foot and jerked out of his grasp. She shoved her right foot backward like a steam-driven piston, and the ball of her foot struck him solidly in the face. He gave a sharp grunt of pain, and she felt a rush of satisfaction.

"You fucking cunt." He spat out the words. "You hit me where I was cut, and now I'm goddamned well going to cut you."

Susan got to her knees, then struggled up from the floor. She wavered a moment, as if slightly drunk, then started to run. She ran blindly through the fog, knowing only that she had to get away from Whip.

She had covered hardly more than a dozen feet when she heard him behind her. His breathing was heavy and ragged, and he was so close she could feel heat radiating from his body. Suddenly, he lunged forward and grabbed her right arm near the shoulder, wrapping his hand around it in a steel grip. She pushed herself forward, trying to break free, and dragged Whip with her.

Then all at once, he braced his feet and pulled her toward him. The force spun her around, jerking her arm free. She fell sideways to the floor, hitting her right shoulder on the edge of the lab bench. She felt a stab of pain, and her arm went numb.

Whip looked down at her stretched out on the floor, but the fog was so thick she could hardly make out his face. He dropped to his knees beside her feet and shoved the machine pistol behind his back. Then before she realized what he was doing, he climbed on top of her, covering her body with his.

He pushed down hard, crushing her chest against the cool concrete floor. Leaning on his forearms, he peered into her eyes and gave her a leering smile. The long raw cut from Mrs. Rostov's knife ran along his left check almost to the corner of his mouth. Her kick had opened the wound, and blood was seeping out and running down his neck. His face was streaked with dried blood, making him look like a participant in some savage ritual.

"You don't want to run away from me, sugar," Whip whispered. He pushed his face close to hers, the death's-head earring dangling over her eye. His hot breath had a foul odor, and she turned her head to the side.

"Let me go," she said. She shifted her hips, trying to get out from under the weight of his body.

"Oh, that feels so good." Whip's voice took on a languid, moaning tone. He thrust himself against her, and she could feel his erection through the layers of clothes separating them. "I love the way you squirm around."

"You're crushing me." Susan gasped out the words. "I can't breathe."

Feeling had returned to her right arm, and she reached out toward the cabinets under the lab bench. Her hand bumped against one of the doors, and she stuck her fingers under the bottom edge and pulled. The door opened silently. She slipped her hand inside and groped around on the lower shelf.

"I'll move—right after I mark your pretty little face." Whip murmured the words, as if they were endearments.

"I'll go back with you." She spoke in a choked, breathy

voice, allowing herself to sound scared. "I won't try to escape."

She strained to stretch her arm more to the right, pushing her hand farther back into the shelf.

"I always wanted to cut me a little piece of a movie star," Whip said. He smiled. but his eyes were as cold and hard as dark glass marbles. "Maybe if you treat me right, I might decide not to carve my initials on your cheek."

Whip shoved his right hand between their bodies and located the fly of her jeans. He raised his body off hers and tugged on the metal button at the top.

Just as the button slipped loose, her fingers touched something cylindrical and ribbed but with the smoothness of plastic. The object was close, but she couldn't get her fingers around it. She shifted her hips again, pushing herself against Whip, then sliding right to extend her grasp.

"I thought you'd start to like it some." Whip forced himself between her legs and began to nuzzle her face, rubbing the stubble of his beard over her cheeks. Her skin stung.

She suddenly lunged to the right, almost pulling her arm out of its socket. As her hand closed around the hard cylinder, she felt a thrill of triumph.

It was a screwdriver. Sticking out of its ribbed plastic handle was a thin six-inch shaft tipped with a narrow, tapered blade. She quickly brought her arm down by her side so that the tool was hidden under her leg.

"Get off me," she ordered Whip. She could hardly get enough breath to speak, but her voice no longer had a pleading tone. Whip was still rubbing his face against hers, and his cheek brushed against her lips. His skin had a sour musty taste.

"I'll get off when I roll off." Whip moved his head slightly, trying to find her mouth with his. As she twisted out of the way, his fingers grasped the zipper of her jeans.

Susan wrapped her hand around the screwdriver handle, squeezing it as if trying to crush it. If she stabbed him in the back, the blade might hit a bone and slide off. That would turn him into an enraged animal. She needed

to stab him someplace soft, someplace that would do serious damage.

She slid the screwdriver along her leg and rotated her
wrist so that the blade pointed upward. The narrow tip
was only a few inches from Whip's stomach. She kept her
head turned to the side and clenched her jaw so hard the
muscles began to ache. Her palms felt cold and sweaty,
and she was glad the handle was ribbed. But she was
ready—her mind was ready.

As Whip started pulling down on her zipper, she
rammed the blade upward with as much force as she
could muster. She could feel the sharp tip tear through his
shirt, catch on his skin, then pop through. The full length
of the long shaft slid smoothly into his stomach. A gush
of hot blood spilled over her hand. She gritted her teeth,
gave the screwdriver an extra push, then jerked it out.

Whip's face froze in a mask of pain. He sucked in a
deep breath with a loud whistling noise. He pulled himself up on his knees, then rocked back to sit on her legs,
pinning her in place. She tried to move, but his weight
was too great.

He looked down at her with a disbelieving expression,
shaking his head, as though stunned. Then, all at once, his
eyes became wild with rage.

"You're going to die, you fucking little whore." His
voice was soft and low, almost caressing. His left hand
was pressed against his side, but blood ran through his
fingers.

He lunged for the screwdriver, and as she jerked it out
of his reach, it flew from her hand. While it was still clattering on the floor, she drew back her right arm and hit
him in the center of his stomach with the heel of her
hand, putting all her strength behind the blow.

Whip gave a sharp cry, and as he doubled over in pain,
she pulled her legs toward her chest. Her movement
threw him off balance and he lurched to one side. Susan
rolled out from under him, scrabbling across the floor and
into the fog.

Then she was on her feet and running.

37

By the time Don Lindsley had started backing out of the parking lot, Hightower was already jogging across the playground. He clasped the shotgun around the middle with the chopped-off barrel pointed toward the sky.

When he reached the sloping bank, he slowed down, then made his way along the edge until he recognized the place where he had come through the bushes. He pushed past the shrubs into the darker hidden area behind them. He felt his neck muscles relax when he saw that he was only a few feet from the tunnel entrance.

As soon as he reached the rusty iron door, he groped for the lock and twisted around so that it was hanging with its broad front toward him. He pulled back the shotgun's slide and dropped in a Shok-Lock round. He pushed the release button, and when the slide snapped into place, he pumped the shell into the chamber.

He should have asked Don for a large flashlight. He held the small one in his left hand, focusing the beam on the lock, then aimed the shotgun with his right hand. Was the muzzle lined up with the lock? *I just goddamned can't see well enough.* The muscles of his hand grew weak, and he lowered the shotgun and flexed his fingers to get the blood to flow.

To solve the aiming problem, he would have to get close to the lock and fire quickly. He moved nearer the door and held out the shotgun, aiming it like a pistol. When its muzzle was a foot from the lock, he pulled the trigger.

The shotgun exploded with a deafening roar and a harsh flash of red and yellow light. Something that felt like a spray of sand hit him in the face, and the force of the discharged shell kicked the gun backward. It twisted and bucked in his hand like a live animal. He held tightly to the stock, but the gun broke free of his grip and clattered to the pavement.

He bent over and examined the lock with the flashlight.

He saw at once that it hadn't been destroyed. His shot had struck the upper part of the lock and bent back a corner so that it resembled a dog-eared page. But the hasp was still fastened. Hightower kicked the door so hard that the chain rattled.

Can't I do anything right anymore? Have I become a helpless cripple? Susan was in there, alone and frightened. He was so close to her, yet he couldn't even break in with a shotgun. He kicked the door again, hard enough to make his foot hurt.

The pain felt almost satisfying, but he knew he was wasting time by giving in to his frustration. He wiped the particles of sand off his face and picked up the shotgun. He kicked aside the spent cartridge and dropped in the remaining Shok-Lock round.

He knelt on the paved area, laid down the shotgun, and started gathering up small stones. Working quickly, he began making a pile of them about four feet from the door. When the mound was several inches high, he turned on the flashlight, rested one end on top of the stones, and focused the beam exactly on the lock. Kneeling down, he rested his left elbow on his knee and held the muzzle of the shotgun six inches from the lock.

He pulled the trigger slowly. The explosion made his ears ring, and the sudden flash of red and yellow blinded him. Once more, a spray of sand hit him in the face. But even before he touched the lock, he could see that the shell had done its job. The body of the lock was twisted metal, and the hasp was hanging loose.

He retrieved his flashlight, then pulled the lock out of the chain and dropped it on the ground. He began to work the links of the heavy chain through the iron staple. He could feel the rust sticking to his fingers like talcum powder. When at last the chain fell free, he put three fingers into the ragged hole and pulled the door toward him. The bottom slid roughly over dirt and grass.

Stepping to the side so he could see past the door, Hightower found himself looking into the dark emptiness of a brick-lined tunnel.

38

Going as fast as she dared, Susan made for the door she had come through. Patches of steam white fog swirled around her and made it hard to see, yet she couldn't stop. Whip was so badly hurt that he might die, but he was going to do his best to kill her first. She had no doubt about that.

As she approached the middle of the room, the fog completely enveloped her. She slowed to keep from stumbling over something. If she fell, Whip would be on her like an attack dog, and she wouldn't get another chance to escape.

"You're going to die in a bad way!" Whip screamed. His voice was raw and hoarse. "I'm going to show you some knife tricks."

Her heart jumped, then beat faster. A high-pitched buzzing filled her ears. He sounded close, maybe only a few feet away. Her teeth began to chatter, and she couldn't stop them.

She glanced behind her and saw the shadowy shape of Whip feeling his way through the fog. He was holding his left hand to his side and carrying the machine pistol in the other.

She realized that she wasn't going to be able to get through the door. Whip was too close. As soon as she opened it, he would spray her with bullets. But if she could just get to the laser, she could at least defend herself.

The steady throbbing of the coolant pump was getting clearer and stronger. The table must be only a few feet away. She held out her right hand and moved it from side to side, sketching an arc in the air. She glanced left and saw the blurry outline of the nitrogen tank. It looked like a boiling cauldron. Thick white clouds were surging up from it, and the supercooled gas had changed the atmosphere of the room. The air had become dank and heavy, and it was cold so near the tank.

Suddenly, her outstretched fingers brushed the edge of the table, and she felt a rush of elation. She kept her hands on the table, then worked her way around to the back. She lifted the laser and cradled it so the lens was pointed in the direction she had come from. Whip could chop her down in a fraction of a second, so she had to be ready to take him by surprise.

But would the damned thing work?

Whip suddenly came into view. He saw her at the same time and stood absolutely still, staring at her. He obviously didn't know what she was pointing at him. She used the time to aim the lens at his face.

The clouds of fog suddenly grew thinner, and for a moment she saw Whip with startling clarity. He was a nightmarish figure, with cold eyes and an expressionless blood-streaked face. He seemed hardly more than a machine, a fabricated zombie lacking all capacity for human warmth.

She pointed the lens toward his left eye.

Whip remained still, then she saw a slight change in his expression. The muscles around his eyes tightened, turning his face into a rigid mask. She saw that he had decided not to take any more chances with her. Even if he couldn't torture her to death, he could still kill her.

The steady thumping of the cooling pump against her chest blended with the surging beat of her heart. Through the shroud of white swirling around Whip, she detected a slight motion of his right hand, and the muzzle of the machine pistol began to swing toward her.

She pushed the discharge button. A pencil-thin beam of green light shot out from the lens, cutting an absolutely straight path through the patchy fog. Almost simultaneously, she heard a brief sizzling sound, like the noise of frying bacon. Whip clawed at his left eye, and Susan felt a sudden flood of horror and relief.

With the bloody fingers of his left hand clasped over his eye, Whip pulled the trigger on the machine pistol.

Susan dropped to the floor behind the table, holding the laser in front of her, and the burst of fire cut through the air above her head. Stretching out flat, she again pointed the lens toward Whip's face. The angle was low, and swirling fog made it impossible to see her target clearly.

Whip fired another burst, and the bullets hit the top of the table above her head. Splinters showered down on her. She felt a sharp pain, like a wasp sting, as one hit her cheek.

Before he could fire again, Susan pushed the discharge button. Once more a thin streak of bright green light stabbed through the fog like a knitting needle rammed into a bundle of white cotton. She could see the light pass harmlessly by Whip's head. But while the sizzling noise of the beam was still in her ears, she shifted the laser to the left and pressed the button another time. Without waiting to see the results, she pressed it again and again, moving the laser in an arc and filling the air with glowing shafts of green light.

Whip suddenly dropped his gun and clapped his hand over his right eye. He stood unmoving in the billowing fog with both eyes covered.

Weak with relief, she set down the laser. As she stood up, her hip bumped the table and it scraped the floor. Whip instantly grabbed for the machine pistol swinging on its strap. Susan fell to the floor, then scuttled to the left. She had hardly moved before shots tore into the vinyl tiles where she had been crouching. She heard the dull twang of bullets ricocheting off the metal case of the laser.

She moved farther left, doing her best not to cause any noise. Even so, the soles of her shoes made small squeaking sounds on the polished vinyl. Whip immediately swiveled in her direction and fired a burst from the machine pistol.

She could hear the peculiar whistling noise of the high-velocity bullets as they tore through the air above her head. She found herself holding her breath, not daring to breathe. Then she made herself exhale and slowly draw in more air.

He had aimed too high, and he was now staring straight ahead. His head didn't seem to be moving, so he wasn't tracking anything with his eyes. She felt sure the laser had blinded him, but he was still dangerous, and he was still trying to kill her.

He took two steps in her direction, then stopped. He cocked his head and listened. He was directly in front of the tank of liquid nitrogen. The nitrogen gave off an almost imperceptible hissing noise as it turned into gas. Plumes of fog spewed up behind him, forming a dense white backdrop. He stood out like a cobra crawling on the snow.

Susan squatted down where she was, hoping her knees wouldn't pop. If Whip started firing again, she wanted to present him with the worst possible target. As she looked up at him looming above her, it suddenly occurred to her how she might win the battle.

She eased herself flat on the floor and stretched out her legs. Doing her best to avoid making the slightest sound, she pulled up her right leg and slipped off her shoe. She took off the other. Holding a shoe in each hand, she got to her knees, then stood up straight.

She looked directly at Whip. He obviously couldn't see her, but she felt only a moment of relief, because her mind was already racing ahead, choreographing her actions. She would have to act fast before she made a noise and gave away her location or before Whip decided to start firing at random.

She grasped the shoe in her right hand by the toe, then pitched it toward the table. It sailed in a graceful arc and hit the floor with a sharp crack. She tossed the second shoe.

Whip wheeled around toward the direction of the noise and fired. He shot one burst, shifted the gun to the right, and shot another. Acrid gray smoke spewed out of the barrel and mixed with the clouds of water vapor.

While the gun was still chattering, Susan ran toward

Whip, hoping that the soft padding of her feet would be drowned out by the shots. Yet Whip seemed to sense that something was happening. He whirled toward her, bringing the machine pistol level with her face. But before he could fire, she lowered her head and ran into him full tilt. Her right shoulder caught him in the midsection, and he stumbled back. The pistol jerked upward, firing shots toward the ceiling.

Susan recovered her balance before Whip did. She braced her feet on the floor, and with as much force as she could muster, she shoved him backward. Whip half turned in the air, gave a single high-pitched scream, then fell against the lip of the tank of liquid nitrogen. He hung balanced on the edge for a moment, as if deciding what to do, then tumbled into the tank. The supercooled nitrogen bubbled up with a loud hiss, and thick white clouds rose to the surface.

Susan bit her lip and watched as Whip flailed his arms, struggling to rise. It was like watching a silent film, because Whip made no sound. Then he somehow managed to get a foothold and stand up in the tank, but suddenly his movements stopped abruptly. His eyes bulged, his mouth dropped open, and his face turned to blue-white as a mask of ice formed over his skin. His body plunged back into the cylinder, partly disappearing below the surface of the liquid gas. He was turning to solid ice.

Susan felt herself go limp. She wasn't sure she could move, but she couldn't bear to watch any longer. She turned and made her way to where she had thrown her shoes. When she reached the table, she knelt down and crawled around, feeling on the floor for them. She found one almost immediately.

Suddenly, a dull *boom!* shook the entire room, rattling the equipment on the lab benches. Susan dropped flat and threw her hands over her head. Her ears rang, and a concussion wave from the explosion made her skin vibrate. White fog rolled over her, then billowed up to form a tower as high as the ceiling.

All at once, small fragments, as delicate as broken

crystal, fell down around her. The pieces were no larger than hailstones, and they bounded off her and onto the floor. The strange rain was over almost as quickly as it began, and she got up from the floor and looked over at the nitrogen tank.

What in the world had happened? Did the gas blow up?

Then she understood. The supercooled nitrogen had changed Whip's body into a crystalline solid, but then the nitrogen had combined with the oxygen in his tissues, and that caused him to explode. The delicate crystalline fragments strewn around the room were pieces of his body.

Whip had literally shattered like glass.

39

Gibson stood in the doorway of Susan's room and glanced around. The powder blue duvet and the top sheet of the bed were pulled down. Susan seemed only to have gone out for a while, and in a moment she would return and climb into bed.

As he stepped inside, he felt a stirring of excitement, a tingling that started at his groin and ran across his stomach to his chest. He could sense Susan's presence. He was invading her territory, and that made him feel close to her. Yet he wanted more than a few slight traces of her.

Talking to her had made him feel shy and awkward. It was as if a shell of ice had suddenly surrounded his heart, and he was unable to respond the way he wanted. Even so, being near her—her pure physical presence—gave him more pleasure than he had imagined possible.

Yet the pleasure came with a sharp edge of frustration. To satisfy the urgency he felt, he needed more. He needed to take control of her body, to possess it. Only then could he enjoy it completely—admire it, appreciate it, and even worship it. Her body would be his shrine, his temple, his altar, the perfect effigy in his necropolis. If only he could take her with him, he could spend as much time as he wanted doing whatever he wanted to her. But he would be traveling alone, and without Cortez or Whip, he would have no way to control her.

Softly closing the door behind him, he crossed the beige carpet and pulled open the middle drawer of the mahogany chest of drawers. He looked down at the orderly rows of clothes, then rifled through a stack of neatly folded shirts. He admired the pale pastels, the soft whites, and the complicated patterns of colors that caught his eye. He began realigning the edges, so that no one could tell what he had done.

He wondered if Whip had found her yet. But he tried to push the question from his mind, because he didn't want to think about what Whip might do to her. He hadn't really wanted him to go after her, but he had no real choice. It was the only way to defuse an explosive situation. Anyway, by the time Whip brought Susan back, she wouldn't be much interested in running anymore. She would be easy to control.

Before the helicopter arrived, he would have her sent to this room, then he would follow her inside and lock the door. He didn't want to leave marks on her beautiful body, so he wouldn't shoot her. He would ask her to take off her clothes, and he would put his hands around her soft neck.

He would be gentle at first, then grip her more tightly, shutting off the carotid artery. Her naked body would twist and curl, thrusting itself against him. Then all of a sudden, it would be as if a string had broken and she would stop moving. She would become quiet and peaceful, her body solid, beautiful, and still hot with blood— *still hot with blood.* She could no longer leave, no longer run from him. He would possess her and worship her, if only for a little while.

On the left side of the drawer, a pile of bikini underpants in a variety of colors were tossed together randomly. He picked up a pair and held them in front of him, spreading out his fingers to stretch the elastic. They were dark blue with a pale pink rose embroidered on the right side.

When Susan was wearing them, the small patch of fabric in front would barely cover her pubic hair, and the blue would look almost black against the pale smooth skin of her thighs. The rose would nestle in the soft hollow area of her pelvis.

Hearing a sharp rap on the door, he dropped the underpants into the drawer and closed it noiselessly. "Come in," he called. He stepped back from the chest and looked across the room. Cortez was standing in the doorway.

"Hey, Cyber. The kid says he's hungry. Can he go to the kitchen by himself?"

"After what the old woman did?" Gibson shook his head. "The kitchen's got too many potential weapons."

"Man, I'm getting hungry too." Cortez's voice took on a whining tone. "How about if I make him stay with Meg and I get something for both of us?"

"If you leave him by himself, he might try something, and I don't want him killed. As I keep saying, hostages are like insurance."

"How about if you stay with them? I'll just be a minute."

"I'm about to go down to use the computer." Gibson suddenly felt the need to explain why he was in Susan's room. "I'm just here to get a blanket to cover up the guy you shot. I'm sick of looking at him."

Cortez said nothing, but he didn't turn to go. Gibson realized that Cortez was waiting for him to work out a solution.

"All right," Gibson said, as if answering a question. "Take the kid with you, and both of you can get something to eat."

"How about Meg?"

"She's not going anywhere." He shook his head and smiled at Cortez. "I clipped her toenails too short."

Cortez laughed, then left without closing the door. Gibson pulled the duvet off the bed. He folded it in half, then rolled it up and tucked it under his arm.

As he left the room, he saw Cortez and Tim going toward the kitchen. Tim was walking in front, and in contrast with the round bulky shape of Cortez, he was slight and extremely thin.

Gibson walked down the marble hall at a fast pace. He should have been down at the computer already, zipping mail out to the cops. Not getting even an acknowledgment was beginning to make him nervous. He had expected the cops to E-mail him immediately, demanding to speak to Susan and trying to persuade him to release some hostages.

Probably what he had told Whip was right; they were playing some mind game, trying to psych him. They would be expecting him to be worried enough by now to start backing down on his demands, so he was going to have to turn the handle on the vise one more round. The best way to do that was by moving up the deadline.

He walked behind the desk and glanced down at Joe Ling's body. Ling's head was turned to the side, and his striped tie hung down at an angle, as though he had been strangled with it. The puddle of blood under him had become dark and thick. His face looked waxy.

Gibson had seen hundreds of photographs of bodies, but this was the first actual damaged body he had seen. It hadn't bothered him particularly while he was with Susan and involved in the business of making ransom demands. Now, though, he found the experience unpleasant. He didn't like looking at the torn and shredded flesh, and he particularly didn't like the sweet, almost rotten stench of the drying blood.

He unfolded the duvet, flapped it in the air, then let it settle gently over the body. With a sense of relief he stepped over to the desk and glanced at the TV monitoring the front door. Nothing had changed. All he could see was the floor and the stainless-steel speaker panel on the wall.

Sitting on the edge of the desk with the keyboard on

his lap, he booted the computer, then flipped the switch on the monitor. The blank screen gradually turned a luminous gray. He called up *Mail received* and glanced at the last name on the time-ordered list. It was Ling, just the way it had been before. The cops still hadn't answered. This time he was goddamned going to *make* them pay attention to him, but before he could do that, he had to change a few lines in the Chernobyl program.

He stroked a few keys, then after a series of sharp beeps he got a long, low tone. He was on the net. He used the same bang path as before, going to MIT, then through a satellite link and the Tymnet international gate to the Oxford Mathematical Laboratory. This time, though, the final hop was from Oxford to Los Angeles.

He entered the password admitting him into his system and called up the Chernobyl program on the living room computer. He went directly to the last subsection, the one containing the time code, then paused to glance at his watch. Would thirty minutes be enough for the cops to arrange for a helicopter? More important, could Whip get Susan back before the deadline he had in mind? He added fifteen minutes.

While he was making the changes, his breathing slowed. He was easing into cyberspace, and he felt relaxed and untroubled. Some code or process might be puzzling, but only for a while. It was never a complete mystery to a software wizard. If you groked the system, deep magic was possible, and cyberspace was heaven.

He erased part of the line containing the program command, substituted the new time, then saved the change to disk. He sent a copy of the altered program to the necropolis computer, along with an overwrite command. The new file would replace the existing one, so the changes would be effective on both machines.

He broke contact with his system and put down the keyboard. He stretched his neck, raised his shoulders, and smiled. He hadn't done anything stupid, anything that would let the cops track down the computer in the necropolis. Some hacker working for them might be able to follow the bang path and get to his machine. But that would probably take a couple of days. Even then, the path would get them only to his living room machine and no farther. It was the cutout between him and the necropolis computer. Somebody might think to try an equipment-number trace on the phone link he used in transferring the file, but that number was untraceable. He had made the assignment himself and so deep inside NYNEX that no record of it appeared in any user file. Any trail would dead-end in his living room, if not long before.

Now he was ready to deal with the cops. He listened to the faint buzzing sound of emptiness, then the rapid tone pattern. He was connected. He pulled down a menu, chose *Chat mode,* then started typing.

THIS IS JOHN ARMSTRONG IN OXFORD FOR THE ASSOCIATION FOR PSYCHIATRICALLY DISABLED PEOPLE. I HAVE NEW ORDERS CONCERNING THE SITUATION IN JOHNSON HALL. GET ME THE PERSON IN CHARGE.

Please wait. I'll get Lt. Augustine.

Augustine must have been only a few feet away, because the response was immediate.

This is George Augustine, John. Glad you decided to get in touch again, because we need to talk. But first, can you assure me the hostages are all okay?

LING AND ROSTOV ARE DEAD AND YOU ARE RESPONSIBLE. I GAVE ORDERS, BUT YOU NEVER ACKNOWLEDGED RECEIVING THEM OR ASSURED ME YOU WOULD CARRY THEM OUT.

John, that's bad news about the hostages. I'm out here doing everything possible to resolve this situation, and killing two innocent people isn't going to make my job easier. People are going to think you can't be trusted.

CUT THE CRAP, AUGUSTINE. YOU'RE STALLING TO TRY TO WAIT OUT THE TAKEOVER, BUT YOU WON'T BE ABLE TO DO IT. THE COST WILL BE TOO GREAT. NOT ONLY WILL YOU FORCE THE LIBERATION FIGHTERS TO KILL MORE HOSTAGES, BUT THE CHERNOBYL PROGRAM WILL MELT DOWN NYNEX. I'M MOVING THE DEADLINE FORWARD.

John, I don't understand what you mean. Please explain.

EVERYTHING WILL BE MADE CLEAR TO YOU IN THE FOLLOWING REVISED ORDERS. DO NOT INTERRUPT.

ESSENTIAL BACKGROUND: THE CHERNOBYL PROGRAM HAS BEEN RESCHEDULED TO BECOME OPERATIVE AT 3:30 A.M. IF YOU FOLLOW THESE ORDERS EXACTLY, THE PROGRAM WILL BE CANCELED. IF YOU DO NOT, YOU MUST ACCEPT RESPONSIBILITY FOR THE TERRIBLE CONSEQUENCES.

1. THE TRANSFER OF THE TWENTY MILLION DOLLARS ($20,000,000) TO THE BAHRAIN ACCOUNT MUST BE COMPLETED WITHIN THIRTY (30) MINUTES—BY 2:30 A.M.

2. THE THREE SUITCASES CONTAINING ONE MILLION DOLLARS ($1,000,000) EACH MUST BE LEFT INSIDE THE ENTRYWAY OF JOHNSON HALL BY THREE (3:00) A.M.

3. THE HELICOPTER MUST LAND IN THE PARKING LOT ON THE NORTH SIDE OF THE RESEARCH TOWER BY TWO-FORTY-FIVE (2:45) A.M. YOU MUST CONFIRM THAT THE HELICOPTER WILL ARRIVE AT THIS TIME BY SENDING ME AN E-MAIL MESSAGE AT TWO-THIRTY (2:30) A.M.

4. THE JET MUST BE WAITING AT LOGAN AIRPORT AND READY TO TAKE OFF IMMEDIATELY. THERE CAN BE NO STALLING. (NO WAITING FOR REFUELING, MECHANICAL CHECKS, ETC.)

THE CHERNOBYL PROGRAM WILL AUTOMATICALLY ACTIVATE UNLESS I CANCEL IT. HENCE, IT IS IN THE INTEREST OF EVERYONE TO AVOID DELAY AND EXPEDITE THE PASSAGE OF THE LIBERATION FIGHTERS.

5. THE LIBERATION FIGHTERS WILL LEAVE JOHNSON HALL, RETRIEVE THE SUITCASES, AND GO DIRECTLY TO THE HELICOPTER FOR TRANSPORTATION TO LOGAN. SUSAN BRADSTREET WILL BE WITH THEM. IF THEY ARE FIRED ON OR HINDERED, SHE WILL BE KILLED IMMEDIATELY.

6. SUSAN BRADSTREET WILL BE RELEASED BY THE LIBERATION FIGHTERS AS SOON AS THEY BOARD THE AIRCRAFT AT LOGAN.

7. THE CHERNOBYL PROGRAM WILL BE ABORTED WHEN THE AIRCRAFT CONTAINING THE LIBERATORS IS OUT OF U.S. AIRSPACE AND ON ITS WAY TO THE DESTINATION THAT THEY WILL GIVE TO THE PILOT.

ACKNOWLEDGE THAT YOU HAVE RECEIVED AND UNDER-

STAND THESE ORDERS AND ARE PREPARED TO CARRY THEM OUT.

John, I understand what you would like for us to do, but you're rushing us. It takes a long time to get a helicopter.

BULLSHIT. IF YOU DON'T HAVE A POLICE HELICOPTER, GET ONE FROM A TV STATION THAT USES TRAFFIC COPTERS. NO MORE EXCUSES. AND DON'T FORGET TO CONFIRM THE HELICOPTER AT 2:30.

Your ideas are good, Johnny. You've obviously given everything a lot of thought. But what we need from you is an indication that you're acting in good faith and will keep your promises. We would consider the release of a hostage a good sign. How about letting Tim walk out the front door? You can gain a lot of goodwill out here by turning loose a kid.

STOP WASTING TIME. YOU HAVE LESS THAN 30 MINUTES TO TRANSFER THE 20 MILLION DOLLARS. I WILL BE EXPECTING A MESSAGE.

Wait, don't go. To show our good faith, we've talked to the Galaxy people, and they've agreed to put up the ransom money.

I'M NOT INTERESTED IN THE PROCESS, ONLY THE RESULTS.

That's what I'm trying to tell you. We've already transferred the money to the account in Bahrain.

DON'T LIE TO ME.

I'm not lying. The transfer is complete. But now we need something from you. We've made the first move to show you that you can trust us, but now you've got to prove we can trust you. Turn Tim loose, and we'll know you're somebody we can work with.

MAKE THE OTHER ARRANGEMENTS. I'LL GET BACK TO YOU ON TIM.

We need to settle it now. I'm going to make a—

Gibson tapped out the hang-up command and cut off Augustine in midsentence. He put down the keyboard, then wrapped his arms across his chest, feeling so elated that he found himself smiling. Twenty million dollars— all his. He was free to do whatever he wanted. He really could build a mansion with underground tunnels and a private mortuary.

But was Augustine telling the truth? His smile died away. Maybe they thought they could bullshit him and get him to turn Tim loose. Then they would say they did something else and tell him to turn Meg loose. They wanted to bargain with him, make swaps for people.

Ultimately, they wanted him to turn everybody loose, then be forced to cut a deal with them to come out and take a lighter prison sentence. The assholes would tell him anything he wanted to hear. They'd lie to him up and down and sideways to get him to bend over so they could fuck him.

A hot surge of fury passed through him, and he felt his face flush. Did they think he was suffering brain burn? Didn't they realize they were dealing with a computer cowboy who could fold cyberspace and go wherever he wanted to?

He snatched up the keyboard and tapped back into the net. Within half a minute he was going up to the satellite again, but this time he passed through the Sorbonne gate. He bent over the keyboard with his fingers flying, and as he typed, he felt himself slipping into the network, blending with it. The world around him turned misty gray and silver, all pale muted colors that soothed his eyes and his mind. He could feel his rage evaporate and a sense of serenity take its place.

He left Paris by using the *mil* address that let him reach the Bahrain army network in Al-Manamah. He spent a couple of minutes smashing through the military ice, but he had done it so often before that it didn't constitute a problem. The programmers in Bahrain were geeks.

Once he got down under the ice, he used a *com* address to cross the city and reach the International Bank of Bahrain's accounts computer. He hit more ice, but nobody had even tried for variations since the last time he was inside. Keeping records in English was challenge enough to the gumbys who had to do it. If the bank didn't require that computer accounts be backed by paper records, he could have made himself a multimillionaire years ago. He employed an ID he had used before and moved to the list of accounts. He requested a statement and typed in his own nine-digit number. In less than five seconds, the record on the screen showed that the last deposit was for $20 million.

They had done it! He found himself smiling foolishly. He was going to get everything he came for. He had all the variables under control—except for Susan.

He was starting to get a little concerned. If she was away for too long, he would lose some of his time with her. Whip should have found her by now.

As soon as she was back under control, he would follow through with his plan to take her into her room and spend whatever time was left with her. Whip and Cortez were sure to wonder where he and Susan were, but the promise of $20 million each waiting outside the front door should make them leave the building. That was all he needed. While the lights were shining on them running to the helicopter, he could escape from the rear of the research building.

The crash of furniture and the sound of footsteps startled him out of his reverie. Someone was running through the living room, bumping into the chairs and turning over lamps. He heard the almost delicate crash of a small table and, immediately afterward, the dull crunch of breaking light bulbs.

Then Cortez was yelling. Gibson couldn't understand what he was saying, but his voice was loud and strangely high pitched.

He took two steps away from the desk, glanced back at the monitor, then hesitated. He couldn't leave his Bahrain account on display for everybody to see. He snapped off the computer. While the storage disk and fan were still whirring to a stop, he was already running down the hall.

40

For the first twenty feet of the tunnel, Hightower had been able to guide himself by the almost bluish light of the night sky that came through the open door. Now, however, the darkness was complete, and when he glanced over his shoulder, he saw no trace of the entrance.

The narrow beam of his flashlight provided barely enough illumination to keep him going straight. The light was a washed-out yellow that occasionally flickered like a candle in a breeze. The batteries probably wouldn't last to the end, and for the second time he wished he had thought to ask Don for another flashlight.

The tunnel itself was a barrel vault constructed of brick. It was six or seven feet across, but the ceiling was so low that to avoid bumping his head, he had to keep to the center of the path. In places he was forced to duck to avoid tree roots that had broken through the brick and hung down in thick tangles. Here and there the roots had punched out several bricks, which weakened the vaulting. Probably even a slight tremor would send sections of the ceiling crashing down.

He walked slowly, taking small, careful steps. He was progressing in a steady, almost mechanical fashion when all at once he felt a surge of frustration. He wanted to speed through the darkness like a demon, yet here he was shuffling along like a blind man. At this rate it would take him an hour to get to Johnson Hall. A lot could happen in an hour.

He had a sudden image of Susan hiding in the research tower, crouched in a dark corner, listening nervously for Cyberwolf or one of his gang, scared of getting captured again. She would be afraid that at any moment death would find her.

He broke into a brisk walk. He scanned the terrain ahead, sweeping the flashlight across the floor. Instead of covering inches, he was covering feet, and he felt satis-

fied with his progress. Then as he raised his foot to step
over a root, the toe of his shoe caught on it. He staggered
forward and threw out his hands, but his head hit the wall
with a crack. He saw flashes in both eyes, although he
managed to save himself from falling.

He stood a moment, rubbing the bump on his right temple. He was breathing hard, and his hands were trembling.
If he had hit his head hard enough to knock himself unconscious, Susan would have to depend on Murphy and
Augustine to negotiate her freedom. He had no more confidence that they could do it than Lindsley did.

Slow and steady, he told himself as he began walking.
That was the lesson of the tortoise and the hare. If he kept
going at a regular pace, he would be more certain of getting to the end.

And what would he do then? The tunnel would lead to
the basement of Rush, and the only way out was the stairs
into the kitchen. Assuming Susan hadn't been recaptured,
he would have to get into the research building. The
sealed doors would make that impossible from the first
floor, so he would need to get to the second, then cross to
the tower. That should be no problem, because the stairs
from the basement to the kitchen continued to the second
floor.

The flashlight flickered, went out, then came on again.
The beam seemed almost gray. Probably the flashlight
had only another six or eight minutes of life. He turned it
off and shoved it into his front pants pocket. He then
stood with his eyes closed, giving them a chance to adjust.

When he opened his eyes, he could see nothing. The
darkness was only slightly paler than that under his eyelids. He felt a shudder run across his back. If he hadn't
turned to speak to Alma, both his eyes would have been
destroyed by the glass splinters. He would have had to try
to live the way he was now—blind and completely shut
off from the world.

As he started walking, he touched the bricks with his

fingertips, letting them drag along the gritty surface. To estimate his progress, he started counting steps.

Just as he reached thirty-five, something hard struck him a sharp blow in the center of his forehead. He put his hand to his head, and he could feel a small cut. His fingers came away wet with blood. His head ached, but the cut wasn't bleeding enough to worry about. He groped in front of him and located what felt like a two-inch iron pipe sticking down from the roof. Probably it was a fence post somebody wanted to be sure was set deep enough not to tip over.

Once again, he was okay, but he didn't relish the idea of getting bashed in the face another time. He started off down the tunnel, then stopped after only a few steps, realizing that he could rig up a warning system. He slipped the shotgun out of the webbed ammunition belt where he had stuck it. Holding the gun in front of him, slightly above eye level, he set off again.

Even without using the flashlight, he felt confident enough to speed up his pace. When the barrel brushed against protruding roots, he ducked low and walked under them.

He forced himself to think practically. He didn't have a clear idea of exactly how long the tunnel was. He guessed that the distance between the park and Johnson Hall was about a quarter of a mile. That would make the tunnel roughly thirteen hundred feet.

If his steps were three feet long, it would take four hundred and thirty of them to reach the end. Since they were shorter and the distance was probably more, five or six hundred would be a better estimate. So if he took thirty steps a minute, it would take him about twenty minutes to get through the tunnel. For the first time since entering the darkness, he felt his spirits rise. In ten or fifteen minutes, he should be out of the tunnel.

Almost without noticing it, he became aware of noises somewhere in the darkness ahead of him. They were so muted that at first he wasn't sure he was hearing them. He stopped and tucked the shotgun under his left arm. He leaned forward and concentrated on listening. Low murmuring sounds, like a crowd of people whispering together at a theater, reached his ears. Without varying in pitch, the sounds grew louder, then softer, ebbing and flowing like ocean waves.

His mouth went dry, and he felt a shiver cross the back of his neck. What was there? For a moment the idea of turning around and getting out of the tunnel had such a powerful appeal that he made himself think about Susan. He called up the image of her narrow face, with its high cheekbones and delicate features, her honey blond hair, and her gray-green eyes that shone like polished opals.

Yet he still found himself wanting to turn and run. *She's not waiting for me. She may even have forgotten who I am. She would think I was an idiot if she knew I was taking a casual flirtation so seriously.*

Even while the ideas floated through his mind, he didn't believe them. Susan hadn't been flirting casually, and he knew she hadn't forgotten about him. Something in each of them had evoked a response in the other. He was sure of it.

This was his chance to do for Susan what he hadn't been able to do for Alma. He couldn't alter the past, but he could make the future different. He could redeem it by saving Susan from the kind of senseless death Alma had suffered.

Hightower ran his tongue around the inside of his mouth and swallowed hard. The noises ahead now sounded more like the mewing of cats mixed with the high-pitched squeals of squirrels. Yet underlying the noise was a dry rustling, like heavy canvas rubbing against itself.

He raised the shotgun and clicked off the safety, then fished the flashlight out of his pocket. He pointed the shotgun down the tunnel, aiming the flashlight in the same direction. After the total darkness, the flashlight's feeble light seemed brighter than a magnesium flare. He had to blink away tears.

He played the beam back and forth, moving the muzzle

of the shotgun in parallel. He saw nothing but brick walls surrounding a dark emptiness. Now, though, he was sure that he could smell something. He couldn't identify the odor, but it was rank and feral, like the smell of animals at a zoo. Something was hidden in the darkness in front of him.

He listened again. The high-pitched murmur was definitely coming from in front of him. It varied in intensity as he moved his head, and it seemed loudest toward the ceiling. He aimed the beam upward, and as he directed the light farther down the tunnel, he detected movement. But what could be moving? Keeping the light pointed upward, he took a few steps forward.

Suddenly, the feeble beam fell on a brown undulating mass clinging to the ceiling. After a moment he realized he was looking at thousands of separate small creatures—bats. Their eyes glittered in the light like small black beads. Somewhere there must be a hole to the outside that let them in to roost. Dozens of bats were flying around below the clinging mass. They flew in tight circles, hovering near the top of the tunnel, then swooping down to the floor. Their curves were graceful and swift and he watched them in amazement, almost hypnotized by the perfection of their skill.

He could see no way to cross under the roosting bats and avoid being splattered with bat shit. He sighed deeply. The sooner he started, the sooner he would get to the other side.

He walked forward, keeping the flashlight pointed toward the ceiling. All at once the gliding bats recognized that he was there. Ten or twelve began to fly around him, skimming close to his face, then sheering off at the last moment. It was unnerving to be at the center of their swirling, intricate flight patterns. He glimpsed their small pointed faces and glittering eyes. Their screeches seemed higher pitched than the mewing chatter above him. People had constructed the tunnel, but now it obviously belonged to the bats. He was the interloper.

He felt the floor grow slick under his shoes, and almost

simultaneously, droppings struck the back of his shirt. He pulled his neck down into his collar and hunched up his shoulders. He had to get out from where he was as fast as he could.

Still holding the shotgun pointed toward the ceiling, he started forward again. Bats whizzed around him, and the leathery flapping of their wings seemed extraordinarily loud. He turned the light on the mass of hanging bats. He was fascinated by their sheer number. The ceiling was crawling with them, and they were crawling over each other.

Abruptly, the solid brick surface seemed to drop from under him. His breath caught in his throat, and he scrambled forward, both feet pawing at the floor, trying to get a grip on it. Too late, he realized that the bricks were tilting downward to a shallow depression and that he was sliding downhill. His flailing feet made contact with the floor, but the bricks were covered with a slick layer of bat guano.

As he pitched forward, he reflexively dropped the shotgun and put out his hand to catch himself. The gun went off with a stupendous blast and a blinding flash of orange and yellow light.

With a sharp cracking sound, the vault of bricks directly overhead came tumbling down. Bricks and bats fell together, filling the air. Hightower hit the floor with his hands, not falling completely. His left hand was tightly wrapped around the flashlight, and he could see the opposite side of the depression. He started scrambling up it, his heart pounding in his chest.

He pushed hard with his feet and hands, but he couldn't get enough grip on the slick floor to avoid slipping back. A hail of bricks from the ceiling fell around him. Then what seemed like hundreds of bricks came down in a single rush. Hightower lunged forward, but he wasn't fast enough.

His left leg was pinned to the floor, and searing pain pushed him to the brink of fainting. Then his leg turned completely numb, as if he had immersed it in a tub of ice water.

41

Gibson slowed down as he approached the end of the hall, then stopped. Trying to ignore the harsh wheezing of his own breathing, he strained his ears to listen.

"Cyber! Help me!" Cortez's voice was high and frantic, verging on the hysterical. "Help me!" Cortez called out the same plea again, recycling like a stuck conduit. Judging by the direction, he was in the kitchen.

Taking a deep breath, Gibson started running again. Without slackening speed, he rounded the corner and raced under the arch into the dining room. He was forced to slow down so he could maneuver his way beside the long mahogany table with its pushed-in chairs.

He halted before he came to the open kitchen door and pulled out the .44 Magnum. The pistol was heavy in his hand, and its very weight gave him a feeling of power. No problem was so big he couldn't blow it out of the way. But he wasn't going to rush inside without taking a look first.

He stood to the right of the kitchen door with his back to the wall. He bent his knees, sinking halfway to the floor, so he would be below eye level of anybody in the kitchen. He peered cautiously around the corner.

Looking left, he saw Cortez and Meg locked in a struggle. Both were breathing hard and grunting with effort, but neither seemed to be winning. Cortez kept glancing down to his right, then looking back at Meg. He was doing something with his right hand, but Gibson couldn't see what it was. Meg's back and shoulders were turned toward him, blocking his view.

Cortez was fighting off Meg with his left hand, pushing

on her chest and trying to shove her away from him. The Street Sweeper hung from its sling on his right shoulder, but Meg was so close he couldn't use it. If he could step back a few feet, he could shoot her, but something kept him from doing it.

"Cyber!" Cortez's voice soared almost into a scream.

Cortez was fighting hard. His jaw was tightly clenched and his lips pulled back from his teeth. Long scratches from Meg's fingernails ran from above his eyes to his chin, and narrow ribbons of blood were trickling down his cheeks.

Meg was pulling at Cortez's right arm, and he was pounding her shoulder with his fist. She was so close to him that he couldn't swing wide enough to put any power behind his punches. Meg had both hands wrapped around his right arm, and despite his blows, she began to shake it back and forth, as if trying to get him to drop something.

Cortez awkwardly lashed out at Meg's head. The blow knocked her to the side. She staggered, then quickly regained her balance. Cortez swung his fist at her, but she took the blow on her forearm. She kept pulling on his right arm.

Cortez lowered his fist, and when he did, Meg turned loose of his arm and slammed him solidly in the face with the back of her closed hand. The blow made a flat, almost wet sound as it struck his cheek. Cortez stumbled backward, but even then he didn't raise his right hand to defend himself.

Gibson stepped into the room with the Magnum raised. Now that he was standing up, he could see what they were fighting about. Tim Kimberly's head and shoulders were barely visible in a metal tilt-down door opening out from the kitchen wall, and Cortez was hanging on to his arm.

Gibson was puzzled a moment, then he realized that the door belonged to a trash chute leading to the outside. Tim must have noticed the chute when he was in the kitchen with Whip.

The hinged flap blocking off the chute from the outside kept Tim pressed flat against the narrow channel. He was squirming around, but all he could do was twist his shoulders from side to side. His thin face was as white as bleached paper, and his blue eyes were wide and staring. Cortez's fingers were clamped around his arm so tightly that Tim's hand looked pale and floppy, as though it had been severed above the wrist. Meg was trying to break Cortez's grip so that Tim could slide down the chute.

Moving quickly and silently, Gibson walked toward Meg with the pistol raised, its muzzle pointing upward. As soon as he was within striking distance, he lifted the gun and tensed the muscles in his arm and shoulder. He was poised to bring down the barrel on her head when she suddenly whirled around.

Her dark eyes shone with rage. A mottled pattern of dried blood still clung to her left cheek, and sweat ran down her face. Her short-cropped black hair was plastered to her head, the short ends sticking to her forehead in a ragged fringe.

Gibson hesitated, and before he could recover the momentum of his downward swing, Meg lashed out at him with her left leg. The hard callused pad on the ball of her foot caught him in the center of his chest, and he felt a spasm of severe pain. Gasping for breath, he lurched backward, his mind reeling with the shock of being attacked. His arms were thrown to the sides, but he hadn't lost his grip on the Magnum.

While he was struggling to breathe, he saw Meg hop nearer to Cortez, dragging her right foot behind her and barely putting any weight on it. Blood was seeping through the bandage wrapped around her toe. The pain had to be terrible, and he wondered how she had ever stumbled from her room into the kitchen. She shoved Cortez's arm, but she was unable to break his grip. He hit the side of her head with a solid *thunk*. She staggered backward, then she seemed to remember Gibson. She took a hop toward him, trying to get close enough to him to kick him again.

He saw her coming. Her lips were drawn back from her teeth, and her breathing was ragged and her chest heaving. He knew he should do something to save himself, but he felt too dazed. He stared up at her and saw that she meant to kill him. She was going to smash his face to a pulp on the red tile floor.

He watched her balance on her left leg and raise her right foot. The haze surrounding him distorted her face, twisting it into a fun-house shape. Except the shape wasn't funny, and he knew the raised foot was going to hurtle down and destroy his own face, splintering the bones and smashing the flesh into pulp.

Meg's foot was hanging in the air, as if she was about to take a giant step, when he shot her. The entire room seemed to explode. A smell of cordite filled the air, and the gun jumped in his hand, jerking his wrist backward. *This fucker will blow a hole as big as your fist in an engine block,* Whip had said.

The .44 slug caught Meg in the middle of the belly and knocked her toward the wall. She stumbled backward, but she didn't fall. She was still gripping Cortez's arm, and that gave her the support she needed to remain upright.

"You're a worthless piece of shit," Meg said. She looked straight at Gibson and spoke in a clear, almost conversational voice. For a moment her face seemed to relax and turn peaceful.

Gibson lowered the Magnum, resting it awkwardly in his lap. The scene was completely motionless. The fight was over, and Meg was a dead woman. He raised his left hand to his chest, as if he could ease the pain by his own touch.

Then everything changed. Meg let go of Cortez's arm, put her hands together, palm to palm, and locked her fingers, making a single fist. The muscles in her powerful shoulders rippled under her black T-shirt as she swung the fist in a long arc.

The blow slammed into Cortez's head with a loud crack. His eyes bulged, and his body slumped to the floor. As he fell, he loosened his grip on Tim's arm. In a frac-

tion of a second Tim slid down the narrow chute, and the
hinged door covering it snapped back into position with a
sharp metallic clack.

Gibson slowly raised the Magnum and shot Meg again.
The slug hit her in the center of her chest, right where she
had kicked him. As though hurled by a giant hand, she
spun backward and smashed into the wall. She slid slowly
to the floor and remained there, motionless as a heap of
empty clothes.

"Goddamn it," Gibson said.

He got to his feet and walked to within a yard of where
Meg was lying. He aimed the gun at the back of her head
and pulled the trigger. Her skull seemed to explode. Fragments of bone, tufts of black hair, and pink-gray pieces of
brain were thrown out in a wide arc around her head.

Gibson looked to make sure that his shoes hadn't been
splattered. He took a deep breath, then exhaled. He was
beginning to breathe easily, but his chest still hurt.

Turning to the left, he saw that Cortez was on his feet
and rubbing the side of his face. Gibson stared at him, not
saying anything. Out of the corner of his eye, in the middle of the kitchen, he glimpsed the body of the old
woman. He looked back at Cortez. Cortez was watching
him, as if he didn't want to interrupt whatever Gibson
was doing. He had a sheepish look, and the bleeding from
the scratches had become a slow ooze.

"Sorry, Cyber." Cortez's voice was almost a whine. "I
didn't know about that hole in the wall, and before I saw
what was happening, the kid was halfway through it.
Then that crazy bitch came swinging out of nowhere." He
shook his head incredulously. "Man, I couldn't get her to
turn loose of my arm no matter what I did. She was like
a fucking alligator."

"Forget it." Gibson blamed himself for letting the boy
outwit him. "We've got Susan, and she's the one who
counts."

"Yeah, but where is she? I thought Whip would be
back by now."

"Me too," Gibson admitted. He pushed on the center of

his chest and found it was still tender. "I'm going to look for him and for her."

"Why don't we both go?"

"Because I'm expecting a message from the cops. They're supposed to confirm that they'll have a helicopter here by two-forty-five."

"Man, I'll be glad to see it." Cortez took a deep breath and sighed. "I've had about all I can take."

"We're leaving at three, so we can't waste any time getting Susan back. Come on down the hall, and I'll open the door to the research tower and let you keep the key card."

Gibson stepped into the dining room with Cortez following close behind him. As soon as they crossed under the arch, Cortez moved up and walked beside him.

"What do I need the key card for?"

"As soon as the message from the cops arrives, I want you to come and tell me what it says."

"And if it doesn't come?"

"Then come and tell me that too. Have you got it?"

"Yeah, sure." Cortez hesitated, then asked, "Are they really going to give us the money?"

"Do you have any reason to think they aren't?" He was in no mood to waste time reassuring Cortez.

"The kid will tell them about Susan escaping. And about the other people getting killed." He stopped walking. "Maybe they'll decide to blow off the front door and nail us."

"Maybe," Gibson agreed. He kept walking and jerked his head toward the end of the hall. "That's one reason we need to get Susan back. So let's go. We don't have time to waste."

"After I let you in the building, can I come back and get me something to eat?" Cortez asked, hurrying to catch up.

"How can you even think of eating?" Gibson wrinkled his face and shook his head. "And all that blood in the kitchen, too."

"Man, I'm hungry. I told you that before."

"Okay, okay," Gibson said. "Eat something fast, then get your ass down there and watch for E-mail."

42

Susan slipped on her second shoe, then stood up. She wasn't dizzy, but her whole body seemed to be quivering. She forced herself to concentrate on getting across the room to the door.

White clouds of nitrogen were still billowing out of the open tank, and visibility was approaching zero. She stretched her hands out in front of her like a sleepwalker in a cartoon. To keep oriented in the fog, she tried to recall where the lab bench was and stay parallel with it.

If she let her mind wander to the struggle with Whip, she would become too upset to function, and she wasn't ready to give up. You didn't have to be the strongest to be the fittest, but if you weren't, you had to rely on intelligence. You had to keep control of your feelings and think things through. She should think of herself as back to searching for a way out. She should concentrate on surviving.

She was good at concentrating. It was her greatest strength as an actress. She could focus her thoughts and virtually become her character. Even when she played Alice Davenport in *Aztec Gold*, a character based on fantasy, she had drawn from sources deep inside that allowed her to think herself into the part. She smiled. Maybe she should become Alice again, because she certainly needed Alice's resourcefulness and determination.

At last her fingertips touched the door, and she slid her hands along the cold metal, groping for the doorknob. Suddenly she heard a shrill squeal, and her heart fluttered. She leaned against the door, listening.

It's the monkeys. They were making a terrible commotion, chattering and squealing. She recognized the rhythmic metallic rattling they produced by jerking at the doors of their cages. Could somebody else be coming through the room? Should she hide behind the table again? The idea was abhorrent to her. *I've got to get out of this goddamned room.*

Probably it was just that the monkeys had been frightened by the gunfire and the explosion. Or maybe they could smell the blood from Whip's stab wound. She thought about the way his blood had spurted over her hand, and she rubbed her knuckles against the seam of her jeans.

She slipped into the room, shutting the door quietly behind her. She looked at the opposite door, then at the door on her left. She took a deep breath. It was a relief to get away from the nitrogen clouds and to be able to see clearly.

Suddenly she realized that the noise from the monkeys had changed. They had been chattering and squealing, but now that they saw her, they sounded wilder and more savage, ready to bite and tear at her, given the chance.

She turned toward the cages, and the screeching monkeys stared into her face with eyes as hard as black marbles. They pulled back their lips to show red gums and long canine teeth. Their hard eyes followed her as she moved, and they snapped their jaws together, as if ripping her flesh. A large male directed a stream of urine at her. The mesh of the cage turned it into a spray, but its rank odor filled the room.

Earlier the monkeys hadn't scared her, but now they did. They were so disturbed that they would attack anybody they could reach. Fortunately, the mesh over the doors kept them from snaking through a hand and pulling back the latch. A shiver ran across her shoulders.

She walked toward the door at the end of the room opposite the monkey cages. She passed by the fifty-pound bags of monkey chow propped against the wall. Should she take a minute and feed them? Then she caught herself. The monkeys weren't starving. Her own survival had to come first.

She glanced to the right at the long counter with its sink and stainless-steel top. She took in the scrub brushes, flea powder, and nail clippers next to the sink. Nothing looked useful. Above the counter were tall cabinets with metal doors. If she searched the shelves, would she find a hammer or some other tool she could use to break through an outside wall?

She didn't have time to search, and it was silly to think about smashing through a wall. Before she could even make a start, Cyberwolf would decide Whip had been gone too long, then either he or Backup would come to investigate. She had to find a faster way.

The door was unlocked, and she stepped into the same large lab she had started from. She had forgotten how dim and shadowy it was. The faint yellow-green fluorescent light didn't allow her to see anything clearly, but she could make out the glassed-in office on the other side of the room and the door at the end that Whip had come through.

The door had to lead to the front hall, but the front of the building would be too well secured. She needed to discover where they threw out the trash or brought in the experimental animals, someplace where every outside opening might not be tightly sealed. If she searched the office, she might be able to locate a floor plan and not have to wander around blindly.

She started across the room, walking fast. Instantly, she could feel the sweat running down her ribs and beading up on her face. The lab was still hot and heavy with humidity, like the atmosphere of a stagnant marsh, and the air still reeked with the odor of spoiled fish.

Susan looked toward the eel pool. The fountain of light still shone up from the murky seawater, but something was different. She was puzzled for a moment, then she realized what it was—the circular guardrail was missing. She could see an indistinct heap of curved pieces on the far side of the pool. Whip must have taken down the rail. But why would he want to?

"Oh, my God," she said in a soft voice as the only reasonable explanation came to her.

He had planned all along to rape her. Maybe he had intended to threaten her with the eel pool if she didn't cooperate. He could have dragged her to the edge and let her get a good look at the eels, with their needle teeth and snakelike bodies. If he had dangled her over the pool, she would have done anything he told her. Then maybe after raping her, he had meant to kill her. He could have thrown her body into the pool. That way, if he was brought to trial, he could claim she died accidentally. No one could prove anything against him.

She blinked to try to get rid of the image of the eels attacking the clay-colored one, ripping out pieces of its flesh with their terrible teeth. She remembered how blood had streamed out of its wounds and polluted the bright water with what looked like dark smoke. A wave of anger swept over her. She was glad Whip was dead. She wasn't glad she had killed him, but she felt no regret.

As she approached the office, she could see the monitor of the computer she had left switched on. The screen gave off a faint blue light, like the beacon of a distant lighthouse. She glanced at the lab bench along the back, then her eyes swept toward the front. In the shadowy nook formed by the office wall and the lab wall, she saw a door she hadn't noticed earlier. She felt a small thrill of surprise.

She crossed over and turned the knob, then let out her breath in a long whoosh. It was unlocked.

43

The silence following the collapse seemed as absolute as the darkness. Even the bats were briefly silent. Hightower felt a momentary sense of relief. Although his leg was trapped, he was still alive, and even though the shotgun was buried under the mountain of fallen bricks, he still had the flashlight.

He twisted around and shone the light into the darkness. White dust as thick as flour filled the air, and the bats were in turmoil. Hundreds flittered below the collapsed ceiling, looking for new places to settle. Their mewings and shrill shrieks had started again.

As the light shone on the roof, Hightower drew in his breath sharply. Directly above him, the tunnel's brick lining had pulled away from the earth behind it and sagged downward. Only the interlocking of the bricks kept the ceiling from collapsing. The vaulting was like a segment of a jigsaw puzzle still hanging together when the puzzle is picked up. The bonds holding the bricks to one another could break at any moment.

His body began to shake, and he felt cold, but he made himself lie quietly. He wasn't dead yet. If he didn't lose his head, he had a good chance of getting out. He turned off the flashlight to save battery power. He needed to think.

He could use the phone in his pocket to call Don for help. But any attempt to rescue him would kill him. He'd have to get himself loose, and he'd better not waste any time before trying.

He flexed his left leg slightly and found that he could move it a little. Bricks covered it only up to the knee, so maybe he could yank the leg loose. He crawled forward, pulling on his leg. The leg moved a fraction of an inch, but then seemed to catch. He pulled again, even harder, but it had too much weight on it.

He was lying flat on his stomach, but by supporting

himself on his right hand, then twisting around, he could reach the bricks on top of his leg. The maneuver was awkward and painful, but he could stand it. He pulled a brick toward him with his fingers, then tossed it to the side. The brick shook the floor as it fell, and he felt a stab of fear. He glanced at the ceiling, but nothing seemed to have changed. He worked as fast as he could. His back began to ache, and the skin on his fingers was cut and abraded by the bricks. Yet in only a few minutes the weight on his leg was noticeably less.

But he had also reached a limit. The remaining bricks were beyond his reach. He turned on the flashlight and shone the beam toward the ceiling. Bats were still flying in the space below the roof, and a few were already hanging from the bricks. He was going to have to get loose before so many roosted that their weight pulled down the structure.

He began kicking at the bricks. His kicks were feeble, but they were effective, and bricks fell to either side. He paused after several minutes and pulled on his leg. It moved forward just a bit. He pointed his toes to reduce resistance, then started pulling on his leg while pushing against the floor with his right foot. He established a regular rhythm of *pull and push, rest; pull and push, rest.*

His leg was beginning to tingle, as if thousands of tiny needles were pricking his skin. It was a good sign, because it meant blood was beginning to circulate.

He stopped the cycle of resting and pulling to check the ceiling once more. The air was so full of bats that he could hardly make out the ragged edge of the vaulting. Yet from what he could see, more and more bats were roosting on the bricks.

He raised himself on his elbows and pulled as hard as he was able. Simultaneously he pushed hard against the floor with his right leg. He kept up the tension, straining everything in his body, concentrating his energy. Then using his elbows as levers, he hurled his body forward with all his force, tugging on his leg. His leg jerked free, popping out of the bricks like a cork out of a bottle.

He pulled himself to a sitting position. The needles were stinging his flesh more than ever, but he was sure his leg wasn't broken. The autopsy knife was in place, and the bandage holding it to his leg was still tightly wrapped.

He got to his knees, then levered himself up. He touched the floor with his left foot to keep his balance, then very slowly, he let it bear some of his weight. The ammunition belt around his waist was throwing him off, and without a shotgun, he saw no more need to carry the shells. He let the belt drop to the floor.

Hightower turned and started limping up the tunnel, but he had taken no more than two steps when he heard several sharp popping noises, like someone breaking sticks to make a fire.

He didn't turn to see what was happening. Instead, he began hobbling up the tunnel as fast as he could, stepping forward with his right leg, then dragging up his left foot. He gasped for breath with the exertion, but in a moment he found he could rest more weight on his left foot. He began to run.

Suddenly he heard a dull roaring sound, as loud as an explosion, and a powerful wave of wind and dust broke against his back. A piece of brick struck his right shoulder a sharp blow, and small fragments fell around him like hailstones.

He switched on the flashlight. The area where he had been lying was covered by a ragged heap of bricks. The narrow space above was filled with bats flapping their wings in the heavy dust. Their shrill cries and soft mewings were eerily mournful.

Relief again flowed through him with an almost physical pleasure. "I could have been killed," he said out loud. He found himself smiling as if he found the idea funny. The white dust stung his nose, and he could taste it on his tongue.

Turning his back on the wreckage of the ceiling, he continued walking. He began counting his steps again, and before he had taken a hundred, the barrel vaulting gave way to straight walls with a short vault at the top.

Then directly ahead and reflecting the flashlight beam was a solid yellow metal door. He had made it! He could feel himself smiling, and he felt himself pick up his pace, like a racehorse in the homestretch.

But when he got to the door, he hesitated. He looked at the round face of the lock above the brass handle, and a feeling of despair swept through him. Without the shotgun he had no way to break open a lock. He grabbed the handle and tugged on it.

He almost fell backward as the door swung open.

44

Gibson watched Cortez close the door. When he heard the spring lock snap into place, he turned to look down the hallway.

The overhead lights were painfully bright, and instantly his eyes started to water. He shielded them with his hand, but the light was as caustic as acid dashed in his face. With his eyes half closed, he stared down at his shoes. He reached into the inside pocket of his blazer and fished out his mirrored sunglasses. He slipped the metal legs over his ears.

The effect was immediate. He might have just stepped out of the fiery desert sun into the soothing shade of a cool shadowy house. The pain in his eyes vanished, and he blinked to clear away the tears. He wiped his cheeks with his handkerchief.

He glanced around to get oriented and to assure himself that he could see all right. The walls of the hallway were stark white, and the vinyl floor was laid in a postmodern pattern of pale gray and dark green triangles. The left wall was as blank as a slab of ice, and at the far end, smooth pillars with Doric capitals flanked the front entrance.

The five doors along the right wall were featureless metal rectangles painted the same shade of gray. Opposite the front entrance round indicator lights marked the elevators.

The first and last doors led to stairways. They would be locked, because the upper floors were sealed off, just as in Johnson Hall. The elevators wouldn't work without a key. So Susan couldn't have left the first floor.

He might end up trying each of the other three doors, but he wouldn't do it now. Susan wasn't stupid. She would probably look for a back door or loading dock. So that's what he was going to do.

45

Susan entered the room cautiously. It was even dimmer than the lab. The glow from above was a pale gray wash that turned prominent objects into silhouettes and shrouded everything else in shadows.

Easing the door closed, she turned and looked around. The room was long and narrow, running the width of the building. So far as she could make out, boxes occupied most of the floor space. A few large wooden packing crates were near her, and a great number of cardboard cartons were stacked in orderly groups. Most stacks rested on rough wooden pallets.

She walked toward the back wall, weaving her way around the pallets. Glancing up, she noticed a long metal track suspended by thin rods from the ceiling. She felt a surge of hope and smiled. She was sure she knew what she was going to find.

As she stepped from behind a high stack of boxes, she saw she was right. Directly in front of her, sealing off the building from the outside, was a wide overhead steel door. She had managed to stumble on to the loading dock.

An open area of smooth, polished concrete was in front of the door. Overhead, bare bulbs screwed into white porcelain fixtures provided better light, and she spotted an ordinary metal door at the left of the overhead door. She hurried over to it and tested it, but as she had expected, it was locked. It was too solid and well armored even to think about trying to break down.

Stepping back a little, she took a careful look at the overhead door, searching for some sort of latch. The door was designed like a rolltop desk. A series of narrow beige panels were hinged to flex backward when the door slid onto the overhead track. The door was too big to be raised by hand, so somewhere there must be an electric motor and a switch to control it.

She ran her eyes along the right side of the door. Attached to the concrete-block wall was a metal box slightly larger than a light switch. She felt a thin current of excitement run through her. *I'm going to get out of here.*

Two buttons were set into the face of the box. She eagerly jabbed the red button at the top, then listened for the sounds of a hoist motor. Nothing happened. She pressed the button again and again, but still nothing happened.

She leaned close to the switch, searching for something to explain why it wouldn't work. Most likely, she would have to do something besides pushing the button. She ran her fingers along the side of the box, and halfway down they encountered the smooth metal circle of a key slot.

"Shit," she said under her breath. She was so close to freedom and yet as trapped as ever. Tears came to her eyes, and she rapped the side of her head with her fist. She was tired to the point of exhaustion, and the idea of looking for another way out was more than she could bear. Getting out, even if it was possible, didn't seem worth the effort.

But in some hidden place beyond her awareness, she knew she wasn't ready to give up and die. Somehow, some way, she was going to survive. It was the isolation and the stress that were making her crazy. After what she had been through, she needed some time to pull herself together.

She let her mind roam, and an image of David Hightower slipped into her consciousness. She saw his face, with his somewhat asymmetrical brown eyes and his serious look. The image was so vivid that he seemed almost present in the murky darkness of the narrow room.

Probably he had heard about the hostage-taking, and maybe he was watching the TV news programs for any new information. If so, he might have heard that she had broken free. She was sure that he was thinking about her. Probably he was worried that she would have another panic attack. She wanted him to know she was okay. She *had* to get out. She still had a life to live.

She wiped her tears with the back of her hand. Maybe the front of the building offered a better chance of breaking out. Maybe there was some glassed-in place she could throw a chair through. *You can't know until you've looked.*

As she turned to leave, she caught sight of the electrical conduit running into the bottom of the switch box, then out through the top. Something stirred at the back of her mind. The conduit suggested something to her. But what? The wires were in the conduit, so she couldn't get to them.

That was it! If she could pop loose the conduit from the top and the bottom of the box, she could get access to the wires. If she pulled them out of the switch, she could bypass it completely. She wouldn't need a key, because she could make a direct connection.

The wires wouldn't be long enough to reach from one side of the switch to the other, so she would have to find some way to bridge the gap. Maybe a lamp cord would do the trick, but to get it she was going to have to go back to the lab office.

Studying the switch, she saw that there was another way. She didn't have to go looking for electrical wire to make a splice. All she needed to do was touch the wires from each side of the switch to the metal cover. The cover would complete the circuit, and that would activate the hoist motor.

She sensed excitement rising in her. She wasn't going to have to stay locked up in this madhouse for long. She smiled; the real lunatics weren't the inhabitants, but those who had broken in from the outside.

She examined the conduit and saw that it was nothing more than thin aluminum pipe. The ends didn't have couplings on them but were simply stuck through the holes in the ends of the box. Putty was pressed around the holes to keep out moisture.

The last several inches of conduit were slightly bowed out from the wall to allow it to enter the bottom of the box. She slipped her fingers under the bow and tugged. The conduit moved, but it was too solid for her to pull loose with only her hand. But if she could find a lever, she could raise the conduit and pop it out of the box.

Just then she heard a metallic clicking and a loud whooshing behind her. She whirled around and stared into the gloom, her eyes searching the shadows. Then she felt a wave of cold air wash over her, cooling the sweat on her face and neck. She shivered. A long moment passed, then she realized that the clicking was nothing more than the air-conditioning system coming on.

Turning away from the switch box, she walked back through the storage area. Her breathing was rough, and her heart was still beating too fast. She needed to try to get out while she still had the nerve and the strength to work at it. Her constant vigilance was exhausting her. She was a rabbit expecting to be torn to pieces by a pack of dogs.

She shook her head. No, that was not what she was. She was a fox, and she had many wiles. The dogs might eventually catch her, but they weren't going to have an easy time of it.

She stopped to examine a wooden shipping crate. One of the slats of the lid had been removed, and although she looked for it on the floor, she couldn't find it. She noticed that the next slat had been loosened, so she leaned over the crate and hit it from underneath with the heel of her hand.

Nothing happened, and she hit it again, harder. An end came loose. She grabbed the slat and began rocking it from side to side. Finally, the slat broke free. She felt a small thrill, but she knew her time was running out fast. She checked the front of the room, then returned to the door.

Susan slipped the slat under the conduit, then lifted and pushed it forward until it hit the wall. She didn't have enough leverage. She raised the end of the slat and planted it on the door frame. She then lifted the slat again, and the conduit pulled away from the wall. The slat bent as she pulled harder, but from the corner of her eye, she saw an inch or so of conduit slide out of the switch box. Was she strong enough to pull it all the way out?

She clenched her jaw and began jerking hard on the slat, making the conduit bounce in and out of the box. It would slide out if only she could get it past the hole. She could feel herself slipping into despair. A sharp click made her heart leap. But then the air blowing on her abruptly stopped, and she realized that what she had heard was just a relay closing someplace.

She spread her feet apart and bent her knees to brace herself. She then gave her end of the slat a short, hard shove, thrusting it toward the ceiling. The conduit popped out of the bottom of the switch box, bringing a bundle of torn wires with it. As the bare ends of the wires touched one another, they made a hissing shower of sparks. The air was foul with the acrid odor of electrical burning, and a thin curl of dark smoke drifted up from the tangle of wires.

She jerked out the slat and used the end to push the wires apart. The sparking stopped, and she splayed out the wires into an array of red, white, green, and black.

I've done it, she thought with satisfaction. But she still had to pop loose the conduit at the top of the box. She slipped the slat under the upper section. She was going to be out the door in five minutes, ten at the most.

Then she heard a slight squeak. She froze in place as if paralyzed. That wasn't a noise made by the air conditioning. It was the sound of a door opening, a door at the other end of the room, someplace in the gray dimness.

She pulled the slat out. She set it down gently on the floor, but she turned loose of it too soon, and it made a flat, slapping noise. The noise was small, no louder than the squeak she had heard. Yet anyone listening would hear it.

She bit her lip, angry with herself, but she forgot her anger as she felt fear spread through her like a cold chill. This wasn't another false alarm. Somebody was in the room with her, hidden in the gloom and darkness at the far end.

She stepped back from the rear wall, out of the direct light. Doing her best to make no noise, she dropped to her knees and began to crawl toward one of the pallets piled high with cardboard boxes.

46

The basement was a vast, open area, with smooth white plaster walls and a green vinyl floor. The space was mostly taken up by metal filing cabinets arranged in orderly rows.

The area on the right seemed to be the dumping ground for abandoned office equipment. Chairs, lamps, and bookcases were huddled together in the back corner, while desks and tables were pushed against the wall. Stacked on top of them were the remains of a dozen computers. Monitors, processors, keyboards, and loops of black cable were scattered around in no apparent order.

Seeing the equipment reminded him that he had promised to call Lindsley. He pulled the phone out of his pocket, flipped it open, and extended the stubby antenna. Holding the receiver close to his mouth, he said, "Don, Don."

"Lindsley," Don said on the second ring.

"I'm in the basement now." Hightower spoke softly.

"Are you okay?"

"I'm fine, but I haven't seen anybody yet."

"We heard from Cyberwolf again," Lindsley said. "You don't have as much time as we thought. He's moved up the deadline. If he's not out of U.S. airspace by three-thirty this morning, he's going to let the Chernobyl program blow."

"Three-thirty?" Hightower couldn't keep the shock out of his voice. "That's when my parents' plane is landing at Kennedy." His throat was so tight that he felt like he was squeezing out the words.

His head spinning, he leaned against the tunnel door. How could he ever find Susan in the next hour? And what could he do to help his parents? Before daylight, he might lose everybody in the world he cared about.

"I wish there was something I could do," Don said.

"How about warning TWA they may have an emergency situation when the flight tries to land?"

Don hesitated. "I can call them, but a police emergency hasn't been declared by the chief. The airline isn't likely to divert the flight on my say-so."

"Shit," Hightower said fiercely. "I'm sure you're right." He clenched his right hand and tapped his knuckles on his leg.

"But LAPD called me five minutes ago, and they've got a list of Pix-Wizard customers. With luck, we might be able to unplug Cyberwolf's computer in time to abort the meltdown."

"When I find him, he'll tell me where it is." Hightower was surprised by his harsh tone. "I've got to go," he said abruptly.

Less than an hour.

"Be careful," Don said.

Hightower folded up the phone and slid it into his pocket. As the Berserker game had taught him, only one set of stairs led out of the basement. He could see the back of the stairwell to the left. He padded silently down the narrow corridor between the wall and the rows of filing cabinets. If Salter was right about the game, he should know his way around Johnson Hall without having to think about it.

He turned down a narrow aisle between two rows of filing cabinets and found himself standing at the foot of the stairs. A single bulb provided just enough light to keep someone from falling. The stairs rose at a steep angle, without a landing, and the centers of the wooden treads were worn into hollows. A closed door was at the top.

He grabbed the handrail and, walking on his toes, sprinted up the first five steps. The fifth tread gave a groaning creak. The loudness of the sound caught him by surprise, and he froze. He kept an eye on the door, ready to bolt back down the stairs.

After a full minute passed, he felt safe enough to resume his climb. But he had been wrong to hurry. He should be crawling slowly, doing his best to make no sound. Also, he should step on the edge of the treads near the wall. He started again, moving with excruciating slowness, pausing at each step.

He thought of Susan and of how close he must be to her, and he could hardly restrain himself. But he had learned the importance of patience as a surgeon. Your eyes might be burning, your back breaking, and your hands cramped, but you had to keep up the tedious business of dissecting out tendons, tying off bleeders, and avoiding severing nerves. Sometimes you just wanted to stop and close up the wound. But you couldn't do that, because too much depended on you. Skill without the patience to use it could be destructive.

He paused on the top step and listened, but all he heard was the steady mechanical humming of a refrigerator. He put his right ear flat against the door. The humming grew louder, then the motor cut off with a solid *chunk*. After that he could hear nothing but the sound of his own heartbeat.

Probably Susan was still free and Cyberwolf and his men were out searching for her. His best course of action, then, was to go directly to the tower and look for her himself. But to get upstairs so he could cross to the tower, he would have to walk through the kitchen. Cyberwolf might have left a guard behind, so he had better stay quiet and move fast.

He turned the doorknob, and to his immense relief, the bolt slid easily out of the latch plate. Holding the knob so the bolt wouldn't slip back, he opened the door a crack and peered out. He saw a gallon can of peanut butter with a red-and-yellow label on the countertop on the opposite side of the room.

Opening the door wider, he noticed splatters of blood on the large blocks of milk-glass tile covering the walls. The splatters were teardrop shaped, with the small ends at the bottom. As he slowly lowered his eyes, he saw the body.

For a moment he was puzzled. The short black hair, the massive head wound, and the crooked line of blood running across the floor seemed such disparate elements that his mind couldn't fit them together. Then the moment passed, and he knew he was looking at a dead woman. Even though he couldn't see the face, he realized it was Meg.

Hightower felt his mouth turn dry as cotton, and a light haze seemed to fall between him and his surroundings. He grabbed on to the door facing to steady himself and swallowed hard. *At least it's not Susan.*

He stepped inside the kitchen and took hold of the outside knob before he released the inside one. He closed the door, then let the knob unwind until the bolt slid back. He turned left, where the second-floor stairs should be. As he turned, he saw another body. Close to the oversized refrigerator, an elderly woman lay on her back with her arms thrown out to the sides. Her face was slack and shrunken, and the front of her pale blue dress was splattered with blood. Her halo of white hair was absurdly neat and well combed.

He took a step toward her, and as he bent over to get a better look, he glimpsed a movement out of the corner of his right eye. Without turning his head, he automatically threw himself to the floor. An explosive blast rattled the room, and fragments of plaster and dust rained down on him from the wall beside the basement door. The air was filled with the sharp odor of gunpowder, but the shot had missed him.

"Don't move! Don't move!" a male voice shouted. It was shrill with stress.

"I'm not moving." Hightower spoke loudly, wanting to make clear that he was obeying the command. He was lying on his stomach, and he could see flecks of dried blood on the floor in front of him.

"Where the hell did you come from?" The man sounded calmer.

"I'm an air-conditioning specialist," Hightower said. "I've been in the basement working on the compressor since late this afternoon. I heard noises that sounded like shots, so I came up to check things out."

"You're a lucky fuck," the man said. "I should've shot you, but I guess I'd better keep you for now. Get up on your knees."

Hightower climbed to his knees. He turned partway around and glimpsed the barrel of a gun and a burly black-haired man in a light blue shirt.

"Don't look at me!" the man yelled. "Keep your fucking eyes straight ahead and start walking to that door."

Hightower turned toward the basement door.

"Not that one, asshole." The man's voice was rough with anger. "The next one."

Hightower shuffled several feet across the floor until he reached the next door. He couldn't recall a door in that location, either from the drawing or from the Berserker game. Yet there it was, a paneled wooden door, painted white, with a brass doorknob and the round flat face of a brass lock above it.

"Open the door and get on in there," the man ordered.

"What are you going to do to me?" Hightower was surprised to hear how creaky his voice sounded.

"That's for Cyberwolf to decide. Maybe if you're lucky, he'll trade you for something."

"What do you mean?"

"That's enough talk." The man sounded rougher. "I've got work to do."

Hightower knee-walked through the doorway. It was light enough inside for him to see that he was in a pantry or storage room. Shelves along both sides were crowded with large institutional-size cans of food. The lower shelves were stacked with roasting pans, baking sheets, and other cooking equipment.

He heard the rattle of keys, then what sounded like a key sliding into a lock. He had started turning around to look behind him when something hit him solidly on the back of the head, knocking him forward and onto the floor.

For a fraction of a second, he was aware that darkness was closing around him, and he felt a flush of anger. How could he help Susan or his parents when he couldn't even help himself?

47

Susan crouched behind the stack of cartons. Her knees rested on the hard concrete floor, and she pressed her face against the cartons so closely that she could smell the glue used to seal them.

Her hands were trembling, and her heart was beating so rapidly that its motions blurred into a continuous throbbing. She took rapid, shallow breaths but tried not to make gasping sounds.

"Hello, Susan." Cyberwolf's voice came from the front of the long room. His tone was conversational and friendly. "I know you're there, so you could save us both a lot of grief if you would just come on back to Johnson Hall with me."

He paused a moment. When he spoke again, he sounded slightly louder, closer to her. "I don't know what happened to Whip. I guess he couldn't find you. I'm glad about that. I don't like to think about the things he might have done to you."

Slowly and deliberately, she took in a breath, then let it all out. If she was going to have any chance at all, she would have to keep thinking and think clearly.

She peered around the carton, doing her best to see Cyberwolf without exposing herself. He was in the middle of the room. Except for the dim light surrounding him, he could have been an actor standing on a bare stage delivering a soliloquy.

"You know you'll be safe with me. I won't let Whip or Backup do anything to hurt you."

He was no more than thirty feet from her. He turned his head slowly from one side of the room to the other, and his sunglasses made his eyes look blank. He reminded her of a cobra swaying back and forth, searching for its prey.

"Do you remember what I told you about wanting to live in one of my possible worlds?" he asked. "Well, the one I most want to make real is the one where you and I can be friends. Maybe you think that's asking too much, but I want you to know that you're safe with me."

He sounded reasonable and agreeable, and there was no hint of anger or threat in his voice. He was ice instead of fire; he was smooth instead of rough. A part of her wanted to believe him. It would be nice to stop struggling and trying to outwit people. Giving up would be easy.

"I can understand why you might be frightened by what's happened. But believe me, nothing's been directed

against you personally. The other two are doing this for
the money, but that's only part of my reason."

She wouldn't give up. She couldn't. He was friendly
and reassuring, like the fox in a dozen fables, and she
wouldn't have trusted him if he told her the sky was blue.

He hesitated, then hurried on, as if to meet an objection
she had raised. "I want money too, but from the beginning I realized this was going to be the only opportunity
I would ever have to spend time with you."

He wanted her. She could hear the yearning in his
voice. He might even want her more than money. The
money was abstract, but she was real and immediate. She
was just a few feet away from him, and he would be able
to imagine reaching out and pulling her to him. But after
that, after he had her, he would think about the money.
She was only first in line.

"I want us to be together for a while and share a few
experiences, so I can have something to look back on
with pleasure. When we get the ransom money, we'll
leave you here by yourself." He paused, then said firmly,
"I'll personally guarantee that you won't have a bad experience."

He took off his sunglasses, folded the legs, then slipped
them into his inside jacket pocket. He started moving forward, taking small, silent steps. He turned his head from
side to side, and now and then he stopped to take a look
at something. If she didn't act soon, he was going to find
her.

If she had a few minutes, she could break loose the top
section of conduit and open the overhead door. But how
could she get him to leave her alone long enough for that?
It would be so easy, yet it looked impossible.

She felt panic rising up in her again. Cold sweat broke
out on her forehead, and her chest seemed paralyzed. She
couldn't get her breath, and she felt certain she was going
to die. Only her lack of breath kept her from screaming.

I am not dying. This will soon go away.

She felt the anxiety disappear like a shadow struck by
light. She wiped the sweat off her face, then rubbed her

hand on her jeans. At least the attacks didn't last very long now. David would be interested in hearing that, if she ever got to tell him. She felt tears well up in her eyes, but she blinked them away. This was no time to get distracted. She had to keep herself focused the way she did when she was acting.

She looked around the side of the cartons and saw Cyberwolf with his hand held up to his eyes, as if the feeble gray light was a threat he needed to ward off.

"I'm the one who planned this whole operation," he called out. Pride was in his voice. "I changed the protocols that opened the doors, and I control the whole system here. But that's all trivial compared to the program I've designed."

Susan pulled her head back and peered around the right side of the stack. She could no longer see Cyberwolf, because another pallet of cartons was blocking her view. That meant he shouldn't be able to see her, either.

The distance between the other pallet and the door into the lab was hardly more than five feet. If she hid behind the pallet, she was almost sure she could get through the door before Cyberwolf could reach her. But what then? Unless she could get out of the building, he would just chase her around in circles.

"My program can melt down NYNEX," he went on. "Do you know what that means?" His voice grew higher with excitement, and he spoke more rapidly. "Every telephone and every computer linkup from Maine to New York is going to crash. Planes will crack up and people will die by the hundreds, maybe the thousands. All communication will stop, and the social organization in this part of the country will completely collapse."

She still couldn't see him, but she could hear him. He sounded fainter, though. He must be moving away from her, searching the other side of the room. He was probably crisscrossing the area, sweeping it from wall to wall, making sure he didn't overlook her hiding place.

Maybe he was talking to convince her to trust him. Or maybe he wanted to keep her distracted so she would stay

in one place while he searched behind the mounds of cartons.

"I really can do all of that," he said. "In fact, it's all
going to happen at three-thirty this morning, unless I stop
it. The program is already running, so there's less than an
hour before disaster strikes."

Whatever his reason for talking, she was sure he would
keep on doing it. He would also keep on looking, and
sooner or later, he was going to find her. Yet she was beginning to get a glimmer of an idea, and if she was ever
going to act, she had better do it. It was now or never.

From her kneeling position, she lowered herself to the
floor, stretching out on her stomach. Lifting her feet to
keep her shoes from making a noise on the concrete, she
crawled forward with a wriggling motion.

As soon as she reached the other pallet, she raised herself to her knees and peeped around the edge of a box.
Cyberwolf was across the room, checking behind one of
the large wooden crates.

"The cops will try to shut down my program," he said.
"But I've taken precautions to see that they won't be able
to. Even if they think they've done it, they'll be wrong.
I've made sure they can't find what they need to know in
time to change anything."

Susan ducked lower behind the boxes. She wasn't paying attention to what Cyberwolf was saying, because she
was concentrating on working out the plan that had half
formed in her mind. If it was successful, she should have
barely enough time to pull loose the rest of the switch
wires and raise the steel door. She just might be able to
escape.

But for the plan to work, everything would have to go
smoothly, and her timing would have to be perfect. She
was going to be taking a big risk, yet it would be an even
bigger risk to stay where she was and do nothing.

"Why don't you walk back to Johnson Hall with me,
and I'll tell you more about my program," Cyberwolf
said. "I'll explain how I slipped past the ice and got down
deep inside NYNEX." His voice took on a bright, encour-

aging tone. "I can show you what it's like to click into the net and slip into cyberspace."

She crawled to the end of the pallet and paused a moment. She ran through a checklist of everything she would have to do, memorizing the sequence the same way she would memorize the blocking for an action scene. This time, though, she wasn't going to have a stunt double, and she was going to have to be her own director.

She raised herself to a crouching position, took a deep breath, then ran for the door. Out of the corner of her eye, she glimpsed Cyberwolf. He was on the opposite side of the room behind an island of cardboard boxes. She pushed the door inward, and as she ducked through the opening, she saw him turn his head and look directly at her.

As he caught sight of her, his lips pulled back from his teeth in a snarl, and his whole face changed into a distorted mask of fury. For an instant, she was reminded of the ghoulish white face, disheveled hair, and long fangs of Lon Chaney in *The Phantom of the Opera*.

She made no effort to keep the heavy door from slamming behind her. She cut left and ran parallel to the lab bench along the rear wall. She wanted to stay far away from the eel pool, but she also wanted to make sure Cyberwolf followed her through the door on the left. It was a crucial element in her plan.

The light was almost too dim for her to see the other side of the room. She had been in the room twice before, though, and knew exactly where she was going. She ran without worrying about the noise she was making, and her feet struck the concrete floor like hammer blows.

She was a quarter of the way across the room when she heard the door leading to the loading dock slam with a dull metallic reverberation. Without slackening her pace, she turned her head and saw what she had expected. Cyberwolf was coming toward her, his amber eyes burning, his blond hair streaming back, and his face still screwed up in fury. He seemed to have lost all human qualities.

Susan jerked her head back around, feeling the chill of fear spread through her body like icy water. She willed herself to move faster, raising her knees higher and throwing herself forward. She snatched her breath in ragged gasps, with her chest heaving and her heart hammering wildly. The blank face of the door seemed miles away from her.

Suddenly, something hard and solid struck her squarely between the shoulder blades, and a thousand lines of burning pain radiated through her neck and back.

Oh, my God, he's shot me.

The blow knocked her off balance, and she stumbled and fell forward. As she reflexively threw out her arms to catch herself, her hands hit the concrete, scraping her palms. She felt a wrenching pain as her right knee twisted sharply to the right.

Turning her head, she saw a snub-nosed pistol like Meg's on the floor several feet behind her. That must be what hit her. Cyberwolf must have thrown it at her.

She felt relief as she recognized that she wasn't shot after all. Then she raised her eyes and saw Cyberwolf coming toward her with easy, loping strides that were erasing the distance between them.

She scrambled to her feet. Ignoring the pain in her knee, she started to run again. She had no more than fifteen feet to cover, and she had to make it. Once she was on the other side of the door, she could dodge into the monkey room. Cyberwolf might rush through the first door, but he would be puzzled for at least a few seconds about where she had gone. And that would be all the time she needed—at least she hoped it would.

She was moving so fast that she was unable to keep herself from running into the door. She broke her speed with her left shoulder, then jerked open the door. She rushed inside and immediately pushed the door shut with the bottom of her foot. Barely glancing at the operating table or the supply cabinets, she rushed into the animal room.

The door between the rooms was propped open, and

without hesitating a moment, she kicked out the wedge holding it in place, then leaned against it to shut it faster. The weight she put on her knee made her bite her lip in pain.

The monkeys were chattering and rattling the metal doors. As Susan turned toward the bank of cages, a large male in the middle row bared long yellow fangs at her and gave a high-pitched screech. Other monkeys began to squeal, producing a deafening din, and a score of eyes, as black and glassy as obsidian, turned toward her. The monkeys had a wild, almost demented, look, as if they were strange small people pushed beyond the point of endurance.

Starting at the left side of the top row, then moving feverishly along the line of cages, she flipped loose the latches that secured the six doors. She didn't pull the doors open, because she knew she didn't have to. The monkeys shaking the doors would realize immediately that the mesh of stainless-steel rods keeping them confined was no longer latched.

She finished work on the top row and was about to start on the second one. Then all at once, despite the shrill chattering of the monkeys, she felt the vibration made by the slamming door in the adjacent room.

She abruptly stopped opening latches and ran for the door opposite the monkey cages. She turned around for a last glance at the room, and as she did so, she saw a large monkey with a ragged ear climbing out of the first cage.

The monkey leaped to the floor and began jumping and strutting in front of the others. He opened his mouth, bared his teeth, then snapped his mouth closed. Some of the others began pushing open their doors and leaping out of their cages. A shudder ran down her spine at the raw power of the animals.

As she turned to leave, the other door burst open and Cyberwolf stepped inside. He was breathing heavily through his half-opened mouth, and his face was wild with rage. He was holding a gun in his right hand, the muzzle pointed toward the ceiling. His eyes darted around the room, examining every shadow and hunting for every possible place of concealment.

As his gaze fell on her, his face seemed to grow more rigid, and his eyes turned hard and impenetrable.

Susan felt a sudden weakness, as if all her bones had dissolved and she had nothing left to support her. Her feet seemed frozen to the floor, and she stood paralyzed for what seemed like minutes. She told herself that she had to do something, she had to move. This man was going to kill her. With a considerable effort of will, she forced herself to reach out and turn the doorknob.

She saw Cyberwolf swing toward her, ready either to shoot her or to chase her, and she didn't know which. She began to run before the door had completely closed behind her.

48

As Hightower slowly came awake, he was increasingly aware of the sharp pain in his head. It was as if a long knitting needle had been shoved through his left eye and out the back of his head. His scarred retina shimmered with the bright sparks of randomly firing neurons, roiling like a pot of boiling light.

He tried to escape the pain by willing himself back into unconsciousness. Yet something deep inside his mind seemed to be pushing him into awareness. He felt like he was floating up from the muddy depths of a dark pond, unable to resist the power of his own buoyancy. He raised his eyelids, blinked, then closed them again. His head was clouded by a red haze of pain that pulsed with the rhythm of his heartbeat.

After what seemed a long time, he opened his eyes and kept them open. Without moving his head, he looked around. He could see nothing but shadowy forms. He was vaguely aware of a pale glimmer of light coming from behind him. His bad eye flickered in the darkness, producing its own distorted and unreal shapes.

He was lying flat with his left cheek pressed against the floor. He knew he had to get up, although he wasn't sure why. With his whole body resisting, he pulled himself to a sitting position. A wave of nausea swept over him, and for a moment he was sure he was going to throw up. Then he began to feel better.

An image of Susan floated into his mind. She was wearing a gold breechcloth that bared her legs to the hips, and a narrow band of red cloth that hardly covered her breasts. Her long blond hair swirled around her face. He remembered that he was searching for her, but his memories were vague and distant. Was he remembering a real person or a character from a movie?

He touched the lump on the back of his head. It was large and tender, but his scalp wasn't bleeding. The man with the mustache must have hit him with the butt of his gun. Hightower rubbed his face with his hands, then shook his head.

The man must have been too busy to search him, because he could feel the familiar bulges made by the phone and the grenade. He rubbed his left leg, and through his pants his fingers detected the hard steel edges of the autopsy knife.

He felt a sudden sense of urgency. *I've got to get out of this pantry.* Otherwise, he was going to get killed without having done anything to help Susan or his parents. Dying while struggling to accomplish something had a point, but being shot dead like a bull in a slaughter pen was pointlessly absurd. That was the way Alma had died. He wasn't going to let it happen to Susan or to himself.

Hightower struggled to his feet, doing his best to ignore the pounding in his head. He stood in the dark, feeling so dizzy that he thought he would collapse. He put out his right hand, fumbling for something to lean against. He grabbed a shelf and steadied himself. He then remembered that both sides of the pantry were lined with shelves.

The pantry itself puzzled him. He was sure he hadn't seen one on the design drawings, and the Berserker hadn't led him into a pantry. His experience of finding his way through the basement convinced him that the Berserker game had trained his body to know the layout of Johnson Hall. That was why being in the pantry felt so wrong. His body didn't recognize its existence.

When he felt steadier on his feet, he let go of the shelf and turned around. The door he had crawled through was directly behind him. It was tightly closed, and the feeble lines of light filtering though the gap between the door and the jamb provided the only illumination.

He groped for the doorknob and turned it right, then left. He could feel the latch slide in and out of the plate, but the bolt was locked into place. He felt along the opposite edge of the door, searching for the hinges. If they were on his side, he might be able to extract the pins with the autopsy knife, then pull the door off its hinges. But his exploring fingers found only the smooth groove where the door met the jamb. The hinges were on the outside.

He turned the doorknob and held it in place. He then leaned backward, and as he threw himself forward, he twisted to the left and hit the door with his shoulder. The latch rattled, but the door hardly moved. A bolt of searing pain shot through his head. He massaged the area beside his eye. Even if he waited until he felt stronger, it was unlikely that he could batter the door down. And if he made too much noise trying, he might get shot.

He was still feeling light-headed, and he turned and leaned his back against the door. He had to think. If he hadn't lost the shotgun, he could shoot off the lock. But it was useless to think that way. He could cut and chisel his way through one of the thin panels with the autopsy knife. However, the hole wouldn't be big enough for him to climb through, and it would take hours to cut through the door's rails or crosspieces to enlarge it. By then Susan would be dead and NYNEX melted down. If the key was in the lock, he could reach through a smaller hole and turn it. But it didn't seem likely that it would have been left behind.

Was there anything in the pantry that could help him get out? He tried to remember what the pantry had looked like. Just before he got hit, he had been glancing at the shelves and noticing that the lower ones were filled with cooking equipment. The upper ones were crowded with large institutional-size cans of tomatoes and the like.

Yet he had noticed something else, too, something that didn't have anything to do with what was in the pantry. It had to do with the pantry itself. What was it? He squeezed his eyes closed and bit at the edge of his lip. It was something obvious.

His first impression of the pantry when he crawled inside was that it seemed small and very narrow. It was only a storage room, yet it was hard to imagine an architect designing it that way. Also, when he was caught, he had just come up the stairs from the basement and was searching for the stairs to the second floor. He had gone to where they were supposed to be, but he couldn't find them.

Why weren't the stairs where they were supposed to be? How could both the architectural drawings and the body-memory he had acquired from the Berserker game be completely wrong?

Suddenly he understood what he should have realized from the first. *The stairs were exactly where he thought they were.*

49

Gibson started after Susan, then paused as he caught a fleeting movement out of the corner of his eye. He whirled around and saw a large monkey with a ragged ear perched on top of the nearest cage. The monkey was staring at him with hard, glittering eyes.

Suddenly, the monkey let out a long screech. The sound triggered a cacophonous din, filling the air with high-pitched screams, grunts, and fierce chattering. Gibson smelled the harsh odor of urine.

Glancing around, he noticed eight or ten monkeys out of their cages and scampering around. The one with the torn ear was the closest to him and the most threatening.

The monkey was staring at him with a steady gaze, as if it had a personal hatred for him. Sticking its head forward, it retracted its lips to display sharp yellow canines, then made a hoarse hissing that was almost a growl.

Keeping his eyes on the animal, Gibson began edging toward the opposite end of the room. Then with amazing quickness the monkey leaped straight at him. With its hands and feet extended, it hit him solidly, causing him to stagger to the side and almost fall. A surge of fear ran through him as he thought that he was going to end up on the floor with the monkey on top of him.

The monkey clung tightly to his jacket. Instinctively, Gibson turned his head to avoid the animal's rank feral odor. Without warning, the monkey sank its teeth into Gibson's left shoulder, then jumped to the floor.

Gibson was stunned by the pain. He whirled around, pointing the Magnum toward the monkey. Yet before he could fire, another hot shaft of pain shot through the calf of his right leg. He automatically kicked out hard, and his toe caught another monkey in the ribs, sending it staggering backward.

The monkey gave a series of sharp squeals and scurried out of range of Gibson's foot. But when it was a safe distance away, it reared up on its bent legs, threw out its chest, and pulled back its lips to show its fangs.

Gibson pointed the Magnum and pulled the trigger. The muzzle of the gun flashed like lightning, and the entire room exploded with noise. The shot hurled the monkey against the wall and left a bloody fist-sized wound in its chest. The screams of the other monkeys grew more hysterical.

Before Gibson could turn back around, the monkey with the ragged ear and another with a black spot on its nose rushed in from the left, barking out high-pitched *kee-kee-kee* sounds that rose above the constant background of squealing.

Torn-ear grabbed two of Gibson's left fingers in a viselike grip and rapidly bit him twice on the thumb. The pain was excruciating, and Gibson flung his arm backward, slamming the monkey against the wall with all the force he could summon.

The monkey's body hit the hard plaster with a dull crunch that seemed to shake the room. The monkey gave a strangled moan and loosened its grip. As the stunned animal slipped to the floor, Gibson jerked his hand free. He turned his pistol toward Torn-ear and fired, blasting off part of the creature's skull in a spray of blood. The animal's ragged ear was blown away with the shot.

The monkey with the black spot was clinging to his left leg, pinching and biting him, as if trying to force him to the floor. Gibson reached around with his right hand, raised the gun shoulder high, then brought it down hard against the monkey's face. The bone made a sharp cracking as it shattered.

The monkey dropped from Gibson's leg and lay stunned on the floor, its bulging eyes staring up at him. Gibson aimed for the center of its chest and fired, again filling the room with smoke and noise. The monkey gave a convulsive jerk that pulled its limbs together like the legs of a dying spider, then collapsed back into the spreading puddle of blood.

Gibson shifted from side to side, checking to see where the next attack was coming from. But the shrieks had died away, and the only noise came from the animals locked in the cages.

Two small monkeys were perched on top of the cages, watching the action like spectators at a sporting event. Two others were cowering against the wall by the door

opposite him. Three were gathered around an open bag of
food pellets, scooping them up and stuffing them into
their mouths. They nervously glanced up at Gibson, then
went back to their eating.

The fight was over, and he had won it decisively. But
he had paid a price. Both legs, his left shoulder, and his
hand were aching with dull pains that throbbed with every heartbeat. If he didn't get them taken care of, they
would probably become infected. Monkeys were such
filthy fucking animals. He tightened his lips in disgust.

His hands shook as he realized how close he had come
to being killed. The big monkey with the torn ear could
have ripped out his throat. A tide of anger swept through
him. Susan had set him up to be killed. She had planned
it, then carried out the plan coldly and deliberately. She
had caught him by surprise and made a fool of him. He
knew she was intelligent, but it had never occurred to him
that she was capable of being so cunning.

He had also underestimated her determination to escape
from him. When they had talked in the living room, she
seemed to like him and be interested in him. She seemed
ready to spend more time with him, just the two of them
together, talking quietly and enjoying each other's company.

For a brief moment, he had glimpsed another possible
world for them to share. He had imagined a life in which
the cloud of dread that floated between him and other
people blew away like smoke, leaving him free of the
sickening terror he felt whenever he thought about having
an ordinary relationship with a woman. If he could live in
that possible world, he and Susan could be together for
years, and he could enjoy the pleasures of her body without having to kill her first.

Now he realized that his pathetic little fantasy was
based on her deliberate deception. She wasn't interested
in him. She cared nothing about him and didn't want to
know him better. She thought he was some disgusting
creature, and she wanted to get away from him. In fact
she wanted to kill him.

It was unfair. He had never done anything to hurt her. He had tried to protect her from Whip, and he had never threatened her with the slightest harm. She had somehow sensed danger and wanted to save her own life. But that was exactly what she wasn't going to be able to do.

He pressed on his left shoulder with the tips of his fingers. The wounds still hurt, but the blood had stopped soaking through his shirt. He needed to find Susan before the helicopter landed.

She was sure to be back where he had discovered her. She had been working at something when he came in. He hadn't seen what she was doing, but she was probably trying to open the loading-dock door. He needed to get to her fast, before she succeeded.

He walked rapidly up the corridor toward the door Susan had run through. Two of the three monkeys gathered around the bag of food pellets stopped eating and pushed themselves tightly against the wall. The third continued to eat, and when he saw Gibson approaching, he made a hissing noise and bared his teeth in a warning grimace.

Hardly slowing his pace, Gibson kicked the monkey in the face, snapping its head back. The animal uttered a high-pitched squeal of pain and fear. It leaped over the bag of food, then scurried toward the cages.

Gibson held up his left hand and shook it to try to ease the pain. He looked at the bite. It was a nasty one. Although there was little blood, the fold of skin at the base of his thumb was torn open, and the area around it had turned an angry red. He located two purple-ringed holes made by the monkey's teeth.

He stopped in front of the stainless-steel sink, slipped the Magnum into its holster, and turned on the cold water. He held his thumb under the sparkling stream. The water burned the raw flesh, but it might wash away some of the germs. He didn't want to die of an infection or maybe lose his hand. He would have a hard time climbing around in the net with only one hand.

He wiped off the water on the side of his khaki pants. As he glanced up at the metal cabinets, he noticed that the monkeys had pulled open several doors. The cabinets were filled with various sorts of medicines and supplies in bottles, tubes, and boxes, most of it marked VETERINARY USE in red letters.

In the cabinet nearest the door he saw what looked like a rifle or shotgun, with a polished wooden stock and an unusually large blue-steel barrel. On the shelf with the gun he noticed a lidless cardboard box filled with strangely shaped cartridges. All at once the pieces fell into place, and he realized that the gun was used to shoot tranquilizing darts.

He picked up the box and saw that it was labeled VETERINARY FLECHETTES, XYLAZINE, 60 MG. He took out one of the darts and examined it. Three fins flared out from the metal base like the feathers of an arrow, and mounted at the tip was a polished-steel hypodermic needle. A clear plastic cap covered the quarter-inch-long needle. Apparently the drug was in the tapered metal base.

He dropped the fléchette back into the box and slid the gun out of its rack. He saw then why the barrel looked unusual. The gun was an air rifle, and attached to the barrel, directly beneath it, was an air chamber twice its size. He unscrewed the cap at the end of the chamber and discovered a long cylinder of compressed air.

He screwed the cap back on, then turned the rifle over to examine its firing mechanism. He flipped up the bolt handle and drew back the bolt. He snapped off the plastic cap covering the needle of a fléchette and slipped the fléchette into the breech. He closed the bolt, locked it down, then used his thumb to slide the safety to the "Off" position.

He aimed the rifle at the closer of the two monkeys still feeding from the open bag. He focused on the animal's chest, lining it up with the blade of the front sight and the notch of the rear sight. He was so close he could hardly miss. He gently squeezed the trigger, and the rifle made a dull thump.

The monkey gave a shrill shriek and jumped into the air. Gibson had almost missed the shot. The small dart was stuck in the monkey's arm. The monkey plucked out the fléchette, looked at it with a puzzled expression, then dropped it on the floor. But by then the animal was having trouble staying upright. It tottered, then fell over on its side beside the bag of food.

Gibson smiled. The rifle worked, and the drug was obviously effective. He was delighted by his good luck. He then felt a moment of disgust as he imagined what the heavy slug of the Magnum, with such incredible power behind it, would do to the slim perfection of Susan's body. It would explode in her chest and leave a giant exit wound in her back.

He wanted to keep her body unblemished, and he could never bear the idea of shooting her. Now he had a way to take control of her without leaving a mark on her larger than a pinprick. He picked up several fléchettes and slipped them into his jacket pocket as he went through the door.

50

Susan pulled hard on the end of the thin slat. Its rough-sawed finish was like coarse sandpaper, and it tore at her hands. Her fingers and palms stung, but she kept up a steady strain. A feeling of desperation was taking hold of her, and she couldn't afford to stop, no matter how much her hands hurt.

Her effort was paying off. The conduit moved smoothly in its round slot, coming up an inch or so above the level of the junction box. She was afraid something might go wrong, yet she also felt a thrill of anticipation. If this conduit was cut like the bottom one, she needed only to force it up another inch. The end should slip out and give her access to the wires. Then she could touch them to the metal faceplate and complete the circuit activating the hoist.

Sweat ran from under her hair and down her face. But she felt chilled through and through, as if she were standing under a cold shower. She had heard three shots coming from the monkey room, and it couldn't be much longer until Cyberwolf burst through the door. The need to hurry nagged at her like a throbbing toothache.

Keeping pressure on the slat, she shifted her weight to her right foot to get more leverage. A sharp stab of pain in her twisted knee made her bite her lip, but she didn't change her position. Just another half inch and the conduit would clear the hole. She added more force to the steady strain, and the conduit moved up at least a half inch—but nothing happened.

"Come on, come on." The words were an almost prayerful murmur, and her tone was urgent and pleading.

There's no reason to panic. The goddamned top piece must be slightly longer than the bottom one. But it couldn't be much longer, because there wouldn't be room for it inside the box. It should definitely come out on the next pull. But first, she should pause and let her muscles recover. Then she would make the big push.

She slacked off the plank, letting the conduit slide back into the box. She held the board in place with her left hand and wiped her right hand on her pants. She flexed her fingers until the blood started flowing again. Her skin stung from the dozens of small scrapes the rough plank had given her. The sheet-metal cuts from the cable channel had stopped bleeding, but now they were starting to pull open and burn.

This isn't the time to fret about trivial wounds. It's time to concentrate on staying alive.

Gibson was careful not to let the door to the monkey room bang shut. Susan would be listening for him, and he didn't want to give her any advantage. In other circumstances, it might be fun to play games with her, but he had no time to waste. Each minute he spent chasing her was a minute subtracted from the very few they would spend together.

Walking as quietly as he could, he headed across the lab toward the loading-dock door. The light filtering down from the fluorescent tubes high overhead comforted his eyes like a cool compress. His shoulder, legs, and left hand ached dully from the monkey bites. It had never crossed his mind that Susan would set him up that way.

He glanced toward the center of the room at the pale golden light spraying up from the floor. The light was so striking that he had marveled at it even while he was running after Susan. If he only had the time, he would investigate its source.

As he approached the door, he raised his feet and put them down with exaggerated caution, being careful not to let his shoes scuff the floor. He switched the dart rifle to his left hand, then stood sideways and put his ear flat against the metal door. He closed his eyes and concentrated on listening.

She was doing something that made faint scraping noises and drew small grunts of effort from her. Exactly what she was up to, he couldn't tell, but probably she was trying to force open one of the outside doors.

Judging by the sounds, she was at the far end of the room. So if he entered where he was, she would see him immediately and either run or fight. He would then have to try to hit a moving target. The best strategy was to go in through the door he had first used. This time, though, he would be quieter.

He walked past the office to the door into the hall, then paused and put on his mirror shades. As he went through the door, he glanced down the stark white passage. The double doors leading into Johnson Hall were still closed. Had Cortez received the message that the helicopter was on its way? If so, he ought to be coming in with the news before long.

And what about Whip? Was he lost someplace in the building or had Susan done something to put him out of action? Maybe she had even flat-lined him. But how could she have done it without some kind of weapon?

He stopped in front of the swinging door leading to the loading dock. Holding the air rifle in his left hand, he pulled back the bolt handle. He cradled the rifle in the crook of his arm while he fished a fléchette out of his pocket. He used his thumb to break off the fléchette's thin plastic cap. Then, being careful not to stick himself with the needle, he placed the dart in the breech of the rifle. He shoved the bolt forward and pushed down the handle to lock it into position.

Smiling, he stuck out the tip of his tongue and licked his upper lip. Loaded and locked, he was ready to go. He was more than ready—he was eager.

Susan grabbed the slat with both hands and pulled until it was lodged firmly against the conduit. She hauled back on it with all the strength she could summon. Now was the time to do or die. She put her shoulders and back into the effort, pulling as hard as if she were working the oars on Lake Erie.

"Pull like you live—hard!" her father would shout to her from the stern. She had been no more than thirteen, but he was determined that she would learn to row. Twice a week for almost the whole summer, with him urging her on, she put all her will and power into making the oars cut through the water. She had surprised herself by how fast she could send the flat-bottomed boat gliding across the gray-green waters. Her father wasn't surprised, though. "If you *think* you can do it, you *can* do it," he had told her.

The conduit slid easily out of the box to the point it had reached before. She held her breath and kept pulling, and another half inch followed. She smiled as she saw the cut end coming up. The bundle of white, black, and red wires was clearing the machined edge of the hole. A little more pressure and they should pull loose the way the others had.

Suddenly, without the slightest warning, the thin slat

snapped in two with a loud crack. All at once she was pulling against no resistance. She staggered backward, clutching the splintered piece of wood in both hands.

Reeling out of control, she took several quick steps, then got tangled in her own feet. She sat down hard, hitting the polished concrete with her left hip. A barb of pain spread through her thigh and down her leg.

She tossed down the broken plank, and it clattered dully on the floor. Worrying about making noise was pointless now. She rubbed her hip with the flat of her hand, trying to blunt the sharpness of the ache. Now both her legs hurt. But she hadn't broken anything.

She got to her feet and walked over to the switch. The other piece of slat was jammed under the conduit, the jagged end broken off even with it. The conduit had slipped back into the junction box, and she was left where she had started. She was actually worse off, because now her lever was broken.

"Goddamn it all to flaming hell," she said aloud, her voice tight with bitterness.

The expression wasn't one she had used before, and she was almost surprised to hear it coming out of her mouth. It was something her mother had said when she felt frustrated beyond endurance. Given her own situation and feelings, maybe that was what made the expression seem exactly right.

The back of the narrow room was as dim as his necropolis. The widely spaced incandescent bulbs emitted a pearl gray glow that was not even bright enough to read by. The packing cases and the loaded pallets looked as insubstantial as shadows, and areas without bulbs directly overhead were pools of darkness. He removed his mirror shades and returned them to his jacket pocket.

Bulbs of a higher power had been screwed into the porcelain fixtures at the end of the room, and the area in front of the overhead door was as brightly lit as a stage. He could see everything Susan was doing with complete clarity.

He made his way to the far side of the room, then, staying in the shadows, he walked along the perimeter until he was no more than fifteen feet from her. She was concentrating so hard on the switch box in front of her that she probably wouldn't notice him even if he walked right up to her.

He knelt down behind a pallet of cardboard boxes. Sweat had made his shirt damp and clammy, and it stuck to the skin of his back. His breathing was getting faster, and he could feel the excitement building inside. He hoped he could keep his hands steady enough not to ruin his aim.

Susan glanced back at the packing case she had taken the slat from. She remembered how hard it had been to pry off, even though it was already loose. Prying off another slat would take too long, so she would have to try to make the broken one work.

She picked it up. She then grabbed the conduit with her fingertips and tugged it toward her, while she simultaneously tried to slide the smooth end of the slat under it. She managed to wedge in one small corner. She worked the slat back and forth, shoving it toward the wall, moving it under the conduit a bit at a time. Her fingertips felt bruised, but she was making progress. She tried to ignore the knotted feeling in her gut. Her stomach hurt with a dull, steady ache.

The end of the slat finally slipped under the conduit and butted against the wall. She levered back the short piece with her right hand, while she pulled on the conduit with her left. She pulled hard and steadily, keeping up the pressure.

The conduit moved slowly out of the junction box, and she felt herself relaxing. She was going to make it out this time.

He rested the barrel of the rifle on the carton at the top of the stack. It was just the height to allow him to look through the notch of the rear sight without having to crouch lower.

He watched Susan a moment, taking pleasure in the smooth way her slim body moved as she tugged on the board she had stuck behind the conduit. An almost over-whelming desire swept through him, mixed with a cold current of anxiety.

The raw lust that shoved aside everything else made it clear why he had mounted such a massive effort just to be with her for a while. He had always known that he didn't have a real choice about such matters. He was guided by a program that he hadn't written and couldn't escape. But that also meant that he was doing exactly what he wanted to do.

He lined up the blade of the front sight with her back, then moved the rifle slightly to the left, until the notch of the rear sight was also in perfect alignment.

He held his breath and gently began to squeeze the trigger.

She slipped her fingers under the conduit, then as she started pulling on it, she heard a short, muffled noise. It reminded her of a puff of air escaping from a can of warm soda, only louder. She paid no attention to it.

Suddenly, she felt a sharp stinging sensation just below her right shoulder blade. She flinched, shrugging her shoulders forward but not letting go of the slat or the con-duit. Probably she'd been stung by an insect, but this wasn't the time to stop and check.

For the second time, she watched the end of the conduit emerge from the junction box, then she began to feel strange. A luminous gray mist swirled around her, and ev-erything she was looking at fragmented into disconnected colored shapes. She no longer recognized what she was pulling on, and she turned it loose.

She could feel herself slipping over the edge of con-sciousness. She sensed panic rising up in her, choking off her breath and making her head spin. She could no longer think coherently. She knew she had to do something, but she didn't know what it was.

When the darkness closed over her, she was still wondering.

51

Gibson watched Susan waver and try to steady herself against the wall in front of her. Finally she slid heavily to the floor.

She fell on her knees, then rolled onto her left side. She lay half curled, her legs bent and her left arm stretched above her head. With her wrist turned slightly inward, the curve of her hand made a graceful arc. As he studied her, he realized that her body had fallen into a classic pinup pose. It suited her perfectly.

He put the air rifle on the floor and stood up slowly, almost cautiously. He sensed an electrical tingling of excitement coursing down his spine. But at the same time he felt uneasy and apprehensive. His stomach was constricted, as if a wide belt around his middle had been cinched up tightly.

Now he was in a position to create one of the possible worlds he had spent so much time imagining. Susan's body belonged to him more than it did to her, and whatever he wished to do with it, she couldn't object. That was arousing and exciting virtually beyond the reach of his fantasies.

Yet he was afraid. Fears hard to identify, much less articulate, kept him from completely giving himself over to the pleasures he had imagined for so long. Could he regard Susan as nothing more than the silent and beautiful body he wanted her to be? Or was he still too aware of her will and desires?

He tried to push such worries from his mind. He had

achieved everything he had set out to achieve. He had $20 million and he had Susan. He was the one with real power. She was nothing more than a toy. No more than movie plastic made flesh.

She was his to possess and control for as long as he wanted. No, that wasn't quite true. She was his for as long as he was able to remain at Rush. Time was severely limited. For that reason, if no other, he should be spending every second with her.

He stepped from behind the pile of boxes and hurried across the few feet separating them. Gazing down at her, he saw at once that she was drugged into oblivion. The muscles of her face were slack, her mouth hung open, and her head lolled to the side.

He picked up her right hand. He pinched the delicate skin of her wrist between his thumb and index finger, then twisted it hard. Her mouth gaped open, but she made no sound. As he let her hand drop to the floor, he saw a glint from the needle of the fléchette. It must have pulled loose from her back when she fell.

Glancing up, he caught sight of the bundle of colored wires splayed out from the electrical box. He got to his feet and walked over to get a closer look. He touched the red button, then he noticed the key slot on the side of the box.

The switch obviously controlled the overhead door, and after studying the setup, he saw how she had been trying to bypass it. He pulled the end of the broken slat toward him. The conduit came up from the wall, and he pulled harder, until it warped and bowed outward. He slipped the fingers of his left hand under it and gave an exploratory tug. He felt the conduit slide up slightly. He would be able to pop the end out of the junction box with no trouble. He moved his hand and slacked off the lever. The conduit settled back into place against the wall.

Susan had solved his escape problem. He would wait for Cortez and Whip to take off in the helicopter, then head for the loading dock. As soon as the copter went up, the cops would most likely call off their watch at the back of the research building. He could raise the back door and slip through it in less than two minutes. Then he could blend in with the crowd, go into Boston and rent a car, then drive to Canada, maybe Toronto. He could get a plane to Paraguay from there.

He knelt by Susan and rolled her onto her back. Probably the drug would start to wear off in about fifteen or twenty minutes. He could stick another needle in her, but he didn't want to do that. He wanted her back in Johnson Hall alive and conscious. She was their sole hostage, so he might have to use her to cut a deal. If so, the cops would want proof that she wasn't already a corpse. She was his insurance policy.

He grabbed her right arm and pulled her into a sitting posture. Her head fell forward, her chin on her chest. A grimy loading dock wasn't where he had imagined spending time with her. Then he suddenly remembered a more comfortable and private place. Holding her upright with one hand, he got to his feet, put his hands under her arms, and pulled her to a standing position.

He leaned her body against his, enjoying its surprising softness and warmth. He put his arm around her shoulders, then paused to enjoy the moment. The way they were posed, they might be in some L.A. club, dancing close and focusing on each another, completely oblivious of their surroundings. He bent his head and rubbed his nose gently back and forth on the top of her head. Her hair felt smooth and soft, and beneath the sweet musky odor of sweat, he could detect the faint jasmine scent of her shampoo.

He shifted his grip to her waist, and he was surprised by how small it was. His hands could almost encircle it; another couple of inches and his fingers would touch. He lifted her off the floor in a single straight jerk, then draped her over his left shoulder. She was heavier than he had expected, probably because she was so well muscled. Yet she also seemed as delicate as a porcelain figurine. He had the distinct feeling that if he dropped her, she would shatter into thousands of tiny fragments.

He looped his left arm over the backs of her thighs, clasping her tightly to him. He walked to the door of the lab and opened it with his right hand. He turned sideways and maneuvered his way through the doorway, being careful not to let any part of her body get scraped on the door frame.

He was determined to preserve her body in the most perfect condition possible, free from any more bruises and abrasions. He was sorry he had been forced to throw the pistol at her, because it almost surely would have made a bruise on the pale skin of her back. But she hadn't given him a choice. He had done his best to convince her to stop resisting and come along in a friendly way. They could have had a nice time talking and joking together.

But she had chosen the hard way, so she had only herself to blame. Now he didn't have to ask her permission or get her to agree to anything. He could do what he wanted with her, and he could do it his way.

52

The stairs were right where they should be.

He hadn't been able to locate them because they had been boarded up. The hall from the kitchen had been turned into a pantry by adding a door at the front and a wall at the rear. To get to the stairs, he would have to smash through the wall.

His head still throbbed with pain, but he was getting excited. He might be able to do something besides sit in the dark and wait to be shot. He hadn't been able to knock down the door, but maybe he could break through the wall.

He fought down the inclination to rush to the back of the pantry. The darkness surrounding him was so dense that he could see virtually nothing. The judicial phrase *all deliberate speed* came to mind. That was exactly how he needed to proceed.

He lowered himself into a squatting position, and a sharp pain shot through his left leg. The whole leg still ached from being battered by the falling bricks. Ignoring the pain, he got down on his hands and knees and began to crawl toward the back of the pantry.

The floor was a seamless vinyl surface so smooth that it felt slick. He advanced by sliding his hands in front of him to explore the territory, and when he encountered no obstacles, he crawled forward. Twice he had to change course to avoid running into a shelf, but he moved ahead steadily.

Finally, the fingers of his left hand touched the strip of quarter-round molding at the junction of the wall and floor. He crawled to the wall, then sat on his haunches in front of it.

He ran his hands over the flat surface. The wall was smooth, but it didn't feel particularly cool, not even as cool as the floor. That was good news, and he found himself quite unselfconsciously smiling in the dark. A wall that didn't feel cool probably wasn't made of plaster. He placed his left ear flat against the wall, then tapped it sharply with his knuckles. *Just like percussing a chest.* To his relief, he heard a dull, hollow sound. Definitely wallboard.

He was going to have to make some noise. He would just have to work fast and hope that the door was thick enough to muffle the sound. He got to his feet and took two steps backward. He leaned on his hands and shifted his weight to his left foot. He drew back his right foot and kicked the wall with the toe of his shoe. The wall shook, but nothing else happened.

He leaned closer, almost touching the wall with his cheek. He pulled his foot back farther than before and kicked again. As he swung his foot through the short arc, he tightened the muscles of his knee, putting as much power into the kick as he was able. He felt the impact all the way up his leg. He heard a sharp crack and his foot moved forward another few inches.

He had broken through!

He felt for the hole. An irregularly shaped piece of wallboard the size of a paperback book had snapped loose and was hanging by a hinge of thick paper. He tore the piece off and dropped it on the floor. The material between the paper layers had the familiar feel of the chalky substance used in drywall. That was good, because drywall was extremely brittle.

He put his hand through the hole and searched around. The wall was only the thickness of the drywall. The stairs must be just on the other side of it, and another wall had probably been constructed at the top of them.

He turned left and shuffled forward with his hands outstretched. When he located the top shelf, he began searching its contents by touch. He encountered cardboard boxes with unidentifiable contents, large cellophane bags of what felt like pasta, and plastic bottles of ketchup or salad dressing.

He found what he was looking for on the middle shelf: a restaurant-size can. Probably it contained vegetables in water, because it sloshed when he shook it. He guessed it weighed five pounds, maybe six.

He knelt in front of the wall and wrapped his hands around the can, holding it near the top. He located the hole, then, turning the can down at an angle, he began to chop away at the edges of the chalky material.

The can made a satisfying *thunk* each time it hit. The raised steel rim bit through the drywall, and the weight of the can knocked out big holes. As he continued to chop, large chalky pieces fell to the floor on the opposite side.

Now that he had started hammering, he seemed to switch into an automatic mode. With no thought about what he was doing or why, he worked furiously. He breathed hard, and his nose clogged up with the heavy dust from the shattered drywall. Sweat trickled down from his forehead and stung his eyes. He squinted and blinked, but he kept on hammering.

He didn't let himself think about the steady thudding noise he was making. If he worked fast, he might be able to break through the wall before anybody came to check. Speed was what he needed.

When the hole seemed large enough to squeeze through, he stopped hammering and set the can down between his feet. He pulled out his handkerchief and wiped his eyes. A gritty powder stuck to the sweat on his cheeks, making a coarse, dry paste. He scraped off the paste with the tip of his index finger, being careful not to get any in his right eye. That could put him out of commission completely.

He placed his hands on each side of the opening, then stuck his right foot through the hole. Ducking his head low, he turned sideways and stepped through to the other side of the wall.

He felt a thrill of exhilaration, but it immediately died away. He had expected to find Susan by now, and he wasn't even in a position to search for her. He thought of his parents flying blindly into risks they knew nothing about. He had to help them.

He peered forward, straining his eyes, but he couldn't see anything. The darkness was too complete. The air was motionless and stale, devoid of any odor except the stale scent of dust. He had the feeling that he now knew what it was like to break into a tomb sealed shut for a thousand years.

He turned and retrieved the heavy can from the floor on the other side of the wall. He still had another curtain of drywall to punch a hole in, and he wasn't likely to find a better tool.

Tucking the can under his left arm, he shuffled forward, moving only inches at a step. The floor wasn't as slick as the one in the pantry; probably it was the original varnished hardwood. Whatever it was, it was coated with a layer of grit, and when he slid his feet forward, the soles of his shoes made a rough, grating noise.

The toe of his left shoe suddenly tapped something. He leaned forward and touched it. He felt the bullnose finish on the front edge of the stair tread, and relief ran through him. *Thank God for Pete Salter and the Berserker.* Without them he would never have found the stairs.

Keeping his toes butted against the riser, he shuffled to the right. He slid his hand along the wall and groped for the railing. Gripping it firmly, he started up the stairs. He took one step at a time, sliding his hand ahead of him.

As he reached the top, he paused. He felt himself swaying in the dark, and for an instant, he had a vivid image of himself falling backward down the stairs, breaking his neck and lying helpless on the gritty floor. A shudder rippled down his back, and he took two quick steps forward.

After another dozen small shuffling steps, he encountered the wall. He used his hands to explore the surface in front of him and determined that it was virtually a mirror image of the one below. He grasped the heavy can in both hands and started hammering. As he worked, a sense of urgency came over him, urgency mixed with doubt so strong that it bordered on despair. *Am I going to be able to find Susan soon enough? Can I make Cyberwolf shut down the Chernobyl program?*

He pushed the doubt to the back of his mind. He might get himself killed, but no matter what happened, he wasn't going to give up. He couldn't face being a survivor again.

53

Gibson moved as quickly as he could through the pale light of the lab. He wrinkled his nose at the fishy odor, and almost at once he felt sweat break out on his forehead. Susan was a dead weight on his shoulder, and the hot, moist atmosphere of the lab made any exertion difficult.

Her hip was nestled by his left cheek, and he pressed

his face hard against her. As her body rubbed his, he could feel the soft resilience of her flesh. The solidity of her body reminded him that she was real and not the poster on his wall or another chapter in his fantasy.

The constant pressure of her hip aroused him. He seemed able to feel the suppleness of the skin on her thighs beneath the heavy fabric of her jeans.

He walked faster. He glanced toward the back wall at the shadowy form of the lab bench, and from the corner of his eye he glimpsed the golden spray of light radiating from the floor. He quickly turned away to keep from being blinded by its brightness.

He liked having Susan's body rubbing against him, but her weight made his shoulder hurt with a burning pain. Shifting her to maintain his balance was like twisting a knife in a wound. The bites on his hand and legs had turned into dull aches that he could ignore.

Suddenly he heard a loud, ragged whooshing noise coming from outside the building. The noise increased and decreased in a regular, repetitive way, sounding like some giant harvesting machine threshing a field of wheat. The noise was puzzling, then he realized that he was hearing a helicopter. He felt a jolt of anger. *That goddamned Cortez.* He hadn't come to tell him that the police had agreed to send it, and now here the fucking thing was.

They had met his demands, and that was a relief, even though the helicopter was early. That might have consequences for his original plans, but what? His mind raced as he considered possibilities.

Cortez and Whip might look for him to get some orders, or if they got nervous, they might decide to forget him and get on board the copter to make a break for the airport. But it really didn't matter what they did. The helicopter was already playing its role as a distraction, and the police would be focusing attention on it. So getting himself out the loading-dock door was the only arrangement he needed to concentrate on.

He suddenly realized that meant he didn't have to take Susan back to Johnson Hall. What's more, he didn't have to keep her alive to talk to the police. He felt a sharp thrill of excitement, and his lips pulled back in a smile. He could turn her into a silent friend right now. He could enjoy her until the helicopter took off and the police started searching the buildings.

He couldn't have worked out a better plan. He would have more time with Susan than he had expected. She wouldn't even have to wake up, because he could give her an overdose with the fléchettes.

But that would be anticlimactic. He wanted the pleasure of feeling her smooth neck under his hands. As he squeezed tighter and tighter, he would be able to feel her body writhe and buck as she made the transition to another, darker possible world. By strangling her he would begin to possess her.

He reached the opposite side of the lab, then stood with his back to the fountain of light as he opened the door to the operating room. Turning sideways, he carried her inside. He shot a glance toward the monkey room to assure himself that the door was completely closed. *I don't want to have anything else to do with those goddamned monkeys.*

He crossed the room and stopped beside the narrow operating table. Letting Susan's body slide down his shoulder, he bent his knees and leaned forward. When she was half sitting on the table, he lifted her legs and swung them to the top. He let her back sink down onto the green drape.

Directly over the table, an array of incandescent bulbs set into metal reflectors provided a flood of light too bright to tolerate. Overlapping circles of hot white light illuminated the operating area without shadows or shading.

He squinted his eyes to shut out the worst of the glare, then scanned the front of the room, looking for a rheostat. He spotted it just inside the door. He glanced at Susan to make sure she was properly positioned on the table, then crossed over and began to adjust the light. As he pushed down a small plastic lever, the light shining directly on

Susan gradually grew weaker and softer. The raw whiteness lost its force and turned into a diffuse, gentle gray.

He could sense some of his anxiety and tension ebbing as the light became muted. Walking back to the operating table, he began to feel that he was completely free to enjoy Susan the way he wanted and the way she deserved. She was made to be admired and adored, and he was prepared to do both.

As though in a dream, he recalled with complete clarity the details of the night he had spent with Bert and Dennis. He saw the small dark room, with its cold sour smell and its black-painted windowpanes. He saw the stainless-steel drawers set into the wall like filing cabinets.

But mostly his mind was filled with the image of the chill, ashen white body of the woman laid out naked on the shiny metal tray that Bert had slid out from one of the drawers. Now he was going to get to repeat that experience with Susan.

And this time Bert and Dennis wouldn't be around to stop him from doing everything that he wanted to do.

54

Hightower stood with his head turned toward the floor and his hand shielding his eyes. After the complete darkness of the pantry, even the dim light made his right eye burn and his left eye flash with scintillations. He needed to move and move fast, but he could do nothing until he was able to see.

Keeping his hand to his forehead, he lifted his head and did his best to look around. He was in some sort of office, maybe the accounting department or patient records. Shoulder-high partitions formed tiny enclosures that were furnished with desks and swivel chairs. But what interested him most was the hallway he could see beyond the open door in front of him.

He walked through the office, and when he reached the hall, he glanced quickly in both directions. To the right were double doors leading into the research tower. As he hurried toward them, he wondered if he'd have to go back for the heavy can and smash the glass panel. But the door he tried swung open smoothly.

The bright down-lights and their reflection from the stark white walls made him squint. He paused to consider what strategy he should follow. The research building was eight stories tall, and if he was going to have a chance of finding Susan, he needed to figure out the most likely places to look.

What would *he* do if he were trying to get away from somebody? He looked down at the pattern of nested dark green and pale gray rectangles on the vinyl floor. Probably he would try to get off the first floor, because it had no windows and the outside doors would be locked. Maybe he would go to the roof and signal for attention. The police would be able to rescue him from there. Anyway, the roof would be a good place to start. He could then work his way down floor by floor.

He covered the space to the stairway in a few rapid steps and pulled open the heavy fire door. A flight of unpainted concrete steps ran up to a landing, then another flight switched back and led up the next floor.

He took the stairs two at a time, hurrying but not running. A single fluorescent fixture attached to the wall of the landing supplied a faded greenish light. He couldn't see the steps clearly, and he made sure he had a firm grip on the handrail.

He was halfway up the stairs to the third floor when it occurred to him that he hadn't considered taking the elevator. "Goddamn it," he said under his breath. Exhaustion and stress were taking their toll. He wasn't thinking clearly. He turned and went back down to the second-floor landing. He should be able to get the elevator on the second floor as well as the third.

He stopped in front of the metal door. He turned the knob and pulled the door toward him, but it wouldn't budge. He then shoved hard, pushing on the door with his shoulder, but it still wouldn't move.

His heart seemed to stop for a moment, and a feeling of dread spread through him. *He was locked in the stairwell.* If he couldn't get into the hall from the second floor, that was probably true for all the floors.

He ran down the stairs to the first floor. Any idea he had of keeping quiet he forgot about. His feet hit the concrete steps with hard slaps that echoed hollowly in the stairwell. He held tight to the railing, and when he reached the landing, he swung around the corner and onto the last flight of stairs.

When he reached the first floor, he crossed the distance to the door in two long steps. He grabbed the smooth brass knob, turned it, and pulled the door toward him. It wouldn't move, and he felt a sickening sinking feeling in his stomach. He was trapped, and there wasn't a goddamned thing he could do about it.

Then he suddenly realized that he was being stupid again. Still holding on to the doorknob, he threw himself forward, hitting the door with his shoulder. The door flew open, and he had to take several running steps to keep from falling on the slick vinyl floor.

Shaking his head, he took a deep breath, then let it out as a long sigh. He should have realized that the doors would open onto the stairs from inside the offices to allow people to go to the ground floor in case of an emergency. But to maintain security, the doors wouldn't open from the stairs into the offices. Only the first-floor door would be set to open from the stair side.

Trying to use the elevator was likely to be equally pointless. It was sure to operate only with a key. Rush was concerned about patient safety and about protecting research projects. Even if patients managed to get into the tower, they would find it impossible to roam freely.

Then, with rising excitement, he saw that he had reached a conclusion without trying to. If the stair doors were locked and the elevator required a key, then Susan had to be on the first floor. He felt resolution take form in him. He would search the building, and if he couldn't find her, he would search Johnson Hall.

He took two steps, then stopped. He was forgetting that if Cyberwolf hadn't recaptured Susan, he was also going to be out looking. It would be wise to be better prepared to fight than he was the last time. Only good luck had saved him from being shot instantly, but luck wasn't something you could count on. Bad surgeons got lucky, but good surgeons got prepared.

Hightower hiked up the left leg of his pants and began unwrapping the self-sticking elastic bandage. The tan fabric made a soft tearing sound as it peeled off. When the autopsy knife slipped to the side, he held it by the handle while he finished the unwrapping.

He put the knife on the floor and took off the rest of the bandage. The skin of his calf was a mottled white and red, and it was indented in odd ways where the knife blade and the handle had pushed hardest. Now that the pressure was off, his leg began to sting as if it had been whipped with nettles. He rubbed his hand over the skin, then kneaded his calf with his fingers. He straightened up. He had no time to waste on trivial irritations.

Someplace outside the building, he heard a ragged whirring sound. It seemed to get louder and then softer, like the noise of a giant rotating fan. He paused a moment, listening. It was a helicopter, probably the one Don told him Cyberwolf had ordered to transport him to Logan Airport.

Hightower felt the muscles of his stomach tighten. If the helicopter was arriving, he couldn't have much time left to find Susan and force Cyberwolf to cancel the Chernobyl program.

He snatched up the autopsy knife and hurried down the hall. He stopped by the first door and grabbed the doorknob. The door was locked, and he didn't have the time to try to force it.

Before he even reached the next door, he smelled the

sharp ammoniac odor of spoiled fish. As he stepped inside the room, the fishy odor intensified. The air was hot
and heavy with moisture, like the swampy, sour air of a
public sauna.

The fluorescent light was so dim that he could make
out few details. But his eyes were strongly attracted to the
center of the room, where a fountain of golden light
spouted up from the floor, surrounding itself with a magical glowing circle.

55

Gibson stood by the head of the table looking down at
Susan and studying her face. It was narrow and perfectly
proportioned, and the ridges of her cheekbones gave it a
sharp definition.

He frowned as he noticed a small cut, crusty with dried
blood, that was half hidden by the ragged fringe of hair
hanging over her forehead. Despite the wound, she was
still beautiful. She looked so different from other women
that he wouldn't have been shocked to learn that she
came from another planet.

He walked to the opposite end of the table and pulled
off her shoes. He put them on the floor under the table so
he wouldn't stumble over them. He took off her socks,
working them down from the top, then yanking them off
by the toes. He rubbed the fabric with his fingers. It felt
incredibly fine, like some special material not available to
ordinary women.

Her feet were long and slim and her toes neatly ordered
in descending length. She wore no nail polish, and each
toe seemed perfectly formed, like those in romantic ads
for sandals or expensive perfumes. He ran his fingers
over her instep, feeling the delicate texture of the thin, almost transparent skin, then wrapped his hand around the

toes of her left foot. Her foot felt cool and dry, and in the throbbing of her pulse, he could detect the strong and regular beat of her heart.

Leaning over her, he began unbuttoning her shirt, starting at the top. As he worked at the buttons, the knuckles of his bent fingers brushed across her soft skin. He pulled the shirt open and let the fabric fall to the sides. He glanced away from her bare breasts as he slipped her arms out of the sleeves. It was hard not to look, but he was waiting for exactly the right view, and looking too soon would spoil the experience.

He unhooked the fastener at the top of her jeans and pulled down the zipper. Spreading open the waist, he exposed the smooth expanse of her stomach, with its neatly formed round navel. He inched the jeans past her hips and down her legs. The jeans were tight, and as he pulled on them, they drew her dark blue bikini underpants along with them.

He stepped back from the table and allowed himself to look at her fully for the first time. She was the perfect Sleeping Beauty, so flawlessly beautiful that she was frightening. Now, though, he could approach her, because now he owned her. He could do anything to her. Her vulnerability thrilled him. As he thought of its implications, he could feel his pulse speed up and his breathing deepen.

He recalled how he had fallen in love with her the moment he had seen her in *Aztec Gold*. It was then that he had decided to use the name Sue for the cadaver in the poster. Until Cortez had called him, he had only fantasized about substituting the real Susan for the Pix-Wizard stand-in. Now here she was, exactly the way he had wanted to see her, her body stretched out naked in front of him.

Her skin was pale ivory, and in the soft light it seemed almost translucent. She was so still that she could already be dead. Her head was turned to the side and her face was more peaceful and relaxed than he had ever seen it. Her lips were parted slightly, as if inviting a kiss.

He wished her eyes were open. He wanted to gaze directly into their gray-green emptiness so that he could enjoy the knowledge that they couldn't see him and wouldn't judge him. It was a pleasure he wouldn't have to postpone long.

He let his eyes rove farther down her body, taking in every aspect, studying it. Her breasts were small and firm, and her nipples and areolas a soft shade of pink. Her body was slender, with long legs, gently flaring hips, and a narrow waist. The small triangle of tightly curled pubic hair was the same shade of honey blond as the fringe of hair framing her face.

She was everything he had imagined. She was a perfect doll, a precise manifestation of all that he wanted. She was hauntingly beautiful, yet silent and acquiescent. She would never belittle him or make him feel inadequate. She would never laugh at him or leave him, and whatever he wanted to do with her, she wouldn't object. She was his, but he was not hers.

Suddenly a shrill scream from the monkey room cut into his thoughts. He jerked his head back in surprise, then anger rose in him like bile. He shot a withering glance at the metal door. Then he heard a short yelping cry, the sound of an animal in pain.

He shook his head and frowned. If the monkeys interrupted him again, he'd shoot the rest of them.

Hightower had spent many days in rooms like this. He took in the lab bench and cabinets along the back wall and the office off to the left. The doors on the right probably led to special facilities. They were places he would have to search.

He didn't know where to start, but the golden fountain in the center of the room drew him in that direction. He walked toward the circle of light, and as he approached it, he saw that the glow was coming from a pool of water. The pool was large, at least ten feet in diameter, and the light shone from its depths.

At first he thought the pool was empty. Then he caught sight of a green snakelike shape gliding and twisting near the surface. He stopped dead still, then walked forward slowly. As he looked more closely, he saw several black and gray shapes, and he realized that the pool was teeming with the creatures. *Eels,* he realized. Not ordinary freshwater ones, but eels from tropical oceans. Probably different varieties of morays.

He stared at the eels in fascination, watching them trace out curving patterns in the murky water. They swiveled their snoutlike heads, searching for prey, and from time to time they opened their mouths and displayed teeth as thin and sharp as needles. Their tar black eyes were round and lidless, and the long flaps of skin along their backs undulated in the turbulence produced by the movement of their own bodies.

He glanced at the stack of iron railing, then turned away from the pool. The office was probably the best place to start searching. He took two steps toward it, then he heard a high-pitched scream, the sound of someone suffering unrelieved agony.

Hightower's heart fluttered. *Is that Susan?* He cocked his head to the side. The second scream was short, hardly more than a sharp cry, but it let him pinpoint the direction. He ran to the right, holding the autopsy knife in front of him like a lance.

By the time he was halfway across the room, he was breathing hard, and he could feel his heart pounding. *What am I getting into?* A part of him wanted to slow down and cautiously investigate the scream, while another part urged him to run faster and throw himself into action.

He opened his eyes wide and stared into the gloom of the lab. As he approached the back corner, he could make out the blank surfaces of two metal doors. The screams had come from behind one of them, but which one? He listened for another sound that would tell him, yet he heard nothing but the whistling of his own breathing and the sharp slaps of his feet striking the floor.

He'd decided to take the closer door. Barely slowing down, he jerked it open, then rushed inside. He was

crouched over and holding the autopsy knife low in front
of him.

He immediately realized he was in an animal facility,
but he had never before seen one where the animals
roamed loose. Four brown-faced monkeys were eating
from an opened bag of monkey chow. While taking out a
handful of food, three of them would look nervously at
the fourth, a large monkey with a white patch on his
chest.

Another large monkey was sitting on top of the cages
at the back end of the room. Hunched over with his head
pulled into his shoulders, he looked scared. With tiny
black fingers, he was gingerly patting the edges of a
bloody rip in his left arm.

Hightower felt some of the tension go out of his muscles. He lowered the autopsy knife and took a deep
breath. The injured monkey was the obvious loser in a
dominance struggle with the white-patch monkey. That
was what the screaming had been about, and now the
matter was resolved.

As he turned to leave, he caught sight of the bodies of
two monkeys on the floor by the cages. Then he noticed
a third body. He felt a shiver that raised the hair on his
arms and neck. He lifted the autopsy knife into fighting
position.

With his head thrust out and his eyes darting from side
to side, he walked forward in an awkward stiff-legged
gait. The entire back end of the room was splattered with
blood. Under the body of one of the dead monkeys, a
pool of blood was beginning to coagulate, and a second
monkey had the side of its head blown off. The body of
the third monkey was stretched out flat, with its arms
thrown out to the sides and a massive hole in its chest.

He stood staring at it for a moment, numb with revul-
sion and horror. *Why would anyone want to slaughter
monkeys?*

Gibson walked to the end of the table and stood looking down the entire length of Susan's body. In the dis-

tance, outside the building, he could hear the rough engine of the helicopter.

He bent over and took the three middle toes of Susan's left foot into his mouth. They tasted faintly of salt and felt strange at first. He slowly ran his tongue over their plump rounded tips, then gently sucked on each toe. A shudder of pleasure ran through him, making his hands quiver. He sucked harder for a moment, then bit at the soft flesh with the edges of his teeth.

He wanted to linger by her feet, just playing with her toes. But he couldn't spend the time, not if he wanted to do anything else with her. Reluctantly, he took the toes out of his mouth and rubbed them lightly between his fingers, feeling the slickness of his own saliva as his skin slipped easily over hers.

He straightened up and wiped his lips with the back of his hand. He felt slightly dazed, as if he had taken one drink too many.

Keeping his hand on the edge of the table to steady himself, he walked forward a few steps, until he was standing just below Susan's shoulders. He took her chin in his hand, and the soft feel of her skin was almost startling. He extended his fingers along her jaw, then turned her head so that her eyes were pointed toward the ceiling.

She had to be face up when he strangled her. He was sure that her lids would open, and he wanted to be able to watch her eyes. He wanted to see the pupils become fixed and dilated as she turned into a corpse. *Into a corpse.* He felt simultaneously horrified and exhilarated by the notion that Susan would be one. She would be irrevocably changed by nothing more than a few seconds of pressure on her throat.

The corpse at the embalming school had been in perfect condition. Her body was beautiful, yet it was also chill and rigid. But Susan would retain her heat for as long as he would have time to spend with her. She would still feel alive, yet he would be free from his own gnawing fears and uncertainties. He could get exactly what he needed from her.

His chest was tight, and his palms felt damp. Probably her body would heave and rise from the table, maybe even go into convulsions. He would have his hands on her, so he would be able to detect the very moment when the last tremor of life left her and she became inert and yielding.

As he thought about what he would do with her, the muscles around his eyes and mouth stiffened and turned his face into an expressionless mask. His surroundings began to blur and recede. Even the rough chopping noise of the helicopter faded away. All he could focus on was Susan's body lying on the narrow green-draped table. He wrapped his hands around Susan's neck, carefully placing the pads of his thumbs over each of her carotid arteries.

Susan stirred and started to rise.

Now that he was at the back of the room, Hightower could see that two other doors led out of it.

When he got to within eight feet of the cages, the monkeys all at once seemed startled by him. One chanted *eeh-eeh-eeh* over and over in a piercing voice, and the others gave high-pitched squeals. As he drew nearer, they bared their teeth and hissed at him, then began rattling the cage doors. The noise was deafening. Suddenly, he heard a male voice yell out, "Shut up! Shut the fuck up!"

Hightower whirled to the left. The shout had come from behind the door. Without giving any thought to what he was about to do, he rushed toward the door. The monkeys let out shrill squeals of fear, and the injured monkey jumped to the floor and cowered against the wall.

Hightower was hardly aware of what was happening around him. He gripped the autopsy knife in his right hand, and in long running strides he covered the distance to the rear of the room.

Without hesitation, he snatched open the heavy door and hurled himself into the room.

56

Hightower halted just inside the door. For a moment he stood paralyzed, peering helplessly into the shadowy dimness.

The autopsy knife trembled in his hand as a mixture of frustration, anger, and panic coursed through him. His face was hot, and he had trouble getting enough breath. Then as his eyes adjusted to the low light he could see the figure in front of him with an almost luminous clarity.

The man had a pale face, with thin lips and strangely yellow eyes, like those of a jungle animal. His hair was as blond as bleached cotton, and it flew back from the crown of his head like a mane. His face showed surprise, but there was also a withering arrogance in his glance. Hightower had no doubt that he was looking at Cyberwolf himself.

Lowering his gaze, Hightower saw the operating table. With an almost physical shock, he realized that someone was stretched out on it. It was a woman, and she was completely naked. Cyberwolf was blocking his view so that he couldn't see her face. Yet who could it be but Susan? He stepped to the side and saw that he was right.

His first thought was that she was dead—dead on an operating table, the way Alma had been when they showed him her body at the hospital. White-hot rage possessed him. His vision blurred, and he seemed to be looking down on the scene from some spot high above it.

He narrowed his eyes into a savage scowl. As he glared at Cyberwolf, his lips pulled back from his teeth, and he made a sound that was almost a snarl. He crouched low, poising himself to rush at Cyberwolf. But Cyberwolf had recovered from his own surprise. Seeing Hightower ready to jump him, he whipped out a large pistol.

Hightower stood frozen in fascination, watching Cyberwolf lower the pistol through a short curve and aim it directly at his face. But before the gun could reach the crucial point in the arc, Hightower's hand was already above his head with the autopsy knife gripped tightly in his fingers.

Heeding his father's lessons during the years of practice on the anatomical chart, he aimed for Cyberwolf's heart. He brought his arm downward, giving the knife a short snap. It spun out of his hand, turned over once, then sped straight toward its target.

Cyberwolf fired two quick shots as he dodged to the left. But by the time he fired the second shot, the narrow wedge of the knife point struck his right arm. His arm jerked upward, and the gun flew out of his hand. The autopsy knife clattered to the floor beside his feet, and he grabbed the wound with his left hand.

Blood ran from the spaces between his fingers and his features were distorted with pain. Yet his yellow eyes still burned with cold fury.

Hightower's ears rang with the shots, and his nostrils stung from the odor of burning gunpowder. He didn't know if he had been hit, and it didn't occur to him to check. The rational part of his brain was no longer exercising control, although he was dimly aware that he was going berserk.

He ran toward Cyberwolf with no other idea than to kill him—to tear out his throat, to smash out his brains, to strangle him, to destroy him in any way possible. His head and hands felt hot with the sudden rush of blood.

Cyberwolf glanced up at him. His face was still twisted with pain, but he hadn't lost control. Deliberately, almost calmly, he scanned the floor around him, searching for the pistol.

Hightower saw it at the same time Cyberwolf did. It was lying between them, some two feet closer to Cyberwolf. Cyberwolf scrambled for it, bending at the waist and lunging forward with his arms stretched out. Hightower reached the gun as Cyberwolf's fingers touched the barrel, but Hightower didn't try to pick it up. He gave it a sharp kick, and it skittered across the floor and under the operating table. Cyberwolf looked at him with wild eyes, then, leaping up, grabbed for Hightower's throat.

Hightower's shoulder smashed into Cyberwolf's chest, sending him reeling backward. Cyberwolf caught himself before he fell, then, with surprising speed, he lashed out with his foot. The kick struck Hightower squarely on his left knee, and the pain made him gasp.

Cyberwolf hopped forward, trying to keep his balance, but before he could recover his stability, Hightower took a step toward him and drew back his fist, ready to swing. When Cyberwolf was within range, Hightower hit him a solid blow in the chest, trying to stop his heart.

Hightower could feel the shock of the impact travel through the bones of his hand. Simultaneously he heard the snap of a rib cracking. Cyberwolf's mouth dropped open, then he staggered backward, gasping. He fell against the outside door and slid to the floor.

Still struggling for breath, he began climbing to his feet. Hightower, out of the corner of his eye, saw Susan stirring on the operating table. As he turned and glanced at her, he felt a surge of joy. She was raising herself on her elbows, trying to sit up. *She's not dead* was all he could think. *At least she's not dead.*

When Hightower looked back, Cyberwolf was opening the door into the lab. As the door slammed shut, Hightower ran headlong after him. Then before he could pull open the door, he heard Susan say, "David?" Her voice was so weak it was barely audible above the noise of his own breathing.

He released the doorknob and hurried back to her. She had fallen back onto the table, and her eyes were closed. His hand was shaking as he rested it on her forehead and used his thumb to raise her eyelid. He watched the pupil grow smaller, then checked the other eye. To his relief, both pupils responded normally to light. She probably didn't have a head injury. Except for a small cut on her forehead, he saw no wounds on her face, and running his fingers over the back of her head, he found no bump.

Susan opened her eyes, then closed them again. She

moved uneasily, twisting from side to side. Hightower put his hand on her chest and held her in place. He then picked up her left arm and searched for her pulse with his fingertips. His heart was pounding so hard that he had to focus carefully to make sure he wasn't monitoring himself. But in a moment, under his own racing pulse, he detected a strong, steady throbbing.

He put his ear to her bare chest, uncomfortably aware of her breast rubbing against his face. Her lungs sounded clear. He wished he could check her more thoroughly, but she seemed fine.

Thank God she's okay. Thank God he didn't kill her.

Her hand slipped off the table, and as he put it back, she opened her eyes again. She blinked several times, then seemed to focus on his face. "Is it really David?" she asked in a slow, thick voice. "Am I hallucinating?"

"You're safe now, and you're going to be all right," he said. He wasn't confident that either was true, but she needed reassurance. She sounded like she had been drugged, and patients fighting their way into consciousness were often confused and worried.

"I still feel dopey." Her voice sounded stronger. "Where's Cyberwolf?"

"He ran out the door."

She started struggling to sit up, but Hightower restrained her with a hand on her shoulder. "Don't try to move yet. I want you to stay here while I go after Cyberwolf. I've got to find him and make him turn off his computer program."

"I want to come." She lifted herself onto her elbows, ignoring his hand. She swung her legs over the edge of the table and sat up. Folding her arms protectively over her breasts, she asked, "Where are my clothes?"

"I'll look for them, but you're too weak to come with me."

Walking to the opposite side of the operating table, he spotted the pistol at the base of the instrument stand. For a moment he considered taking it with him. He wanted its almost magical power to deliver death at a distance. He brushed the thought away, because it was that very power he wished to put into Susan's hands. He could take care of himself.

As he came back around the table, he noticed Susan's clothes on the floor. He handed them to her.

"I know where he's gone." Susan's voice was still thick and fuzzy, but she was making an effort to be clear. "He probably thinks you're leading an army of cops, and he's going to try to escape through the loading-dock door. That's where he caught me."

"Take this gun," Hightower said, putting it on the table beside her. "Shoot anybody who threatens you." He lifted her right hand and placed it on top of the gun. "The safety is off, so be careful. Now where's the loading dock?"

"Through the door across the lab." She was struggling into her shirt. "But I still want to come."

He didn't answer her. He located the autopsy knife near the wall and picked it up. He examined the blade in the light. The first two inches were dark with blood. He clenched his jaw, revolted by the sight.

Yet if he had no other choice, he was prepared to darken the whole length of the blade.

57

As Hightower saw the loading-dock door looming in front of him, a sudden cramp of fear twisted his stomach. He rubbed his hand across his middle, as if soothing an ache.

But I don't have any reason to be afraid. I've got the autopsy knife, and Cyberwolf has lost his gun.

The odds were on his side. He was only scared because of anticipation, the way he used to be right before surgery. Cyberwolf was just one person, and he possessed no magic that couldn't be overcome by the sharp edge of a knife.

Hightower stepped quietly into the room with the autopsy knife held at the ready. He braced his left hand against the door and let it close silently behind him. Once again the light was so faint that he found it hard to orient himself. All he could make out was that the room was narrow and filled with shadowy mounds of cartons.

From his right, at the rear of the room, he heard the sharp, rasping sound of wood scraping against concrete, then a series of short grunts. He turned and peered into the shadows.

Cyberwolf was absorbed in something attached to the wall, and he showed no sign that he had heard Hightower enter the room. Suddenly, a shower of hot yellow sparks lighted up the corner, and the acrid smell of electrical burning filled the air. Cyberwolf jumped back, but then immediately resumed work.

Hightower slipped silently from one stack of cartons to another until Cyberwolf was no more than fifteen feet away. With one flick of the wrist, he could skewer Cyberwolf like a kabob.

But now that Susan was safe, that was something he definitely shouldn't do. When he had been wild to kill Cyberwolf, he hadn't given a thought to the Chernobyl program or his parents. He felt a flash of embarrassment at the memory. Leaving the cover of the stacks of cartons, he stepped into the narrow aisle.

"Stop and turn around!" Hightower shouted. His throat felt constricted, and his voice sounded reedy in his ears.

Cyberwolf glanced over his shoulder, then turned back and went on working, pulling at electrical wires. It was as if he didn't understand the language Hightower was speaking.

"I'm an expert at throwing a knife. At this range I can sink it so deep in your back that it goes through your heart."

Cyberwolf stopped and turned around slowly. Hightower walked forward, holding the autopsy knife by the point and resting the handle in his left hand. He kept his gaze fixed on Cyberwolf. Cyberwolf's amber eyes seemed to glow in the shadowy light.

"I didn't expect you to find me so quickly." Cyberwolf's voice was level and unworried. It revealed no emotion at all.

"Put your hands up where I can see them. We need to talk."

Cyberwolf slowly raised his hands shoulder high, letting his fingers bend lazily toward his palms. Still holding the autopsy knife by the point, Hightower walked a few feet nearer. He stopped while he still had enough distance for a throw. He saw that Cyberwolf had tied a handkerchief around his upper right arm where the knife had sliced him. Blood had already soaked through both the jacket and the makeshift bandage.

"I know about the Chernobyl program," Hightower said.

"Then you know it's only ... how many minutes?" Without lowering his hands, Cyberwolf rotated his left wrist and glanced at his watch. "About forty-seven minutes before NYNEX shuts down."

"My parents are flying into Kennedy." Hightower kept his voice level. "They're scheduled to arrive at three-thirty."

"Sorry about that." Cyberwolf sounded understanding and apologetic. "If it's any comfort, thousands of other people are going to be in trouble, and a lot of them are going to die." He shook his head. "It really is a shame."

"I want you to stop the program." Hightower paused. "Kill it, cancel it, whatever you need to do to keep it from going into operation."

"I wish I could." Cyberwolf smiled sadly.

"You can." Hightower was matter-of-fact. "We'll find a computer, and you can send a canceling command." He stared at Cyberwolf's face, looking for a clue as to what he might be thinking. "If you can't do it from here, we'll get the police to unplug the computer that's running the program. That would work, wouldn't it?"

"Of course it would," Cyberwolf admitted. "But you're missing the point. When I say I can't shut down the program, I'm not talking about a technological difficulty." His lips stretched out in a tight smile. "The problem is what you might call social."

"I don't know what you mean."

"The Chernobyl program is my only ticket out of here," Cyberwolf said. "But if you'll go away and leave me alone for fifteen minutes, I promise to kill the program before meltdown."

"I can't be sure you'll do what you say." Hightower shook his head. "If you didn't, NYNEX would melt down, and you would be long gone. I'd lose both ways." He gave Cyberwolf a cold smile. "This way I've at least got you."

Cyberwolf shrugged. "Having me won't do you any good, because I won't cooperate."

"You might change your mind," Hightower said. "I'm not a cop, so I don't have to obey legal rules. I'm a surgeon, and I know a lot of ways to cause pain. I could start by severing the cervical nerves and paralyzing you from the neck down." He caught Cyberwolf's eyes and held them. "Under the circumstances, any inquiry into your death would be perfunctory."

Suddenly, the room behind him seemed to explode. Fire flashed, and bullets produced a rapid series of high-pitched twangs as they ricocheted off the wall in front of him.

"You goddamned idiot, don't shoot *me!*" Cyberwolf yelled.

Hightower whirled around, simultaneously raising the autopsy knife above his head. Directly behind him, he saw the plump man with the thick mustache. He was pointing his peculiar gun with the short barrel and round canister toward Hightower.

"Drop that knife!" He spoke fast, in an excited voice. "Let it drop, man, I'm telling you."

Hightower lowered the knife, then let it slip out of his fingers and onto the floor.

"It's about time you got here," Cyberwolf said. "Where's Whip?"

"Man, I haven't seen him since you did." He kept his eyes on Hightower. "And me, I waited for the message about the helicopter, but they didn't send it. Then I heard the helicopter come, and I thought I'd better go find you."

"I've got everything under control," Cyberwolf said. "Susan is knocked out in the other room. As soon as we deal with this guy, you can go get on the helicopter. I'll pick her up, then join you there."

The man's eyes looked into Hightower's face. "Step over to the side," he said. "Get up against those boxes."

"So you can shoot me." Hightower couldn't keep the bitterness out of his voice.

"You should have accepted my offer," Cyberwolf said, coming up behind him. "You'd be alive, even if a few hundred other people would be dead."

"That's what you've got to live with."

"And that's what you've got to die with." Cyberwolf's tone had turned vicious, and he spat out the words. "Shoot the asshole in the head, Backup."

Hightower's attention focused automatically on the muzzle of the gun Backup was aiming at his forehead. The beveled hole looked immense, surrounded by satin-finished, blue-black metal. In a moment the hole would be filled with flames and hot gases, but before his mind could register the fact, his body would be shredded by chunks of flying metal. The muzzle was a metallic eye of death staring holes into his body.

"I'm out of the way." Cyberwolf had moved back against the wall. "Keep the Sweeper pointed toward him and away from me."

A vivid image of Alma's bright smile flashed into Hightower's mind. He thought about his parents on the plane, his father reading a novel, his mother asleep. And then he thought about Susan. She was going to die too, just like Alma, just like his parents. A bitter taste filled his mouth.

He could see Backup alter his stance, spreading his feet

apart and bracing to absorb the gun's recoil. Backup took his left hand off the grip, wiped it on his blue uniform shirt, then grasped the gun again. Hightower could see Backup's fingers tense as he started to squeeze the trigger.

Then a sharp explosive crack tore the air. Backup leaped toward him, his eyes wide open, his mouth gaping, and a look of incredulity on his face. His gun flew out of his hands, hit a pile of cartons, then clattered to the floor.

Hightower dodged to the side and looked intently into the dimness. He drew in his breath sharply when he saw Susan. She was in a firing stance, holding Cyberwolf's heavy pistol in both hands, and pointing it at Backup.

She had obviously hurried to the loading dock. She had zipped her jeans, but her shirt was unbuttoned. It hung open in the front, barely covering her breasts. Like Backup, she had come in through the upper door, and that had put her in a position to control the situation.

Backup grabbed the fallen gun and turned toward Susan. He was raising the barrel and aiming when the second shot hit him. His head burst apart like a melon dropped onto concrete. Hightower drew back as bloody skull fragments seemed to float through the air in slow motion.

He glanced at Susan. Her jaw was set, and her expression was grim. She was still holding the pistol in front of her, both hands wrapped around the grip. She looked as if she were playing a movie scene she had rehearsed many times.

Hightower ran forward and snatched Backup's gun off the floor, but as soon as he was bent over, Cyberwolf shoved him forward with a powerful thrust of his foot. Hightower threw out both hands, but he kept a firm grip on the gun. He felt a dull pain in his chest as he hit the concrete floor and the gun's canister dug into his ribs.

Gasping for breath, he pushed himself up without taking his hand off the gun stock. When he had raised himself only halfway, Cyberwolf stepped on his back, shoving him to the floor again. Struggling to rise, Hightower lifted his head to see Cyberwolf snatch the autopsy knife off the floor, then rush toward Susan.

She was more than twenty feet away, on the far side of the door leading to the lab, and she took her time responding. She watched Cyberwolf jump over Backup's body, then she took up a firing stance and pointed the pistol at him. She pulled the trigger, and Hightower could hear a sharp click.

No ammunition. Cyberwolf must have known the gun was empty.

Susan looked stunned. Recovering quickly, she drew back her arm and hurled the pistol at Cyberwolf. The gun hit him in the chest and bounced off. As he kept coming, she grabbed a carton from the stack beside her. Turning to the side to get more torque, she hurled the carton down the narrow aisle.

Cyberwolf slowed his rush, waited until the box reached him, then kicked it to the side. He glanced back at Hightower, then turned toward Susan again. He waved the knife in front of him, and it flashed like fire as it caught the light from an overhead bulb.

Hightower finally struggled to his feet. He raised the gun and pointed it at Cyberwolf's back, then realized that he couldn't fire without hitting Susan.

Step to the side and get out of the way!

He was still gasping and too out of breath to yell at her. He motioned her to move with his left hand, but her attention was focused on Cyberwolf, and she didn't see him.

He dropped the gun to free both hands. Then, following Susan's example, he picked up a cardboard carton. It weighed only a few pounds, and he lifted it high over his head. He then launched it forward with as much strength as he could muster.

For no apparent reason Cyberwolf abruptly moved to the right. The box hit him on the back, low and to the left, but it was only a glancing blow. He grabbed at his back with his left hand and staggered. He turned his head toward Hightower, then looked back at Susan. She was taking another carton from the stack.

Suddenly, Cyberwolf turned sharply left, then disappeared through the door into the lab. The heavy metal door banged shut behind him with a crack like a rifle shot.

Hightower looked at Susan. She stood holding the carton she had picked up, with an almost shocked expression on her face. She, too, had been taken by surprise at Cyberwolf's disappearance.

Hightower picked up the gun from the floor. He took four long strides, then jumped over the dead man's body. Rushing up to Susan, he was on the verge of taking her in his arms, but then he held back, suddenly overcome by doubt. How would she react?

Susan leaned forward and wrapped her arms around him. She felt soft, yet solid and real. As she pushed her body against his, squeezing him tightly, his doubts evaporated.

"I imagined that you would come and rescue me," she said. Her head was pressed against his chest, and her words came out in a hoarse whisper. "But I thought it was only a fantasy."

"You're the one who did the rescuing." He held the gun out to the side, and smoothed down her hair with his free hand. Leaning into her so that they were supporting one another, he kissed the top of her head.

"I'm not letting myself think about what I did," she said.

"It was necessary," he reassured her.

"I know," she said softly. "But that's the second one."

"You killed the other gang member?"

She nodded. "It's all so horrible." She pulled away from him, then looked up into his eyes.

"It's still not over," he told her. "I'm going after Cyberwolf." The meltdown clock was still ticking, and only Cyberwolf knew how to stop it.

Susan made no objection. "Be careful," she said. Fear made her voice sound fragile. "He's still got the knife."

"I saw him."

He wrapped his left hand around her arm and squeezed it gently. She gave him a worried smile as he turned and walked back down the narrow aisle.

Dodging around a pallet piled high with cartons, he shoved his way through the door and into the lab.

58

Grasping the stock of the gun with his right hand, Hightower wrapped his left hand tightly around the pistol grip jutting out from the barrel. With his right hand around the lower grip and his finger on the trigger, he stood just inside the door and moved the muzzle in a wide arc, sweeping the room from one side to the other.

His eyes followed the line of the lab bench and cabinets along the back wall, then moved past the two doors in the opposite wall. The bright fountain of light spouting up from the eel pool made it difficult to see clearly into the corner beyond it, but he wouldn't be able to miss something as large as a man.

When he reached the front of the room, he turned to the right. He moved the gun as he revolved, training the muzzle onto the area at the far side of the lab office. But it was as empty as the rest.

He peered through the large window of the office. Inside, he saw nothing but the shadowy shapes of desks and office equipment and the ghostly blue glow of a computer screen.

He pushed open the office door with the toe of his shoe and walked into the darkness. He stood for a moment, scanning each sector of the small room. Nothing. He moved from the desk to the table pushed against the wall, then crouched down and looked under each. Still nothing.

He went out the door and walked to the opposite side

of the office. The hot, swampy atmosphere of the lab, with its pervasive odor of rotting fish, made him feel vaguely sick.

Where the hell is Cyberwolf? Did he have enough time to escape through one of the other doors? Or is he still somewhere in the lab?

He felt his stomach grow tight. Sweat began to trickle from under his hair and run down his face. If he couldn't find Cyberwolf in the next few minutes, there would be no chance of shutting down the Chernobyl program.

Still gripping the gun tightly, Hightower bent his head toward the floor and strained his ears for any unusual sounds. He heard the muted throbbing of the pump circulating the water in the eel pool and a few metallic pops and creaks from the building's support beams.

Then he heard the high-pitched squeal of a door opening. His heart thumped, then fluttered. He whirled around, pointing the muzzle of the gun behind him.

"It's me," Susan said in a stage whisper.

As soon as her words registered, he felt his heart rate slow. He lowered the gun and looked at her. She was standing behind the loading-dock door with only her head showing through the opening. She was cautious and shrewd. She hadn't managed to stay alive just by luck.

"I can't find him," Hightower said.

Susan stepped from behind the door and walked toward him. She had done up the buttons on her shirt, but he noticed for the first time that she wasn't wearing shoes. Her bare feet looked too vulnerable for the hard surface of the lab floor.

"He had enough time to get out of the lab," Hightower went on. "So I'd better check behind the other doors."

"Do we have to find him? Can't we just get the police to come in now?"

"Not if we want to stop the NYNEX meltdown, because we don't have enough time." He paused, then added, "My parents are on a plane that's scheduled to land at Kennedy."

She looked puzzled a moment, then she saw the

consequences. "Oh, that's awful." She reached out and squeezed his arm. "We'd better get busy."

"You've done enough." He shook his head. "Why don't you leave the building and get the police?"

"Don't be ridiculous." Susan's tone was sharp. "I'm not leaving until this is over."

Hightower was surprised by how relieved he felt at not having to face Cyberwolf alone. He didn't try to change her mind. Susan was at least as able as he was, and the two of them together would have a better chance of capturing Cyberwolf than he would alone.

"Then let's get going," he said. "We've got a lot of looking to do."

"Wait," Susan said. "Maybe not so much. That's what I came to tell you." She paused, trying to find the right words. "I slipped a tracer bracelet into Cyberwolf's pocket. Unless he's found it and thrown it away, we should be able to locate him on the computer."

Hightower felt almost lighthearted as he realized the implications of what she was saying.

"My God, you're wonderful," he said. "Let's check the computer." Without glancing back to see if she was following, he hurried toward the open door of the office.

Susan was two steps behind him when he went inside. "I know how to use this computer," she said.

He followed her across the office. She slipped into the typing chair in front of the glowing screen, and he took up a position behind her. He found the safety on the gun, pushed it in, then set the gun down on the floor.

Susan moved the mouse to the right and up until the arrow was pointing to the "Exit" icon. She double-clicked the button, and the menu appeared in yellow and red letters.

"I don't know the name of the program, but it should be something obvious." She moved the mouse down, highlighting one item after another.

"How about that one?" Hightower pointed at a line on the screen. "*Locator* sounds like what we want."

"Let's take a look."

Susan clicked the mouse, and the computer made faint thumping noises as the program loaded. Then, almost instantly, the menu blinked off, and a query appeared: *Locations? Individuals?*

"It's got to be locations," Susan said. "The computer doesn't have his name listed." She clicked the mouse, and an alphabetical list appeared.

"Find the research tower," Hightower said. He then realized that he didn't need to tell Susan the obvious. He had only spoken out of the frustration of not having anything to do.

Locations produced a list of the eight floors in the research tower. Susan selected the first. When she clicked, a schematic drawing of the floor plan appeared on the screen.

"That's where we are," she said. "I recognize every inch."

"How do we search for him?"

"Room by room, I imagine." Susan glanced up at him. "Where do you want to start?"

"With this one."

He leaned over her shoulder to get a better view of the screen. He was close enough to smell the faintly floral odor of her hair and to feel the warmth radiating from her body.

The image on the screen was wiped away, and a drawing of the room appeared. Doors were represented by two short lines perpendicular to the wall; the office was a rectangular box, and the eel pool was a circle.

"There it is!" Susan's voice was high with excitement. She tapped the screen beside a small white silhouette of a person. The icon was blinking at a regular rate.

Hightower bent closer to the screen. "It says he's in the left back corner of the room." He shook his head. "But that's not possible. We were just there. Try the other places."

One by one, Susan brought up drawings of the hall, the operating room, the monkey room, and the loading dock. The white silhouette didn't appear in any of them. She switched back to the main lab, and the tiny figure was still blinking in the same location as before.

"I don't know what to make of it," Susan said, shaking her head. She sounded discouraged. "Maybe he threw the bracelet on the floor."

"Let's go take a look."

Hightower picked up the gun. Before they stepped out of the office, he paused by the door and clicked off the safety. He wrapped his hand around the pistol grip and kept his finger on the trigger as they walked toward the back of the lab. He wasn't planning on shooting Cyberwolf, but he wasn't going to let him hurt Susan, either.

Susan walked beside him, her head down, scanning the floor for the plastic bracelet. The greenish fluorescent light was too faint for Hightower to be able to make out anything so small. He looked forward, watching for any movement in the shadows. His eyes swept down the line of the lab bench, then back.

He glanced up at the acoustical panels in the ceiling and wondered if Cyberwolf could hide behind them. Maybe, but he would need a ladder to climb up, and he wouldn't have had time to find one. Just then Hightower recognized the obvious possibility.

He reached out and put a hand on Susan's arm. She stopped and gave him a questioning look. He leaned over so he could whisper in her ear.

"The cabinets under the lab bench," he said. He pointed toward the back corner.

Susan glanced at the cabinets, then nodded. She leaned toward him. "It makes sense. He could wait for us to rush to some other place, then go back and leave by the loading-dock door."

Her physical closeness and her warm breath against his ear were distracting, and he found it hard to concentrate on what she was saying.

"Let's check them out," Susan said.

He nodded in agreement, then put his mouth to her ear. "Let's climb on top of the bench," he whispered. "You

reach over the edge and open a door, and I'll be ready
with the gun."

She formed the word "okay" with her lips. She smiled
at him, then started for the back corner of the room.

59

Susan hoisted herself into a sitting position on the lab
bench and swung her legs up. She then drew her feet beneath her into a crouch. Hightower handed her the gun,
placed his left foot on the edge of the bench, then, bending low, climbed up in a single step. Susan gave him back
the gun.

She put the palms of her hands together prayer-fashion,
turned her head back, and rolled her eyes upward. He
smiled and nodded. He then gave her a stern look and
wagged a finger at her to indicate that she should be careful. She put her fingertips to her lips and threw him a
kiss.

She turned away from him and got down on her knees.
She bent over the edge of the lab bench until she could
reach the stainless-steel door pull near the middle of the
first cabinet. He could see the perspiration glistening on
her face.

Hightower stood with his eyes fixed on the area directly in front of the cabinet. The muzzle of the gun was
pointed where he was looking, and his finger was on the
trigger. Sweat from his hand had made the plastic pistol
grip wet, and he could feel each of his fingers pressed
into the molded grooves. He made himself keep taking
breaths regularly so he wouldn't get dizzy.

He could hear the creaking of a hinge as Susan pulled
open the first door. The muscles of his shoulders tensed,
and his arms trembled slightly.

Nothing happened.

Susan glanced up at him and shrugged. She duck-walked three steps toward him and again reached over the edge of the bench to open the second door.

Suddenly, the door of the cabinet flew open with a loud metallic screeching and Cyberwolf leaped out. Susan gave a short "Hunh" of surprise and jerked her hand back.

Cyberwolf whirled around to face them. The autopsy knife was in his right hand, and he glared at them with hatred, his pale yellow eyes burning into them. For a moment all three of them seemed paralyzed, frozen in time. Then without warning, Cyberwolf lunged forward like a fencer and thrust the point of the autopsy knife at Susan.

"You fucking bitch!" he shouted. "You worthless whore!"

Susan threw herself backward on the lab bench, managing to avoid all but the tip of the knife. The sharp point raked the back of her hand, making a long, thin gash, and a gush of bright red blood trickled down her fingers.

Ignoring Hightower, Cyberwolf drew back from his lunge and then held the knife level, preparing to make another thrust at Susan. But before he could attack again, Hightower extended the barrel of the gun, stuck the muzzle under Cyberwolf's chin, then, holding tight to the pistol grips, levered the barrel sharply upward. The muzzle clipped Cyberwolf under the chin, knocking his head back and splitting open his skin with a splattering of blood.

Cyberwolf stumbled backward, his amber eyes looking blank and dazed. He shook his head violently from side to side and put his hand to his chin. He then glared up at Hightower crouched on the lab bench. Hightower shifted the gun, bringing the muzzle to bear on Cyberwolf.

"Drop the knife." Hightower snapped out the words.

"You won't shoot me." Cyberwolf fixed his eyes on Hightower's face, then smiled. "If you do, you're likely to kill your parents. Most people couldn't live with that, and I'm betting you're one of them."

He stood completely still for a moment, but his eyes

flitted from Hightower to Susan. Then without saying another word, he turned and started running toward the front
door of the lab.

"Stop him!" Susan yelled. She got to her feet. "He's
going to try to reach the helicopter."

"Stop!" Hightower shouted. He got up off the bench.
"I'll shoot you!"

He squeezed the trigger, and the noise from the exploding shells bounced off the hard surfaces of the walls and
floor, then ran together to form a single rolling boom.
Plumes of smoke whirled around him, and the harsh taste
of gunpowder coated the back of his throat.

Cyberwolf slowed and looked behind him, but he
didn't stop. Hightower had aimed over his head, hoping
to make him feel threatened enough to surrender. But he
hadn't surrendered, and now he was getting away.

Hightower pointed the gun again, aiming lower this
time. Then, his mind churning, he hesitated. He needed
information to cancel the Chernobyl program, but he
couldn't let Cyberwolf escape. He felt himself shaking his
head.

What the hell can I do?

He thrust the gun at Susan. "I'm going after him." He
was almost shouting. "If he gets me, then shoot him."

Susan's eyes locked on his, and her face looked gaunt
and horror stricken. She nodded and took the gun from
him without a word.

Hightower jumped out as far as he could from the lab
bench. He hit the floor running. The sharp pain in his left
knee made him grit his teeth.

He tried to gauge the distance he would have to cross.
He thought he could do it. Cyberwolf had almost reached
the eel pool.

Hightower lifted his knees higher and tried to throw his
body forward. As his heaving chest pumped breath in and
out, he could feel the air tearing at his lungs. His heart
was thumping hard, as if he were running up a mountain.
Was he going to drop dead before he could catch up with
Cyberwolf?

Cyberwolf glanced over his shoulder. Hightower had expected him to speed up, but he didn't. Instead, he abruptly stopped and turned around.

Hightower kept going, rapidly closing the distance between them. But why had Cyberwolf stopped?

When he saw Cyberwolf raise the autopsy knife over his head, everything became clear. But it was too late to do anything but keep running toward him and try to crash into him.

Cyberwolf's arm snapped downward, and Hightower saw the long blade of the knife flashing through the air. The knife seemed to move slowly at first, then to speed up as it got nearer.

Hightower's mouth went dry, and fear surged through him like a jolt of electricity. With only one functioning eye, he had no depth perception, so he couldn't get a fix on the knife's position. He made his best guess and jogged sharply to the left.

A searing pain cut through his right leg. He had avoided a knife in the chest, but he hadn't avoided getting stabbed. He stopped and looked down to see the knife in his thigh.

Without letting himself think about what he was doing, he grabbed the handle and yanked out the blade. Hot blood ran down his leg and seeped into his shoe. He shifted the knife to his left hand and pressed on the wound with his right.

He looked up in time to see Cyberwolf turn away and resume running. Ironically, he must have felt sure that if he reached the police, they would escort him to the helicopter and take him to Logan to meet his plane.

Without even making a decision, Hightower started after Cyberwolf again. Blood squelched in his shoe, and each time his foot struck the floor, a hot bolt of pain shot through his thigh.

He rolled the handle of the autopsy knife in his hand. *Am I close enough to be sure to hit him?* Probably he could, but not with any accuracy. He was as likely to injure him in a minor way as to kill him, and he couldn't risk killing him.

Cyberwolf was almost within the golden circle of light flowing from the eel pool. Hightower felt despair sweep over him. If only he could make Cyberwolf slow down and let him get within range.

Suddenly, he realized that he had a weapon that might do exactly that. He reached into his pocket and took out the flash-bang grenade. It was shaped like an explosive grenade and even had fragmentation scoring on its surface. He didn't know how much an ordinary grenade weighed, but the flash-bang version felt heavy in his hand. It would be weighted and shaped to throw.

He slid the autopsy knife under his belt until the hilt caught. He then held the grenade in his right hand and pulled the pin with his left. He kept the timing handle pushed down.

He stopped running and stood as still as his hard breathing would allow, getting a fix on his target. Cyberwolf was on the right side of the eel pool, just entering the circle of light.

Hightower lifted his right arm, rotated his wrist, then brought his hand down in a smooth overhand pitch that sent the grenade sailing through the air.

He started running again, but he kept an eye on the grenade. It traced a graceful parabolic arc, and for a moment he was afraid he had aimed too far left and that it was going to fall into the pool.

No, no, no. Don't let that happen.

With relief he realized that he had misjudged the trajectory. He nodded as he watched the grenade hit the floor on Cyberwolf's right. It bounced once, rolled toward Cyberwolf, then detonated with a loud *crack* that was like a tremendous clap of thunder. The suspended ceiling quivered, and the whole room reverberated with the sound.

Simultaneously, a burst of intense blue-white light— brighter than a bolt of lightning—illuminated the room with stark clarity. The fountain of golden light was wiped away, as if it were nothing more than a shadow.

Hightower blinked, but the brightness didn't blind him. His damaged retinas lacked the sensitivity. He saw Cyberwolf lunge sharply to the left and clap his hands over his eyes. Hightower tried to run faster, hoping to reach him while he was still blinded by the light.

Cyberwolf took down his hands, but he still didn't seem able to see. He stood motionless with his head turned toward the floor. He looked dazed, as if he didn't know where he was or what he was doing. He put his hands over his eyes again, then tried to run.

He staggered forward a few steps along a line tangent to the pool. He uncovered his eyes, and for a moment stared into the golden light that again flowed up through the water. He made a sharp turn to the right as if to walk away from the pool, but as he put down his left foot, nothing was there to support it.

His foot seemed to hover in the air for a long time, and he pumped his leg desperately, as if he could by that effort create a place to stand. In a fraction of a second the expression on his face changed from confusion into surprise, then into terror, his mouth opening wide and his eyes bulging.

"Aaahhha!" Cyberwolf screamed.

The scream was long and drawn out, and as he teetered above the water his arms flailed in the air uselessly, like a small child trying to fly. Then his body hit the surface of the pool with a flat smacking sound followed by splashing as the displaced water splattered onto the concrete floor.

Hightower rushed to the edge of the pool and looked into the murky water. The pool was a dense mass of writhing eels. At the center of the mass were Cyberwolf's white face and flowing hair. Under the weight of his sodden clothes, he had sunk low into the pool, and all the eels seemed to have attacked him at once. He was beating his arms and kicking his legs, but too many eels were crowded around him, the weight of their bodies keeping him down. Lines of bubbles streamed to the top and noiselessly burst.

Hightower stuck his arm shoulder deep into the water, but Cyberwolf was too far out of his reach. He fluttered his hand back and forth, trying to draw the eels from their prey, but the effort was useless.

An iridescent emerald green eel darted under a black one and swam toward Cyberwolf's face. The eel's lipless mouth curved upward slightly at the corners, giving the impression of a grotesque smile. The eel lunged forward and sank its needlelike teeth into one of Cyberwolf's eyes. The eel twisted its blunt snout to one side, and when it pulled its head back, a cloud of blood burst into the water. Cyberwolf's mouth opened in a noiseless scream, and his body twisted and flopped from side to side like a hooked fish.

Hightower stood up and shouted to Susan, "Bring the gun! Hurry!" He then lay down flat on the concrete so that he could extend his reach.

Attracted by the blood, a black-spotted eel twisted around and changed direction. It launched itself toward the other eye, its own lidless, pale yellow eyes showing no more emotion than a burnished topaz.

The eel struck, and another cloud of blood bloomed in the water. Cyberwolf struck out at the eel, but his blows were feeble and slow in the density of the water. The eel swam off, the flanges of skin along its back and belly rippling in the currents.

Gripping the autopsy knife in his right hand, Hightower plunged his arm into the pool, trying once more to distract the eels. Again he failed. Even with the knife, they were too far away for him to reach. He pulled his arm out of the water.

The ribbons of blood streaming out of Cyberwolf's empty eye sockets unleashed a frenzy of feeding. Darting toward Cyberwolf's flailing body, the eels sank their thin teeth into his flesh, then pulled away. Time after time they struck at him.

Cyberwolf's movements grew more feeble, then finally

his body went lax. The bubbles breaking at the top of the water became sparse, then stopped altogether.

Hightower stood up and peered into the pool, but blood had turned the water even more murky, and all he could see was the vague shape of Cyberwolf's body, surrounded by a writhing mass of alien, inhuman creatures.

He looked up as he heard the soft sound of Susan's bare feet on the concrete. Arriving breathless, she held the gun out to him.

"We don't need it anymore," Hightower said. He shook his head.

60

"Let's get away from here," Hightower said. "I can't stand to watch." His hands were shaking, and his wet shirt felt clammy against his skin.

He took the gun from Susan, snapped on the safety, and laid it down on the floor. They walked side by side toward the lab office, both of them limping.

"I was ready to kill him to make him shut down the computer program." Hightower shook his head, then said bitterly, "Now all we can do is wait for the end to come."

"Your parents might be lucky," Susan said, touching his shoulder. "When they come in, the airport won't be jammed yet, so maybe they can land without crashing."

"They've got a chance, I guess," he admitted. He glanced down and shook his head. "Some people won't have that."

"I need to go back into Johnson Hall and find Meg and Tim," Susan said. "Do you want to stay here and wait for us?"

Despite the overheated room, Hightower felt a sudden chill. He looked toward the lighted office. "I've got some bad news about Meg," he said gently.

Susan stared at him with stricken eyes. "She's dead, isn't she?"

"I don't know who did it or how it happened, but I saw her body. She was shot in the kitchen."

"In the kitchen? That's where they killed Mrs. Rostov. She must have been fighting them." Susan hesitated, then asked, "What about Tim? Did they kill him too?"

"I didn't see him. Maybe he found a place to hide. We can go look for him, but I need to bandage my leg first."

"I'm going to miss Meg." Susan's voice was ragged and choked, and she was on the verge of tears. "She was good to me. And she was so brave."

"Maybe you can tell me about her when we get out of here." He gave her arm a tight squeeze, and she put her hand on top of his for a moment.

"I'd like to," Susan said softly. "I'd like to very much."

Hightower turned on the light in the office and sat heavily in the chair beside the cluttered desk. Susan slid into the swivel chair behind it.

He blinked at the brightness of the light for a moment, then pulled his handkerchief out of his back pocket and held it out to Susan. "Wrap this around your hand," he said. "It'll keep your cut from getting contaminated."

"You need it more than I do," Susan said, nodding at his leg. Blood from the knife wound had soaked through his pants and a dark irregular patch had formed near his crotch.

"Take it," he insisted. "I need something bigger to make a pressure bandage."

He handed Susan the handkerchief, then began to work on himself. He held the pant leg taut with his left hand, jabbed the knife point into the fabric, then cut off the leg with a single continuous sweep of the blade.

"I'm sorry I couldn't get there sooner," Susan said.

"You did fine," he said, glancing up at her. "If it's anybody's fault, it's mine for throwing the grenade."

He looked at the cut in his thigh. It was no more than two inches across, but it was probably deeper than that.

The pain had become a steady, aching throb. Clots had formed in the wound, but it was still seeping blood.

He cut the loose fabric into broad strips. Folding a strip into a pad, he put it on top of the wound and tied it in place with another strip. As he finished the knot, he looked at Susan. She had wrapped the handkerchief around her hand and was tucking the loose end underneath. She didn't need his help.

He leaned his right elbow on the desk and rested his head in his hand, cradling his forehead. He felt defeated and exhausted. He would have to stop worrying about his parents. If he couldn't do anything to help them, he should put them out of his mind.

He rubbed his hand over his face and massaged his eyes with his fingertips. It would be nice to rest for a while, but they needed to look for Tim. Before that, though, he had one more thing to do. He sat up straight in the chair.

"I have to call Don Lindsley and let him know that Cyberwolf is dead," he said.

"The phones aren't working." Susan picked up the handset of the phone on the desk and held it up so that he could hear that it lacked a dial tone. She dropped the handset back onto its cradle.

"Don sent me prepared," Hightower said. He shifted onto his left hip and slipped the thin black telephone out of his front pocket. He flipped it open and pulled out the short antenna. He put the phone to his ear and waited until he heard a gentle buzzing. Speaking distinctly, he said, "Don, Don, Don" into the small round grid. He listened to the faint, thin electronic noises of empty space, not sure that the phone was working. Then the noises were replaced by a ringing sound.

"Lindsley here," Don said, answering immediately.

"I've got Susan Bradstreet with me," Hightower said. "She's a little bruised and knocked around, but she's all right. Meg O'Hare is dead, and we don't know anything about the boy, Tim."

"He's safe," Lindsley said. "He escaped, and we've got

him in the hospital, even though he doesn't have a scratch on him."

"Tim got out," Hightower said to Susan. "He's not hurt."

Susan nodded and smiled, but tears welled up in her eyes. She raised her left hand and wiped them away with the handkerchief wrapped around it.

"What about you?" Lindsley asked.

"I'm okay," Hightower said. "But all the takers are dead."

"Will you repeat that?" Lindsley's voice was full of surprise. "All three of them?"

"All three, including Cyberwolf," Hightower said. "So we don't have a way to shut down the Chernobyl program."

"That's no longer a problem," Lindsley said. He gave a short laugh. "I was tempted to call and tell you that the L.A. police traced the Pix-Wizard machine to somebody named Gibson, who runs a store selling outdated computer manuals. They got the photo of him out of Miss Bradstreet's album and found some neighborhood people who identified it as Gibson, even though the hair was different."

"I don't know anything about a photo," Hightower interrupted. "But did they find the computer?"

"They did," Lindsley said, sounding excited and happy. "Gibson lives above the store, and the computer was in his living room. The L.A. police had one of their experts check the machine, and it was running something. She took a look at it, and she was sure it was the Chernobyl program. So they just unplugged the computer and disconnected the phone wire." Lindsley paused, then said, triumphantly, "End of story."

"You're sure about that?" Hightower could feel himself getting lightheaded. This was not news he had expected.

"Absolutely," Lindsley said. "I've got the L.A. police on an open line, and I know they pulled the plug on the computer about fifteen minutes ago."

"My God, that's a relief," Hightower said. He was having trouble believing everything Lindsley was telling him.

"The ironic thing is that the L.A. people didn't find the Pix-Wizard device," Lindsley said. "It was the clue that broke the case, but it didn't turn up in the apartment or the store."

"At least they found the computer," Hightower said. He turned to face Susan and smiled. She smiled back, but her smile was tentative and her face was drawn with exhaustion. He realized that he'd better make arrangements to get them out of the building.

"We're in some lab in the research tower," he said. "Can you open the front door so we can leave here?"

"I wish I could," Lindsley said. "But it's not that easy. The doors are computer controlled, and the codes aren't working. Cyberwolf apparently changed them." He paused to think. "We can put a ladder to one of the upper floors and come down for you, but we'll have to get the fire department out here."

"Shit," Hightower said. "It'll take an hour before everything is in place. Susan was almost out the loading-dock door, so we'll just come out that way."

"I can't stop you," Lindsley said. He sounded like someone having a good time at a party.

"Tell your people we're coming out, then. We don't want to get shot by somebody who's not clear about what's happening."

"I'll pass the word," Lindsley said. "But wait there ten or fifteen minutes, until I can send somebody over to meet you. I don't want you gunned down by some hot dog who didn't get the message."

"We can wait," Hightower said. "And try to get Murphy to spare us making any statements until tomorrow. We're both about to collapse from exhaustion and traumatic shock."

"I'll do what I can," Lindsley promised. "Congratulations to you both." His rich voice sounded as if he were awarding them a prize. "I can't imagine how you did what you did. Believe me, I'm relieved and amazed."

"See you in a few minutes." Hightower flipped the telephone shut and slipped it back into his pocket. He turned to Susan and asked, "Did you follow all that?"

"Most of it," she said. "They located the computer and unplugged it?"

"That's right," he looked at her and smiled. "But Don said they didn't find some kind of device called a Pix-Wizard." He shrugged. "I never heard of it."

"It's a machine he used to fake a picture of him and me together. He sent it to me about a year ago. That's how I eventually recognized him."

"You couldn't tell the picture was a fake?"

"Not at all," Susan said. "And I looked at it very closely, because I didn't recognize him. The way he explained it, he put together two computer images, then made a print." She paused. "A picture from a possible world, he called it."

"He was crazy," Hightower said. He reached out and took her right hand. He found himself smiling again. Despite the throbbing pain in his thigh and the almost overwhelming fatigue that was making his hands shake, he couldn't remember when he had felt better. Probably it was in Paris with Alma, that morning before the explosion.

"I'll go get your shoes," he said. "Then we can break out of this place and maybe get something to eat. I'm starving."

He gave her hand a final squeeze, then turned it loose. He slid forward in his chair and heaved himself up with considerable effort. Sharp pain shot through his left leg. All his muscles seemed to have grown stiff in just a few minutes.

"I can get them myself," Susan said absently. She glanced up at him, but he had the impression that she wasn't really seeing him. She seemed to be looking through him, her eyes focused on something visible only to her. "You shouldn't go. Your leg is hurt."

"Exercise won't do it any harm. It may even help."

She raised no further objection and stayed seated as he walked out of the office and started across the lab toward the operating room. The yellowish green light seemed almost soothing now. It was the end of the battle, and he and Susan had won. He had done what he had set out to do. This time he hadn't had to stand idly by while calamity struck, the way he had with Alma.

He glanced in the direction of the eel pool, then quickly looked away. The halo of light was so closely associated with images of the eels tearing out Cyberwolf's eyes that he found he could no longer bear to look at it.

He stopped and shifted his weight to his right leg. He was only about halfway across the lab, but his leg was making it hard to go on. At each step pain stabbed through his thigh. Maybe if he rested a minute, it would ease up. He smiled ironically. Probably dozens of his surgical patients had told themselves the same thing.

He shifted some weight to his left leg and took a step forward. He clenched his teeth at the sharp pain. Then he heard Susan's voice.

"David! Come back! Quick!"

61

Susan's voice had a sharp edge of alarm that made his stomach contract. He spun around and saw her standing in the door of the lab office. As soon as she started to run after him, he hurried toward her. They met several feet outside the office, and she grabbed his right arm with both hands, as if she were going to force him to follow her someplace.

"What's the matter?" he asked. "Are you all right?" He could hear the high pitch of surprise in his voice.

"Cyberwolf's program is still running," she said.

She released his arm, but her face continued to reflect her panic. Her eyes were staring and her lips parted. She made an obvious effort to control herself.

Standing straight with her hands clasped in front of her, she added in a calmer tone, "I'm sure that it is."

"What makes you so sure?" Hightower shook his head. He felt more puzzled than alarmed. "Lindsley said that a police computer expert—"

"Because I remember what Cyberwolf told me when he was trying to talk me into giving up." She spoke rapidly, hardly stopping to snatch a breath. "He said, 'The cops will think they've found out how to shut down the program, but they'll be wrong. I've made sure they can't find what they need to find.' And that sounds exactly like what's happened. They think they've turned off his program, but they really haven't." She twisted her hands together, rubbing one against the other.

Hightower stood watching her, but his mind was whirling like a top. Would Cyberwolf have told Susan the truth? If he had wanted to impress her, he might have bragged about how much smarter he was than the cops. Hightower nodded his head, then he realized something that persuaded him even more. Cyberwolf wouldn't care if Susan knew the truth about the program, *because he believed she wouldn't live to make use of it.*

"Oh, Jesus," Hightower said softly. "I think you're right." Then he added more forcefully, "I'm sure you are."

He felt a shiver run up his neck, and he hunched his shoulders forward. He tried to get control of himself again. "I'd better call Don," he said. He slipped the thin phone out of his pocket, flipped it open, and jerked up the antenna. Lindsley didn't answer until the second ring.

"Don, listen carefully. Susan and I think the Chernobyl program is still running," Hightower said. He did his best to sound calm, because any suggestion of hysteria would undercut what he was saying. "Let me repeat that. We think the Chernobyl program is still in operation."

Lindsley paused for a long moment. "That can't be," he said at last. "Since I talked to you, the L.A. computer experts have been looking line by line at the content of the program they located, and they're convinced it was meant to melt down NYNEX."

"I'm sure they're right," Hightower said. "But I suspect that what they've found is a *copy* of the Chernobyl program. Maybe it was even in control until they pulled the plug on it, and now the other copy is running."

"I guess that's possible," Lindsley admitted. "But it's all completely speculative."

"Don, we don't have time for a philosophical debate." Hightower fought to stay calm, but his head reeled, and his words sounded as if they were coming from some far-off place. "You've got to get the L.A. police to find the other computer that's running the program."

"But how do you know there *is* another computer?" Lindsley's voice took on a sharp edge of irritation. "The L.A. people are satisfied with the one they've got, and I can't tell them to look for another computer without giving them a good reason."

"Talk to Susan," Hightower said. "She'll tell you what Cyberwolf told her, then see if you don't think we're right."

Susan took the telephone from Hightower. "I don't have any details," she said. "But Cyberwolf told me that he'd planned things so the police would think they had stopped the program, but they would be wrong. He said he'd made sure they wouldn't be able to find what they needed to find." She paused to listen. Then, sounding very tired, she said, "No, that's absolutely all I know. Now here's David again." She handed the phone back to him.

"That's not much of a basis for requesting that L.A. go on with a search they think they've completed," Lindsley said.

"But, Don, the fact that they now think it's over with was just what Cyberwolf was counting on," Hightower said. He could hear his voice rising in frustration, but he no longer cared much about sounding reasonable. "Cyberwolf designed in a cutout so we wouldn't find both programs. Isn't it obvious? Isn't that exactly the kind of thing he would do? And wouldn't you expect him to have a backup program? His whole plan depended on threatening NYNEX."

"I'm not saying you're wrong, Dr. Hightower." Lindsley suddenly turned formal. "I'm only saying that I don't have much to convince a police department to conduct a new search."

"Are the L.A. police at Cyberwolf's apartment?"

"They're still securing evidence and inventorying the scene."

"Will you please just *ask* them to look for another computer?"

"Hang on a second. I've got them on the open line."

Lindsley put down the phone, and Hightower could hear him talking to somebody else. The words were mostly indistinct, and he could catch a phrase only now and then.

Then Lindsley was back. "It's no go," he said. "I told them what you and Miss Bradstreet told me, but they don't put any stock in it. They've traced out the phone wires coming into the apartment and the bookstore, and none of them lead to another computer."

"For Christ's sake, the fucking computer could be somewhere else," Hightower said. "Don't be so dense, Don. He could have rented another apartment somewhere."

"If that's so, we're just screwed, aren't we?" Lindsley said flatly. "There's no way we could find it in time to stop the meltdown."

"Yeah," Hightower admitted. His throat felt tight, and he knew nothing else to say. "I guess we just have to wait and see."

"Now come on out of there and let us take care of you," Lindsley said. His tone was warm and friendly again. "You've got to be tired and hungry."

"Right," Hightower said. "But will you do me a favor?

Will you call up Logan Airport and see if my parents' flight is still scheduled to arrive at three-thirty?"

"That's TWA one-o-one from London?" Lindsley asked.

"That's it." Hightower's voice sounded more stiff and strained than he had expected. He cleared his throat. "Maybe the weather's been bad and the flight was delayed."

"I'll get somebody to check it."

"Thanks, Don," Hightower said softly. He snapped the phone closed and put it back into his pocket. His shoulders sagged inward, and he felt completely defeated.

"Maybe I'm wrong," Susan said, obviously trying to sound hopeful. "Maybe there isn't another computer."

Hightower held out his arms, and she stepped into them. As he held her tightly, she wrapped her arms around him. They stood holding each other, swaying gently together, neither of them saying anything. He tried to think only of the moment and only of how good it felt to be hugging Susan. He had done all he could do. It was time to give up the struggle and accept whatever might happen.

"Let's get your shoes," he said at last. "We can walk over together."

They moved apart but held on to each other's fingers. Then as if they were performing some choreographed movement, they stepped toward one another, raising their hands, and kissed softly. Susan's eyes looked into his for what seemed a long time. The telephone in his front pocket buzzed sharply. Before he could get the phone out of his pocket, it buzzed again.

"Are you someplace near a computer?" Lindsley asked. His deep voice sounded strained.

"Yeah," Hightower said. He automatically looked toward the lab office and saw the blue glow of the computer screen through the front window. "What's up?"

"Get on Internet and you'll see for yourself," Lindsley said. "But do it right now."

"I'll get back to you," Hightower said. He flipped the

phone shut and turned to Susan. "Don says plug into Internet."

"Why?" She looked at him, and the lines of her face were drawn tight with anxiety.

Hightower shrugged. "I'm sure it's got something to do with Cyberwolf."

"Then let's go," she said. Her voice was strong with resolution. "Maybe it's not too late to shut down the Chernobyl program."

"I doubt it." Hightower shook his head, but he felt a shiver of anticipation run down his back. *Was it possible?*

Despite their sore legs they covered the distance to the office at a dead run. Susan turned right and hurried back to the computer with Hightower close behind her.

"You do it," Hightower said, rolling out the typing chair in front of the computer. "You're the expert on this machine."

Susan sat down in the chair and clicked the mouse, bringing back the main menu. She quickly scanned the options, moved the mouse to the right, putting the arrow on *COMMTALK*. When she double-clicked, the menu disappeared, and she was offered the same options presented to her earlier. She selected *Directory,* and a long list of nine-digit numbers with identifying names appeared on the screen. She slid the mouse down to point at *Internet,* then clicked twice.

"Listen for the connection," she said. "This program does everything for you."

Hightower sat down in the straight chair he had pulled over from the desk. Leaning forward to get close enough to read the monitor, he heard the buzz of a dial tone followed by a sequence of tones of varying pitch. A sudden silence signaled that the connection was made.

Yet instead of a blank screen emerging, bright yellow numbers three inches tall suddenly appeared against a blue background:

Hightower shifted his chair closer. As he stared at the numbers, twenty-three changed to twenty-two, which was replaced almost immediately by twenty-one.

"It's a countdown," he said. He couldn't take his eyes off the numbers. "Those are seconds zipping by, and the others must be minutes."

Suddenly, the minutes' register was one fewer, and the seconds' countdown was starting over. Hightower looked at the screen in fascination. *Fifteen more minutes to zero.*

"A countdown for what?" Susan asked. "Do you think it's for the NYNEX meltdown?" She rolled the typing chair away from the computer so that Hightower could pull his chair even with hers.

"It must be," he said softly, then nodded his head. The realization struck him with the shock of a plunge into icy water.

62

Hightower whipped the phone out of his pocket, and this time Lindsley answered on the first ring.

"What am I looking at, Don? Is it the time until meltdown?"

"We think so," Lindsley said.

"Then the Chernobyl program is still operating?"

"We think so," Lindsley repeated. "One of our computer people noticed it right before you called me, and when he checked, he discovered that it affected every computer dialed into the network through NYNEX."

"So it's acting like a virus," Hightower said. Ironically, he felt his spirits rise. At least Don and the L.A. police were prepared to admit that the Chernobyl program was still running. But would they be able to stop the goddamned thing or was it already too late?

"What do you think about the chances of disabling the program?" Hightower realized he was pushing Don to give him grounds for hope.

"The L.A. police are going through Gibson's apartment with a sieve, but they haven't come up with anything yet," Lindsley said. "They hope they can find some of his notes for the Chernobyl program, and then maybe they can find a way to abort it. The computer experts are also talking to the NYNEX experts, and they're searching the system."

"What do the NYNEX people think the chances are that they can do something?"

"Not good," Lindsley said. "They say a cyberpunk like Gibson could go down deep in the system and hide lines of code in files nobody ever looks at. And even if they did look at them, they wouldn't be able to tell the difference between what code belongs in the file and what Gibson put there."

"Killing the program that way looks hopeless," Hightower said. "It sounds like locating the computer running it is still the best bet." He expelled his breath in a sigh. "And if that's not hopeless, it's next door to it." He felt his initial excitement begin to seep away like air from a child's balloon.

"The L.A. police are ready to take you seriously now," Lindsley said. "Have you got any suggestions?"

"None," Hightower said. He paused, not knowing what to say. It was maddening to have to give up so easily, but what could he suggest? He knew little about computers, compared to Cyberwolf.

Then he suddenly realized that if he knew more about Cyberwolf, he might be able to make some reasonable conjectures about his behavior.

I'm a psychiatrist now, goddamn it. I know a lot about what makes people tick. So get some data, then try to figure out a few basic things about him. Maybe the conjectures could narrow down the search for the computer. He felt himself getting excited again at the prospect of being able to do something.

"Can you brief me on what the L.A. police have learned about Cyberwolf?"

"I've got Sergeant Tagore of the LAPD on the line," Lindsley said. "I'll ask him to talk to you. Hang on." The line went dead, then Lindsley suddenly came back. "Tagore's going to hook up with the computer you're using."

"I don't know the address here."

"We know it, though," Lindsley said. "By the way, TWA flight one-o-one is scheduled to land on time. Now hang on."

"Oh, God," Hightower groaned.

Hightower put the phone in his lap and turned to look at Susan. She was sitting bolt upright, the skin of her face stretched tight with worry.

"An L.A. cop is going to tell us what they know about Cyberwolf," he said.

She nodded and took a deep breath, but she said nothing. He suspected she was on the verge of physical collapse. He felt exhausted, and she had been through a lot more than he had.

Tagore's voice came through the computer speaker with surprising clarity. "Dr. Hightower, we don't know much," he said. "Just what we found out from a quick search of public records and interviews with neighbors." His voice had no noticeable accent, but it rose and fell in a musical way, suggesting that he had learned English in some other country.

Hightower leaned forward, unsure of what to do so that Tagore could hear him. Susan reached out and tapped the grille of the condenser microphone on the front of the computer.

"Anything you say will be more than I know," Hightower said, speaking into the microphone.

"His full name is Thomas Arthur Gibson," Tagore said. "He's thirty-four years old and was born in Dallas, Texas, where his parents still live. He got a B.S. in electrical engineering from MIT, and a bit later served an eight-month sentence at Chino for theft of phone services. He seems to be a computer hacker turned bad, what some people call a cracker or a cyberpunk."

Tagore paused in his rapid, almost singsong recital. Hightower could hear him take a deep breath, then he began again. "When Gibson got out of Chino, he worked a year or so for ITT, then taught computer science for a couple of years at L.A. Community College. He now owns Specialty Books, which sells out-of-date computer and software manuals."

Hightower turned his head slightly and looked at Susan. Her face was ashen, and her mouth was pulled into a straight line. She was squeezing her interlocked fingers together so tightly that she seemed to be trying to crush them.

Hightower put a hand on her leg and leaned over. "You don't have to listen to this," he said gently. "Would you like to sit somewhere else until I finish talking? Maybe you could find someplace to lie down."

"I'm okay. Don't worry about me." Susan shook her head. She had brushed back her hair so that it formed a soft frame for her face. Despite the circumstances, he couldn't help noticing how astonishingly beautiful she was.

"You'll have to say that again, Dr. Hightower," Tagore said. "I didn't catch any of it."

"Sorry," Hightower said. "Have you found a wife, or an ex-wife, or friends of any kind?"

"No, sir. He seems to be a loner, but we haven't had much time to check yet."

"Has the search of the apartment turned up anything?"

"Nothing about the Chernobyl program and nothing pertaining to his interest in Ms. Bradstreet or the hostage situation. The only thing unusual is a letter that must have been delivered yesterday from Ocean View Funeral Home in San Diego."

"What was strange about it?"

"It's hard to know what to make of it," Tagore said.

"The only text was *20 yo F A+ 500 per 5,* then it was signed with the initials B.W."

"Is anybody trying to find out who B.W. is and what the note is about?"

"Lieutenant Chang has been talking to San Diego, but I don't know if he's come up with anything yet. It's hard to get anything done in the middle of the night." Tagore paused, then said, "Would you like me to get the camera crew to give you a quick look around the apartment so you can see things for yourself?"

"Is that possible?" Hightower asked. "Even with the numbers on the screen?"

"Yes, sir," Tagore said. "You'll still see them, but they'll go into a screen-in-screen format. Hang on, and I'll ask the camera crew to show you the scene."

"Wait," Hightower said. "What am I going to see?"

"A kitchen, living room, bedroom, and bathroom upstairs, then the store downstairs, which is just one large room."

"I'll be waiting."

Hightower looked at the computer screen. The countdown clock was now reading *14:19,* and the seconds were disappearing so fast that the numbers seemed to be rolling backward.

"Are you all right?" He turned so that he could see Susan.

"I'm just so tired." Her eyes met his. "But I wish I could do something to help you."

"Oh, Susan, you are helping me. I'm just so glad that you're alive."

Hightower glanced back at the screen. All at once, the numbers jumped to a box in the upper right and he was looking at a scene from a kitchen: stove, countertop, refrigerator, narrow table of some kind of natural wood. The walls were white and blank and the room cramped and windowless. A short woman in a white lab coat was taking containers out of the cabinet. She emptied a box of salt into a white plastic bucket, then set the box down on the countertop. Through the computer's speaker he could hear a low shuffle of sound.

The camera swept around the kitchen a final time, then pointed through the door and into the living room. People kept stepping in front of the lens, but Hightower noted the location of a desk, a boxy couch, a couple of upholstered chairs, and a line of windows along the side. Two people were gathered around a computer, and three or four others were in the process of going through the desk drawers, looking under several small rugs, and slitting open upholstery to search inside. The walls were as blank as those in the kitchen, and Hightower saw nothing that suggested anything of interest about Gibson.

As the camera entered the bedroom door, Hightower saw a flash of color on the wall beside the bed. It was a picture of some kind, the first picture he had seen in the apartment. He leaned toward the microphone and said, "Sergeant Tagore! Ask the camera operator to focus on the picture on the wall."

The camera continued to pan the room. Hightower saw more bare white walls with only a minimum of furniture: a chest with four drawers, a nightstand with a row of paperback books on the lower shelf, a platform bed with a plain green spread.

The only window in the room was at the head of the bed, and the opening had been covered over with heavy black fabric. The fabric was nailed to the window frame so that all light would be excluded. Through a doorway he could see the pink tile of the bathroom floor. A man in a white shirt was standing in front of the open medicine cabinet, sorting through its contents.

Hightower was about to decide that Tagore hadn't heard him when the camera suddenly jumped to the picture on the wall. The image was fuzzy, but as the operator adjusted the lens, it slowly came into focus.

Hightower leaned forward and stared into the monitor, doing his best to ignore the yellow numbers in the corner of the screen. He found himself looking at the naked body of a slender young woman lying on a sofa draped in black cloth. Standing at the foot of the sofa and gazing down at the woman was Cyberwolf.

"That's him," Susan said. "Look at his eyes, the way he's staring at her." He glanced around and saw her wrap her arms over her chest in a protective way. "That's how he stared at me."

Hightower focused briefly on Gibson, but his eyes were drawn back to the woman. She was young and beautiful, yet something about her was peculiar. Her head rested on a small red cushion, and her long black hair was draped over her rounded breasts. Her eyes were a brilliant blue, and her skin had a dusky, ashen hue.

"Do you notice anything strange about the woman?" Hightower asked.

Susan leaned toward the monitor, then drew back. "Not really," she said. "She's attractive, if that's what you mean."

"Tagore," Hightower said, speaking into the microphone. "Ask the camera operator to give me a close-up on the woman's face."

The camera locked onto the face, then it expanded to fill the screen. Hightower looked at the woman's eyes. In the scleral membrane, he could make out petechiae, tiny dots of blood produced by hemorrhaging. Her pupils were as round and open as the lenses of a pair of binoculars. Being "fixed and dilated" were the classic pupillary signs. He had no way to check whether the pupils were fixed, but they were obviously dilated.

"She's dead," he said, thinking aloud.

"What?" Susan's voice was rough with surprise. She let her arms drop and sat up straight in the chair. She turned toward him. "You mean the woman in the picture?"

"Right," he said absently.

"Oh, my God." Disbelief slowed her speech. "Why would anybody want his picture taken with a dead body?"

He stared into the woman's brilliant blue eyes and

thought about Susan's question. The woman was obviously a neomort at the time the photograph was made, and Gibson was in it with her. He was thinking how peculiar that was when he realized with a flash of understanding that it was more than peculiar. The obvious answer to Susan's question was that *Gibson was a necrophile.*

Some psychiatrist he was turning out to be. He should have noticed the resemblance between the picture of the nude woman lying on the couch and the way Gibson had arranged Susan. He had stripped her naked, stretched her out on the operating table, and was about to strangle her. He was obviously acting out some dark fantasy that he had played out many times in his mind. The picture was probably the trigger for the fantasy, as well as the model for what he wanted to do with Susan.

Suddenly, Hightower recalled the letter from the San Diego funeral home. Now it made sense. Somebody working at the mortuary, probably an embalmer, was offering Gibson five pictures of a beautiful—an A-plus—twenty-year-old for $500.

"Is that long enough on the face, Dr. Hightower?" Tagore asked over the speaker.

"That's great," Hightower said. He felt the prickling of a growing frustration that was making it hard for him to sit still. "Now maybe a quick look downstairs."

"Okay," Tagore said. "We'll cut transmission until we get inside the bookstore."

How would Gibson get access to the corpse of the woman in the photograph? He could have killed her, then had somebody take a picture of the two of them together. Or maybe he didn't kill her, but he somehow got hold of her body. Maybe through somebody at a mortuary.

Or maybe he only got the picture from a mortuary. Maybe the body in the picture was from another photograph sold to him by somebody like B.W. in San Diego.

Hightower turned to face Susan. "Tell me about that machine again," he said. "The Pix-Wizard."

"I've told you all I know." Susan shrugged. "Cyberwolf said he used it to put a picture of himself into a picture of me at a movie opening so that it looked like we were attending the opening together."

"And you couldn't tell the difference?"

She shook her head. "I really studied the picture, because I didn't recognize the guy standing beside me, and it looked like an ordinary photograph." She gave him a puzzled glance. "Why do you want to know?"

"I think Gibson put himself into the picture of the dead woman," he said. "I think he's a necrophile."

"Oh, God," Susan said. "That's what he wanted to do to me." She stood up and put her hands over her face. "I might need to throw up." She swallowed hard twice, then she began to cry. Her chest heaved with heavy sobs.

Hightower shoved his chair back and pulled Susan to him. "It's okay, it's okay," he said softly. She leaned against him, and he held her close. "It didn't happen."

"But it could have." Susan's voice was choked, and her shoulders were trembling. "It's what he would call a possible world."

"Yes, but you're all right now."

She sniffed and wiped the tears out of her eyes with the handkerchief. "I'm sorry," she said in a husky voice. "This isn't the time for a breakdown."

"Don't worry about it." Hightower searched her face carefully, trying to get a sense of how she was feeling. "Are you going to be all right now?"

She nodded, then sniffed again and rubbed her nose with her forearm. Her eyes were wet and red, but her face was composed. She sat back down and gave him a small smile.

Hightower smiled back, then ruffled his hair with his fingers. Something about Gibson's use of the Pix-Wizard was important, but what? He had been about to make a connection when Susan had started crying.

A picture of the inside of Specialty Books suddenly appeared on the computer screen. Lining the walls were floor-to-ceiling unpainted wooden bookcases packed tightly with an enormous variety of pamphlets, loose-leaf notebooks, and thick reference manuals. The camera scanned one long windowless wall, and Hightower saw nothing that looked helpful.

But now he had to begin thinking like a psychiatrist. Since he had started looking for Susan, he had reverted to his old ways. He had been thinking like a surgeon and seeing everything as a practical problem that could be fixed by direct action. He hadn't been wrong to believe that at the beginning of the search, but the nature of the problem had changed. He needed to figure out what somebody like Gibson would do to cover his tracks. Where would he hide the computer with the Chernobyl program?

The camera traveled along the back wall of the store, then turned the corner and ranged along the side wall. Nothing but more manuals, some looking ragged and ancient.

What he had been thinking about the Pix-Wizard began to come back to him. He was sure that the key to finding the computer was connected with where the Pix-Wizard was. If Gibson used the Pix-Wizard to produce necrophilic materials to satisfy his fantasies, he would conceal the machine in some secret place. People found necrophilia disgusting, so he wouldn't risk getting caught with pictures of dead bodies. He would hide them away, and he would hide himself away with them.

The camera traversed the front of the store, and Hightower noticed that the dark green curtain was pulled over the glass of the front door. Cyberwolf liked dim, shadowy places. Wherever he had made his hiding place, it was sure to be shut off from the light.

Hightower forced himself to try to recall all that he had heard or read about necrophiles. It wasn't much, because not much was known about them. They almost never sought psychiatric help and were rarely charged with a crime connected with their activities.

He remembered, though, that necrophiles were always

socially and personally immature. They were frightened of having to deal with people in a personal way. They were happier when people literally became objects so that they could do whatever they wanted with them without feeling anxiety or risking humiliation.

If Gibson was typical, he spent most of his time alone. Probably, too, he spent it in a place that only he knew about. It would be dark and isolated, a place where he could be sheltered from the rest of the world. In effect, he would construct a mausoleum for himself to live in.

Most likely the Pix-Wizard would be in that place, and because Gibson would think of it as his safe place, the Chernobyl computer would be there too. And the place would be one he could get to easily and often.

Hightower shook his head in puzzlement. He was surprised that Gibson hadn't kept both machines in his apartment. It was about the only place satisfying the conditions of complete privacy and easy and speedy access. Yet now that he had received the camera's-eye tour of all the rooms, that seemed impossible.

But maybe there was something he had overlooked. He leaned forward and called "Tagore" into the speaker. While he was waiting for an answer, he looked at the shelves of books on the opposite side of the room.

"Yes, Dr. Hightower," Tagore responded. "Have you seen enough of the scene?"

"Just one more thing. Is there a basement?"

"Only a crawl space," Tagore said. "We've explored it, but we didn't find anything."

Hightower felt his last hope blink out like a light. Don was right, if the computer was hidden in some rented apartment, they had no chance of finding it soon enough. He glanced at the screen display. Not in thirteen minutes and a few odd seconds.

"Thanks, Sergeant," Hightower said.

"No problem," Tagore said.

The computer screen went blank, except for the bright yellow numerals, which resumed their previous size and

location. The seconds were draining away like water leak-
ing out of a cracked bottle, and he made himself look
away. He couldn't think if he let himself become trans-
fixed by watching the seconds disappear.

Maybe it would have been better if Susan hadn't remembered what Cyberwolf told her until later. Then at
least they could have avoided the almost unendurable
frustration of trying to do something when there was
nothing that could be done.

He pounded his fist into the palm of his hand. The
blow made a slapping noise, and Susan gave him a startled glance. Neither of them said anything. He stood up
and turned around, feeling like he might explode with the
need to act. Through the office window he could see the
golden light rising up from the eel pool. It must take a lot
of electricity to keep the pool heated and lighted twenty-
four hours a day.

Then some mechanism clicked in one of the deep structures of his mind.

A lot of electricity.

It probably took a lot of electricity for the Pix-Wizard
to produce the prints that Gibson made. Gibson would be
charged for the electricity, so Pacific Power or whoever
did the billing in L.A. would know if he had two accounts. If he did, the second account would be his hiding
place, the place with the Pix-Wizard and the Chernobyl
computer.

If it was only across the street or a block away, there
might be enough time to get to it—barely.

63

Hightower snatched the phone out of his pocket and
shouted Don's name into the receiver.

While he was listening to the phone ring, he repeatedly tapped himself on the knee with his fist. He left leg was still throbbing, but he hardly noticed it.

"I need some information immediately," he said, as soon as Don answered. "I want to know if the L.A. power company records show that Gibson has two accounts."

"Why do you want . . ." Lindsley started to say. Then he stopped and said, "Don't hang up."

Lindsley put down the phone, and Hightower could hear him on another line. "Check and see how many electricity accounts Gibson has." Someone said something Hightower couldn't hear. "If that's the fastest way, that's great," Lindsley said. Then to Hightower he whispered, "They're searching company computer records. It'll just take a second."

"You're trying to figure out where his hiding place is, aren't you?" Susan said.

Hightower turned away from the office window and looked at her. She was leaning back in the typing chair with her legs stretched out in front of her and her ankles crossed. Despite her pose, she didn't look relaxed.

"If it's close, we could still shut down the program."

Then Lindsley came back on the line. "Sorry, Dr. Hightower. Gibson's got only one billing account."

Hightower felt his body grow slack, and he suddenly needed to sit down. That was the end, the last idea. The Chernobyl program was as unstoppable as a juggernaut, as inevitable as death itself.

"It's a big account, though," Lindsley went on. "Almost thirty-two thousand kilowatt hours. Looks like he uses about twice as much power as an ordinary house."

"Probably the bookstore has an electric sign," Hightower said absently. He was wondering if checking Gibson's phone account would show anything and was only half listening.

"That's what's peculiar," Lindsley said. "I saw a scan of the outside, and the store's got a painted sign that's not even lighted up with light bulbs."

Hightower felt a current of excitement as he saw the implication of what Don was saying. It was as if the salt making a glass of water murky had instantaneously crystallized, leaving the water lucidly clear.

"That's it!" Hightower shouted. "By God, that's it! He doesn't have an apartment somewhere else." Hightower thrust out his left arm and made a sweeping gesture. "His hiding place is right where he spends most of his time."

"What do you mean?" Lindsley asked.

"Look for a hidden room somewhere in the apartment or the bookstore. Maybe it's at the back of a big closet or maybe it's a whole closet, but I'm sure it's there." Hightower paused, then said, "It's *got* to be there, given the kind of person he is."

"You're basing that on your psychiatric judgment?"

"And the fact that his electric bill is twice what it ought to be."

"I'm going to say to Lieutenant Chang in L.A. that it's my understanding that Miss Bradstreet heard Gibson mention something about a secret room."

"Tell him whatever the hell you have to," Hightower said. "Just get them to look."

"The bookcases—tell them to check behind the bookcases," Susan suggested. She got up from the typing chair and stood beside Hightower. He placed a hand on her back, then pulled her toward him. She slid under the arch of his arm, nestling against him. Her body was warm against his, but his hand felt the tension in the muscles of her back.

"Did you hear that?" Hightower said into the phone. "Check behind the bookcases." He rubbed a piece of her hair between his fingers, feeling the fineness of its texture. "And don't hang up, Don. I want to know what's happening." He was almost yelling into the phone.

"Then keep quiet a minute," Lindsley said calmly.

Susan stepped away from him and extended her arms to the sides in a stretch. She then looked at him and asked, "It's still possible, isn't it?"

"I think so," he said. He could hear Lindsley talking to someone. He thought he caught the phrase "secret room," but everything else was too indistinct to be intelligible.

"But it's going to be close," Hightower added.

"You don't give up." Susan nodded in approval. "I'm a bit that way myself."

"A *bit*?" He smiled at her.

Then suddenly Lindsley was talking to him again. "Lieutenant Chang is willing to search," he said. "And God help us all if a room doesn't turn up."

"It will," Hightower said. "I can feel it there somewhere."

"Lieutenant Chang is accepting you as the expert consultant," Lindsley said. "They're sending you pictures again."

"Good," Hightower said. "And thanks for taking a chance."

The computer screen was suddenly filled with an image of six or eight L.A. detectives inside the bookstore. The men were in shirtsleeves and ties and the women in skirts and blouses. They all had the slightly overgroomed look of police officers.

"I'll call you later," Hightower said, then snapped the phone closed.

Susan sat down in the typing chair, and he took the other chair again. He leaned closer to the monitor, trying to ignore the yellow numbers in the upper right that now read *12:46.*

"It looks like they're going to take my advice," Susan said.

The detectives hurriedly spread themselves out along the floor-to-ceiling bookshelves that covered the walls. One group went right, one left, and another concentrated on the shelves opposite the front door.

Working at a frantic pace, the detectives began pulling the manuals and guides off the shelves. They made no effort to be systematic or careful. They started with the shelves at eye level, grabbed the manuals at the top, then tumbled them to the floor. A detective would open up a space on the shelf, slip an arm behind the manuals, then shove them all to the floor in a single sweep. Through the speaker Hightower could hear the muffled crashes of hundreds of falling books.

As the camera panned back and forth, he could see books accumulating in front of the shelves. They formed low heaps that reminded him of long burial mounds. The pages flying out of falling loose-leaf binders glided for a moment in the air, rocking swiftly back and forth, then dropped solidly to the cracked green vinyl tile floor.

"Here's something!" a man's voice called.

Immediately the camera swung to the shelves at the front of the room. A husky detective in a short-sleeved white shirt and red tie was pulling back a section of the bookcase. The section was hinged along the right edge, but because of the manuals heaped on the floor, the bottom could no longer move forward.

The detective was hanging on to the bookcase with one hand and kicking the books out of the way. Three other officers joined him, and in seconds the floor was clear. The bookcase glided forward.

"Stand back and let me get a look," another male voice said.

The detectives moved aside, and a thin middle-aged Asian in a tan suit walked into camera range. When he reached the shelves, he turned slightly to the side and stepped into the gap between them. Hightower decided that the man must have been Lieutenant Chang.

Chang put his hand flat against the wall, then rapped the wall with his knuckles. He turned right and touched a small panel set into the wall. He shoved on the panel with his fingers, and it slid back like the lid on a box. Chang peered inside for a moment. He then turned around to face the camera and the circle of detectives gathered around the opening.

"The door is steel, and the locking mechanism is controlled by a retina scan," Chang announced. "We've got *eleven* minutes to get the door open and disable the computer." He looked in the direction of the front door. "I asked Joe Stein to get ready, and I'm going to let him handle the problem now."

Hightower looked at the seconds running backward and made fists out of both hands. As he squeezed his fingers, he could feel his nails biting into his palms. It hurt, but not enough to distract him. Susan sat staring at the screen, biting at her lower lip.

"The computer has to be behind that door," she said. She shot Hightower a quick glance. "Where else could it be?"

"Anywhere," he said. His voice sounded husky and strangled. "But are they even going to get the goddamned door open in time?" He stood up and turned away from the screen, then immediately turned back around. He crossed his arms over his chest and tucked his hands into his armpits.

A dark-haired man in a blue shirt slipped into the opening between the bookcases—Joe Stein, Hightower figured. Stein was carrying a black toolbox in one hand and a cordless drill in the other. Without bothering to examine the door, he started drilling the wall near the upper left corner.

The drill punched through the plaster without difficulty, and a heavy cloud of white powder floated in the air. Stein then drilled five more holes, one by each corner of the door and one near the middle on each side. The holes looked to be about an inch in diameter.

Stein put down the drill, opened his toolbox, and took out what looked like a bar of pink putty. "This is C-Four plastic explosive," he said, glancing behind him. Some of the detectives moved back a few steps. Breaking off pieces from the bar, Stein rapidly filled the holes, pressing the plastic in with his fingers.

"Everybody out of the way now," Stein said. "I'm going to use smart caps with built-in ignition chips, and there's a danger of accidental detonation."

The detectives all hurried out the front door, and for a moment the screen contained only images too dark to make out. The sound became garbled with too many people talking at once. But then the camera operator got Stein back into focus. He was pressing what looked like small brass cylinders into the soft plastic in each drill hole.

Hightower let himself glance at the yellow numbers in the corner of the screen: *02:24*. His parents' plane would be making its final descent now. Susan must have seen his expression change, because she reached out and took his hand. She gave it a tight squeeze, but she said nothing.

Hurry up! Don't be so goddamned slow and cautious.

Stein came through the front door carrying a small gray box about the size of a pocket calculator. He walked directly toward the camera, then turned to face the open door of the building. Hightower saw him bend his head to look at something and make some small movement with his right hand.

Suddenly, the steel door was ringed with flames and black smoke, and a resounding *boom!* shook the wall like a piece of flimsy cardboard. The upright supports of the wooden bookcases splintered, and the ends of the shelves sagged, dumping more books onto the floor. The computer speaker rattled from the concussion, and the picture on the screen jerked wildly. As the shattered wall crumbled to the floor, a white cloud of plaster dust rolled toward the outside door.

Shrouded by the dust, the steel door seemed to stand alone for a moment, not needing the wall to support it. But it finally fell forward, hitting the floor with a solid crash that shook the entire building. The broken ends of laths stuck out from the ragged edges of the shattered plaster.

"Great job," somebody said. Then over a short smattering of applause, others called out, "Way to go, Joe."

"Get inside the goddamned room," Hightower muttered

through clenched teeth. "Pat yourselves on the fucking back later." He jumped up from his chair, then stood beside it, looking down at the screen and pounding his fist on the chair back.

Lieutenant Chang cut through the group of detectives and darted inside the store. He was carrying a red-handled fire ax with a broad blade and a spike at the top. Without stopping, he stepped onto the prone steel door, then walked through the opening torn into the wall. The camera operator was right behind him, and the long-focus lens provided a close-up of the ragged hole. Inside, it was too dark for Hightower to make out anything at all. Even Chang had disappeared.

Chang must have found the switch, because suddenly the lights came on. He was standing at the entrance, and on the wall to his right, Hightower saw a copy of the picture of Gibson with the naked dead woman that was in Gibson's bedroom. He felt a surge of satisfaction—he was sure they were in the right place.

But why wasn't Chang doing something?

As the camera moved closer, Hightower saw that at the end of the room, past Chang, was the gray box of a computer. The glowing yellow screen of Gibson's computer displayed the time in heavy black numbers: *0:12.*

"Smash the fucking thing!" Hightower shouted. Rubbing his left hand through his hair repeatedly, he stood looking down at the scene, as helpless to act as if he were in a dream.

Chang finally spied the computer and ran toward it, dodging around a large table and a chair. When he got to within three feet of the computer, he paused, then hoisted the ax above his head. He swung the ax toward the floor, cutting through the bundle of cables leading into the back of the computer.

A torrent of yellow and orange sparks arced upward, then cascaded to the floor. The computer screen turned blank, its internal light extinguished.

Simultaneously, Hightower saw the yellow *0:02* in the

upper right of the screen in front of him blink out of existence.

"They're safe now," Susan said with wonder in her voice. She turned toward him. "Everybody is safe."

Epilogue

Susan scooped up a handful of sand, then let a thin stream of it trickle out of her fist. The sand was as white and fine as granulated sugar. She made a circular motion with her wrist, and the line of sand formed an intricate overlapping spiral on the beach.

"What are you making?" Hightower asked.

He was sitting beside her under the shade of the umbrella, leaning back on his elbows with his heels dug into the sand. Floppy khaki pants hid the bandage covering his stab wound and the bruises on his left leg.

"Nothing," she said.

As she turned to look at him, she could feel herself almost physically pulled in his direction. He smiled at her, but he still looked tired. The lines at the corners of his eyes were deep, and the skin under them had a dark purplish look.

"I never do anything the least bit constructive at the beach." She returned his smile.

"Not even when you were a kid playing on the beautiful shores of Lake Erie?" His tone was ironic, but he gave her a dreamy, wistful look, as if for a moment he had glimpsed a remote image of her as a child.

"Not even then," she said. "When I was a little girl, my parents took me for a swim every Sunday afternoon in the summer, and I never built sand castles or even houses."

"You swam all the time?"

"I made patterns in the sand." She paused to concentrate on making a loop with the sand drizzling out of her hand. "Whorls, zigzags, wavy lines, and things that don't have names. I still make them when I'm happy."

Hightower leaned over and gazed at the pattern she was

making. His eyes seemed to be tracing out the intricate design.

She looked at him and said, "My parents always found something nice to say about my designs."

"That's probably why you became an actress. You're always looking for more applause."

"Maybe so," she said. "And then I had to meet a man who doesn't go to movies and never even heard of me."

She held out her left hand. He interlocked his fingers with hers. He sat up, then lifted her hand and kissed the back of it.

"That still didn't make me much of a challenge," he said. "You swept me away with a single look and two minutes of conversation. And that was even before I saw you reading a book about Darwin."

"That's flattering," Susan said. "I'm afraid I was the real challenge." She shook her head in mock seriousness. "So few men nowadays are willing to be beaten up, shot at, and knifed to show a woman that they're serious about her."

"Only because they have so few chances," Hightower said. "On the other hand, very few men can find a woman willing to risk her life to save theirs."

"Only because there are never as many good roles for women as for men."

They smiled at each other, then looked out at the ocean in front of them. It was a flawless blue, and the waves sparkled in the sun as they gently rolled onto the white beach. Off to the side, Susan could see the bright green foliage that covered the upland hills. A mild breeze carried the odor of flowering plants.

She shook her head in wonder. Time had stopped for a moment, and she wasn't sure she ever wanted it to start again. The day was as perfect as any she had ever known or perhaps would ever know.

Notes and References

In depicting the events of this novel I have assumed one major development in computers. Although the cult film *Wax: Or the Discovery of Television Among the Bees* was digitized and sent over the Internet on May 23, 1993, current packet-switching technology does not permit the transmission of moving images as I have represented them. Asynchronous transfer mode (ATM) may offer an improvement, but perhaps only optical computing will be able to move enough data fast enough over a fiber optic network to permit television-quality moving images.

I am indebted to Jack Hitt and Paul Tough's article "Terminal Delinquents" (*Esquire*, December 1990) for an account of the way hackers operate. I also benefited from Clifford Stoll's *The Cuckoo's Egg* (Doubleday, 1989), which tells how Stoll traced an intruder from the Lawrence-Berkeley Laboratory computer through the networks to uncover a spy ring in Germany. *The New Hacker's Dictionary,* edited by Eric S. Raymond (MIT Press, 1991), is a readable guide to the world of hacking that I found invaluable.

Criminal practices of hackers are discussed in Paul Mungo's *Approaching Zero: The Extraordinary World of Hackers, Phreakers, Virus Writers, and Keyboard Criminals* (Random House, 1992). The threat to civil liberty posed by governmental attempts to control hacking is discussed in *Hacker Crackdown* by Bruce Sterling (Bantam, 1992). Howard Rheingold's *Virtual Reality* (Summit Books, 1991) is a good introduction to the subject.

William Gibson launched *cyberpunk* fiction in his now classic novel *The Neuromancer* (Ace Books, 1984). A range of cyberpunk can be found in *Mirrorshades,* edited by Bruce Sterling (Arbor House, 1986). Cyberpunk as an attitude and lifestyle is best represented in magazines like *Mondo 2000* and *Wired.*